The howling bore through my head like a drill bit. I strained to make out words amid the torrent but heard only the pain.

Louder.

I leaped up to turn down the volume on the machine. Found it already set low.

I started to turn it off, but before I could, the screaming died.

More static-quiet.

Then a new voice.

Soft. High-pitched. Nasal.

A child's voice:

> Bad love. Bad love.
> Don't give me the bad love.

Child's timbre—but with no childish lilt.

Unnaturally flat—*robot*like. . . .

Almost like a prayer. . . .

No. Too hollow for prayer—too faithless.

Idolatrous.

A prayer for the dead.

By the dead.

—from *Bad Love*

Please turn the page. . . .

TIME BOMB

"A marvelous read." —*The New York Times Book Review*

"Though a time bomb is ticking away at the heart of this novel, readers will forget to watch the clock once they begin it."
—*Chicago Sun-Times*

SILENT PARTNER

"A complex and haunting story . . . hits the reader right between the eyes."
—*Los Angeles Times Book Review*

"Kellerman possesses a voice of authority and an uncanny gift for perfectly placing each chilling revelation."
—*Booklist*

WHEN THE BOUGH BREAKS

"Suspenseful, neatly spun, fascinating . . . One helluva good, spooky book." —*Philadelphia Daily News*

"An engrossing thriller . . . This knockout of an entertainment is the kind of book which establishes a career in one stroke." —*New York Newsday*

AND PRAISE FOR
THE BUTCHER'S THEATER

"Spellbinding . . . A vivid, fascinating tale." —*Time*

"This one is going to scare the hell out of a lot of people on its way to the bestseller lists." —Elmore Leonard

"Roller-coaster suspense." —*Los Angeles Times*

Books by Jonathan Kellerman

Fiction
BAD LOVE (1994)
DEVIL'S WALTZ (1993)
PRIVATE EYES (1992)
TIME BOMB (1990)
SILENT PARTNER (1989)
THE BUTCHER'S THEATER (1988)
OVER THE EDGE (1987)
BLOOD TEST (1986)
WHEN THE BOUGH BREAKS (1985)

Nonfiction
HELPING THE FEARFUL CHILD (1981)
PSYCHOLOGICAL ASPECTS OF
    CHILDHOOD CANCER (1980)

JONATHAN
KELLERMAN

BAD
LOVE

BANTAM BOOKS
NEW YORK · TORONTO · LONDON · SYDNEY · AUCKLAND

BAD LOVE

A Bantam Book

PUBLISHING HISTORY

Bantam hardcover edition published February 1994
Bantam large print edition / February 1994
Bantam International edition / June 1994
Bantam paperback edition / December 1994

ISBN: 0-553-56870-1

Published simultaneously in the United States and Canada

Bantam Books are published by Bantam Books, a division of Bantam
Doubleday Dell Publishing Group, Inc. Its trademark, consisting of
the words "Bantam Books" and the portrayal of a rooster, is
Registered in U.S. Patent and Trademark Office and in other
countries. Marca Registrada. Bantam Books, 1540 Broadway,
New York, New York 10036.

PRINTED IN THE UNITED STATES OF AMERICA

OPM   0 9 8 7 6 5 4 3 2 1

To my daughter Rachel.
Brains, beauty, grace, wit, style.
And a heart of gold.

Special thanks to Sheriff's Deputy Kurt Ebert.

BAD
LOVE

1

It came in a plain brown wrapper.

Padded envelope, book rate, book sized. I assumed it was an academic text I'd forgotten ordering.

It went on to the mail table, along with Monday's bills and announcements of scholarly seminars in Hawaii and St. Croix. I returned to the library and tried to figure out what I was going to do in ten minutes when Tiffani and Chondra Wallace showed up for their second session.

A year ago their mother had been murdered by their father up on a ridge in the Angeles Crest Forest.

He told it as a crime of passion and maybe he was right, in the very worst sense. I'd learned from court documents that absence of passion had never been a problem for Ruthanne and Donald Dell Wallace. She'd never been a strong-willed woman, and despite the ugliness of their divorce, she had held on to "love feelings" for Donald Dell. So no one had been surprised when he cajoled her into taking a night ride with sweet words, the promise of a lobster dinner, and good marijuana.

Shortly after parking on a shaded crest overlooking the forest, the two of them got high, made love, talked, argued, fought, raged, and finally clawed at one another. Then Donald Dell took his buck knife to the woman who still bore his name, slashed and stabbed her thirty-three times, and kicked her corpse out of his pickup, leaving behind an Indian-silver clip stuffed with cash and his membership card in the Iron Priests motorcycle club.

A docket-clearing plea bargain landed him in Folsom Prison on a five to ten for second-degree murder. There he was free to hang out in the yard with his meth-cooking Aryan Brotherhood bunkmates, take an auto mechanics course he could have taught, accrue good behavior brownie points in the chapel, and bench press until his pectorals threatened to explode.

Four months into his sentence, he was ready to see his daughters.

The law said his paternal rights had to be considered.

An L.A. family court judge named Stephen Huff —one of the better ones—asked me to evaluate. We met in his chambers on a September morning and he told me the details while drinking ginger ale and stroking his bald head. The room had beautiful old oak paneling and cheap country furniture. Pictures of his own children were all over the place.

"Just when does he plan on seeing them, Steve?"

"Up at the prison, twice a month."

"That's a plane ride."

"Friends will chip in for the fare."

"What kind of friends?"

"Some idiocy called The Donald Dell Wallace Defense Fund."

"Biker buddies?"

"Vroom vroom."

"Meaning it's probably amphetamine money."

His smile was weary and grudging. "Not the issue before us, Alex."

"What's next, Steve? Disability payments because he's stressed out being a single parent?"

"So it smells. So what else is new? Talk to the poor kids a few times, write up a report saying visitation's injurious to their psyches, and we'll bury the issue."

"For how long?"

He put down the ginger ale and watched the glass raise wet circles on his blotter. "I can kibosh it for at least a year."

"Then what?"

"If he puts in another claim, the kids can be reevaluated and we'll kibosh it again. Time's on their side, right? They'll be getting older and hopefully tougher."

"In a year they'll be ten and eleven, Steve."

He picked at his tie. "What can I tell you, Alex? I don't want to see these kids screwed up, either. I'm asking you to evaluate because you're tough-minded —for a shrink."

"Meaning someone else might recommend visitation?"

"It's possible. You should see some of the opinions your colleagues render. I had one the other day, said the fact that a mother was severely depressed was good for the kid—teach her the value of true emotions."

"Okay," I said. "But I want to do a real evaluation, not some rubber stamp. Something that may have some use for them in the future."

"Therapy? Why not? Sure, do whatever you want. You are now shrink of record. Send your bill straight to me and I'll see you get paid within fifteen working days."

"Who's paying, our leather-clad friends?"

"Don't worry, I'll make sure they pay up."

"Just as long as they don't try to deliver the check in person."

"I wouldn't worry about it, Alex. Those types shy away from insight."

The girls arrived right on time, just as they had last week, linked, like suitcases, to the arms of their grandmother.

"Well, here they are," Evelyn Rodriguez announced. She remained in the entry and pushed them forward.

"Morning," I said. "Hi, girls."

Tiffani smiled uneasily. Her older sister looked away.

"Have an easy ride?"

Evelyn shrugged, twisted her lips and untwisted them. Maintaining her grip on the girls, she backed away. The girls allowed themselves to be tugged, but unwillingly, like nonviolent protesters. Feeling the burden, Evelyn let go. Crossing her arms over her chest, she coughed and looked away from me.

Rodriguez was her fourth husband. She was Anglo, stout, bottom-heavy, an old fifty-eight, with dimpled elbows and knuckles, nicotine skin, and lips as thin and straight as a surgical incision. Talk came hard for her and I was pretty sure it was a character trait that preceded her daughter's murder.

This morning she wore a sleeveless, formless blouse—a faded mauve and powder blue floral print that reminded me of a decorative tissue box. It billowed, untucked, over black stretch jeans piped with red. Her blue tennis shoes were speckled with bleach spots. Her hair was short and wavy, corn colored above dark roots. Earring slits creased her lobes but

she wore no jewelry. Behind bifocals, her eyes continued to reject mine.

She patted Chondra's head, and the girl pressed
her face against a thick, soft arm. Tiffani had walked
into the living room and was staring at a picture on
the wall, tapping one foot fast.

Evelyn Rodriguez said, "Okay, then, I'll just wait
down in the car."

"If it gets too hot, feel free to come up."

"The heat don't bother me." She raised a forearm
and glanced at a too-small wristwatch. "How long we
talking about this time?"

"Let's aim for an hour, give or take."

"Last time was twenty minutes."

"I'd like to try for a little longer today."

She frowned. "Okay . . . can I smoke down
there?"

"Outside the house? Sure."

She muttered something.

"Anything you'd like to tell me?" I said.

"Me?" She freed one finger, poked a breast, and
smiled. "Nah. Be good, girlies."

Stepping out on the terrace, she closed the door.
Tiffani kept examining the picture. Chondra touched
the doorknob and licked her lips. She had on a white
Snoopy T-shirt, red shorts, and sandals with no socks.
A paper-wrapped Fruit Roll-Up extended from one
pocket of the shorts. Her arms and legs were pasty
and chubby, her face broad and puggish, topped by
white-blond hair drawn into very long, very tight pigtails. The hair gleamed, almost metallic, incongruous
above the plain face. Puberty might turn her pretty. I
wondered what else it might bring.

She nibbled her lower lip. My smile went unno-
ticed or unbelieved.

"How are you, Chondra?"

She shrugged again, kept her shoulders up, and

looked at the floor. Ten months her sister's senior, she was an inch shorter and seemed less mature. During the first session, she hadn't said a word, content to sit with her hands in her lap as Tiffani talked on.

"Do anything fun this week?"

She shook her head. I placed a hand on her shoulder and she went rigid until I removed it. The reaction made me wonder about some kind of abuse. How many layers of this family would I be able to peel back?

The file on my nightstand was my preliminary research. Before-bed reading for the strong stomached.

Legal jargon, police prose, unspeakable snapshots. Perfectly typed transcripts with impeccable margins.

Ruthanne Wallace reduced to a coroner's afternoon.

Wound depths, bone rills . . .

Donald Dell's mug shot, wild-eyed, blackbearded, sweaty.

"And then she got mean on me—she knew I didn't handle mean but that didn't stop her, no way. And then I just—you know—lost it. It shouldn'ta happened. What can I say?"

I said, "Do you like to draw, Chondra?"

"Sometimes."

"Well, maybe we'll find something you like in the playroom."

She shrugged and looked down at the carpet.

Tiffani was fingering the frame of the picture. A George Bellows boxing print. I'd bought it, impulsively, in the company of a woman I no longer saw.

"Like the drawing?" I said.

She turned around and nodded, all cheekbones and nose and chin. Her mouth was very narrow and crowded with big, misaligned teeth that forced it open and made her look perpetually confused. Her hair was dishwater, cut institutionally short, the bangs hacked crookedly. Some kind of food stain specked her upper lip. Her nails were dirty, her eyes an unremarkable brown. Then she smiled and the look of confusion vanished. At that moment she could have modeled, sold anything.

"Yeah, it's cool."

"What do you especially like about it?"

"The fighting."

"The fighting?"

"Yeah," she said, punching air. "Action. Like WWA."

"WWA," I said. "World Wrestling?"

She pantomimed an uppercut. "Pow poom." Then she looked at her sister and scowled, as if expecting support.

Chondra didn't move.

"Pow poom," said Tiffani, advancing toward her. "Welcome to WWA fighting, I'm Crusher Creeper and this is the Red Viper in a grudge match of the century. *Ding!*" Bell-pull pantomime.

She laughed, nervously. Chondra chewed her lip and tried to smile.

"Aar," said Tiffani, coming closer. She pulled the imaginary cord again. "Ding. Pow poom." Hooking her hands, she lurched forward with Frankenstein-monster unsteadiness. "Die, Viper! *Aaar!*"

She grabbed Chondra and began tickling her arms. The older girl giggled and tickled back, clumsily. Tiffani broke free and began circling, punching air. Chondra started chewing her lip, again.

I said, "C'mon, guys," and took them to the library. Chondra sat immediately at the play table. Tiffani paced and shadowboxed, hugging the periphery of the room like a toy on a track, muttering and jabbing.

Chondra watched her, then plucked a sheet of paper off the top of a stack and picked up a crayon. I waited for her to draw, but she put the crayon down and watched her sister.

"Do you guys watch wrestling at home?" I said.

"Roddy does," said Tiffani, without breaking step.

"Roddy's your grandmother's husband?"

Nod. Jab. "He's not our grampa. He's Mexican."

"He likes wrestling?"

"Uh-huh. Pow poom."

I turned to Chondra. She hadn't moved. "Do you watch wrestling on TV, too?"

Shake of the head.

"She likes *Surfriders*," said Tiffani. "I do, too, sometimes. And *Millionaire's Row*."

Chondra bit her lip.

"*Millionaire's Row*," I said. "Is that the one where rich people have all sorts of problems?"

"They *die*," said Tiffani. "Sometimes. It's really for real." She put her arms down and stopped circling. Coming over to us, she said, "They die because money and materials are the roots of sins and when you lay down with Satan, your rest is never peaceful."

"Do the rich people on *Millionaire's Row* lay down with Satan?"

"Sometimes." She resumed her circuit, striking out at unseen enemies.

"How's school?" I asked Chondra.

She shook her head and looked away.

"We didn't start yet," said Tiffani.

"How come?"

"Gramma said we didn't have to."

"Do you miss seeing your friends?"

Hesitation. "Maybe."

"Can I talk to Gramma about that?"

She looked at Chondra. The older girl was peeling the paper wrapper off a crayon.

Tiffani nodded. Then: "Don't do that. They're his."

"It's okay," I said.

"You shouldn't destroy other people's stuff."

"True," I said. "But some things are meant to be used up. Like crayons. And these crayons are here for you."

"Who bought them?" said Tiffani.

"I did."

"Destroying's Satan's work," said Tiffani, spreading her arms and rotating them in wide circles.

I said, "Did you hear that in church?"

She didn't seem to hear. Punched the air. "*He* laid down with Satan."

"Who?"

"*Wallace.*"

Chondra's mouth dropped open. "Stop," she said, very softly.

Tiffani came over and dropped her arm over her sister's shoulder. "It's okay. He's not our dad anymore, remember? Satan turned him into a bad spirit and he got all his sins wrapped up like one. Like a big burrito."

Chondra turned away from her.

"Come on," said Tiffani, rubbing her sister's back. "Don't worry."

"Wrapped up?" I said.

"Like one," she explained to me. "The Lord counts up all your good deeds and your sins and wraps them up. So when you die, He can look right away and know if you go up or down. *He's* going down. When he gets there, the angels'll look at the package and know all he done. And then he'll burn."

She shrugged. "That's the truth."

Chondra's eyes pooled with tears. She tried to

remove Tiffani's arm from her shoulder, but the younger girl held fast.

"It's okay," said Tiffani. "You got to talk about the truth."

"Stop," said Chondra.

"It's okay," Tiffani insisted. "You got to talk to him." She looked at me. "So he'll write a good book for the judge and *he'll* never get out."

Chondra looked at me.

I said, "Actually, what I write won't change how much time he spends in jail."

"Maybe," insisted Tiffani. "If your book tells the judge how evil he is, then *maybe* he could put him in longer."

"Was he ever evil to you?"

No answer.

Chondra shook her head.

Tiffani said, "He *hit* us."

"A lot?"

"Sometimes."

"With his hand or something else?"

"His hand."

"Never a stick or a belt or something else?"

Another headshake from Chondra. Tiffani's was slower, reluctant.

"Not a lot, but sometimes," I said.

"When we were bad."

"Bad?"

"Making a mess—going near his bike—he hit Mom more. Right?" Prodding Chondra. "He *did*."

Chondra gave a tiny nod, grabbed the crayon, and started peeling again. Tiffani watched but didn't stop her.

"That's why we left him," she said. "He hit her all the time. And then he came after her with lust and sin in his heart and killed her—tell the judge that, you're rich, he'll listen to you!"

Chondra began crying. Tiffani patted her and said, "It's okay, we got to."

I got a tissue box. Tiffani took it from me and wiped her sister's eyes. Chondra pressed the crayon to her lips.

"Don't eat it," said Tiffani. "It's poison."

Chondra let go and the crayon flew out of her hand and landed on the floor. Tiffani retrieved it and placed it neatly alongside the box.

Chondra was licking her lips. Her eyes were closed and one soft hand was fisted.

"Actually," I said, "it's not poisonous, just wax with color in it. But it probably doesn't taste too good."

Chondra opened her eyes. I smiled and she tried to smile, producing only a small rise in one corner of her mouth.

Tiffani said, "Well, it's not food."

"No, it isn't."

She paced some more. Boxed and muttered.

I said, "Let me go over what I told you last week. You're here because your father wants you to visit him in jail. My job is to find out how you feel about that, so I can tell the judge."

"Why doesn't the judge ask *us*?"

"He will," I said. "He'll be talking to you, but first he wants me to—"

"Why?"

"Because that's my job—talking to kids about their feelings. Finding out how they really—"

"We don't *want* to see him," said Tiffani. "He's an insument of Satan."

"An—"

"An *insument*! He laid all down with Satan and became a sinful spirit. When he dies, he's going to burn in hell, that's for sure."

Chondra's hands flew to her face.

"Stop!" said Tiffani. She rushed over to her sister, but before she got there, Chondra stood and let out a single, deep sob. Then she ran for the door, swinging it open so hard it almost threw her off balance.

She caught it, then she was out.

Tiffani watched her go, looking tiny and helpless. "You got to tell the truth," she said.

I said, "Absolutely. But sometimes it's hard."

She nodded. Now her eyes were wet.

She paced some more.

I said, "Your sister's older but it looks like you take care of her."

She stopped, faced me, gave a defiant stare, but seemed comforted.

"You take good care of her," I said.

Shrug.

"That must get hard sometimes."

Her eyes flickered. She put her hands on her hips and jutted her chin.

"It's okay," she said.

I smiled.

"She's my sister." She stood there, knocking her hands against her legs.

I patted her shoulder.

She sniffed, then walked away.

"You got to tell the truth," she said.

"Yes, you do."

Punch, jab. "Pow poom . . . I wanna go home."

Chondra was already with Evelyn, sharing the front seat of the thirty-year-old, plum-colored Chevy. The car had nearly bald blackwalls and a broken antenna. The paint job was homemade, the color nothing GM had ever conceived. One edge of the car's rear bumper had been broken and it nearly scraped the ground.

I got to the driver's window as Tiffani made her way down the steps from the landing. Evelyn Rodriguez didn't look up. A cigarette drooped from her lips. A hardpack of Winstons sat on the dashboard. The driver's half of the windshield was coated with greasy fog. Her fingers were busy tying a lanyard keychain. The rest of her was inert.

Chondra was pressed up against the passenger door, legs curled beneath her, staring at her lap.

Tiffani arrived, making her way to the passenger side while keeping her eyes on me. Opening the rear door, she dove inside.

Evelyn finally took her eyes off her work, but her fingers kept moving. The lanyard was brown and white, a diamond stitch that reminded me of rattlesnake skin.

"Well, that was quick," she said. "Close that door now, don't kill the battery."

Tiffani scooted over and slammed the door.

I said, "The girls haven't started school yet."

Evelyn Rodriguez looked at Tiffani for a second, then turned to me. "That's right."

"Do you need any help with that?"

"Help?"

"Getting them started. Is there some kind of problem?"

"Nah, we been busy—I make 'em read at home. They're okay."

"Planning to send them soon?"

"Sure, when things calm down—so what's next? They have to come again?"

"Let's try again tomorrow. Same time okay?"

"Nope," she said. "Matter of fact, it isn't. Got things to do."

"What's a good time for you, then?"

She sucked the cigarette, adjusted her glasses,

and placed the lanyard on the seat. Her slash lips twitched, searching for an expression.

"There are no good times. All the good times already been rolled."

She started the car. Her lips were trembling and the cigarette bobbed. She removed it and turned the wheel sharply without shifting out of park. The car was low on steering fluid and shrieked in protest. The front tires swung outward and scraped the asphalt.

"I'd like to see them again fairly soon," I said.

"What for?"

Before I could answer, Tiffani stretched herself out along the back seat, belly down, and began kicking the door panel with both feet.

"Cut that *out!*" said Mrs. Rodriguez, without looking back. "What for?" she repeated. "So we can be told what to do and how to do it, as usual?"

"No, I—"

"The problem is, things are upside *down. Nonsensical.* Those that *should* be dead *aren't,* and those that *are,* shouldn't *be.* No amount of talking's gonna change that, so what's the difference? Upside down, completely, and now I got to be a mama all over again."

"He can write a book," said Tiffani. "So that—"

Evelyn cut her off with a look. "You don't worry yourself about things. We got to be heading back—if there's time, I'll get you an ice cream."

She yanked the gear lever down. The Chevy grumbled and bucked, then drove off, rear bumper flirting with the road.

I stood there a while, sucking up exhaust fumes, then went back up to the house, returned to the library, and charted:

"*Strong resistance to eval. on part of m.g.m. T overtly*

angry, hostile to father, talks in terms of sin, retribution. C still not communic. Will follow."

Profound.

I went to the bedroom and retrieved Ruthanne Wallace's police file.

Big as a phone book.

"Trial transcripts," Milo had said, hefting it as he handed it over. "Sure isn't because of any hotshot detection. Your basic moron murder."

He'd pulled it from Foothill Division's CLOSED files, filling my request without question. Now I flipped pages, not knowing why I'd asked for it. Closing the folder, I took it into the library and crammed it down into a desk drawer.

Ten in the morning and I was already tired.

I went to the kitchen, loaded some coffee into the machine, and started going through the mail, discarding junk mail, signing checks, filing paper, then coming to the brown-wrapped package that I'd assumed was a book.

Slitting the padded envelope, I stuck my hand in, expecting the bulk of a hardcover. But my fingers touched nothing and I reached deeper, finally coming upon something hard and smooth. Plastic. Wedged tightly in a corner.

I shook the envelope. An audiocassette fell out and clattered onto the table.

Black, no label or markings on either side.

I examined the padded envelope. My name and address had been typed on a white sticker. No zip code. No return address either. The postmark was four days old, recorded at the Terminal Annex.

Curious, I took the tape into the living room, slipped it into the deck, and sank back onto the old leather couch.

Click. A stretch of static-fuzzed nothing started me wondering if this was some sort of practical joke.

Then a shock of noise killed that theory and made my chest tighten.

A human voice. Screaming.

Howling.

Male. Hoarse. Loud. Wet—as if gargling in pain.

Unbearable pain. A terrible incoherence that went on and on as I sat there, too surprised to move.

A throat-ripping howling interspersed with trapped-animal panting.

Heavy breathing.

Then more screams—louder. Ear-clapping expulsions that had no shape or meaning . . . like the soundtrack from the rancid core of a nightmare.

I pictured a torture chamber, shrieking black mouths, convulsing bodies.

The howling bore through my head. I strained to make out words amid the torrent but heard only the pain.

Louder.

I leaped up to turn down the volume on the machine. Found it already set low.

I started to turn it off, but before I could, the screaming died.

More static-quiet.

Then a new voice.

Soft. High-pitched. Nasal.

A child's voice:

> Bad love. Bad love.
> Don't give me the bad love.

Child's timbre—but with no childish lilt.
Unnaturally flat—*robot*like.

> Bad love. Bad love.
> Don't give me the bad love . . .

Repeating it. Three times. Four.

A chant, Druidish and mournful—so oddly metallic.

Almost like a prayer.

Bad love. Bad love . . .

No. Too hollow for prayer—too faithless.

Idolatrous.

A prayer for the dead.

By the dead.

2

I turned the recorder off. My fingers were stiff from clenching, my heart thumped, and my mouth was dry.

Coffee smells drew me to the kitchen. I filled a cup, returned to the living room, and rewound the tape. When the spool filled, I turned the volume to near inaudible and pressed PLAY. My gut knotted in anticipation. Then the screams came on.

Even that soft, it was hideous.

Someone being *hurt*.

Then the child's chant again, even worse in replay. The robotic drone conjured a gray face, sunken eyes, a small mouth barely moving.

Bad love. Bad love . . .

What had been done to strip the voice so completely of emotion?

I'd heard that kind of voice before—on the terminal wards, in holding cells and shelters.

Bad love . . .

The phrase was vaguely familiar, but why?

I sat there for a long time, trying to remember, letting my coffee go cold and untouched. Finally I got up, ejected the tape, and took it into the library.

Down into the desk drawer, next to Ruthanne's file.

Dr. Delaware's Black Museum.

My heart was still chopping away. The screams and chants replayed themselves in my mind.

The house felt too empty. Robin was not due back from Oakland till Thursday.

At least she hadn't been home to hear it.

Old protective instincts.

During our years together I'd worked hard at shielding her from the uglier aspects of my work. Eventually, I realized I'd erected the barrier higher than it needed to be and had been trying to let her in more.

But not this. No need for her to hear this.

I sank lower into my desk chair, wondering what the damned thing meant.

Bad love . . . what should I do about it?

A sick joke?

The child's voice . . .

Bad love . . . I knew I'd heard the phrase before. I repeated it out loud, trying to trigger a memory. But the words just hovered, chattering like bats.

A psychological phrase? Something out of a textbook?

It did have a psychoanalytic ring.

Why had the tape been sent to *me*?

Stupid question. I'd never been able to answer it for anyone else.

Bad love . . . most likely something orthodox Freudian. Melanie Klein had theorized about good breasts and bad breasts—perhaps there was someone

out there with a sick sense of humor and a side interest in neo-Freudian theory.

I went to my bookshelves, pulled out a dictionary
of psychological terms. Nothing. Tried lots of other
books, scanning indexes.

Not a clue.

I returned to the desk.

A former patient taunting me for services poorly
rendered?

Or something more recent—Donald Dell Wallace,
festering up in Folsom, seeing me as his enemy and
trying to play with my head?

His attorney, a dimwit named Sherman Bucklear,
had called me several times before I'd seen the girls,
trying to convince me his client was a devoted father.

"It was Ruthanne neglected them, Doctor. Whatever
else Donald Dell did, he cared about them."

"How was he on child support?"

"Times are rough. He did the best he could—does that
prejudice you, Doctor?"

"I haven't formed an opinion yet, Mr. Bucklear."

"No, of course not. No one's saying you should. The
question is, are you willing to form one at all or do you
have your mind made up just because of what Donald Dell
did?"

"I'll spend time with the girls. Then I'll form my opinion."

" 'Cause there's a lot of potential for prejudice against
my client."

"Because he murdered his wife?"

"That's exactly what I mean, Doctor—you know, I
can always bring in my own experts."

"Feel free."

"I feel very free, Doctor. This is a free country. You'd
do well to remember that."

Other experts. Was this bit of craziness an attempt to intimidate me so that I'd drop out of the case

and clear the way for Bucklear's hired guns? Donald Dell's gang, the Iron Priests, had a history of bullying rivals in the meth trade, but I still didn't see it. How could anyone assume I'd make a connection between screams and chants and two little girls?

Unless this was only the first step in a campaign of intimidation. Even so, it was almost clownishly heavyhanded.

Then again, Donald Dell's leaving his ID at the murder scene didn't indicate finesse.

I'd consult an expert of my own. Dialing the West L.A. police station, I was connected to Robbery-Homicide, where I asked for Detective Sturgis.

Milo was out of the office—no big surprise. He'd endured a demotion and six months' unpaid suspension for breaking the jaw of a homophobic lieutenant who'd put his life in danger, then a butt-numbing year as a computer clerk at Parker Center. The department had hoped inertia would finally drive him into disability retirement; the LAPD still denied the existence of gay cops, and Milo's very presence was an assault upon that ostrich logic. But he'd stuck it out and finally gotten back into active service as a Detective II. Back on the streets now, he was making the most of it.

"Any word when he'll be back?" I asked the detective who answered.

"Nope," he said, sounding put upon.

I left my name. He said, "Uh-huh," and hung up.

I decided nothing further could be gained by worrying, changed into a T-shirt, shorts, and sneakers, and trotted out the front door, ready for a half-hour run, knees be damned.

Bounding down the steps, I jogged across the motor court, passing the spot where Evelyn Rodriguez's car had leaked oil. Just as I rounded the eugenia hedge that blocked my house from the old bridle path winding above the Glen, something stepped in front of me and stopped.

And stared.

A dog, but I'd never seen one like it.

Small dog—about a foot high, maybe twice that in length. Short, black coat brindled with yellow hairs. A lot of muscle crammed into the compact package; its body bulged and gleamed in the sunlight. It had thick legs, a bull neck, a barrel chest, and a tight, tucked-in belly. Its head was disproportionately wide and square, its face flat, deeply wrinkled, and pendulously jowled.

Somewhere between frog, monkey, and extraterrestrial.

A strand of drool dangled from its flews.

It continued to look me straight in the eye, arching forward, as if ready to spring. Its tail was an inch of stub. Male. Neutered.

I stared back. He snorted and yawned, showing big, sharp, white teeth. A banana-sized tongue curled upward and licked meaty lips.

A diamond of white hair in the center of his chest throbbed with cardiac excitement. Around his beefy neck was a nailhead-studded collar, but no tag.

"Hi, fella."

His eyes were light brown and unmoving. I thought I detected a softness that contradicted the fighter's stance.

Another yawn. Purple maw. He panted faster and remained rooted in place.

Some kind of bulldog or mini-mastiff. From the crust around his eyes and the heaving of his chest, the early autumn heat wasn't doing him any good. Not a pug—considerably bigger than a pug, and the ears stood upright, like those of a Boston terrier—in fact, he looked a bit like a Boston. But shorter and a lot heavier—a Boston on steroids.

An exotic dwarf fighter bred to go for the knee-caps, or a pup that would turn massive?

He yawned again and snorted harshly.

We continued to face off.

A bird chirped.

The dog cocked his head toward the sound for half a second, then peered back at me. His eyes were preternaturally alert, almost human.

He licked his lips. The drool strand stretched, broke, and fell to the pavement.

Pant, pant, pant.

"Thirsty?"

No movement.

"Friend or foe?"

Another display of teeth that seemed more smile than snarl, but who knew?

Another moment of standoff, then I decided letting something this pint-sized obstruct me was ridiculous. Even with the bulk, he couldn't weigh more than twenty or twenty-five pounds. If he did attack, I could probably punt-kick him onto the Glen.

I took a step forward, then another.

The dog came toward me deliberately, head lowered, muscles meshing, in a rolling, pantherish gait. Wheezing.

I stopped. He kept going.

I lifted my hands out of mouth range, suddenly aware of my exposed legs.

He came up to me. Up to my legs. Rubbed his head against my shin.

His face felt like hot suede. Too hot and dry for canine health.

I reached down and touched his head. He snorted and panted faster, letting his tongue loll. I lowered my hand slowly and dangled it, receiving a long lick on the palm. But my skin remained bone dry.

The pants had turned into unhealthy-sounding clicks.

He tremored for a second, then worked his tongue over his arid face.

I kneeled and patted his head again, feeling a flat plate of thick, ridged bone beneath the glossy coat. He looked up at me with a bulldog's sad-clown dignity. The crust around his eyes looked calcified. The folds of his face were encrusted, too.

The nearest water source was the garden-hose outlet near the pond. I stood and gestured toward it.

"Come on, buster—hydration."

The dog strained but stayed in place, head cocked, letting out raspy breaths that grew faster and faster and began to sound labored. I thought I saw his front legs quaver.

I began walking to the garden. Heard soft pads and looked behind me to see him following a few paces behind. Keeping to the left—a trained heeler?

But as I opened the gate to the pond, he hung back, remaining well outside the fence.

I went in. The pond water was greening due to the heat, but still clear. The koi were circling lazily. A couple of them saw me and approached the rim for feeding—babies who'd survived the surprise spawn of two summers ago. Most were over a foot long now. A few were colored brilliantly.

The dog just stood there, nose pointed at the water, suffering.

"Come on, pal." I picked up the hose.

Nothing.

Uncoiling a couple of feet, I opened the valve. The rubber hummed between my fingers.

"C'mere. H_2O."

The dog stared through the gateway, panting, gasping, legs bowed with fatigue. But he didn't budge.

"C'mon, what's the problem, sport? Some kind of phobia, or don't you like seafood?"

Blink. He stayed in place. Swayed a bit.

The hose began to dribble. I dragged it out the gate, sprinkling plants as I walked.

The dog stood his ground until the water was an inch from his fleshy mouth. Then he craned his neck and began lapping. Then gulping. Then bathing in it, shaking his head and showering me before opening his maw and heading in for more.

Long time since the last tipple.

He shook and sprayed me again, turned his head away from the water, and sat.

When I returned from replacing the hose, he was still there, settled on his ample haunches.

"What now?" I said.

He ambled up to me, jauntily, a bit of roll in his stride. Putting his head against my leg, he kept it there.

I rubbed him behind the ears and his body went loose. He stayed relaxed as I used my handkerchief to wipe the crust from his face. When I was through, he let out a grumble of contentment.

"You're welcome."

He put his head against my leg once more, blowing out breath as I petted.

What a morning. I sighed.

He snorted. A reply?

I tried it again, sighing audibly. The dog produced an adenoidal grunt.

"A conversationalist," I said. "Someone talks to you, don't they? Someone cares about you."

Grunt.

"How'd you get here?"

Grumble.

My voice was loud against the quiet of the Glen, harsh counterpoint to the flow of the waterfall.

Nut mail and talking to a dog. This is what it's come to, Delaware.

The dog gazed up at me with a look I was willing to classify as friendship.

You take what you can get.

He watched as I pulled the Seville out of the carport, and when I opened the passenger door, he jumped in as if he owned the vehicle. For the next hour and a half, he looked out the window as I drove around the canyon, watching for LOST DOG posters on trees and talking to neighbors I'd never met. No one belonged to him and no one recognized him, though the checkout girl at the Beverly Glen Market opined that he was "a little stud," and several other shoppers concurred.

While I was there, I bought a few groceries and a small bag of kibble. When I got home, the dog bounced up the stairs after me and watched as I unloaded the staples. I poured the kibble into a bowl and set it on the kitchen floor, along with another bowl of water. The dog ignored it, choosing instead to station himself in front of the refrigerator door.

I moistened the kibble but that had no effect. This time the stubby tail was wagging.

I pointed to the bowl.

The dog began nudging the fridge door and looking up at me. I opened the door and he tried to stick his head in. Restraining him by the collar, I scrounged and found some leftover meatloaf.

The dog jumped away from my grasp, leaping nearly to my waist.

"A gourmet, huh?"

I crumbled some meatloaf into the kibble and mixed it with my fingers. The dog was snarfing before my hand was free, coating my fingers with a slick layer of drool.

I watched him feast. When he finished, he cocked his head, stared at me for a moment, then walked toward the back of the kitchen, circling and sniffing the floor.

"What now? Sorbet to clean your palate?"

He circled some more, walked to the service porch door, and began butting and scratching at the lower panel.

"Ah," I said, bounding up. I unlatched the door and he zipped out. I watched him race down the stairs and find a soft, shaded spot near a juniper bush before lifting his leg.

He climbed back up, looking content and dignified.

"Thank you," I said.

He stared at me until I petted him, then trailed me into the dining room, settling next to my leg, frog face lifted expectantly. I scratched him under his chin and he promptly flipped onto his back, paws upright.

I scratched his belly and he let out a long, low, phlegmy moan. When I tried to stop, one paw pressed down on my hand and bade me continue.

Finally he turned back on his belly and fell asleep, snoring, jowls shaking like mudflaps.

"Someone's got to be looking for you."

I slid the morning paper across the table. Plenty of lost-dog ads in the classifieds, but none of the animals remotely matched the creature stretched out on the floor.

I got animal control's number from information and told the woman who answered it what I'd found.

"He sounds cute," she said.

"Any idea what he is?"

"Not offhand—could be some kind of bulldog, I guess. Maybe a mix."

"What should I do with him?"

"Well," she said, "the law says you have to try to return him. You could bring him in and leave him with us, but we're pretty crowded and I can't honestly tell you he'll get anything more than basic care."

"What if you have him and no one claims him?"

"Well . . . you know."

"What're my alternatives?"

"You could put an ad in the paper—'founds' are sometimes free. You might also want to take him to a vet—make sure he's not carrying anything that could cause you problems."

I thanked her, called the newspaper, and placed the ad. Then I pulled out the Yellow Pages and looked under veterinarians. There was an animal hospital on Sepulveda near Olympic that advertised "walk-ins and emergencies."

I let the the dog sleep for an hour, then took him for another ride.

The clinic was a milky blue, cement-block building set between a wrought iron foundry and a discount clothing barn. The traffic on Sepulveda looked angry, so I carried my guest to the front door, upping the weight estimate to thirty pounds.

The waiting room was empty except for an old man wearing a golf cap, comforting a giant white German shepherd. The dog was prone on the black linoleum floor, weeping and trembling from fright. The man kept saying, "It's okay, Rexie."

I tapped on a frosted glass window and registered, using my name because I didn't know the dog's. Rex was summoned five minutes later, then a college-age girl opened the door and called out, "Alex?"

The bulldog was stretched on the floor, sleeping

and snoring. I picked him up and carried him in. He opened one eye but stayed limp.

"What's the matter with Alex, today?" said the girl.

"Long story," I said and followed her to a small exam room outfitted with lots of surgical steel. The disinfectant smell reminded *me* of traumas gone by, but the dog stayed calm.

The vet arrived soon after—a young, crewcut, Asian man in a blue smock, smiling and drying his hands with a paper towel.

"Hi, I'm Dr. Uno—ah, a Frenchie, don't see too many of those."

"A what?"

He one-handed the towel into a waste bin. "A French bulldog."

"Oh."

He looked at me. "You don't know what he is?"

"I found him."

"Oh," he said. "Well, that's a pretty rare dog you've got there—*someone'll* claim him." He petted the dog. "These little guys are pretty expensive, and this one looks like a good specimen." He lifted his flews. "Well cared for, too—these teeth have been scaled pretty recently and his ears are clean—these upright ears can be receptacles for all kinds of stuff . . . anyway, what seems to be your problem with him?"

"Apart from a fear of water, nothing," I said. "I just wanted him checked out."

"Fear of water? How so?"

I recounted the dog's avoidance of the pond.

"Interesting," said the vet. "Probably means he's been perimeter trained for his own safety. Bulldog pups can drown pretty easily—real heavy boned, so they sink like rocks. On top of that, they have no nose to speak of, so they have trouble getting their head clear. Another patient of mine lost a couple of English bull babies that way. So this guy's actually being smart by shying away."

"He's housebroken and he heels, too," I said.

The vet smiled and I realized something very close to owner's pride had crept into my voice.

"Why don't you put him up here on the table and let's see what else he can do."

The dog was probed, vaccinated, and given a clean bill of health.

"Someone definitely took good care of him," said Uno. "The basic thing to watch out for is heatstroke, specially now, when the temperature is rising. These brachycephalic dogs are really prone to it, so keep him out of the heat."

He handed me some brochures on basic dog care, reiterated the heat danger, and said, "That's about it. Good luck finding the owner."

"Any suggestions along those lines?"

"Put an ad in the paper, or if there's a local Frenchie club, you could try getting in touch with them."

"Do you have a list of club addresses?"

"Nope, sorry, we do mostly ER work. Maybe the AKC—American Kennel Club—could help. They register most of the purebreds."

"Where are they?"

"New York."

He walked me to the door.

"These dogs generally have good temperament?" I said.

He looked down at the dog, who was staring up at us and wagging his stub.

"From the little I've heard and read, what you're seeing right now is pretty much it."

"They ever attack?"

"Attack?" He laughed. "I guess if he got attached to you he might try to protect you, but I wouldn't count on it. They're really not good for much but being a friend."

"Well, that's something," I said.

"Sure it is," he said. "That's where it's at, bottom line, right?"

3

I drove away from the clinic stroking the dog and thinking of the child's voice on the tape. I wasn't hungry but figured I'd need some lunch eventually. Spotting a hamburger stand farther up on Sepulveda, I bought a takeout half-pounder. The aroma kept the dog awake and drooling all the way home, and a couple of times he tried to stick his nose in the bag. Back in the kitchen, he convinced me to part with a third of the patty. Then he carried his booty to a corner, sat, masticated noisily, and promptly went to sleep, chin to the floor.

I phoned my service and found out Milo had called back. This time he answered at Robbery-Homicide. "Sturgis."

"How's it going, Joe Friday?"

"The usual buckets of blood. How's by you?"

I told him about receiving the tape. "Probably just a prank, but imagine getting a kid to do that."

I expected him to slough it off, but he said, " 'Bad love'? That's weird."

"What is?"

"Those exact same words popped up in a case a couple of months ago. Remember that social worker who got murdered at the mental health center? Rebecca Basille?"

"It was all over the news," I said, remembering headlines and sound bites, the smiling picture of a pretty, dark-haired young woman butchered in a soundproof therapy room. "You never said it was your case."

"It wasn't really anyone's case because there was no investigation to speak of. The psycho who stabbed her died trying to take another caseworker hostage."

"I remember."

"I got stuck filling out the paperwork."

"How did 'bad love' pop up?"

"The psycho screamed it when he ran out after cutting Becky. Clinic director was standing in the hall, heard him before she ducked into her office and hid. I figured it was schizo talk."

"It may be something psychological—jargon that he picked up somewhere in the mental health system. 'Cause I think I've heard it, too, but I can't remember where."

"That's probably it," he said. "A kid, huh?"

"A kid chanting in this strange, flat voice. It may be related to a case I'm working on, Milo. Remember that file you got me—the woman murdered by her husband?"

"The biker?"

"He's been locked up for six months. Two months ago he started asking for visitation with his daughters—around the same time as the Basille murder, come to think of it. If Becky's murderer screaming 'bad love' *was* in the news, I guess he could have taken notice and filed it away for future use."

"Intimidate the shrink—maybe remind you of

what can happen to therapists who don't behave themselves?"

"Exactly. There'd be nothing criminal in that, would there? Just sending a tape."

"Wouldn't even buy him snack bar demerits, but how could he figure you'd make the connection?"

"I don't know. Unless this is just an appetizer and there's more coming."

"What's this fool's name, again?"

"Donald Dell Wallace."

He repeated it and said, "I never read the file. Refresh me on him."

"He used to hang out with a biker gang called the Iron Priests—small-time Tujunga bunch. In between prison sentences, he worked as a motorcycle mechanic. Dealt speed on the side. I think he's a member of the Aryan Brotherhood."

"Well, there's a character reference for you. Let me see what I find out."

"You think this is something I should worry about?"

"Not really—you might think of locking your doors."

"I already do."

"Congratulations. You going to be home tonight?"

"Yup."

"How's Robin?"

"Fine. She's up in Oakland, giving a seminar— medieval lutes."

"Smart kid, working with inanimate objects. All right, I'll come by, rescue you from your hermitude. If you want me to I can fingerprint the tape, check it against Wallace's. If it's him, we'll report him to his keepers, at least let him know you're not going to roll over."

"Okay—thanks."

"Yeah . . . don't handle it anymore, hard plastic's a real good surface for preservation. . . . *Bad love*. Sounds like something out of a movie. Sci-fi, splatter flick, whatever."

"I couldn't find it in any of my psych books, so maybe that's it. Maybe that's where Becky's murderer got it, too—all of us are children of the silver screen. The tape was mailed from the Terminal Annex, not Folsom. Meaning if Wallace *is* behind it, someone's helping him."

"I can check the rest of his gang, too. At least the ones with records. Don't lose any sleep over it. I'll try to get by around eight. Meanwhile, back to the slaughter."

"Buckets of blood, huh?"

"Big *sloshing* buckets. Every morning I wake up, praise the Lord, and thank Him for all the iniquity—how's that for perverse?"

"Hey," I said, "you love your work."

"Yeah," he said. "Yeah, I do. Demotion never felt so goddamn glorious."

"Department treating you well?"

"Let's not lapse into fantasy. The department's *tolerating* me, because they think they've wounded me *deeply* with their pissanty pay cut and I'll eventually cave in and take disability like every other goldbricking pension junkie. The fact that one night of moonlighting more than makes up for the difference in take-home has eluded the brass. As has the fact that I'm a contrary bastard."

"They're not very observant, are they?"

"That's why they're administrators."

After he hung up, I called Evelyn Rodriguez's house in Sunland. As the phone rang, I pictured the

man who'd carved up her daughter playing with a
tape recorder in his cell.

No one answered. I put the phone down.

I thought of Rebecca Basille, hacked to death in a
soundproof room. Her murder had really gotten to
me—gotten to lots of therapists. But I'd put it out of
my head until Milo reminded me.

I drummed my fists on the counter. The dog
looked up from his empty bowl and stared. I'd forgotten he was there.

*What happens to therapists who don't behave them-
selves . . .*

What if Wallace had nothing to do with the tape?
Someone else, from my past.

I went into the library and the dog followed. The
closet was stacked with boxes of inactive patient files,
loosely alphabetized with no strict chronological order, because some patients had been treated at several
different time periods.

I put the radio on for background and started
with the A's, looking for children whom I'd tagged
with psychopathic or antisocial tendencies and
cases that hadn't turned out well. Even long-term
deadbeats I'd sent to collections.

I made it halfway through. A sour history lesson
with no tangible results: nothing popped out at me.
By the end of the afternoon, my eyes hurt and I was
exhausted.

I stopped reading, realized grumbly snores had
overpowered the music. Reaching down, I kneaded
the bulldog's muscular neck. He shuddered but remained asleep. A few charts were fanned on the desk.
Even if I came up with something suggestive, patient
confidentiality meant I couldn't discuss it with Milo.

I returned to the kitchen, fixed kibble and
meatloaf and fresh water, watched my companion

sup, burp, then circle and sniff. I left the service door open and he bounced down the stairs.

While he was out, I called Robin's hotel in Oakland again, but she was still out.

The dog came back. He and I went into the living room and watched the evening news. Current events were none too cheerful, but he didn't seem to mind.

The doorbell rang at eight-fifteen. The dog didn't bark, but his ears stiffened and tilted forward and he trailed me to the door, remaining at my heels as I squinted through the peephole.

Milo's face was a wide-angle blur, big and pocked, its paleness turned sallow by the bug light over the doorway.

"Police. Open up or I'll shoot."

He bared his teeth in a Halloween grimace. I unlocked the door and he came in, carrying a black briefcase. He was dressed for work: blue hopsack blazer, gray slacks, white shirt stretched tight over his belly, blue and gray plaid tie tugged loose, suede desert boots in need of new soles.

His haircut was recent, the usual: clipped short at sides and back, long and shaggy on top, sideburns down to the earlobes. Country yokels had looked that way back in the fifties. Melrose Avenue hipsters were doing it nowadays. I doubted Milo was aware of either fact. The black forelock that shadowed his forehead showed a few more gray streaks. His green eyes were clear. Some of the weight he'd lost had come back; he looked to be carrying at least two hundred and forty pounds on his seventy-five inches.

He stared at the dog and said, "*What?*"

"Gee, Dad, he followed me home. Can I keep him?"

The dog gazed up at him and yawned.

"Yeah, I'm bored, too," Milo told him. "What the hell *is* it, Alex?"

"French bulldog," I said. "Rare and pricey, according to a vet. And this one's a damned good specimen."

"Specimen." He shook his head. "Is it civilized?"

"Compared to what you're used to, very."

He frowned, patted the dog gingerly, and got slurped.

"Charming," he said, wiping his hand on his slacks. Then he looked at me. "*Why*, Marlin Perkins?"

"I'm serious—he just showed up this morning. I'm trying to locate the owner, have an ad running in the paper. The vet said he's been well cared for. It's just a matter of time before somebody claims him."

"For a moment I thought this tape stuff had gotten to you and you'd gone out and bought yourself some protection."

"This?" I laughed, remembering Dr. Uno's amusement. "I don't think so."

"Hey," he said, "sometimes bad things come in small packages—for all I know it's trained to go for the gonads."

The dog stood on his hind legs and touched Milo's trousers with his forepaws.

"Down, Rover," he said.

"What's the matter, you don't like animals?"

"Cooked, I do. Didja name it yet?"

I shook my head.

"Then 'Rover' will have to do." He took his jacket off and tossed it onto a chair. "Here's what I've got so far on Wallace. He keeps a low profile in slam and has some associations with the Aryan Brotherhood, but he's not a full member. As for what kind of hardware he's got in his cell, I don't know yet. Now where's the alleged tape?"

"In the alleged tapedeck."

He went over and turned on the stereo. The dog stayed with me.

I said, "You know where the meatloaf comes from, don't you?"

He cocked his head and licked my hand.

Then the screams came on and the hairs rose on the back of his neck.

Hearing it the third time was worse.

Milo's face registered revulsion, but after the sound died, he said nothing. Taking his briefcase over to the deck, he switched it off, ejected the tape, and removed it by inserting a pencil in one of the reel holes.

"Black surface," he muttered. "Ye olde white powder."

Placing the cassette atop the plastic cover of my turntable, he removed a small brush and a vial from the case. Dipping the brush into the vial, he dusted the cassette with a pale, ashlike powder, squinting as he worked.

"Well, looks like we've got some nice ridges and swirls," he said. "But they could all be yours. Your prints are on file with the medical board, right, so I can check?"

"They printed me when I got my license."

"Meaning a week or two going through channels in order to pry it loose from Sacramento—noncriminal stuff's not on PRINTRAK yet. You haven't been arrested for anything recently, have you?"

"Nothing I can remember."

"Too bad. Okay, let's get a quick fix on your digits right now."

He took an inkpad and fingerprint form from the case. The dog watched as he inked my fingers and rolled them on the form. The audiocassette was near my hand and I looked at the concentric white patches on its surface.

"Keep that pinkie loose," said Milo. "Feel like a scumbag felon yet?"

"I don't say squat without my lawyer, pig."

He chuckled and handed me a cloth. As I wiped my fingers, he took a small camera out of the case and photographed the prints on the tape. Flipping the cartridge over with the pencil, he dusted, raised more prints on the other side, and took pictures of them, muttering, "Might as well do it right." Then he lowered the cassette into a small box lined with cotton, sealed the container, and put it into the case.

"What do you think?" I said.

He looked at my print form, then at the tape, and shook his head. "They always look the same to me. Let the lab deal with it."

"I meant about the tape. Sound like any movie you know?"

He ran his hand over his face, as if washing without water. "Not really."

"Me neither. Didn't the kid's voice have a brainwashed quality to it?"

"More like brain *dead*," he said. "Yeah, it was ugly. But that doesn't make it real. Far as I'm concerned, it's still filed under B for 'bad joke.'"

"Someone getting a child to chant as a joke?"

He nodded. "We're living in weird times, Doc."

"But what if it *is* real? What if we're dealing with a sadist who's abducted and tortured a child and is telling me about it in order to heighten the kick?"

"The *screamer* was the one who sounded tortured, Alex. And that was an adult. Someone's messing with your head."

"If it's not Wallace," I said, "maybe it's some psychopath picking me as his audience because I treat kids and sometimes my name gets in the papers.

Someone who read about Becky's murderer screaming 'bad love' and got an idea. And for all I know, I'm
not the only therapist he's contacted."

"Could be. When was the last time you *were* in
the papers?"

"This summer—when the Jones case went to
trial."

"Anything's possible," he said.

"Or maybe it's more direct, Milo. A former patient, telling me I failed him. I started going through
my files, got halfway and couldn't find anything. But
who knows? My patients were all children. In most
cases I have no idea what kind of adults they turned
into."

"If you found anything funny, would you give
me the names?"

"Couldn't," I said. "Without some kind of clear
danger, I couldn't justify breaking confidentiality."

He scowled. The dog watched him unwaver-
ingly.

"What're *you* staring at?" he demanded.

Wag, wag.

Milo began to smile, fought it, picked up his case,
and put a heavy hand on my shoulder.

"Listen, Alex, I still wouldn't lose any sleep over
it. Let me take these to the lab right now instead of
tomorrow, see if I can get some night-shifter to put
some speed on. I'll also make a copy and start a case
file—private one, just for my eyes. When in doubt, be
a goddamn clerk."

After he left, I tried to read a psychology journal
but couldn't concentrate. I watched the news, did fifty
pushups, and had another go at my charts. I made it
through all of them. Kids' names, vaguely remem-

bered pathologies. No allusions to "bad love." No one I could see wanting to frighten me.

At ten, Robin called. "Hi, honey."

"Hi," I said. "You sound good."

"I am good, but I miss you. Maybe I'll come home early."

"That would be great. Just say when and I'll be at the airport."

"Everything okay?"

"Peachy. We've got a visitor."

I described the bulldog's arrival.

"Oh," she said, "he sounds adorable. Now I definitely want to come home early."

"He snorts and drools."

"How cute. You know, we should get a dog of our own. We're nurturant, right? And you had one when you were a kid. Don't you miss it?"

"My father had one," I said. "A hunting cur that didn't like children. It died when I was five and we never got another, but sure, I like dogs—how about something big and protective?"

"Long as it's also warm and furry."

"What breeds do you like?"

"I don't know—something solid and dependable. Let me think about it and when I get back we can go shopping."

"Sounds good, bowwow."

"We can do other stuff, too," she said.

"Sounds even better."

Just before midnight, I fashioned a bed for the dog out of a couple of towels, placed it on the floor of the service porch, and turned out the light. The dog stared at it, then trotted over to the fridge.

"No way," I said. "Time to sleep."

He turned his back on me and sat. I left for the

bedroom. He heeled along. Feeling like Simon Legree, I closed the door on his supplicating eyes.

As soon as I got under the covers I heard scratching, then heavy breathing. Then something that sounded like an old man choking.

I jumped out of bed and opened the door. The dog raced through my feet and hurled himself up on the bed.

"Forget it," I said and put him on the carpet.

He made the choking sound again, stared, and tried to climb up.

I returned him to the floor.

A couple more tries and he gave up, turning his back on me and staying hunkered against the dust ruffle.

It seemed a reasonable compromise.

But when I awoke in the middle of the night, thinking about pain screams and robot chants, he was right next to me, soft eyes full of pity. I left him there. A moment later, he was snoring and it helped put me back to sleep.

4

The next morning I woke up tasting the metal and bite of bad dreams. I fed the dog and called the Rodriguez house again. Still no answer, but this time a machine fed me Evelyn's tired voice over a background of Conway Twitty singing "Slow Hand."

I asked her to call me. She hadn't by the time I finished showering and shaving. Neither had anyone else.

Determined to get outdoors, I left the dog with a big biscuit and walked the couple of miles to the university campus. The computers at the biomed library yielded no references to "bad love" in any medical or psychological journals, and I returned home at noon. The dog licked my hand and jumped up and down. I petted him, gave him some cheese, and received a drool-covered hand by way of thanks.

After boxing my charts, I carried them back to the closet. A single carton had remained on the shelf. Wondering if it contained files I'd missed, I pulled it down.

No patient records: it was crammed with charts

and reprints of technical articles I'd set aside as references. A thick roll of papers bound with a rubber band was wedged between the folders. The word "PROFUNDITIES" was scrawled across it, in my handwriting. I remembered myself younger, angrier, sarcastic.

Removing the band from the roll, I flattened the sheaf and inhaled a snootful of dust.

More nostalgia: a collection of articles I'd authored, and programs from scientific meetings at which I'd presented papers.

I leafed through it absently until a brochure near the bottom caught my eye. Strong black letters on stiff blue paper, a coffee stain on one corner.

GOOD LOVE/BAD LOVE

Psychoanalytic Perspectives and
Strategies in a Changing World

November 28–29, 1979
Western Pediatric Medical Center
Los Angeles, California

A Conference Examining the Relevance
and Application of de Boschian Theory
to Social and Psychobiological Issues

and Commemorating Fifty Years of
Teaching, Research, and Clinical Work by

ANDRES B. DE BOSCH, PH.D.

Co-sponsored by WPMC
and
The de Bosch Institute
and Corrective School,
Santa Barbara, California

Conference Co-Chairs
Katarina V. de Bosch, Ph.D.
Practicing Psychoanalyst
and Acting Director,
The de Bosch Institute
and Corrective School

Alexander Delaware, Ph.D.
Assistant Professor of Pediatrics
and Psychology, WPMC

Harvey M. Rosenblatt, M.D.
Practicing Psychoanalyst
and Clinical Professor of Psychiatry
New York University School of Medicine

Headshot photos of all three of us. Katarina de Bosch, thin and brooding; Rosenblatt and I, bearded and professorial.

The rest was a list of scheduled speakers—more photos—and details of registration.

"Good Love/Bad Love." I remembered it clearly now. Wondered how I could have forgotten.

Nineteen seventy-nine had been my fourth year on staff at Western Peds, a period marked by long days and longer nights on the cancer ward and the genetic disorders unit, holding the hands of dying children and listening to families with unanswerable questions.

In March of that year, the head of psychiatry and the chief psychologist both chose to go on sabbatical. Though they weren't on speaking terms and the chief never returned, their last official cooperative venture was designating me interim chief.

Slapping my back and grinding their teeth around their pipe bits, they worked hard at making it sound like a stepping-stone to something wonderful. What it had amounted to was more administrative chores and just enough of a temporary pay raise to kick me into the next tax bracket, but I'd been too young to know any better.

Back then, Western Peds had been a prestigious place, and I learned quickly that one aspect of my new job was fielding requests from other agencies and institutions wanting to associate with the hospital. Most common were proposals for jointly sponsored conferences, to which the hospital would contribute its good name and its physical premises in return for continuing-education credits for the medical staff and a percentage of the box office. Of the scores of requests received yearly, a good many were psychiatric or psychological in nature. Of those, only two or three were accepted.

Katarina de Bosch's letter had been one of several I received, just weeks after assuming my new post. I scanned it and rejected it.

Not a tough decision—the subject matter didn't interest me or my staff: the front-line battles we were waging on the wards placed the theorizations of classical psychoanalysis low on our want list. And from my readings of his work, Andres de Bosch was a middleweight analyst—a prolific but superficial writer who'd produced little in the way of original thought and had parlayed a year in Vienna as one of Freud's students and membership in the French resistance into an international reputation. I wasn't even sure he was still alive; the letter from his daughter didn't make it clear, and the conference she proposed had a memorial flavor to it.

I wrote her a polite letter.

Two weeks later I was called in to see the medical director, a pediatric surgeon named Henry Bork who favored Hickey-Freeman suits, Jamaican cigars, and sawtooth abstract art, and who hadn't operated in years.

"Alex." He smiled and motioned to a Breuer chair. A slender woman was sitting in a matching nest of leather and chrome on the other side of the room.

She looked to be slightly older than me—early thirties, I guessed—but her face was one of those long, sallow constructions that would always seem aged. The beginnings of worry lines suggested themselves at crucial junctures, like a portrait artist's initial tracings. Her lips were chapped—all of her looked dry—and her only makeup was a couple of grudging lines of mascara.

Her eyes were large enough without the shadowing, dark, heavy lidded, slightly bloodshot, close set. Her nose was prominent, down tilted, and sharp, with a small bulb at the tip. Full wide lips were set sternly. Her legs were pressed together at the knees, feet set squarely on the floor.

She wore a coarse, black, scallop-necked wool sweater over a pleated black skirt, stockings tinted to mimic a Caribbean tan, and black loafers. No jewelry. Her hair was straight, brown, and long, drawn back very tightly from a low, flat brow, and fastened above each ear with wide, black, wooden barrettes. A houndstooth jacket was draped over her lap. Near one shoe was a black leatherette attaché case.

As I sat down, she watched me, hands resting upon one another, spindly and white. The top one was sprinkled with some sort of eczematous rash. Her nails were cut short. One cuticle looked raw.

Bork stepped between us and spread his arms as if preparing to conduct a symphony.

"Dr. Delaware, Dr. Katarina de Bosch. Dr. de Bosch, Alex Delaware, our acting chief psychologist."

I turned to her and smiled. She gave a nod so tiny I might have imagined it.

Bork backed away, rested a buttock on his desk, and cupped both his hands over one knee. The desk surface was twenty square feet of lacquered walnut shaped like a surfboard, topped with an antique padded leather blotter and a green marble inkwell. Centered on the blotter was a single rectangle of stiff blue paper. He picked it up and used it to rap his knuckles.

"Do you recall Dr. de Bosch's writing to you suggesting a collaborative venture with your division, Alex?"

I nodded.

"And the disposition of that request?"

"I turned it down."

"Might I ask why?"

"The staff's been asking for things directly related to inpatient management, Henry."

Looking pained, Bork shook his head, then handed the blue paper to me.

A program for the conference, still smelling of printer's ink. Full schedule, speakers, and registration. My name was listed below Katarina de Bosch's as co-chair. My picture below, lifted off the professional staff roster.

My face broiled. I took a deep breath. "Looks like a fait accompli, Henry." I tried to hand him the brochure, but he put his hands back on his knees.

"Keep it for your records, Alex." Standing, he sidled in front of the desk, taking tiny steps, like a man on a ledge. Finally, he managed to get behind the surfboard and sat down.

Katarina de Bosch was inspecting her knuckles.

I considered maintaining my dignity but decided against it. "Nice to know what I'm doing in November, Henry. Care to give me my schedule for the rest of the decade?"

A small, sniffing sound came from Katarina's chair. Bork smiled at her, then turned to me, shifting his lips into neutral.

"An unfortunate misunderstanding, Alex—a snafu. 'Something naturally always fouls up,' right?"

He looked at Katarina again, got nothing in return, and lowered his eyes to the blotter.

I fanned the blue brochure.

"Snafu," Bork repeated. "One of those interim decisions that had to be made during the transition between Dr. Greiloff's and Dr. Franks' sabbaticals and your stepping in. The board offers its regrets."

"Then why bother with a letter of application?"

Katarina said, "Because I'm polite."

"I didn't know the board got involved in scheduling conferences, Henry."

Bork smiled. "Everything, Alex, is the province of the board. But you're right. It's not typical for us to get directly involved in that type of thing. However . . ."

He paused, looked again at Katarina, who gave another tiny nod. Clearing his throat, he began fingering a cellophaned cigar—one of a trio of Davidoffs sharing pocket space with a white silk handkerchief.

"The fact that we *have* gotten involved should tell you something, Alex," he said. His smile was gone.

"What's that, Henry?"

"Dr. de Bosch—*both* Dr. de Bosches are held in extremely high esteem by . . . Western's medical community."

Are. So the old man was still alive.

"I see," I said.

"Yes, indeed." The color had risen in his cheeks, and his usual glibness had given way to something tentative, shaky.

He removed the cigar from his pocket and held it between his index fingers.

From the corner of my eye I saw Katarina. Watching me.

Neither of them spoke; I felt as if the next line was mine and I'd flubbed it.

"High esteem," said Bork finally, sounding more tense.

I wondered what was bugging him, then remembered a rumor of a few years ago. Doctors' dining room gossip, the kind I tried to avoid.

A Bork problem child, the youngest of four daughters. A teenaged chronic truant with learning disorders and a tendency toward sexual experimentation, sent away, two or three summers ago, hush-hush, for some kind of live-in remediation. The family tight-lipped with humiliation.

One of Bork's many detractors had told the story with relish.

The de Bosch Institute and Corrective School . . .

Bork was watching me. The look on his face told me I shouldn't push it any further.

"Of course," I said.

It sounded hollow. Katarina de Bosch frowned.

But it made Bork smile again. "Yes," he said. "So obviously, we're eager for this conference to take place. Expeditiously. I hope you and Dr. de Bosch will enjoy working together."

"Will I be working with both Drs. de Bosch?"

"My father isn't well," said Katarina, as if I should have known it. "He had a stroke last winter."

"Sorry to hear that."

She stood, smoothed her skirt with brief flogging movements, and picked up her attaché. In the chair she'd seemed tall—willowy—but upright she was only five two or three, maybe ninety-five bony pounds. Her legs were short and her feet pointed out. The skirt hung an inch below her knees.

"In fact, I need to get back to take care of him," she said. "Walk me back to my car, Dr. Delaware, and I'll give you details on the conference."

Bork winced at her imperiousness, then looked at me with some of that same desperation.

Thinking of what he was going through with his daughter, I stood and said, "Sure."

He put the cigar in his mouth. "Splendid," he said. "Thank you, Alex."

She said, "Henry," without looking at him and stomped toward the door.

He rushed from behind his desk and managed to get to it soon enough to hold it open for her.

He was a politician and a hack—a skilled physician who'd lost interest in healing and had lost sight of the human factor. In the coming years he never acknowledged my empathy of that afternoon, never displayed any gratitude or particular graciousness to me. If anything, he became increasingly hostile and obstructive and I came to dislike him intensely. But I never regretted what I'd done.

The moment we were out the door, she said, "You're a behaviorist, aren't you?"

"Eclectic," I said. "Whatever works. Including behavior therapy."

She smirked and began walking very fast, swinging the attaché in a wide, dangerous arc through the crowded hospital corridor. Neither of us talked on the way to the glass doors that fronted the building. She moved her short legs furiously, intent upon maintaining a half-step advantage. When we reached the entrance, she stopped, gripped the attaché with both hands, and waited until I held one of the doors open, just as she'd done with Bork. I pictured her growing up with servants.

Her car was parked right in front, in the NO STOPPING ambulance zone—a brand-new Buick, big and heavy, black with a silver vinyl top, buffed shiny as a general's boot. A hospital security guard was standing watch over it. When he saw her approaching he touched his hat.

Another door held open. I half expected to hear a bugle burst as she slid into the driver's seat.

She started the car with a sharp twist, and I stood there, looking at her through a closed window.

She ignored me, gunned the engine, finally looked at me and raised an eyebrow, as if surprised I was still there.

The window lowered electrically. "Yes?"

"We were supposed to discuss details," I said.

"The *details*," she said, "are, I'll do everything. Don't worry about it, don't complicate things, and it will all fall into place. All right?"

My throat got very tight.

She put the car into drive.

"Yes, *ma'am*," I said, but before the second word was out she'd roared off.

I went back into the hospital, got coffee from a machine near the admittance desk, and took it up to my office, trying to forget about what had happened and determined to focus myself on the day's challenges. Later, seated at my desk, charting the morning's rounds, my hand slipped and some of the coffee spilled on the blue brochure.

I didn't hear from her again until a week before the conference, when she sent a starchily phrased letter inquiring if I cared to deliver a paper. I called and declined and she sounded relieved.

"But it would be nice if you at least welcomed the attendees," she said.

"Would it?"

"Yes." She hung up.

I did show up on the first day to offer brief words

of welcome and, unable to escape graciously, remained on stage for the entire morning, with the other co-chair—Harvey Rosenblatt, the psychiatrist from New York. Trying to feign interest as Katarina strode to the podium, wondering if I'd see another side of her, softened for public consumption.

Not that there was much of a public. Attendance was thin—maybe seventy or eighty therapists and graduate students in an auditorium that seated four hundred.

She introduced herself by name and title, then read a prepared speech in a strident monotone. She favored complex, meandering sentences that lost meaning by the second or third twist, and soon the audience was looking glazed. But she didn't seem to care—didn't seem to be talking to anyone but herself.

Reminiscing about her father's glory days.

Such as they were.

Anticipating the symposium, I'd taken the time to review Andres de Bosch's collected writings, and I hadn't raised my opinion of him.

His prose style was clear, but his theories about child rearing—the good love/bad love spectrum of maternal involvement that his daughter had used to title the conference—seemed nothing more than extensions and recombinations of other people's work. A little Anna Freud here, a little Melanie Klein there, tossed with croutons of Winnicott, Jung, Harry Stack Sullivan, Bruno Bettelheim.

He leavened the obvious with clinical anecdotes about the children he'd treated at his school, managed to work both his Vienna pilgrimage and his war experiences into his summaries, name dropping and adopting the overly casual manner of one truly self-impressed.

Emperor's new clothes, and the audience at the conference didn't show any great excitement. But from the rapt look on Faithful Daughter's face, she thought it was cashmere.

By the second day, attendance was down by half and even the speakers on the dais—three L.A.-based analysts—looked unhappy to be there. I might have felt sorry for Katarina, but she seemed unaware of it all, continuing to flash slides of her father—dark-haired and goateed in healthier days—working at a big, carved desk surrounded by talismans and books, drawing in crayon with a young patient, writing in the brandied light of a Tiffany lamp.

Then another batch: posing with his arm around *her*—even as a teenager, she'd looked old, and they could have been lovers—followed by shots of a blanket-swaddled old man sunk low in an electric wheelchair, positioned atop a high, brown bluff. Behind him the ocean was beautiful and blue, mocking his senescence.

A sad variation upon the home-movie trap. The few remaining attendees looked away in embarrassment.

Harvey Rosenblatt seemed especially pained; I saw him shade his eyes and study some scribbled notes that he'd already read from.

A tall, shambling, gray-bearded fellow in his forties, he struck up a conversation with me as we waited for the afternoon session to begin. His warmth seemed more than just therapeutic veneer. Unusually forthcoming for an analyst, he talked easily about his practice in mid-Manhattan, his twenty-year marriage to a psychologist, and the joys and challenges of raising three children. The youngest was a fifteen-year-old boy whom he'd brought with him.

"He's back at the hotel," he said, "watching movies on pay-TV—probably the dirty ones, right? I promised to get back in an hour and take him out to

Disneyland—do you have any idea how late they're open?"

"During the winter, I think only till six or so."

"Oh." He frowned. "Guess we'll have to do that tomorrow; hopefully, Josh can deal with it."

"Does he like arcade games?" I said.

"Does a duck quack?"

"Why don't you try the Santa Monica pier. It's open late."

"Okay—that sounds good, thanks. Do they have good hot dogs by any chance?"

"I know they have hot dogs, but I can't vouch for them being gourmet."

He smiled. "Josh is a hot dog connoisseur, Alex." He puffed his cheeks and smoothed his beard. "Too bad about Disneyland. I hate to disappoint him."

"Challenges of parenthood, huh?" I said.

He smiled. "He's a sweet kid. I brought him with me hoping to turn it into a semi-vacation for both of us. I try to do that with each of them when they're old enough. It's hard to reconcile working with other people's kids when you can't find time for your own— you have any?"

I shook my head.

"It's an education, believe me. Worth more than ten years of school."

"Do you treat only children?" I said.

"Half and half. Actually, I find myself doing less and less child work as time goes on."

"Why's that?"

"To be honest, kid work's just too nonverbal for me. Three hours in a row of play therapy makes my eyes cross—narcissistic, I know, but I figure I'm not doing them much good if I'm fading away. My wife, on the other hand, doesn't mind. She's a real artist with it. Great mom, too."

We walked to the cafeteria, had coffee and

donuts, and chatted for a while about other places he could take his son. As we headed back to the auditorium, I asked him about his connection to the de Bosches.

"Andres was my teacher," he said, "in England. I did a fellowship eleven years ago at Southwick Hospital—near Manchester. Child psychiatry and pediatric neurology. I'd toyed with the idea of working for the government and I wanted to see how the Brits ran their system."

"Neurology?" I said. "Didn't know de Bosch was interested in the organic side of things."

"He wasn't. Southwick was heavily biological—still is—but Andres was their token analyst. Kind of a . . ." He smiled. "I was about to say 'throwback,' but that wouldn't be kind. It's not as if he was some sort of relic. Quite vital, actually—a gadfly to the hard-wire boys, and don't we all need gadflies."

We entered the conference room. Ten minutes until the next speech and the place was nearly empty.

"Was it a good year?" I said after we were seated.

"The fellowship? Sure. I got to do lots of long-term depth work with kids from poor and working-class families, and Andres was a wonderful teacher —great at communicating his knowledge."

I thought: it's not genetic. I said, "He is a clear writer."

Rosenblatt nodded, crossed his legs, and looked around the deserted auditorium.

"How's child analysis accepted here?" he said.

"It's not used much," I said. "We deal mostly with kids with serious physical illnesses, so the emphasis is on short-term treatment. Pain control, family counseling, compliance with treatment."

"Not much tolerance for delayed gratification?"

"Not much."

"Do you find that satisfying—as an analyst?"

"I'm not an analyst."

"Oh." He blushed around his beard. "I guess I assumed you were—then how'd you get involved in the conference?"

"Katarina de Bosch's powers of persuasion."

He smiled. "She can be a real ball-breaker, can't she? When I knew her back in England she was just a kid—fourteen or fifteen—but even then she had a forceful personality. She used to attend our graduate seminars. Spoke up as if she was a peer."

"Daddy's girl."

"Very much so."

"Fourteen or fifteen," I said. "So she's only twenty-five or -six?"

He thought for a moment. "That's about right."

"She seems older."

"Yes, she does," he said, as if coming up with an insight. "She has an old soul, as the Chinese say."

"Is she married?"

He shook his head. "There was a time I thought she might be gay, but I don't think so. More likely asexual."

I said, "The temptation to think Oedipally is darn near irresistible, Harvey."

"For girls it's Elektra," he said, wagging a finger with amusement. "Get your complexes straight."

"She drives one, too."

"What?"

"Her car's an Electra—a big Buick."

He laughed. "There you go—now if that doesn't convert you to fervid belief in Freud, I don't know what will."

"Anna Freud never married, either, did she?" I said. "Neither did Melanie Klein."

"What, a neurotic pattern?" he said, still chuckling.

"Just presenting the data, Harvey. Draw your own conclusions."

"Well, *my* daughter's damned *boy* crazy, so I wouldn't get ready to publish just yet." He turned serious. "Though I'm sure the impact of such a powerful paternal—"

He stopped talking. I followed his gaze and saw Katarina heading toward us from the left side of the auditorium. Carrying a clipboard and marching forward while looking at her watch.

When she reached us, Rosenblatt stood.

"Katarina. How's everything going?" There was guilt in his voice—he'd make a very bad liar.

"Fine, Harvey," she said, looking down at her board. "You're up in two minutes. Might as well take your place on stage."

I never saw either of them again, and the events of that autumn soon faded from memory, sparked briefly, the following January, by a newspaper obituary of Andres de Bosch. Cause of death was suicide by overdose—prescription tranquilizers. The eighty-year-old analyst was described as despondent due to ill health. His professional achievements were listed in loving, inflated detail, and I knew who'd provided them.

Now, years later, another spark.

Good love/*bad love*. De Bosch's term for mothering gone bad. The psychic damage inflicted when a trusted figure betrays the innocent.

So Donald Dell Wallace probably wasn't behind it. Someone else had picked me—because of the *conference*?

Someone with a long, festering memory? Of what? Some transgression committed by de Bosch? In the name of de Boschian therapy?

My co-chairmanship made me seem like a disciple, but that was my only link.

Some kind of grievance? Was it even real, or just a delusion?

A psychotic sitting at the conference, listening, boiling . . .

I thought back to the seventy strangers in the auditorium. A collective blur.

And why had Becky Basille's murderer howled "bad love"?

Another madman?

Katarina might have the answer. But she hadn't had much use for me back in seventy-nine, and there was no reason to believe she'd talk to me now.

Unless she'd gotten a tape, too, and was frightened.

I punched 805 information. There was no Santa Barbara listing for either the de Bosch Institute or the Corrective School. Neither was there an office number for Katarina de Bosch, Ph.D. Before the operator could get away, I asked her to check for a home number. Zilch.

I hung up and pulled out the latest American Psychological Association directory. Nothing there, either. Retrieving some older volumes, I finally found Katarina's most recent entry. Five years ago. But the address and number were those of the Santa Barbara school. On the off chance the phone company had messed up, I called.

A woman answered, "Taco Bonanza." Metallic clatter and shouts nearly drowned her out.

I cut the connection and sat at my desk, stroking the top of the bulldog's head and gazing at the coffee stain on the brochure. Wondering how and when enlightenment had given way to enchiladas.

Harvey Rosenblatt.

Half past one made it four-thirty in New York. I

got the number for NYU's med school and asked for the department of psychiatry. After a couple of minutes on hold, I was informed that there was no Dr. Harvey Rosenblatt on either the permanent or the part-time clinical staff.

"We do have a *Leonard* Rosenblatt," said the secretary. "His office is out in New Rochelle—and a Shirley Rosenblatt in Manhattan, on East Sixty-fifth Street."

"Is Shirley an M.D. or a Ph.D.?"

"Um—one second—a Ph.D. She's a clinical psychologist."

"But no Harvey?"

"No, sir."

"Do you have any old rosters on hand? Lists of staff members who've retired?"

"There may be something like that somewhere, sir, but I really don't have the time to search. Now if you'll—"

"Could I have Dr. Shirley Rosenblatt's number please?"

"One moment."

I copied it down, called Manhattan information for a listing on Harvey Rosenblatt, M.D., learned there was none, and dialed Shirley, Ph.D.'s exchange.

A soft, female voice with Brooklyn overtones said, "This is Dr. Shirley Rosenblatt. I'm in session or out of the office, and can't come to the phone. If your call is a true emergency, please press one. If not, please press two, wait for the beep, and leave your message. Thank you and have a lovely day."

Mozart in the background . . . *beep*.

"Dr. Rosenblatt, this is Dr. Alex Delaware, from Los Angeles. I'm not sure if you're married to Dr. Harvey Rosenblatt or even know him, but I met him several years ago at a conference out here and wanted to touch base with him on something—for research purposes. If you can help me reach him, I'd appreciate your passing along my number."

I recited the ten digits and put the phone back in its cradle. The mail came a half hour later. Nothing out of the ordinary, but when I heard it drop into the bin, my hands had clenched.

5

I went down to feed the fish, and when I got back the phone was ringing.

The operator at my service said, "This is Joan, Dr. Delaware, are you free? There's someone on the line about a dog, sounds like a kid."

"Sure."

A second later a thin, young voice said, "Hello?"

"Hi, this is Dr. Delaware."

"Um . . . this is Karen Alnord. My dog got lost and you said in the paper that you found a bulldog?"

"Yes, I did. He's a little French bulldog."

"Oh . . . mine's a boxer." Dejected.

"Sorry. This one's not a boxer, Karen."

"Oh . . . I just thought—you know, sometimes people think they're bulldogs."

"I can see the resemblance," I said. "The flat face—"

"Yeah."

"But the one I've found's much smaller than a boxer."

"Mine's a puppy," she said. "He's not too big yet."

I put her age at between nine and eleven.

"This one's definitely full-grown, Karen. I know because I took him to the veterinarian."

"Oh . . . um . . . okay. Thank you, sir."

"Where'd you lose your dog, Karen?"

"Near my house. We have a gate, but somebody left it open and he got out."

"I'm really sorry. Hope you find him."

"I will," she said, in a breaking voice. "I've got an ad, too, and I'm calling all the other ads, even though my mom says none of them are probably the right one. I'm paying a reward, too—twenty dollars, so if you do find him you can get it. His name's Bo and there's a bone-shaped tag on his collar that says Bo and my phone number."

"I'll keep an eye out, Karen. Whereabouts do you live?"

"Reseda. On Cohasset between Sherman Way and Saticoy. His ears haven't been cropped. If you find him, here's my phone number."

I wrote it down, even though Reseda was over the hill to the north, fifteen or twenty miles away.

"Good luck, Karen."

"Thank you, sir. I hope your bulldog finds his owner."

That reminded me that I hadn't yet called the Kennel Club. Information gave me the number in New York and another one in North Carolina. Both answered with recorded messages and told me business hours were over.

"Tomorrow," I told the bulldog.

He'd been observing me, maintaining that curious, cocked head stance. The fact that someone was probably grieving for him bothered me, but I didn't know what else to do other than take good care of him.

That meant food, water, shelter. A walk, when it got cool enough.

A walk meant a leash.

He and I took a drive to a pet store in south Westwood and I bought a lead, more dog food, biscuits in various flavors, and a couple of nylon bones the salesman assured me were excellent for chewing. When we returned, it seemed temperate enough for a stroll if we stayed in the shade. The dog stood still, tail wagging rapidly, while I put the leash on. The two of us explored the Glen for half an hour, hugging the brush, walking against traffic. Like regular guys.

When I got back, I called my service. Joan said, "There's just one, from a Mrs. Rodriguez—hold on, that's your board . . . there's someone ringing in right now."

I waited a moment, and then she said, "I've got a Mr. Silk on the line, says he wants to make an appointment."

"Thanks, put him on."

Click.

"Dr. Delaware."

Silence.

"Hello?"

Nothing.

"Mr. Silk?"

No answer. Just as I was about to hang up and redial the service, a low sound came through the receiver. Mumbles—no. Laughter.

A deep, throaty giggle.

"Huh huh huh."

"Who is this?" I said.

"Huh huh huh." Gloating.

I said nothing.

"Huh huh huh."

The line went dead.

I got the operator back on the line.

"Joan, that guy who just called. Did he leave anything other than his name?"

"No, he just asked if you treated adults as well as children and I said he'd have to speak to you about that."

"And his name was Silk? As in the fabric?"

"That's what I heard. Why, doctor, is something wrong?"

"He didn't say anything, just laughed."

"Well that's kind of crazy, but that's your business, isn't it, doctor?"

Evelyn Rodriguez answered on the first ring. When she heard my voice, hers went dead.

"How's everything?" I said.

"Fine."

"I know it's a hassle for you, but I would like to see the girls."

"Yeah, it's a hassle," she said. "Driving all the way out there."

"How about if I come out to you?"

No answer.

"Mrs. Rodriguez?"

"You'd do that?"

"I would."

"What's the catch?"

"No catch, I'd just like to make this whole thing as easy as possible for you."

"Why?"

To show Donald Dell Wallace I can't be intimidated. "To help the girls."

"Uh-huh . . . *they're* paying for your time, right? His . . . bunch a heathens."

"The judge made Donald Dell responsible for the

costs of the evaluation, Mrs. Rodriguez, but as we talked about the first time, that doesn't obligate me to him in any way."

"Uh-huh."

"Has that been a problem for you?" I said. "The fact that he's paying?"

She said nothing for a moment, then: "Bet you're charging plenty."

"I'm charging my usual fee," I said, realizing I sounded like a Watergate witness.

"Bet it includes your driving time and all. Door to door, just like the lawyers."

"Yes, it does."

"*Good*," she said, stretching the word. "Then *you* can drive instead of me—drive *slow*. Keep your meter running and make them devils *pay*."

Angry laughter.

I said, "When can I come out?"

"How 'bout right now? They're running around like wild Injuns, maybe you can settle 'em down. How about you drive out here right this *minute* and see 'em? You ready for that?"

"I can probably be there in forty-five minutes."

"Whenever. We'll be right here. We're not taking any vacations to Hono-*lu*lu."

She hung up before I could ask for directions. I looked up her address in my case file—the ten thousand block of McVine Terrace in Sunland—and matched it to my Thomas map. Setting the dog up with water, food, and a bone, I left, not at all unhappy about running up the Iron Priests' tab.

The 405 freeway deposited me in a scramble of northbound traffic just beginning to clot, facing hills so smogged they were no more than shrouded, gray lumps on the horizon. I did the L.A. stop-and-go boogie for a while, listening to music and trying to be patient, finally made it to the 118 east, then the 210, and cruised into the high desert northeast of the city, picking up speed as both the road and the air got clearer.

Exiting at Sunland, I hooked north again and got onto a commercial stretch of Foothill Boulevard that ran parallel to the mountains: auto parts barns, body shops, unfinished furniture outlets, and more roofers than I'd ever seen in one area.

I spotted McVine a few minutes later and turned left. The street was narrow, with grass growing down to the curb instead of sidewalks, and planted haphazardly with eucalyptus and willow. The curb grass was dry and yellow. The houses behind it were small and low, some of them no more than trailers on raised foundations.

The Rodriguez residence was on a northwest corner, a boxcar of mocha stucco with a gutterless, black composition roof and a flat, porchless face broken by three metal-sashed windows. One of the windows was blocked by a tilting sheet of lattice. The squares were broken in spots, warped in others, and a few dead branches wormed around them. A high, pink block wall enveloped the rear of the property.

I got out and walked up a hardpack lawn stippled with blemishlike patches of some sort of low-growing succulent and split by a foot-worn rut. Evelyn's plum-colored Chevy was parked to the left of the pathway, next to a red half-ton pickup with two stickers on the bumper. One sang the praises of the Raiders, the other dared me to keep kids off drugs. A stick-on sign on the door said R AND R MASONRY.

I pressed the bell and a wasp-buzz sounded. A woman opened the door and looked at me through the smoke vining upward from a freshly lit Virginia Slim.

In her late twenties, five seven and lanky, she had dirty blond hair gathered in a high, streaked ponytail and pale skin. Slanted, dark eyes and broad cheek-bones gave her a Slavic look. The rest of her features were sharp, beginning to pinch. Her shape was per-fect for the hardbody era: sinewy arms, high breasts, straightedge tummy, long legs leading up to flaring hips just a little wider than a boy's. She wore skin-tight, low-riding jeans and a baby-blue, sleeveless midriff top that showcased an apostrophe of a navel some obstetrician should have been mighty proud of. Her feet were bare. One of them tapped arrhythmi-cally.

"You the doctor?" she said, in a husky voice, talking around the cigarette, just the way I'd seen Evelyn Rodriguez do.

"Dr. Delaware," I said, and extended my hand.

She took it and smiled—amusement rather than friendliness—gave a hard squeeze, then dropped it.

"I'm Bonnie. They're waiting for you. C'mon in."

The living room was half the width of the boxcar and smelled like a drowned cigar. Carpeted in olive shag and paneled with knotty pine, it was darkened by drawn drapes. A long, brown corduroy sofa ran along the back wall. Above it hung a born-again fish symbol. To the left was a console TV topped with some sort of cable decoder and a VCR, and a beige velveteen recliner. On a hexagonal table, an ashtray brimmed over with butts.

The other half of the front space was a kitchen–dining area combo. Between the two rooms was an ochre-colored door. Bonnie pushed it open, letting in a lot of bright, western light, and took me down a short, shagged hall. At the end was a den, walled in grayish mock birch and backed by sliding glass doors that looked out to the backyard. More recliners, another TV, porcelain figurines on the mantel, below three mounted rifles.

Bonnie slid open a glass door. The yard was a small, flat square of scorched grass surrounded by the high pink walls. An avocado tree grew at the rear, huge and twisted. Barely out of its shade was an inflatable swimming pool, oval and bluer than anyone's heaven. Chondra sat in it, splashing herself without enthusiasm. Tiffani was in a corner of the property, back to us, jumping rope.

Evelyn Rodriguez sat between them in a folding chair, working on her lanyard and smoking. She had on white shorts, a dark blue T-shirt, and rubber beach sandals. On the grass next to her was her purse.

Bonnie said, "Hey," and all three of them looked up.

I waved. The girls stared.

Evelyn said, "Go get him a chair."

Bonnie raised her eyebrows and went back into the house, putting some wiggle in her walk.

Evelyn shaded her face, looked at her watch, and smiled. "Forty-two minutes. Couldn't ya have stopped for coffee or something?"

I forced a chuckle.

"Course," she said, "don't really matter what you actually do, you can always *say* you done it, right? Just like a lawyer. You can say anything you *please.*"

She stubbed her cigarette out on the grass.

I went over to the pool. Chondra returned my "Hi" with a small, silent smile. Some teeth this time: progress.

Tiffani said, "You write your book yet?"

"Not yet. I need more information from you."

She nodded gravely. "I got lots of truth—we don't want to ever see him."

She grabbed hold of a branch and started swinging. Humming something.

I said, "Have fun," but she didn't answer.

Bonnie came out with a folded chair. I went and took it from her. She winked and went back into the house, rear twitching violently. Evelyn wrinkled her nose and said, "Well, does it?"

I unfolded the chair. "Does it what?"

"Does it matter? What actually happens? You're just gonna do what you want to, write what you want to anyway, right?"

I sat down next to her, positioning myself so I could see the girls. Chondra was motionless in the pool, gazing at the trunk of the avocado.

Evelyn humphed. "You ready to come out?"

Chondra shook her head and began splashing herself again, doing it slowly, as if it were a chore. Her white pigtails were soaked the color of old brass. Above the pink walls the sky was static and blue, bottomed by a soot-colored cloud bank that hid the horizon. Someone in the neighborhood was barbecuing, and a mixture of scorching fat and lighter fluid spread its cheerful toxin through the autumn heat.

"You don't think I'll be honest, huh?" I said. "Been burned by other doctors, or is it something about me?"

She turned toward me slowly and put her lanyard in her lap.

"I think you do your job and go home," she said. "Just like everyone else. I think you do what's best for *you*, just like everyone else."

"Fair enough," I said. "I'm not going to sit here and tell you I'm some saint who'd work for free or that I really know what you've been going through, 'cause I don't—thank God. But I think I understand your rage. If someone had done it to my child, I'd be ready to kill him, no question about it."

She took her Winstons out of her pocket and knocked a cigarette loose. Sliding it out and taking it between two fingers, she said, "Oh you would, would you? Well that would be revenge, and the Bible says revenge is a negational action."

She lit up with a pink disposable lighter, inhaled very deeply, and held it. When she let the smoke out, her nostrils twitched.

Tiffani began jumping very fast. I wondered if we were within her earshot.

Evelyn shook her head. "Gonna break her head one of these days."

"Lots of energy," I said.

"Apple don't fall far."

"Ruthanne was like that?"

She smoked, nodded, and started to cry, letting her tears drip down her face and wiping them with short, furious movements. Her torso pushed forward and for a moment I thought she was going to leave.

"Ruthanne was *just* like that when she was little. Always moving. I never felt I could . . . she had spirit, she was—she had . . . wonderful spirit."

She tugged her shorts down and sniffed.

"Want some coffee?"

"Sure."

"Wait right here." She went into the house.

"Hey, girls," I called out.

Tiffani kept jumping. Chondra looked up. Her mouth hung slightly open and water droplets bubbled her forehead, like oversized sweat.

I went over to her. "Swim a lot?"

She gave a very small nod and splashed one arm, turning away and facing the avocado tree. Young fruit hung from the branches, veiled by a cloud of white-flies. Some of it was blackened with disease.

Tiffani waved at me. Then she began to chant in a loud voice:

"I went to the Chinese restaurant,
to get a loaf of bread bread bread,
a man was there with a big mustache,
and this is what he said said said.
El eye el eye chicholo beauty, pom-pom
    cutie . . ."

Evelyn came back holding a couple of mugs.
Bonnie marched behind her carrying a small plate of
sugar wafers. The look on her face said she'd been
created for better things.

I walked back to the lawn chairs.

Bonnie said, "Here you go," handed me the
plate, and sashayed off.

Evelyn gave me a mug. "Black or cream?"

"Black."

We sat and sipped. I balanced the cookie plate on
my lap.

"Have one," she said, "or are you one of those
health-food types?"

I took a wafer and chewed on it. Lemon-flavored
and slightly stale.

"I dunno," she said, "maybe *I* shoulda been a
health fooder, too. I always gave my kids sugar and
stuff, whatever they wanted—maybe I shouldn'ta.
Got a boy went AWOL over in Germany two years
ago, don't even *know* where he is, the baby don't
know *zero* about what she wants to do with her life,
and Ruthie . . ."

She shook her head and looked over at Tiffani.
"Watch your head on that *branch*, you!"

"Bonnie's the baby?" I said.

Nod. "She got all the brains and the looks. Just
like her daddy—he coulda been a movie star. Only
time I ever went gaga for the looks, and boy, what a
mistake *that* was."

She gave a full smile. "He cleaned me out thirteen months after we were married. Left me with the baby in diapers and went down to Louisiana to work the deep-sea rigs. Got killed soon after in a fall that they *said* was an accident. Never took out the right insurance for himself, so I got nothing."

She smiled wider. "He had a temper on him. All my men do. Roddy's got a fuse on him, too, though it takes a while to get it lit. He's a Mexican, but he's the best of the lot."

She patted the T-shirt pocket that held the cigarette pack. "Sugar and bad tempers and cancer sticks. I really go for all the good things in life, huh?"

Her eyes watered again. She lit up.

"All the good things," she said. "All the blessed good things."

She kept the cigarette in her mouth, busied her hands by squeezing them together, letting go, repeating the motion. The lanyard lay on the grass, neglected.

"There's no room for your guilt," I said.

She yanked the cigarette out of her mouth and stared at me. "*What'd* you say?"

"There's no room for your guilt. All the guilt belongs to Donald Dell. One hundred percent of it."

She started to say something, but stopped.

I said, "No one else should carry that burden, Evelyn. Not Ruthanne for going with him that night, and certainly not you for the way you raised her. Junk food had nothing to do with what happened. Neither did anything but Donald Dell's impulses. It's *his* cross to bear now."

Her eyes were on me, but wavering.

I said, "He's a bad guy, he does bad things, no one knows why. And now you're having to be a mom, all over again, when you weren't planning on it. And you're going to do it without complaining too much and you're going to do your best. No one's going to pay you or give you any credit, so at least give *yourself* some."

"You talk sweet," she said. "Telling me what I want to hear." Wary, but not angry. "Sounds like you got a temper on you, too."

"I talk straight. For my own sake—you're right about that. All of us do what we think's best for us. And I do like to make money—I went to school a long time to learn what I do. I'm worth a high fee, so I charge it. But I also like to sleep well at night."

"Me, too. So what?" She smoked, coughed, ground out the cigarette with disgust. "Been a long time since I slept peacefully."

"Takes time."

"Yeah . . . how long?"

"I don't know, Evelyn."

"Least you're honest." Smile. "Maybe."

"What about the girls?" I said. "How do they sleep?"

"Not good," she said. "How could they? The little one wakes complaining she's hungry—which is a laugh, 'cause she eats all day, though you wouldn't know it to look at her, would you? I used to be like that, believe it or not." Squeezing her thigh. "She gets up two, three times a night, wanting Hersheys and licorice and *ice* cream."

"Does she ever get those things?"

"Hel—heck no. There's a *limit.* I give her a piece of orange or something—maybe a half a cookie—and send her right back. Not that it stops her the next time."

"What about Chondra?"

"*She* don't get up, but I hear her crying in her bed —under the blanket." She looked over at the older girl, who was sitting motionless in the center of the pool. "She's the soft one. Soft as jelly."

She sighed and looked down at her coffee with disdain. "Instant. Shoulda made real stuff."

"It's fine," I said, and drank to prove it.

"It's okay, but it's not great—don't see great around here too often. My second husband—Brian's dad—owned a big place up near Fresno—table grapes and alfalfa, some quarter horses. We lived up there for a few years—that was *close* to great, all that space. Then he went back to his drinking—Brian, Senior—and it all went to—straight down the tubes. Ruthie used to love that place—especially the horses. There's riding stables around here, too, out in Shadow Hills, but it's expensive. We always said we'd get over there but we never did."

The sun dropped behind the cloud bank, and the yard dimmed.

"What're you gonna do to us?" she said.

"*To* you?"

"What's your plan?"

"I'd like to help you."

"If you wanna *help* them, keep them away from *him*, that's all. He's a devil."

"Tiffani called him an instrument of Satan."

"I told her that," she said defiantly. "You see something wrong with that?"

"Not at all."

"It's my faith—it props me up. And he *is* one."

"How'd Ruthanne meet him?"

Her shoulders dropped. "She was waitressin' at a place out in Tujunga—okay, it was a bar. He and his *bunch* hung out there. She went out with him for months before tellin' me. Then she brought him home and the first look I got I said no, no, no—my experiences, I can spot a bad apple like that." Snap of fingers. "I warned her, but that didn't do no good. Maybe I gave up too easy, I don't know. I was havin' problems of my own, and Ruthie didn't think I had a single intelligent thing to say to her."

She lit another cigarette and took several hard, fast drags. "She was stubborn. That was her only real sin."

I drank more coffee.

"Nothing to say anymore, doc? Or am I boring you?" She flicked ashes onto the dirt.

"I'd rather listen."

"And they pay you all that money for that? Good racket you got there."

"Beats honest labor," I said.

She smiled. First friendly one I'd seen.

"Stubborn," she said. She smoked and sighed and called out, "Five more minutes, then into the house for homework, both a you!"

The girls ignored her. She kept looking at them. Drifted off, as if she'd forgotten I was there. But then she turned and looked at me.

"So, Mr. Easy Listener, what *do* you want from me and my little girls?"

Same question she'd asked me the first time she met me. I said, "Enough time to find out exactly how they've been affected by their mom's death."

"How do you *think* they've been affected? They loved their mama. They're crushed to dirt."

"I need to get specific for the court."

"What do you mean?"

"I need to list symptoms that prove they're suffering psychologically."

"You gonna say they're crazy?"

"No, nothing like that. I'll talk about symptoms of anxiety—like the sleep problems, changes in appetite, things that make them vulnerable to seeing him. Otherwise they're going to get swept up in the system. Some of it you can tell me, but I'll also need to hear things directly from them."

"Won't that mess them up more, talking about it?"

"No," I said. "Just the opposite—keeping things inside is more likely to create problems."

She gave a skeptical look. "I don't see them talkin' to you much, so far."

"I need time with them—need to build up their trust."

She thought about that. "So what do we do, just sit here jawing?"

"We could start with a history—you telling me as much as you remember about what they were like as babies. Anything else you think might be important."

"A history, huh?" She took a deep drag, as if trying to suck maximum poison out of the cigarette. "So now we've got a history . . . yeah, I've got *plenty* to tell you. Why don't you get out a pencil and start writing?"

She talked as the sky darkened further, letting the girls play on as she recounted nightmares and weeping spells, the terrors of orphanhood. At five-thirty Bonnie came out and switched on floodlights that turned the yard sallow. It stilled her mother's voice, and Evelyn stood and told the girls, "Go in the house, you."

Right after they did, a man came out, rubbing his hands together and sniffing the air. Five three or so, in his late fifties or early sixties, low waisted, dark skinned and weak chinned, with long, tattooed arms. Bowlegs gave him a tottering walk. His eyes were shadowed by thick, gray thatches, and a drooping, iron-colored Zapata mustache obscured his mouth. His bushy gray hair was slicked straight back. He wore a khaki workshirt and blue jeans with hand-rolled cuffs. His hands were caked with plaster and he rubbed them more vigorously as he approached.

Evelyn saluted him.

He returned the gesture and looked at me, stretching to stand taller.

"This here's that doctor," she said. "We been having a nice talk."

He nodded. The shirt was embroidered with a white oval tag that said "Roddy" in red script. Up close I saw that his face was severely pockmarked. A couple of crescent-shaped scars ran down his chin.

I held out a hand.

He looked at his palm, gave an embarrassed smile, and said, "Dirty." His voice was soft and hoarse. I put my hand down. He smiled again and saluted me.

"Dr. Delaware."

"Roddy. Pleased to meetchu." Boyle Heights accent. As he lowered his fingers, I noticed tattooed letters across the knuckles. L-O-V-E. Homemade job. On the other hand was the inevitable H-A-T-E. In the fold between his thumb and forefinger was a crude blue crucifix. Next to that, a tiny red-eyed spider climbed a tiny web above the legend NR.

He put his hands in his pockets.

"How's your day?" Evelyn asked him. She looked as if she wanted to touch him.

"Okay." He sniffed.

"Hungry?"

"Yeah, I could eat." The tattooed hands emerged and rubbed together. "Gotta wash up."

"Sure, *patron*."

He went into the house.

"Well," she told me, "I'd better get into the kitchen. Guess it's too late for you to talk to them, but you can come back tomorrow."

"Great."

We walked inside. Chondra and Tiffani were on the sofa in the rear den, watching cartoons on TV. A cat was being cheerfully decapitated. Tiffani held the remote control.

"Bye, girls."

Glazed eyes.

"Say bye to the doctor."

The girls looked up. Small waves and smiles.

"I'm leaving now," I said. "I'll be coming out here tomorrow—maybe we can get a chance to talk."

"See you," said Tiffani. She nudged her sister. Chondra said, "Bye."

Evelyn was gone. I found her out in the kitchen, pulling something out of the freezer. Rodriguez was stretched back in the velveteen recliner, eyes closed, a beer in his hand.

"See you tomorrow," I said.

"One sec." Evelyn came over. The package in her hand was a diet frozen entree. Enchilada Fiesta. "Better be the day after—I forgot there's some things I got to do."

"Okay. Same time?"

"Sure." She looked at the frozen package and shook her head.

"How 'bout New York steak?" she called out to her husband.

"Yeah," he said, without opening his eyes.

"He likes his steak," she said quietly. "For a fella his size, he's a real meat eater."

She followed me all the way out to the front lawn. Looked at the TV dinner in her hand. "No one likes this one. Maybe I'll have it."

I hit bad traffic on the western end of the 210, and by the time I pulled into the carport, it was after seven. When I got in the house, the dog greeted me, but he had his head down and looked subdued. I smelled the reason first, then saw it, on the service porch floor near the door.

"Oh," I said.

He drooped lower.

"My mistake for locking you in." I rubbed his

neck, and he gave me a grateful lick, then trotted over to the fridge.

"Let's not push things, bucko."

I cleaned up the mess, reflecting on the responsibilities of pet foster-parenthood, and phoned in for messages, wondering if anyone had responded to my ad. No one had. Nothing from Shirley Rosenblatt, Ph.D., either. Or Mr. Silk. The operator gave me a few business calls. I decided to put the tape out of my mind, but the child's chant stayed there and I couldn't sit still.

I fed the dog and was contemplating what to do about my own dinner when Milo called at eight-ten.

"No prints on the tape except yours. Any mail problems today?" He sounded tired.

"No, but I did get a call." I told him about the giggling man.

"Silk, huh? Well, that's a pisser."

"What is?"

"Sounds like you've got a nutcase on your hands."

"You don't think it's serious?"

Pause. "Most of these guys are cowards, like to stay in the background. But to be honest, Alex, who knows?"

I said, "I think I may have found what 'bad love' means," and filled him in about the symposium.

"Seventy-nine," he said. "Nut with a real long memory."

"Think that's a bad sign?"

"I—let's put our heads together and hash it out. You eat yet?"

"Nope."

"I'm over in Palms, got to finish up a few things. I could meet you at that place on Ocean in about half an hour."

"Don't think I'd better," I said. "Left my guest alone too long already."

"What guest? Oh, him. Why can't you leave him? Is he lonely and depressed?"

"It's more of a gastrointestinal issue," I said, rubbing the dog behind the ears. "He just ate and will be needing easy ingress and egress."

"Ingr—oh . . . *fun*. Well, get a dog door, Alex. Then, get a *life*."

"A dog door means sawing a hole. He's only a short-term lodger."

"Suit yourself."

"Fine," I said. "I'll put a door in—Robin wants a dog anyway. How about you bring one over, I'll install it, and then we can go out."

"Where the hell am I gonna find a dog door at this hour?"

"You're the detective."

Slam.

He arrived at nine-fifteen, pulling an unmarked Ford into the carport. His tie was loose, he looked wilted, and he carried two bags—one from a pet store, the other from a Chinese restaurant.

The dog came up and nuzzled his cuffs and he gave the animal a grudging pat and said, "Ingress and egress."

Removing a metal and plastic contraption from the pet store bag, he handed it to me. "Seeing as I don't feel like manual labor before dinner and the *handy* resident of this household is out of town, I figured we'd better do takeout."

He went over to the fridge, dog following.

Watching his slow trudge, I said, "You look wiped. New blood buckets?"

He got a Grolsch, opened it, and nodded. "Armed robbery, what I was working on in Palms. Little mom-and-pop grocery. Pop died a few months ago, mom's eighty, barely hanging on. Two little shits came in this afternoon, flashed knives, and threatened to rape her and cut off her breasts if she didn't hand over the cashbox. Old lady puts them at around thirteen or fourteen. She's too shook to say much else, chest pains, shortness of breath. They admitted her to St. John's for observation."

"Poor thing. Thirteen or fourteen?"

"Yeah. The timing of the robbery might mean the little assholes waited till after school to do it—how's that for your extracurricular activities? Or maybe they're just your basic truant psychopaths out for a fun day."

"Urban Huck and Tom," I said.

"Sure. Smoke a corncob of crack, gangbang Becky Thatcher."

He sat down at the table and sniffed the top of the beer bottle. The dog had remained at the refrigerator and was looking at him, as if contemplating approach, but Milo's tone and expression stilled him and he came over and settled at my feet.

I said, "So no one else's prints were on the tape."

"Not a one."

"What does that mean? Someone took the trouble to wipe it clean?"

"Or handled it with gloves. Or there *were* prints and they got smeared when you touched the tape." He stretched his legs. "So show me this brochure you found."

I went to the library, got the conference program, and gave it to him. He scanned it, "No one named Silk here."

"Maybe he was in the audience."

"You look intense," he said, pointing to my photo. "That beard—kind of rabbinic."

"Actually, I was bored." I told him how I'd become a co-chair.

He put down his bottle. "Nineteen seventy-nine. Someone carrying around a grudge all this time?"

"Or something happened recently that triggered a recollection from seventy-nine. I tried calling Katarina and Rosenblatt, to see if maybe they'd gotten anything in the mail, but she's closed up shop in Santa Barbara and he's no longer practicing in Manhattan. I found a psychologist in New York who may be his wife and left her a message."

He examined the brochure again. "So what could the grudge be about?"

"I have no idea, Milo. Maybe it's not even the conference, maybe it's someone who sees himself as victimized by the therapist—or the therapy. Maybe the grievance isn't even real—something paranoid—a delusion that would never occur to you or me."

"Meaning we're normal?"

"Everything's relative."

He smiled. "So you can't remember anything weird happening at the conference."

"Nothing at all."

"This de Bosch—was he controversial in any way? The kind to make enemies?"

"Not that I know, but my only contact with him was through his writings. They're not controversial."

"What about the daughter?"

I thought about that. "Yeah, she could have made enemies—a real sourpuss. But if she's the target of someone's resentment, why would I be? My only link to her was the conference."

He waved the brochure. "Reading this, someone could believe you were esteemed colleagues. She hemmed you in, huh?"

"Expertly. She had clout with the medical director of the hospital. My guess was that it was because she'd treated one of his daughters—a kid with problems—and called in a marker. But it could have been something else completely."

He put his beer bottle down on the coffee table. The dog looked up, then lowered his chin to the floor.

"The kid's voice on the tape," I said. "How does that figure in? And the guy who killed Becky Basille—"

"Hewitt. Dorsey Hewitt. Yeah, I know—what does he have to do with it?"

"Maybe he was treated by the de Bosches, too. Maybe 'bad love' was a phrase they used in therapy. But what does that mean? A whole slew of therapy graduates freaking out—getting back at their doctors?"

"Wait a second," said Milo. "I'm sorry about your tape and your nut-call, but that's a far cry from murder." He handed the brochure back to me. "Wonder if Donald Wallace was ever treated by the de Bosches—still waiting for more info from the prison. How're those girls doing?"

"The kinds of problems you'd expect. Documenting a good case against visitation shouldn't be a problem. The grandmother's opening up a bit, too. I went out to the house this afternoon. Her latest husband looks like a retired cholo—lots of homemade tattoos." I described Rodriguez's skin art.

"Dealing with the elite," he said. "You and me both." He crossed his legs and glanced down at the dog: "C'mere, Rove."

The dog ignored him.

"Good dog," he said, and drank his beer.

He left at ten-thirty. I decided to put off installing the dog door till the next day. Robin called at ten-fifty and told me she'd decided, definitely, to come home early—tomorrow evening at nine. I wrote down her flight number and said I'd be at LAX to pick her up, told her I loved her, and went to sleep.

I was dreaming about something pleasantly sexual when the dog woke me just after three in the morning, growling and pawing the dust ruffle.

I groaned. My eyes felt glued shut.

He pawed some more.

"What?"

Silence.

Scratch scratch.

I sat up. "What is it?"

He did the old-man-choking bit.

Ingress and egress . . .

Cursing myself for not installing the door, I forced myself out of bed and made my way, blindly, through the dark house to the kitchen. When I opened the service porch door, the dog raced down the stairs. I waited, yawning and groggy, muttering, "Make it fast."

Instead of stopping to squat near the bushes, he kept going and was soon out of sight.

"Ah, exploring new ground." I forced one eye to stay open. Cool air blew in through the door. I looked outside, couldn't see him in the darkness.

When he didn't return after a minute or so, I went down to get him. It took a while to find him, but I finally did—sitting near the carport, as if guarding the Seville. Huffing, and moving his head from side to side.

"What is it, guy?"

Pant, pant. He moved his head faster but didn't budge his body.

I looked around some more, still unable to see much. The mixed smells of night-blooming plants hit my nose, and the first spray of dew moistened my skin. The night sky was hazy, just a hint of moonlight peeking through. Just enough to turn the dog's eyes yellow.

"Hound of the Basketballs," I said, remembering an old *Mad* magazine sketch.

The dog scratched the ground and sniffed, started turning his head from side to side.

"*What?*"

He began walking toward the pond, stopping several feet from the fence, just as he had during our first encounter. Then he came to a dead halt.

The gate was closed. It had been hours since the timed lights had shut off. I could hear the waterfall. Peering over the fence, I caught a glimpse of moon-streaked wetness as my eyes started to accommodate.

I looked back at the dog.

Still as a rock.

"Did you hear something?"

Head cock.

"Probably a cat or a possum, pal. Or maybe a coyote, which might be a little too much for you, no offense."

Head cock. Pant. He pawed the ground.

"Listen, I appreciate your watchfulness, but can we go back up now?"

He stared at me. Yawned. Gave a low growl.

"I'm bushed, too," I said, and headed for the stairs. He did nothing until I'd gotten all the way up, then raced up with a swiftness that belied his bulk.

"No more interruptions, okay?"

He wagged his stub cheerfully, jumped on the bed, and sprawled across Robin's side.

Too exhausted to argue, I left him there.

He was snoring long before I was.

Wednesday morning I assessed my life: crank letters and calls, but I could handle that if it didn't accelerate. And my true love returning from the wilds of Oakland. A balance I could live with. The dog licking my face belonged in the plus column, too, I supposed. When I let him out, he disappeared again and stayed out.

This time he'd gotten closer to the gate, stopping only a couple of feet from the latch. I pushed it open and he took another step.

Then he stopped, stout body angling forward.

His little frog face was tilted upward at me. Something had caused it to screw up, the eyes narrowing to slits.

I anthropomorphized it as conflict—struggling to get over his water phobia. Canine self-help hampered by the life-saving training some devoted owner had given him.

He growled and jutted his head toward the gate.

Looking *angry*.

Wrong guess? Something near the pond bothering him?

The growls grew louder. I looked over the fence and saw it.

One of my koi—a red and white *kohaku*, the largest and prettiest of the surviving babies—was lying on the moss near the water's edge.

A jumper. Damn.

Sometimes it happened. Or maybe a cat or coyote *had* gotten in. And that's what he'd heard . . .

But the body didn't look torn up.

I opened the gate and went in. The bulldog stepped up to the gatepost and waited as I kneeled to inspect the fish.

It *had* been torn. But no four-legged predator had done it.

Something was sticking out of its mouth—a twig, thin, stiff, a single shriveled red leaf still attached.

A branch from the dwarf maple I'd planted last winter.

I glanced over at the tree, saw where the bough had been cut off, the wound oxidized almost black.

Clean cut. Hours old. A knife.

I forced my eyes back to the carp.

The branch had been jammed down its gullet and forced down through its body, like a spit. It exited near the anus, through a ragged hole, ripping through beautiful skin and letting loose a rush of entrails and blood that stained the moss cream-gray and rusty brown.

I filled with anger and disgust. Other details began to leap out at me, painful as spattering grease.

A spray of scales littering the moss.

Indentations that might have been footprints.

I took a closer look at them. To my untrained eye, they remained characterless gouges.

Leaves beneath the maple, where the branch had been sheared.

The fish's dead eyes stared up at me.

The dog was growling.

I joined in and we did a duet.

7

I dug a grave for the fish. The sky was Alpine clear, and the beauty of the morning was a mockery of my task.

I thought of another beautiful sky—Katarina de Bosch's slide show. Azure heavens draping her father's wheelchaired form.

Good love/bad love.

Definitely more than just a sick joke now.

Flies were divebombing the koi's torn corpse. I nudged the body into the hole and shoveled dirt over it as the bulldog watched.

"Should have taken you more seriously last night."

He cocked his head and blinked, brown eyes gentle.

The dirt over the grave was a small umber disc that I tamped with my foot. After taking one last look, I dragged myself up to the house. Feeling like a dependent child, I called Milo. He wasn't in and I sat at my desk, baffled and angry.

Someone had trespassed on my property. Someone had watched me.

The blue brochure was on my desk, my name and photo—the perfect logic of trumped-up evidence. *Reading this, someone could believe you were esteemed colleagues.*

I phoned my service. Still no callback from Shirley Rosenblatt, Ph.D. Maybe she wasn't Harvey's wife. . . . I tried her number again, got the same recorded message, and slammed down the phone in disgust.

My hand started to close around the brochure, crumpling it, then my eyes dropped to the bottom of the page and I stopped and smoothed the stiff paper.

Other names.

The three other speakers.

Wilbert Harrison, M.D., FACP
Practicing Psychoanalyst
Beverly Hills, California

Grant P. Stoumen, M.D., FACP
Practicing Psychoanalyst
Beverly Hills, California

Mitchell A. Lerner, M.S.W., ACSW
Psychoanalytic Therapist
North Hollywood, California

Harrison, chubby, around fifty, fair, and jolly looking, with dark-rimmed glasses. Stoumen older, bald and prune faced, with a waxed, white mustache. Lerner, the youngest of the three, Afroed and turtlenecked, full bearded, like Rosenblatt and myself.

I had no memory beyond that. The topics of their papers meant nothing to me. I'd sat up on the dais, mind wandering, angry about being there.

Three locals.

I opened the phone book. Neither Harrison nor Lerner was in there, but Grant P. Stoumen, M.D., still had an office on North Bedford Drive—Beverly Hills couch row. A service operator answered, "Beverly Hills Psychiatric, this is Joan."

Same service I used. Same voice I'd just spoken to.

"It's Dr. Delaware, Joan."

"Hi, Dr. Delaware! Fancy talking to you so soon."

"Small world," I said.

"Yeah—no, actually, it happens all the time, we handle lots of psych docs. Who in the group are you trying to reach?"

"Dr. Stoumen."

"Dr. Stoumen?" Her voice lowered. "But he's gone."

"From the group?"

"From—uh . . . from life, Dr. Delaware. He died six months ago. Didn't you hear?"

"No," I said. "I didn't know him."

"Oh . . . well, it was really pretty sad. So unexpected, even though he was pretty old."

"What did he die of?"

"A car accident. Last May, I think it was. Out of town, I forget exactly where. He was at some kind of convention and got run over by a car. Isn't that terrible?"

"A convention?"

"You know, one of those medical meetings. He was a *nice* man, too—never lost patience the way some of the—" Nervous laugh. "Scratch *that* comment, Dr. D. Anyway, if you're calling about a patient, Dr. Stoumen's were divided up among the rest of the doctors in the group, and I can't be sure which one took the one you're calling about."

"How many doctors are in the group?"

"Carney, Langenbaum, and Wolf. Langenbaum's on vacation, but the other two are in town—take your pick."

"Any recommendations?"

"Well . . ." Another nervous laugh. "They're both—all right. Wolf tends to be a little better about returning calls."

"Wolf'll be fine. Is that a him or a her?"

"A him. Stanley Wolf, M.D. He's in session right now. I'll put a message on his board to call you."

"Thanks a lot, Joan."

"Sure bet, Dr. D. Have a nice day."

I installed the dog door, making slow progress because I kept pausing between saw swings and hammer blows, convinced I'd heard footsteps in the house or unwarranted noise out on the terrace.

A couple of times I actually went down to the garden and looked around, hands clenched.

The grave was a dark ellipse of dirt. Dried fish scales and a slick gray-brown stain marked the pond bank.

I went back up, did some touch-up painting around the door frame, cleaned up, and had a beer. The dog tried his new passageway, ingressing and egressing several times and enjoying himself.

Finally, tired and panting, he fell asleep at my feet. I thought about who'd want to scare me or hurt me. The dead fish stayed in my head, a cognitive stench, and I remained wide-awake. At eleven, he awoke and raced for the front door. A moment later, the mail chute filled.

Standard-sized envelopes that I sorted through. One had a Folsom POB return address and an eleven-digit serial number hand-printed above it in red ink.

Inside was a single sheet of ruled notebook paper, printed in the same red.

Doctor A. Delaware, Ph.D.

Dear Dr. Delaware, Ph.D.:

I am writing to you to express my feelings about seeing my daughters, namely Chondra Wallace and Tiffani Wallace, as their natural father and legal guardian.

Whatever was done to our family including done by myself and no matter how bad is in my opinion, water under the bridge. And such as it is, I should not be denied permission and my paternity rights to see my lawful, legal daughters, Chondra Wallace and Tiffani Wallace.

I have never done anything to hurt them and have always worked hard to support them even when this was hard. I don't have any other children and need to see them for us to have a family.

Children need their fathers as I'm sure I don't have to tell a trained doctor like yourself. One day I will be out of incarceration. I am their father and will be taking care of them. Chondra Wallace and Tiffani Wallace need me. Please pay attention to these facts.

Yours sincerely,
Donald Dell Wallace

I filed the letter in the thick folder, next to the coroner's report on Ruthanne. Milo called at noon and I told him about the fish. "Makes it more than a prank, doesn't it?"

Pause. "More than I expected."

"Donald Dell knows my address. I just got a letter from him."

"Saying what?"

"One day he'll be out and wanting to be a full-time dad, so I shouldn't deny him his rights now."

"Subtle threat?"

"Could you prove it?"

"No, he could have gotten your address through his lawyer—you're reviewing his claim, so he'd be entitled to it legally. Incidentally, according to my sources he doesn't have an audio recorder in his cell. TV and VCR, yes."

"Cruel and unusual. So what do I do?"

"Let me come over and check out your pond. Notice any footprints or obvious evidence?"

"There were some prints," I said, "though they didn't look like much to my amateur eyes. Maybe there's some other evidence that I wasn't sophisticated enough to spot. I was careful not to disturb anything—oh, hell, I buried the fish. Was that a screw-up?"

"Don't worry about it, it's not like we're gonna do an autopsy." He sounded uneasy.

"What's the matter?" I said.

"Nothing. I'll come by and have a look as soon as I can. Probably the afternoon."

He spoke the last words tentatively, almost turning the statement into a question.

I said, "What is it, Milo?"

"What it *is*, is that I can't do any full-court press for you on this. Killing a fish just isn't a major felony —at the most, we've got trespassing and malicious mischief."

"I understand."

"I can probably take some footprint molds myself," he said. "For what it's worth."

"Look," I said, "I still don't consider it a federal case. This is cowardly bullshit. Whoever's behind it probably doesn't want a confrontation."

"Probably not," he said. But he still sounded troubled, and that started to rattle me.

"Something else," I said. "Though it's also probably no big deal. I was looking at the conference brochure again and tried to contact the three local therapists who gave speeches. Two weren't listed, but the one who was had been killed this past spring. Hit by a car while attending a psychiatric symposium. I found out because his answering service just happens to be the same one I use and the operator told me."

"Killed here in L.A.?"

"Out of town, she didn't remember where. I've got a call in to one of his associates."

"Symposium," he said. "Curse of the conference?"

"Like I said, it's probably nothing—the only thing that is starting to bug me is I can't reach anyone associated with the de Bosch meeting. Then again, it's been a long time, people move."

"Yeah."

"Milo, *you're* bugged about something. What is it?"

Pause. "I think, given everything that's been happening—putting it all together—you'd be justified getting a little . . . watchful. No paranoia, just be extra careful."

"Fine," I said. "Robin's coming home early—tonight. I'm picking her up at the airport. What do I tell her?"

"Tell her the truth—she's a tough kid."

"Some welcome home."

"What time are you picking her up?"

"Nine."

"I'll get over well before then and we'll put our heads together. You want, I can stay at the house while you're gone. Just feed me and water me and tell Rover not to make demands."

"Rover's a hero as far as I'm concerned—he's the one who heard the intruder."

"Yeah, but there was no *follow-through*, Alex. Instead of *eating* the sucker, he just stood around and watched. What you've *got* is a four-legged bureaucrat."

"That's cold," I said. "Didn't you ever watch *Lassie*?"

"Screw that, my thing was *Godzilla*. There's a useful pet."

By three, no one had returned my calls and I felt like a cartoon man on a desert island. I did paperwork and looked out the window a lot. At three-thirty, the dog and I hazarded a walk around the Glen, and when I arrived back home, there were no signs of intrusion.

Shortly after four, Milo arrived, looking hurried and bothered. When the dog came up to him, he paid no mind.

He held an audiocassette in one hand, his vinyl attaché case in the other. Instead of making his usual beeline to the kitchen, he went into the living room and loosened his tie. Putting the case on the coffee table, he handed me the tape.

"The original's in my file. This is your copy."

Seeing it brought back the screams and the chants. That child. . . . I put it in my desk and we went down to the pond, where I showed him the footprints.

He kneeled and inspected for a long time. Stood, frowning. "You're right, these are useless. Looks to me like someone took the time to mess them up."

He checked around the pond area some more, taking his time, getting his pants dirty. "Nope, nothing here worth a damn. Sorry."

That same troubled tone in his voice that I'd heard over the phone. He was holding back something, but I knew it was useless to probe.

Back in the living room, I said, "Something to drink?"

"Later." He opened the vinyl case and took out a brown plastic box. Removing a videocassette from it, he bounced it against one thigh.

The tape was unmarked, but the box was printed with the call letters of a local TV station. Rubber-stamped diagonally across the label was the legend PROPERTY LAPD: EVIDENCE RM. and a serial number.

"Dorsey Hewitt's last stand," he said. "Definitely not for prime time, but there's something I want you to check out—if your stomach can take it."

"I'll cope."

We went into the library. Before inserting the cartridge into the VCR, he peered into the machine's load slot.

"When's the last time you lubricated this?"

"Never," I said. "I hardly use it except to record sessions when the court wants visuals."

He sighed, slid the cartridge in, picked up the remote control, pressed PLAY, and stood back, watching the monitor with his hands folded across his waist. The dog jumped up on a big leather chair, settled, and regarded him. The screen went from black to bright blue and a hiss filtered through the speakers.

A half minute more of blue, then the TV station logo flashed over a digital date, two months old.

Another few moments of video stutter were followed by a long shot of an attractive, one-story brick building, with a central arch leading to a courtyard and wood-grilled windows. Tile roof, brown door to the right of the arch.

Close up on a sign: LOS ANGELES COUNTY MENTAL HEALTH CENTER, WESTSIDE.

Swing back to a long shot: two small, dark-garbed figures crouched on opposite sides of the arch —toylike: G.I. Joe figurines holding rifles.

A side shot revealed police barriers fencing the street.

No sound other than static, but the dog's ears had perked and pitched forward.

Milo raised the volume, and a soup of incomprehensible background speech could be heard above the white noise.

Nothing for a few seconds, then one of the dark figures moved, still squatting, and repositioned itself to the left of the door. Another figure came from around a corner and lowered itself to a deep crouch, both hands on its weapon.

A close-up inflated the new arrival, turning dark cloth into navy blue, revealing the bulk of protective vesting, white letters spelling out LAPD across a broad back. Combat boots. Blue ski mask revealing only eyes; I thought of Munich terrorists and knew something bad was going to happen.

But nothing did for the next few moments. The dog's ears were still stiff and his breathing had quickened.

Milo rubbed one shoe with another and ran his hand over his face. Then the brown door on the screen swung open on two people.

A man, bearded, long-haired, scrawny. The beard, a matted frenzy of blond and gray corkscrews. Above a blemished, knotted forehead, his hair haloed in spiky clumps, recalling a child's clumsily drawn sun.

The camera moved in on him, highlighting dirty flesh, sunken cheeks, bloodshot eyes so wide and bulging they threatened to shoot off the shaggy launchpad of his face.

He was naked from the waist up and sweating

furiously. The wild eyes began rotating madly, never blinking, never settling. His mouth was agape, like a dental patient's, but no sound issued forth. He appeared to be toothless.

His left arm was clamped around a heavy black woman, imbedded so tightly in her soft, skirted waist that the fingers disappeared.

The skirt was green. Over it the woman wore a white blouse that had come partially untucked. She was around thirty-five and her face was wet, too—perspiration and tears. *Her* teeth were visible, lips stretched back in a rictus of horror.

The man's right arm was a bony yoke around her neck. Something silvery flashed in his hand as he pressed it up against her throat.

She closed her eyes and kept them clenched.

The man was leaning her back, pressing her to him, convexing her neck and revealing the full breadth of a big, shiny carving knife. Red-stained hands. Red-stained blade. Only her heels touched the pavement. She was off balance, an unwilling dancer.

The man blinked, darted his eyes, and looked at one of the SWAT cops. Several rifles were aimed at him. No one moved.

The woman trembled and the collaring hand moved involuntarily and brought forth a small red mark from her neck. The blotch stood out like a ruby.

She opened her eyes and stared straight ahead. The man screamed something to her, shook her, and they closed again.

The camera stayed on the two of them, then shifted smoothly to another of the SWAT men.

No one moved.

The dog was standing on the chair, breathing hard.

The bearded man's knife elbow quivered.

The man closed his mouth, opened it. Looked to

be screaming at the top of his lungs, but the sound wasn't carrying.

The woman's mouth was still open. Her wound had already coagulated—just a nick.

The man propelled her onto the sidewalk, very slowly. One of her shoes came off. He didn't notice it, was looking from side to side, cop to cop, screaming nonstop.

All at once the sound came on. Very loud. New microphone.

The dog began barking.

The man with the knife screamed, a howling, hoarse and wet.

Panting. Wordless.

Pain scream.

My hands dug into my thighs. Milo faced the screen, immobile.

The bearded man shifted his head from side to side some more, faster, harder, as if being slapped. Screaming louder. Pressing the knife up under the woman's chin.

Her eyes shot open.

The dog's barks turned to growls, guttural and bearish, loud enough to be scary and a lot more threatening than the warning sounds he'd uttered last night.

The man with the knife was directing his screams at a SWAT man to his left, haranguing wordlessly, as if the two of them were friends turned hateful.

The cop might have said something because the madman upped his volume.

Roaring. Shrieking.

The man backed away, hugging the woman more tightly, concealing his face behind hers as he dragged her into the doorway.

Then a smile and a short, sharp twist of his wrist.

Another spot of blood—larger than the first—formed on the woman's throat.

She raised her hands reflexively, trying to bend out from under the knife, losing her balance and stumbling.

Her weight and the movement surprised the man, and for one brief moment, as he tried to keep her upright and haul her backward, he lowered his right arm.

A quick, sharp sound—like a single handclap—and a red dot appeared on the man's right cheek.

He spread his arms. Another dot materialized, just left of the first one.

The woman fell to the pavement as a rain of gunfire sounded—corn popping in an echo chamber. The man's hair blew back. His chest burst, and the front of his face turned into something amoebic and rosy—a pink and white kaleidoscope that seemed to unfold as it imploded.

The hostage was facedown, fetal. Bloodspray showered down on her.

The man, now faceless, slumped and sagged, but he remained on his feet for one hellish second, a gore-topped scarecrow, still gripping the knife as red juice poured out of his head. He had to be dead but he continued to stand, bending at the knees, his ruined head shadowing the hostage's shoulder.

Then all at once he let go of the knife and collapsed, falling on the woman, limp as a blanket. She twisted and struck out at him, finally freed herself and managed to rise to her knees, sobbing and covering her head with her hands.

Policemen ran to her.

One of the dead man's bare feet was touching her leg. She didn't notice it, but a cop did and kicked it away. Another officer, still ski-masked, stood over the faceless corpse, legs spread, gun pointed.

The screen went black. Then bright blue.

The dog was barking again, loud and insistent.

I made a shushing sound. He looked at me, cocked his head. Stared at me, confused. I went over to him and patted his back. His back muscles were jumping and drool trickled from his flews.

"It's okay, fella." My voice sounded false and my hands were cold. The dog licked one of them and looked up at me.

"It's okay," I repeated.

Milo rewound the tape. His jaw was bunched.

How long had the scene lasted—a few minutes? I felt as if I'd aged watching it.

I stroked the dog some more. Milo stared at the numbers on the VCR's counter.

"It's him, isn't it?" I said. "Hewitt. Screaming on my tape."

"Him or a good imitation."

"Who's the poor woman?"

"Another social worker at the center. Adeline Potthurst. She just happened to be sitting at the wrong desk when he ran out after killing Becky."

"How is she?"

"Physically, she's okay—minor lacerations. Emotionally?" He shrugged. "She took disability leave. Refused to talk to me or anyone else."

He ran a hand along the edge of a bookshelf, grazing book spines and toys.

"How'd you figure it out?" I said. "Hewitt on the 'bad love' tape?"

"I'm not sure what I figured, actually."

He shrugged. His forelock cast a hat-brim shadow over his brow, and in the weak light of the library, his green eyes were drab.

The tape ejected. Milo put it on an end table and sat down. The dog waddled over to him, and this time Milo looked pleased to see him.

Rubbing the animal's thick neck, he said, "When I first heard *your* tape, something about it bugged me —*reminded* me of something. But I didn't know what it was, so I didn't say anything to you. I figured it was probably 'bad love'—Hewitt's using the phrase, my reading about it in the clinic director's witness report."

"Had you watched the video before?"

He nodded. "But at the station, with half an ear— a bunch of other detectives sitting around, cheering when Hewitt bit it. Splatter's never been my thing. I was filling out forms, doing paperwork. . . . When you told me about the tape, it still didn't trigger, but I wasn't that bugged. I figured what you did—a bad joke."

"The phone call and the fish make it more than a joke, don't they?"

"The phone call, by itself, is stupidity—like you said, cowardly shit. Someone coming on your property in the middle of the night and *killing* something *is* more. All of it put *together* is more. How *much* more I don't know, but I'd rather be a little paranoid than get taken by surprise. After we spoke on the phone this afternoon I really wracked my brains about what was bothering me. Went back into the Basille files, found the video, and watched it. And realized it wasn't the phrase that I remembered, it was the *screams*. Someone had stuck Hewitt's screams on your little gift."

He pulled his wet hand away from the dog's maw, looked at it, wiped it on his jacket.

"Where'd the video come from?" I said. "TV station's raw footage?"

He nodded.

"How much of it was actually broadcast?"

"Not much at all. This TV station has a twenty-four-hour crime-watch van with a scanner—anything for the ratings, right? They got to the scene first and were the only ones to actually record the whole thing. Their total footage is ten minutes or so, mostly no-action standoff before Hewitt comes out with Adeline. What you just saw is thirty-five seconds."

"That's all? It seemed a lot longer."

"Seemed like a goddamn eternity, but that's what it was. The part that actually made it to the six o'clock news was *nine* seconds. Five of Hewitt with Adeline, three of Rambo close-ups on the SWAT guys, and one second of Hewitt down. No blood, no screaming, no standing dead man."

"Wouldn't sell deodorant," I said, pushing the image of the teetering corpse out of my head. "Why was the sound off for most of it? Technical difficulties?"

"Yup. Loose cable on their parabolic mike. The sound man caught it midway through."

"What did the other stations broadcast?"

"Postmortem analysis by the department mouthpiece."

"So if the screams on my tape were lifted, the source had to be this particular piece of footage."

"Looks that way."

"Meaning what? Mr. Silk's an employee of the TV station?"

"Or a spouse, kid, lover, pal, significant other, whatever. If you give me your patient list, I can try to get hold of the station's personnel records and cross-check."

"Be better if you give me the personnel list," I said. "Let me check it against my patients, so I can preserve confidentiality."

"Fine. Another list you might try to get is the one for your 'bad love' conference. Anyone who attended. It was a long time ago, but maybe the hospital keeps records."

"I'll call tomorrow."

He got up and touched his throat. *"Now* I'm thirsty."

We went into the kitchen, opened beers, and sat at the table, drinking and brooding.

The dog positioned himself between us, licking his lips.

Milo said, "He doesn't get to go for the gusto?"

"Teetotaler." I got up and slid the water bowl over. The dog ignored it.

"Bullshit. He wants hops and malt," said Milo. "Looks like he's closed a few taverns in his day."

"There's a marketing opportunity for you," I said. "Brew a hearty lager for quadrupeds. Though I'm not sure you could set your criteria too high for a species that imbibes out of the toilet."

He laughed. I managed a smile. Both of us trying to forget the videotape. And everything else.

"There's another possibility," I said. "Maybe Hewitt's voice wasn't lifted from the video footage. Maybe he was taped simultaneously by someone at the mental health center. Someone who happened to have a recorder handy the day of the murder and switched it on during the standoff. There'd probably be machines lying around the center, for therapy."

"You're saying there's a therapist behind this?"

"I was thinking more of a patient. Some paranoids make a fetish of keeping records. I've seen some lug tape recorders around with them. Someone who'd been bearing a grudge since seventy-nine could very well be highly paranoid."

He thought about that. "Nutcase with a pocket Sony, huh? Someone you once treated who ended up at the mental health center?"

"Or just someone who remembered me from the conference and ended up at the center. Someone tying me in with bad love—whatever it means to him. Probably anger at bad therapy. Or therapy he perceived as bad. De Bosch's theory has to do with bad mothers letting their kids down. Betrayal. If you think of therapists as surrogate parents, the stretch isn't hard to make.''

He put down his bottle and looked at the ceiling. "So we've got a nut, one of your old patients, gone downhill, can't afford private treatment so he's getting county help. Happens to be at the center the day Hewitt freaks out and butchers Becky. Recorder in his pocket—keeping tabs on all the people talking behind his back. He hears the screams, presses RECORD . . . I guess it's possible—anything's *possible* in this city.''

"If we're dealing with someone who's been stewing for a long time, witnessing Becky Basille's murder and the SWAT scene could have set him off. Hearing Hewitt screaming about bad love could have done it, too, if he'd had experiences with de Bosch or a de Boschian therapist.''

He rolled the bottle between his palms. "Maybe. But two nuts with a 'bad love' fixation just *happening* to show up at the same place on the same day is too damned cute for my taste.''

"Mine, too," I said.

He drank some more.

"What if it wasn't a coincidence at all, Milo? What if Hewitt and the taper *knew* each other—even shared a common rage about bad love, de Bosch, therapists in general? If the mental health center's typical, it's a crowded place, patients waiting for hours. It wouldn't be that strange for two disturbed people to get together and discover a mutual resentment, would it? If they were paranoid to begin with, they could have played upon each other's fears and delusions. *Confirming* for each other that the way they saw the world was valid. The taper might even be someone who wouldn't have been violent under different circumstances. But seeing Hewitt murder *his* therapist and then seeing Hewitt's face blown off could have pushed him over."

"So now he's ready to do his own therapist? So what's the tape and the call and the fish?"

"Preparing the scene. Or maybe he won't go any further—I don't know. And something else: I might not even be his only target. He might have a current therapist who's in danger."

"Any idea who it could be? From your patient list?"

"No, that's the thing. There's no one who fits. But my patients were all kids. Lots can happen over time."

He sat back in his chair and looked up at the ceiling.

"Speaking of kids," he said. "Where does the kid's voice fit in with your two-nut scenario?"

"I don't know, dammit. Maybe the taper's got a kid. Or he's abducted one—God, I hope not, but that voice stank of coercion, didn't it? So flat—did *Hewitt* have any children?"

"Nope. The report has him as unmarried, unemployed, un-everything."

"Be good to know who he hung out with at the center. We could also try to verify that my tape was taken from the video footage. Because if it wasn't, we wouldn't have to bother cross-referencing the station personnel list."

He smiled. "And you wouldn't have to expose your patient list, right?"

"Right. That would be a major betrayal. I still can't justify it."

"You're sure it's not any of them?"

"No, I'm not sure, but what am I going to do? Call hundreds of people and ask them if they've grown up to be hate-crazed nuts?"

"No Mr. Silk in your past, huh?"

"Only silk I know is in my ties."

"One thing I can tell you, your tape's not an *exact* lift off the video. The footage has Hewitt screaming for just over twenty-seven seconds out of the thirty-five, and your segment only lasts sixteen. I had a brief go at it before I came over here—tried running both tapes simultaneously on two machines to see if I could pick out any segments that coincided exactly. I couldn't—it was tricky, going from machine to machine, on-off, on-off, trying to synchronize. And it's not like we're dealing with words, here—doesn't take long before all the screaming starts to sound the same."

"What about doing some kind of voiceprint analysis? Trying to get an electronic match."

"From what I know, you need actual words for a match. And the department doesn't do voiceprints anymore."

"Why not?"

"Probably not enough call. What they're useful for, mostly, is kidnapping ransom calls, and that's usually the FBI's game. Also phone scams, bunco stuff, which is low priority with all the buckets of blood. I think one guy at the sheriff's is still doing them. I'll find out."

The dog finally put his head in the bowl and began slurping water. Milo lifted his bottle, said, "Cheers," and emptied it.

"Why don't you and I try a little bit of low-tech teamwork right now?" I said. "You take audio, I'll take video—"

"And I'll be in Screamland afore ye."

He took the portable tapedeck into the library and loaded the video. We sat across from one another, listening to screams, trying to shut out the context. Even with two people it was difficult—hard to divide the howls into discrete segments.

We played and rewound, doing it over and over, trying to locate the sixteen seconds of the bad love tape amid the pain and noise of the longer video segment. The dog tolerated only a minute or so before scooting out of the room.

Milo and I stayed and sweated.

After half an hour, a triumph of sorts.

A discrepancy.

A second or two of sing-song, wordless jabber at the tail end of my tape that didn't materialize anywhere on the soundtrack of the video.

Ya ya ya . . . the screamer lowering his volume just a bit—a barely discernible shift not much longer than an eyeblink. But once I pointed it out, it mushroomed, as obvious as a billboard.

"Two separate taping sessions," I said, as stunned as Milo looked. "Has to be, otherwise why would the shorter tape have something on it that's missing from the longer segment?"

"Yeah," he said quietly, and I knew he was angry at himself for not catching it first.

He sprang to his feet and paced. Looked at his Timex. "When'd you say you were going to the airport?"

"Nine."

"If you're comfortable leaving the place unguarded, I could go get something done."

"Sure," I said, rising. "What?"

"Talk to the clinic director about Hewitt's social life."

He collected his things and we walked to the door.

"Okay, I'm off," he said. "Got the Porsche and

the cellular, so you can always reach me if you need to."

"Thanks for everything, Milo."

"What're friends for?"

Ugly answers flashed in my head, but I kept them to myself.

8

Just as I was preparing to head out for LAX, Dr. Stanley Wolf returned my call. He sounded middle-aged and spoke softly and hesitantly, as if doubting his own credibility.

I thanked him and said I'd called about Dr. Grant Stoumen.

"Yes, I got the message." He asked several tortuous questions about my credentials. Then: "Were you a student of Grant's?"

"No, we never met."

"Oh . . . what do you need to know?"

"I'm being harassed by someone, Dr. Wolf, and I thought Dr. Stoumen might be able to shed some light on it."

"Harassed?"

"Annoying mail. Phone calls. It may be linked to a conference I co-chaired several years ago. Dr. Stoumen delivered a paper there."

"A conference? I don't understand."

"A symposium on the work of Andres de Bosch

entitled 'Good Love/Bad Love.' The term 'bad love' was used in the harassment."

"How long ago was this?"

"Seventy-nine."

"De Bosch—the child analyst?"

"Did you know him?"

"No, child analysis is outside of my . . . purview."

"Did Dr. Stoumen ever talk about de Bosch—or this particular conference?"

"Not to my recollection. Nor did he mention any . . . annoying mail?"

"Maybe 'annoying' is too mild," I said. "It's fairly nasty stuff."

"Uh-hm." He didn't sound convinced.

I said, "Last night it went a little further. Someone trespassed on my property. I have a fish pond. They took a fish out, killed it, and left it for me to see."

"Hmm. How . . . bizarre. And you think this symposium's the link?"

"I don't know, but it's all I've got so far. I'm trying to contact anyone who appeared on the dais, to see if they've been harassed. So far everyone I've tried to reach has moved out of town. Do you happen to know a psychiatrist named Wilbert Harrison or a social worker named Mitchell Lerner?"

"No."

"They also delivered papers. The co-chairs were de Bosch's daughter, Katarina, and a New York analyst named Harvey Rosenblatt."

"I see. . . . Well, as I mentioned I'm not a child analyst. And unfortunately, Grant's no longer with us, so I'm afraid—"

"Where did his accident take place?"

"Seattle," he said, with sudden strength in his voice. "At a conference, as a matter of fact. And it wasn't a simple accident. It was a hit-and-run. Grant was heading out for a late-night walk; he stepped off the curb in front of his hotel and was struck down."

"I'm sorry."

"Yes, it was terrible."

"What was the topic of the conference?"

"Something to do with child welfare—the Northwest Symposium on Child Welfare, I believe. Grant was always an advocate for children."

"Terrible," I said. "And this was in May?"

"Early June. Grant was on in years—his eyesight and hearing weren't too good. We prefer to think he never saw it or heard it coming."

"How old was he?"

"Eighty-nine."

"Was he still in practice?"

"A few old patients stopped by from time to time, and he kept an office in the suite and insisted on paying his share of the rent. But mostly he traveled. Art exhibitions, concerts. And conferences."

"His age made him a contemporary of Andres de Bosch," I said. "Did he ever mention him?"

"If he did, I don't recall it. Grant knew lots of people. He was in practice for almost sixty years."

"Did he treat especially disturbed or violent patients?"

"You know I can't discuss his cases, Dr. Delaware."

"I'm not asking about specific cases, just the general tenor of his practice."

"The little that I saw was pretty conventional—children with adjustment problems."

"Okay, thanks. Is there anyone else who could talk to me about him?"

"Just Dr. Langenbaum, and he knows about as much as I do."

"Did Dr. Stoumen leave a widow?"

"His wife died several years ago and they had no children. Now I really do have to get going."

"Thanks for your time, Dr. Wolf."

"Yes . . . hmm. Good luck on . . . working this through."

I got my car keys, left a lot of lights on in the house, and turned on the stereo to loud jazz. The dog was sleeping noisily on his towel bed, but he roused himself and followed me to the door.

"Stay and guard the home front," I said, and he harrumphed, stared for a moment, finally sat down.

I walked out, closed the door, listened for a protest, and when I didn't hear any, went down to the carport. The night had cooled, massaged by sea current. The waterfall seemed deafening and I drove away listening to it diminish.

As I coasted down toward the Glen, a sense of dread dropped over me, dark and smothering, like a condemned man's hood.

I paused at the bottom of the road, looking at black treetops and slate sky. A faint bit of light from a distant house blinked through the foliage like an earthbound star.

No way to gauge its distance. I had no real neighbors because an acre-wide strip of county land, unbuildable due to a quirky water table, cut through this section of the Glen. Mine was the only buildable site on the plot plan.

Years ago the isolation had been just what I wanted. Now a nosy streetmate didn't seem half bad.

A car sped down the Glen from the north, appearing suddenly around a blind curve, going too fast, its engine flatulent with power.

I tensed as it passed, took another look backward, and hooked right, toward the Sunset on-ramp of the 405 south. By the time I got on the freeway, I was thinking of Robin's smile and pretending nothing else mattered.

Slow night at the airport. Cabbies circled the terminals and skycaps looked at their watches. I found a space in the passenger loading zone and managed to stay there until Robin came out, toting her carry-on.

I kissed her and hugged her, took the suitcase, and put it in the trunk of the Seville. A man in a Hawaiian shirt was looking at her over cigarette smoke. So were a couple of kids with backpacks and surfer hair.

She had on a black silk T-shirt and black jeans, and over that a purple and red kimono-type shirt tied around her waist. The jeans were tucked into black boots with tooled silver toes. Her hair was loose and longer than ever—well past her shoulder blades, the auburn curls bronzed by the light from the baggage claim area. Her skin gleamed and her dark eyes were clear and peaceful. It had been five days since I'd seen her, but it seemed like a long separation.

She touched my cheek and smiled. I leaned in for a longer kiss.

"Whoa," she said, when we stopped, "I'll go away more often."

"Not necessary," I said. "Sometimes there is gain without pain."

She laughed and hugged me and put her arm around my waist. I held the door open as she got in the car. The man in the Hawaiian shirt had turned his back on us.

As I drove away she put her hand on my knee and looked over at the back seat. "Where's the dog?"

"Guarding hearth and home. How was your talk?"

"Fine. Plus I may have sold that archtop guitar I did last summer—the one Joey Shah defaulted on. I met a jazz musician from Dublin who wants it."

"Great," I said. "You put a lot of time into that one."

"Five hundred hours, but who's counting."

She stifled a yawn and put her head on my shoulder. I drove all the way to Sunset before she woke up, shaking her curls. "Boy . . . must have hit me all of a sudden." Sitting up, she blinked at the streets of Bel Air.

"Home sweet home," she said softly.

I waited until she'd roused herself before telling her the bad news.

She took it well.

"Okay," she said, "I guess it goes with the territory. Maybe we should move out for a while and stay at the shop."

"Move out?"

"At least till you know what's going on."

I thought of her studio, separated from the mean streets of Venice by a thin veneer of white windows and locks. Saws and drills and wood shavings on the ground floor. The sleeping loft in which we'd made love so many times . . .

"Thanks," I said, "but I can't stay away indefinitely—the house needs maintenance. Not to mention the fish that're left."

That sounded trivial, but she said, "That poor fish. And you worked so hard to keep them alive."

She touched my cheek.

"Welcome home," I said glumly.

"Don't worry about *that*, Alex. Let's just figure

out how to deal with this stupidity until it's re-
solved."

"I don't want to put you in any danger. Maybe
you should move to the shop—"

"And leave you alone in the middle of this?"

"I just want to make sure you're okay."

"How okay do you think I'm going to be, worrying every minute about you? I mean, the fish are wonderful, Alex, but you can hire someone to feed them.
Hire someone to look after the whole house, for that
matter."

"Pack up the wagons and head out?"

"What's wrong with being a little cautious,
honey?"

"I don't know . . . it just seems awfully drastic
—all that's really happened is malicious mischief."

"So why were you so upset when you told me
about it?"

"Sorry. I didn't want to upset you."

"Of *course* it upsets me," she said. "Someone
sending you weird tapes, sneaking in and . . ." She
put her arm around my shoulder. The light changed
to green and I turned left.

"Goes with the territory," she repeated. "All
those troubled people you've worked with over the
years. All that misdirected passion. The surprising
thing isn't that it happened. It's how long it took."

"You never said it worried you."

"It wasn't a matter of worry—I didn't obsess on
it. Just thought about it from time to time."

"You never said anything."

"What would have been the point? I didn't want
to upset *you*."

I lifted her hand from my shoulder and kissed it.

"Okay," she said, "so we protect each other,
Curly. Ain't that what true love's all about?"

*   *   *

I pulled up in front of the house. No obvious signs of intrusion.

I said, "Just let me check around for a sec before you get out."

"Oh, really," she said. But she stayed in the car.

I gave the pond a quick inspection. The fish moved with nighttime languor, and none was missing.

I jogged up the stairs to the landing, checked the front door, peered in through the living room window. Something moved as the drapes parted. The dog's face pressed against the glass, wetting it. I raised my hand in greeting. He pawed the window. I could hear the jazz through the redwood walls.

By the time I got back down, Robin was lifting her valise from the trunk. When I tried to take it from her, she said, "I've got it," and headed for the steps.

As I unlocked the front door, she said, "We could at least get an alarm. Everyone else has one."

"Never been a slave to fashion," I said, but when she didn't smile, I added, "Okay. I'll call a company tomorrow."

We walked in and almost tripped over the bulldog, who'd positioned himself on the welcome mat. He stared from Robin to me, then back to her, where he lingered with Churchillian dignity.

Robin said, "My God."

"What?" I said.

"He *invented* cute, Alex. Come here, sweetie." She bent down to his level with one hand extended, palm down.

He trotted forward without hesitation, jumped up, put his paws on her shoulders, and embarked on a lick-fest.

"Ooh!" She laughed. "What a *handsome* boy you are—what a *cutie*—look at those *muscles*!"

She stood, wiping her face, still laughing. The dog continued to nuzzle and paw her legs. His tongue was out and he was panting.

She placed a hand on my shoulder and gave me a grave look. "Sorry, Alex. There is now another man in my life." Bending, she rubbed him behind the ears.

"Crushed," I said, placing a hand over my heart. "And you might reconsider—he doesn't have gonads."

"Them's the breaks," she said, smiling. "Look at that *face*!"

"Also, he snores."

"So do you, once in a while."

"You never told me."

She shrugged. "I kick you and usually you stop —well, just look at *you*, you little hunk. Apathy's not *your* problem, *is* it?"

She knelt back down and got her face rebathed. "What a doll!"

"Think of the ramifications on your social life," I said. "Meatloaf and kibble by candlelight."

She laughed again and roughed the dog's fur.

As the two of them played, I picked up the suitcase and carried it into the bedroom, checking rooms as I passed, trying not to be obvious. Everything looked fine. I took Robin's clothes out and arranged them on the bed.

When I got back, she was on the leather couch, the dog's head in her lap. "I know this is heartless, Alex, but I hope his owner never calls. How long, legally, do you have to run the ad?"

"I'm not sure."

"There's got to be a limit, right? Some sort of statute of limitations?"

"Probably."

Her smile disappeared. "With my luck someone'll show up tomorrow and cart him off."

She covered another yawn. The dog looked at her, fascinated.

"Tired?" I said.

"A little. Everything okay around here? I'm sure you looked."

"Perfect."

"I'll get unpacked."

"Did it," I said. "Why don't you run a bath? I'll put your stuff away, then join you."

"That's sweet of you, thanks." She looked at the dog. "See, he really is a nice guy, our Dr. D. How 'bout you—you like baths, too?"

"As a matter of fact, he hates the water. Won't even get near it. So it's just you and me, kid."

"How Machiavellian of you—where does he sleep?"

"Last night he slept in the bed. Tonight he moves back into the kitchen."

She pouted.

I shook my head. "Uh-uh, no way."

"Oh, c'mon, Alex. It's just temporary."

"Do you want those eyes watching us?"

"Watching us do what?"

"The crossword puzzle."

"He'll be lonely out there, Alex."

"All of a sudden we're into voyeurism?"

"I'm sure he's a gentleman. And as you so unkindly pointed out, he has no . . ."

"Balls or no balls, he's a *nudist*, Robin. And he's got the hots for you. The kitchen."

She tried a bigger pout.

I said, "Put it out of your mind."

"Cruel," she said. "Heartless and cruel."

"Sounds like a law firm. Heartless, Cruel, and Horny—think I'll put 'em on retainer."

*   *   *

The dog posted himself at the bathroom door as Robin stepped into the suds. She soaped up, and I picked him up and carried him, grumbling, to his towel bed. The moment I put him down, he tried to escape. I closed the kitchen doors and gave him a Milk-Bone and as he began chewing, I snuck out.

He fussed for a while, attempting a sonorous rendition of the old-man-choking bit, but I applied sound behavior theory principles and ignored him, while trying to suppress my guilt. After a minute or so he calmed down and soon I heard him snoring in two-four time.

When I got back, Robin looked at me reproachfully. Her hair was up and the water's soapy surface reached just below her nipples.

"He's fine." I got out of my clothes. "Enjoying the slumber of the truly virtuous."

"Well," she said, putting her arms behind her head and watching, "I suppose it's best."

"Forgiven?" I said, sinking into the heat of the bath.

She contemplated. Breathed in. Smiled.

"I don't know . . ."

I kissed her. She kissed back. I touched one breast, kissed a soapy nipple.

"Umm," she said, breaking away. "Well . . ."

"Well, what?"

"You can forget Mr. Cruel and Mr. Heartless, but I think it's time to take a meeting with their partner—what's his name?"

9

Thursday morning she was up and out of the shower by six-fifteen. When I got to the kitchen I expected to see her dressed for work, that restless look in her eyes.

But she was still in her robe, drinking coffee and reading *ArtForum*. She'd set out food for the dog and only a few bits remained. He was at her feet and looked up at me only briefly before returning his head to the side of her leg.

She put the magazine down and smiled up at me.

I kissed her and said, "You can get going, I'll be fine."

"What if I just want to be with you?"

"That would be great."

"Of course, if *you* have other plans . . ."

"Nothing till the afternoon."

"What's then?"

"Patient appointment out in Sun Valley at three-thirty."

"Making a house call?"

I nodded. "Custody case. Some resistance and I want to see the kids in their natural environment."

"Three-thirty? That's good. We can hang out together till then."

"Terrific." I poured myself a cup, sat down, and pointed to the magazine. "What's new in the art world?"

"The usual foolishness." She closed it and pushed it aside. "Actually I have no idea what's going on in the art world or anywhere else. I can't concentrate, Alex. Woke up in the middle of the night, thinking about everything that's been happening to you and that poor psychiatrist up in Seattle. Do you really think there is a connection?"

"I don't know. It was a hit-and-run, but he was eighty-nine and couldn't see or hear well. Like Freud said, sometimes a cigar is just a cigar—did you get any sleep?"

"A bit."

"Was I snoring?"

"No."

"Would you tell me if I was?"

"Yes!" She gave my hand a gentle cuff.

"Why didn't you wake me to talk?" I said.

"You were deep asleep. I didn't have the heart."

"Next time wake me."

"We can talk right now, if you want. This whole thing's giving me very definite creeps the more I think about it. I'm worried about you—what will the next call or mail delivery bring?"

"Milo's looking into it," I said. "We'll get to the bottom of it."   •

I took her hand and squeezed it. She squeezed back hard. "You can't think of anyone who'd want to get back at you? Out of all the patients you've known?"

"Not really. When I worked at the hospital, I saw

physically ill kids. In practice, it was basically normal children with adjustment problems." The same kinds of patients Grant Stoumen had treated.

"What about your legal cases? All that custody garbage?"

"Anything's possible, theoretically," I said. "But I've gone through my files and found nothing. The conference has to be the link—bad love."

"What about that madman—Hewitt? Why was he shouting it?"

"I don't know," I said.

She let go of my hand. "He killed his therapist, Alex."

"Guess I could switch careers. But I'm really not good for anything else."

"Be serious."

"Okay—what happened to Becky Basille is the extreme. It's a long way from tapes and a crank call and a mangled carp to murder."

The look on her face made me add: "I'll be careful—scout's honor. I'll call an alarm company—get a referral from Milo."

"You won't consider moving out—just for a while?"

"Let's just see what happens over the next few days."

"What are you waiting for, Alex? Things to get worse? Oh, never mind, let's not bicker."

She got up, shaking her head, and went to the coffeepot for a refill. Stayed there drinking and looking out the window.

"Honey, I'm not trying to tough it out," I said. "I just want to see what Milo comes up with before I shake up our lives completely. Let's at least give him a day or two to look into it, okay? If he doesn't, we'll move to the studio temporarily."

"A day or two? You've got a deal." The dog padded over to her. She smiled at him, then at me. "Maybe I'm overdoing it. Was the tape that bad?"

"Bizarre," I said. "Like some kind of sick gag."

"It's the *sick* part that bothers me."

The dog snorted and jangled his collar. She took some cheese out of the fridge, told him to sit, and rewarded his obedience with small bites. He gobbled noisily and licked his flews.

"What do you call this?" she said. "Operant conditioning?"

"A-plus," I said. "Next week's topic is stress management."

She grinned. The last bit of cheese disappeared amid the soft folds of the dog's mouth. Robin washed her hands. The dog continued to sit and stare at her. "Shouldn't we give him a name, Alex?"

"Milo calls him Rover."

"Figures."

"I've stuck with 'hey, you' because I keep expecting someone to call and claim him."

"True . . . why get attached . . . are you hungry? I can dish something up."

"Why don't we go out?"

"Go out?"

"Like normal people."

"Sure, I'll go change."

The sparkle in her eyes made me say, "How about changing into something semi-fancy and we can hit the Bel Air?"

"The Bel Air? What are we celebrating?"

"The new world order."

"If only there was one. What about him?"

"Milk-Bone *en le kitchen*," I said. "I don't have a suit that fits him."

*   *   *

She put on a silver crepe de chine blouse and a black skirt and I found a lightweight sportcoat, brown turtleneck, and khaki slacks that looked decent. I told my service where I'd be and we took Sunset to Stone Canyon Road and drove up the half mile to the Bel Air Hotel. Pink-shirted valets opened our doors and we walked across the covered bridge to the main entrance.

Swans glided below in the still, green pond, cutting through the water with blissful ignorance. A white lattice marriage canopy was being set up on the banks. Huge pine and eucalyptus umbrellaed the grounds, air-conditioning the morning.

We passed through the pink stucco arcade hung with black-and-white photos of monarchs gone by. The stone pathways had been freshly watered, the ferns dripped dew, and the azaleas were in bloom. Room service waiters rolled carts to sequestered suites. An emaciated, androgynous, long-haired thing in brown velvet sweats walked past us unsteadily, carrying *The Wall Street Journal* under one atrophied arm. Death was in its eyes, and Robin bit her lip.

I held her arm tighter and we entered the dining room, exchanged smiles with the hostess, and were seated near the French doors. Several years ago—soon after we'd met—we'd lingered right here over dinner and seen Bette Davis through those same doors, gliding across the patio in a long, black gown and coronation-quality diamonds, looking as serene as the swans.

This morning, the room was nearly empty and none of the faces had a measurable Q-rating, though all looked well tended. An Arab in an ice cream suit drank tea, alone, at a corner table. An elderly, dew-lapped couple who could have been pretenders to a minor throne whispered to each other and nibbled on toast. In a big booth at the far end, half a dozen dark suits sat listening to a crewcut, white-haired man in a red T-shirt and khakis. He was telling a joke, gesturing expansively with an unlit cigar. The other men's body language was half humble servant, half Iago.

We had coffee and took a long time deciding what to eat. Neither of us felt like talking. After a few moments, the silence began to feel like a luxury and I relaxed.

We finished a couple of fresh grapefruit juices and put in our breakfast order, holding hands until the food came. I'd just taken the first bite of my omelet when I spotted the hostess approaching. Two steps ahead of someone else.

A tall, broad someone, easily visible over her coiffure. Milo's jacket was light blue—a tint that clashed with his aqua shirt. Pigeon-gray pants and brown-and-blue-striped tie rounded off the ensemble. He had his hands in his pockets and looked dangerous.

The hostess kept her distance from him, clearly wanting to be somewhere else. Just before she reached our table, he stepped ahead of her. After kissing Robin, he took a chair from another table and pulled it up perpendicular to us.

"Will you be ordering, sir?" said the hostess.

"Coffee."

"Yes, sir." She walked away hastily.

Milo turned to Robin. "Welcome home. You look gorgeous, as ever."

"Thank you, Milo—"

"Flight okay?"

"Just fine."

"Every time I'm up in one of those things I wonder what gives us the right to break the law of gravity."

Robin smiled. "To what do we owe the honor?"

He ran his hand over his face. "Has he told you about what's going on?"

She nodded. "We're thinking of moving into the shop until things clear up."

Milo grunted and looked at the tablecloth.

The waiter brought the coffee and a place setting. Milo unfolded the napkin over his lap and drummed a spoon on the table. As the coffee was being poured, he glanced around the room, lingering on the suits in the far booth.

"Meals and deals," he said, after the waiter left. "Either showbiz or crime."

"There's a difference?" I said.

His smile was immediate but very weak—it seemed to torment his face.

"There's a new complication," he said. "This morning I decided to have a go at the computer, tracking down any references to 'bad love' in the case files. I really didn't expect to find anything, just trying to be thorough. But I did. Two unsolved homicides, one three years old, the other five. One beating, one stabbing."

"Oh God," said Robin.

He covered her hand with his. "Hate to spoil your breakfast, kids, but I wasn't sure when I'd be able to catch both of you. Service said you were here."

"No, no, I'm glad you came." She pushed her plate away and gripped Milo's hand.

"Who got killed?" I said.

"Does the name Rodney Shipler mean anything to you?"

"No. Is he a victim or a suspect?"

"Victim. What about Myra Paprock?"

He spelled it. I shook my head.

"You're sure?" he said. "Neither of them could have been old patients?"

I repeated both names to myself. "No—never

heard of them. How does 'bad love' figure into their murders?''

"With Shipler—he was the beating—it was scrawled on a wall at the crime scene. With Paprock, I'm not sure what the connection is yet. The computer just threw out 'bad love' under 'miscellaneous factors' —no explanation.''

"Did the same detectives work both cases?''

He shook his head. "Shipler was in Southwest Division, Paprock over in the valley. Far as I can tell, the cases were never cross-referenced—two years apart, different parts of the city. I'm going to try to get the actual case files this afternoon.''

"For what it's worth,'' I said, "I spoke to Dr. Stoumen's associate last night. The accident was a hit-and-run. It happened in Seattle, in June of last year.''

Milo's eyebrows rose.

"It may have just been a hit-and-run,'' I said. "Stoumen was almost ninety, couldn't see or hear well. Someone ran into him as he stepped off a curb.''

"At a psych conference.''

"Yes, but unless Shipler or Paprock were therapists, what link could there be?''

"Don't know what they were yet. The computer doesn't give out that level of detail.''

Robin's head had dropped, curls spilling onto the table. She looked up, clear eyed. "So what do we do?''

"Well,'' said Milo, "you know I'm not Mr. Impulsive, but with everything we've got here—nut mail, nut call, dead fish, two cold-case homicides, hazardous conferences—'' He looked at me. "Moving's not a bad idea. At least till we find out what the hell's going on. But I wouldn't go to the shop. Just in case whoever's bothering Alex has done enough research on him to know the location.''

She looked out the window and shook her head. He patted her shoulder.

She said, "I'm fine. Let's just figure out where we're going to live." She looked around. "This place ain't shabby—too bad we're not oil sheiks."

"As a matter of fact," said Milo, "I think I've got an option for you. Private client of mine—investment banker I moonlighted for last year. He's in England for a year, put his house up for rent, and hired me to keep an eye on the premises. It's a nice size place and not that far from you. Beverly Hills PO, off Benedict Canyon. It's still empty—you know the real estate market—and he's coming back in three months, so he unlisted it. I'm sure I can get his permission for you to use it."

"Benedict Canyon." Robin smiled. "Close to the Sharon Tate house?"

"Not far, but the place is as safe as you're gonna get. The owner's security conscious—has a big art collection. Electric gates, closed-circuit TV, screaming siren alarm."

It sounded like prison. I didn't say a thing.

"The alarm's hooked up to Beverly Hills PD," he went on. "And their response time's averaging two minutes—maybe a little longer up in the hills, but still damn good. I'm not going to tell you it's home, chillun, but for temporary lodgings you could do worse."

"And this client of yours won't mind?"

"Nah, it's a piece of cake."

"Thanks, Milo," said Robin. "You're a doll."

"No big deal."

"What do I do about my work? Can I go to the shop?"

"Wouldn't hurt to avoid it for a few days. At least until I find out more about these unsolveds."

She said, "I had orders piled up before I went to Oakland, Milo. The time I spent up there already set me back." She grabbed her napkin and crushed it.

"I'm sorry, here you are getting threatened, baby, and I'm griping . . ."

I took her hand and kissed it.

Milo said, "In terms of work, you could set up shop in the garage. It's a triple and there's only one car in it."

"That's big enough," said Robin, "but I can't just pack up the table saw and the band saw and cart them over."

"I may be able to help you with that, too," said Milo.

"An alternative," I said, "would be moving to the studio and hiring a guard."

"Why take a chance?" said Milo. "My philosophy is when trouble calls, don't be there to answer the doorbell. You can even take Rover with you. Owner keeps cats—a friend's taking care of them now, but we're not talking pristine environment."

"Sounds good," I said, but my throat had gone dry and a refugee numbness was rising up from my feet. "As long as we're talking critters, there're the rest of the koi. The pond maintenance people can probably board them for a while—time to get organized."

Robin began folding her napkin, over and over, ending up with a small, thick wad that she pressed between her hands. Her knuckles were ivory knobs and her lips were clamped together. She gazed over my shoulder, as if peering into an uncertain future.

The waiter came over with the coffeepot, and Milo waved him away.

From the big booth came the sound of male laughter. The levity had probably been going on for a while, but I heard it now because the three of us had stopped talking.

The Arab got up from his table, smoothed his suit, put cash on the table, and left the dining room.

Robin said, "Guess it's time to hitch up the wagons," but she didn't move.

"This whole thing seems so unreal," I said.

"Maybe it'll turn out we've hassled for nothing," Milo said, "but you two are among the few humans I hold any positive regard for, so I do feel an obligation to protect and serve."

He looked at our barely touched food and frowned. "This'll set you back some."

"Have some." I pushed my plate toward him.

He shook his head.

"The stress diet," I said. "Let's write a book and hit the talk-show circuit."

He followed us home in an unmarked Ford. When the three of us stepped into the house, the dog thought it was a party and began jumping around.

"Take a Valium, Rover," said Milo.

"Be nice to him," said Robin, kneeling and holding her arms out. The dog charged her and she tussled with him for a second, then stood. "I'd better figure out what I'm going to need to take."

She left for the bedroom, dog at heel.

"True love," said Milo.

I said, "Is there anything more you want to tell me?"

"You mean, am I shielding her from gory details? No. Didn't figure I should."

"No, of course not," I said. "I just—I guess I still want to protect her."

"Then you're doing the right thing by moving."

I didn't answer.

"Nothing to be ashamed of," he said. "The protective instinct. I keep my work out of Rick's face, he does the same for me."

"If anything happened to her . . ." From the

back of the house came Robin's footsteps, rapid and intermittent.

Pause and decision.

Dull sounds as clothing hit the bed. Soft, sweet words as she talked to the dog.

I paced some more, circling, trying to focus . . . what to take, what to leave . . . looking at things I wouldn't be seeing for a while.

"Ring around the rosy," he said. "Now you're looking like me when I'm uptight."

I ran my hand over my face. He laughed, unbuttoned his jacket, and pulled a notepad and pen out of an inner pocket. He was wearing his revolver in a brown cowhide hip holster.

"Do *you* have any more details for me?" he said. "Like about the psychiatrist—Stoumen?"

"Just the approximate date—early June—and the fact that the conference was the Northwest Symposium on Child Welfare. I'm pretty sure it's sponsored by the Child Welfare League, and they have an office here in town. Maybe you can pry an attendance roster out of them."

"You have a go at the Western Pediatric roster yet?"

"No. I'll try right now."

I called the hospital and asked for the Office of Continuing Education. The secretary told me records of past symposia were only kept for one year. I asked her to check anyway and she did.

"Nothing, doctor."

"There're no archives or anything?"

"Archives? With our budget problems we're lucky to get bedpans, doctor."

Milo was listening in. When I hung up, he said, "Okay, scratch that. Onward. I'm going to hook up with the FBI's violent crime data bank and see if 'bad love' shows up on any out-of-town homicides."

"What about Dorsey Hewitt?" I said. "Could he have killed Shipler and Paprock?"

"Let me try to find out if he was living in L.A. during their murders. I'm still trying to get hold of Jean Jeffers, the clinic director—see if Hewitt had clinic buddies."

"The taper," I said. "You know, that second session could have taken place the day of the murder— someone taping Hewitt right after he killed Becky. Before he ran out and the TV mikes picked him up. That's pretty damn cold—almost premeditated. Same kind of mind who could turn a child's voice robotic. What if the taper knew exactly what Hewitt was going to do and was ready to tape him?"

"An accomplice?"

"Or at least a knowing confederate. Someone who knew Becky was going to die, but didn't stop it."

He stared at me. Grimaced. Wrote something down. Said, "Ready to start packing now?"

It took an hour or so for Robin and me to throw together suitcases, plastic shopping bags, and cardboard cartons. A smaller collection than I would have expected.

Milo and I carried all of it into the living room, then I called my pond maintenance people and arranged for them to collect the fish.

When I returned to the pile, Milo and Robin were staring at it. She said, "I'm going to go over to the shop and get the small tools and the breakable things together—if that's okay."

"Sure, just be careful," said Milo. "Anyone weird hanging around, just turn around and come back."

"Weird? This is Venice we're talking about."

"Relatively speaking."

"Gotcha." She took the dog with her. I walked

her down to her truck and watched as they drove away. Milo and I had a couple of Cokes, then the doorbell rang and he went to get it. After looking through the peephole, he opened the door and let in three men—boys, really, around nineteen or twenty.

They were thick faced and had power lifters' rhino physiques. Two white, one black. One of the white ones was tall. They wore perforated tank tops, knee-length baggies in nauseating color combinations, and black lace-up boots that barely closed around their tree-stump calves. The white boys had their hair cut very short, except at the back, where it fringed around their excessive shoulders. The black's head was shaved clean. Despite their bulk, all three seemed awkward—intimidated.

Milo said, "Morning, campers, this is Dr. Delaware. He's a psychologist, so he knows how to read your minds. Doctor, this is Keenan, Chuck, and DeLongpre. They haven't figured out what to do with their lives yet, so they abuse themselves over at Silver's Gym and spend Keenan's money. Right, boys?"

The three of them smiled and cuffed one another. Through the open door I saw a black van parked near the carport. Jacked-up suspension, black-matte reversed hubcaps, darkened windows, diamond-shaped bulb of black plastic set into the side panel, a skull-and-crossbones decal just below that.

"Tasteful, huh?" said Milo. "Tell Dr. Delaware who recovered your wheels for you, after a miscreant scumbag junkie made off with it because you left it on Santa Monica Boulevard with the key in the ignition."

"You did, Mr. Sturgis," said the shorter white boy. He had a crushed nose, puffy lips, a very deep voice, and a slight lisp. The confession seemed to relieve him and he gave a big grin. One of his canines was missing.

"And who didn't charge you his usual private

fee because you'd run out of trust fund that month, Keenan?''

"*You* didn't, sir."

"Was that a gift?''

"No, sir.''

"Am I a chump?''

Shake of the thick head.

"What did I demand in return, boys?''

"Slave labor!'' they shouted in unison.

He nodded and rapped the back of one hand against the palm of the other. "Payoff time. All this stuff goes into the Deathmobile. The really heavy gear's over in Venice—Pacific Avenue. Know where that is?''

"Sure,'' said Keenan. "Near Muscle Beach, right?''

"Very good. Follow me there and we'll see what you're made of. Once you're finished, you'll keep your mouths shut about it. Period. Understood?''

"Yes, sir.''

"And be careful with it—pretend it's bottles of liver shake or something.''

10

We met up with Robin and loaded her pickup. Watching her shop empty made her blink, but she wiped her eyes quickly and said, "Let's go."

We set up a caravan—Milo in the lead, Robin and the dog in the truck, me in the Seville, the van trailing —and headed back to Sunset, passing Beverly Glen as if it were someone else's neighborhood, entering Beverly Hills, and driving north onto Benedict Canyon.

Milo turned off on a narrow road, poorly paved and sided with eucalyptus. A cheerless, white iron gate appeared fifty feet up. He slipped a card key into a slot and it opened. The caravan continued up a steep pebbled drive hedged with very high columns of Italian cypress that looked slightly moth-eaten. Then the road kinked and we descended another two or three hundred feet, toward a shallow bowl of an unshaded lot, maybe half an acre wide.

A low, off-white one-story house sat in the bowl. A long, straight, concrete drive led to the front door. As I got closer I saw that the entire property was hilltop, the depression an artificial crater scalped from the tip.

Canyon and mountain views surrounded the property. Lots of brown slopes and a few green spots, flecked with the lint of occasional houses. I wondered if mine could be seen from up here, looked around but couldn't get my bearings.

The house was wide and free of detail, roofed too heavily with deep brown aluminum tile supposed to simulate shake, and windowed with aluminum-cased rectangles.

A flat-topped detached garage was separated from the main building by an unfenced paddle tennis court. A ten-foot satellite dish perched atop it, aimed at the cosmos.

A few cactus and yuccas grew near the house, but that was it in terms of landscaping. What could have been front lawn had been converted to concrete pad. An empty terra cotta planter sat next to the coffee-colored double doors. As I got out of the car, I noticed the TV camera above the lintel. The air was hot and smelled sterile.

I got out and went over to Robin's truck.

She smiled. "Looks like a motel, doesn't it?"

"Long as the owner's not named Norman."

The black van dieseled as its ignition shut down. The three beef-boys exited and threw open the rear doors. Tarped machines filled the cabin. The boys did some squats and grunts and began unloading.

Milo said something to them, then waved to us. His jacket was off but he still wore his gun. The heat had returned.

"Crazy weather," I said.

Robin got out and lifted the dog out of the pickup. We walked to the front door, and Milo let us into the house.

The floor was white marble streaked with pink,

the furniture teakwood and ebony and bright blue velour. The far wall was taken up by single, light French doors. All the others were covered with paintings—hung frame to frame, so that only scraps of white plaster were visible.

The doors looked out onto a yard encircled by a nearly invisible fence—glass panes in thin iron frames. A strip of sod-grass separated a cement patio from a long, narrow lap pool. The pool had been dug at the edge of the lot—someone aiming for a merge-with-the-sky effect. But the water was blue and the sky was gray and the whole thing ended up looking like an off-balance cubist sculpture.

The dog ran to the French doors and tapped the glass with his paws. Milo let him out and he squatted in the grass before returning.

"Make yourself right at home, why don't you." To us: "Called London, everything's set up. There'll be a token rent, but you don't have to worry about it until he gets back."

We thanked him. He dusted off one of the couches and I studied the art. Impressionist pictures that looked French and important nudged up against pre-Raphaelite mythology. Syrupy, Orientalist harem scenes neighbored with English hunt paintings. Modern pieces, too: a Mondrian, a Frank Stella chevron, a Red Grooms subway cartoon, something amorphous fashioned out of neon.

The dining area was all Maxfield Parrish: cobalt skies, heavenly forests, and beautiful blond boys.

Lots of nude male statuary, too. A lamp whose black granite base was a limbless, muscular torso—Venus de Milo in drag. A framed cover from *The Advocate* commemorating the Christopher Street riot side by side with a Paul Cadmus drawing of a reclining Adonis. A framed Arrow Man shirt ad from an old issue of *Collier's* kept company with a black-and-white gelatin print of a Paul Newman lookalike in nothing but a G-string. I felt less comfortable than I would have expected. Or maybe it was just the suddenness of the move.

Milo brought us back to the door and demonstrated the closed-circuit surveillance system. Two cameras—one in front, the other panning the rear of the house, two black-and-white monitors mounted over the door. One of them captured the three behemoths, shlepping and swearing.

Milo opened the door and shouted, "Careful!" Closing it, he said, "What do you think?"

"Great," I said. "Plenty of space—thanks a lot."

"Beautiful view," said Robin. "Really gorgeous."

We followed him into the kitchen and he opened the door of a Sub-Zero cooler. Empty except for a bottle of cooking sherry. "I'll get you some provisions."

Robin said, "Don't worry, I can take care of that."

"Whatever. . . . Let's get you a bedroom—you've got your choice of three."

He took us down a wide, windowless hallway lined with prints. A wall clock in a mother-of-pearl case read two thirty-five. In less than an hour, I was expected in Sunland.

Robin read my mind: "Your afternoon appointment?"

"What time?" said Milo.

"Three-thirty," I said.

"Where?"

"Wallace's mother-in-law. I'm supposed to see the girls out there. No reason not to go, is there?"

He thought for a moment. "None that I can see."

Robin caught the hesitation. "Why should there be a reason?"

"This particular case," I said, "is potentially ugly. Two little girls, their father killed their mother and now wants visitation—"

"That's absurd."

"Among other things. The court asked me to evaluate and make a recommendation. In the very beginning Milo and I talked about the father possibly being behind the tape. Trying to intimidate me. He's got a criminal record and hangs with an outlaw motorcycle gang that's been known to use strongarm tactics."

"This creep's walking free?"

"No, he's locked up in prison. Maximum security at Folsom, I just got a letter from him, telling me he's a good father."

"Wonderful," she said.

"He's not behind this. It was just a working guess, until I learned about the 'bad love' symposium. My problems have something to do with de Bosch."

She looked at Milo. He nodded.

"All right," she said, taking hold of my jacket lapel and kissing my chin. "I'm going to stop being Mama Bear and go about my business."

I held her around the waist. Milo looked away.

"I'll be careful," I said.

She put her head on my chest.

The dog began pawing the floor.

"Oedipus Rover," said Milo.

Robin pushed me away gently. "Go help those poor little girls."

I took Benedict into the valley and picked up the Ventura Freeway at Van Nuys Boulevard. Traffic was hideous all the way to the 210 and beyond, and I didn't make it to McVine until 3:40. When I got to the Rodriguez house, no cars were parked in front and no one answered my ring.

Evelyn showing her displeasure at my tardiness? I tried again, knocked once, then harder, and when that brought no response, went around to the back. Managing to hoist myself up high enough to peer over the pink block wall, I scanned the yard.

Empty. Not a toy or a piece of furniture in sight. The inflatable pool had been put away, the garage was shut, and drawn drapes blocked the rear windows.

Returning to the front, I checked the mailbox and found yesterday's and today's deliveries. Bulk stuff, coupon giveaways, and something from the gas company.

I put it back and looked up and down the street. A boy of around ten zoomed by on rollerblade skates. A few seconds later, a red truck came speeding down from Foothill and for an instant I thought it was Roddy Rodriguez's. But as it passed, I saw that it was lighter in shade than his and a decade newer. A blond woman sat in the driver's seat. A big yellow dog rode in the bed, tongue out, watchful.

I returned to the Seville and waited for another twenty-five minutes, but no one showed up. I tried to recall the name of Rodriguez's masonry company and finally did—R and R.

Driving back to Foothill Boulevard, I headed east until I spotted a phone booth at an Arco station. The directory had been yanked off the chain, so I called information and asked for R and R's address and phone number. The operator ignored me and switched over to the automated message, leaving me only the number. I called it. No one answered. I tried information a second time and got a street address— right on Foothill, about ten blocks east.

The place was a gray-topped lot, forty or fifty feet behind a shabby brown building. Surrounded by barbed link, it had a green clapboard beer bar on one side, a pawnshop on the other.

The property was empty except for a few brick

fragments and some paper litter. The brown building looked to have once been a double garage. Two sets of old-fashioned hinge doors took up most of the front. Above them, ornate yellow letters shouted R AND R MASONRY: CEMENT, CINDER, AND CUSTOM BRICK. Below that: RETAINING WALLS OUR SPECIALTY, followed by an overlapping R's logo meant to evoke Rolls-Royce fantasies.

I parked and got out. No signs of life. The padlock on the gate was the size of a baseball.

I went over to the pawnshop. The door was locked and a sign above a red button said, PRESS AND WAIT. I obeyed and the door buzzed but didn't open. I leaned in close to the window. A man stood behind a nipple-high counter, shielded by a Plexiglas window.

He ignored me.

I buzzed again.

He made a stabbing motion and the door gave.

I walked past cases filled with cameras, cheap guitars, cassette decks and boomboxes, pocket knives and fishing rods.

The man was managing to examine a watch and check me over at the same time.

He was sixty or so, with slicked, dyed-black hair and a pumpkin-colored bottle tan. His face was long and baggy.

I cleared my throat.

He said, "Yeah?" through the plastic and kept looking at the watch, turning it over with nicotined fingers and working his lips as if preparing to spit. The window was scratched and cloudy and outfitted with a ticket-taker remote speaker that he hadn't switched on. The store had soft, wooden floors and stank of WD-40, sulfur matches, and body odor. A sign over the gun display said NO LOONIES.

"I'm looking for Roddy Rodriguez next door," I said. "Have some work for him to do on a retaining wall."

He put the watch down and picked up another.

"Excuse me," I said.

"Got something to buy or sell?"

"No, I was just wondering if you knew when Rodriguez was—"

He turned his back on me and walked away. Through the Plexiglas I saw an old desk full of papers and other timepieces. A semiautomatic pistol served as a paperweight. He scratched his butt and held the watch up to a fluorescent bulb.

I left and walked over to the bar two doors down. The green board was rubbed to raw timber in spots and the front door was unmarked. A sun-shaped neon sign said, SUNNY'S SUN VALLEY. A single window below it was filled with a Budweiser sign.

I walked in, expecting darkness, billiard clicks, and a cowboy jukebox. Instead, I got bright lights, ZZ Top going on about a Mexican whore, and a nearly empty room not much larger than my kitchen.

No pool table—no tables of any kind. Just a long, pressed-wood bar with a black vinyl bumper and matching stools, some of them patched with duct tape. Up against the facing wall were a cigarette machine and a pocket comb dispenser. The floor was grubby concrete.

The man working the bar was thirtyish, fair, balding, stubbled. He wore tinted eyeglasses and one of his ears was double pierced, hosting a tiny gold stud and a white metal hoop. He had on a soiled white apron over a black T-shirt, and his chest was flabby. His arms were soft looking, too, white and tattooed. He wasn't doing much when I came in, and he continued along those lines. Two men sat at the bar, far from each other. More tattoos. They didn't move either. It looked like a poster for National Brain Death Week.

I took a stool between the men and ordered a beer.

"Draft or bottle?"

"Draft."

The bartender took a long time to fill a mug, and as I waited I snuck glances at my companions. Both wore billed caps, T-shirts, jeans, and work shoes. One was skinny, the other muscular. Their hands were dirty. They smoked and drank and had tired faces.

My beer came and I took a swallow. Not much head and not great, but not as bad as I'd expected.

"Any idea when Roddy'll be back?" I said.

"Who?" said the bartender.

"Rodriguez—the masonry guy next door. He's supposed to be doing a retaining wall for me and he didn't show up."

He shrugged.

"Place is closed," I said.

No answer.

"Great," I said. "Guy's got my goddamned deposit."

The bartender began soaking glasses in a gray plastic tub.

I drank some more.

ZZ gave way to a disc jockey's voice, hawking car insurance for people with bad driving records. Then a series of commercials for ambulance-chasing lawyers polluted the air some more.

"When's the last time you've seen him around?" I said.

The bartender turned around. "Who?"

"Rodriguez."

Shrug.

"Has his place been closed for a while?"

Another shrug. He returned to soaking.

"Great," I said.

He looked over his shoulder. "He never comes in here, I got nothing to do with him, okay?"

"Not much of a drinker?"

Shrug.

"Fucking asshole," said the man on my right.

The skinny one. Sallow and pimpled, barely above drinking age. His cigarette was dead in the ashtray. One of his index fingers played with the ashes.

I said, "Who? Rodriguez?"

He gave a depressed nod. "Fucking greaser don't pay."

"You worked for him?"

"Fucking A, digging his fucking ditches. Then the roach coach comes by for lunch and I wanna advance so's to get a burrito. He says sorry, amigo, not till payday. So I'm adios, amigo, man."

He shook his head, still pained by the rejection.

"Asshole," he said, and returned to his beer.

"So he shafted you, too," I said.

"Fucking A, man."

"Any idea where I can find him?"

"Maybe Mexico, man."

"Mexico?"

"Yeah, all a them beaners got second homes there, got they extra wives and they little taco-tico kids, send all they money there."

I heard a metallic click to the left, looked over, and saw the muscular man light up a cigarette. Late twenties or early thirties, two-day growth of heavy beard, thick, black Fu Manchu mustache. His cap was black and said CAT. He blew smoke toward the bar.

I said, "You know Rodriguez, too?"

He gave a long, slow headshake and held out his mug.

The bartender filled it, then extended his own hand. The mustachioed man jostled the pack until a cigarette slid forward. The bartender took it, nodded, and lit up.

Guns 'n Roses came on the radio.

The bartender looked at my half-empty mug. "Anything else?"

I shook my head, put money down on the bar, and left.

"Asshole," said the skinny man, raising his voice to be heard over the music.

I drove back to the Rodriguez house. Still dark and empty. A woman across the street was holding a broom, and she began looking at me suspiciously.

I called over: "Any idea when they'll be back?"

She went inside her house. I drove away and got back on the freeway, exiting on Sunset and heading north on Beverly Glen. I realized my error just as I completed the turn, but continued on to my house anyway, pulling up in front of the carport. Looking over my shoulder with paranoid fervor, I decided it was safe to get out of the car.

I walked around my property, looking, remembering. Though it made no sense, the house already looked sad.

You know how places get when they're empty . . .

I took a quick look at the pond. The fish were still there. They swam up to greet me and I obliged with food.

"See you guys," I said, and left, wondering how many would survive.

11

I made it to Benedict a few minutes later.

The black van and the unmarked were gone. Two of the three garage doors were open and I saw Robin inside, wearing work clothes and goggles, standing behind her lathe.

She saw me coming and turned off the machine. A gold BMW coupe was parked in the third garage. The rest of the space was a near duplicate of the Venice shop.

"Looks like you're all set up," I said.

She pushed her goggles up on her forehead. "This isn't too bad, actually, as long as I leave the door open for ventilation. How come you're back so soon?"

"No one home."

"Flake out on you?"

"It looks like they're gone for a while."

"Moved out?"

"Must be the week for it."

"How could you tell?"

"Two days' mail in the box and her husband's business was padlocked."

"Considerate of her to let you know."

"Etiquette isn't her strong suit. She wasn't thrilled about my evaluation in the first place, though I thought we were making progress. She probably took the girls out of state—maybe Hawaii. When I spoke to her yesterday she made a crack about a Honolulu vacation. Or Mexico. Her husband may have family there. . . . I'd better call the judge."

"We set up an office for you in one of the bedrooms," she said, leaning over and pecking my cheek. "Gave you the one with the best view, plus there's a Hockney on the wall—two guys showering." She smiled. "Poor Milo—he was a little embarrassed about it—started muttering about the 'atmosphere.' Almost apologizing. After all he did to help us. I sat him down and we had a good talk."

"About what?"

"Stuff—the meaning of life. I told him you could handle the *atmosphere*."

"What he say to that?"

"Just grunted and rubbed his face the way he does. Then I made coffee and told him if he ever learned to play an instrument I'd build one for him."

"Safe offer," I said.

"Maybe not. When we were talking, it came up that he used to play the accordion when he was a kid. And he sings—have you ever heard him?"

"No."

"Well, he sang for me this afternoon. After some prodding. Did an old Irish folk song—and guess what? He's got a really nice voice."

"Basso profundo?"

"*Tenor*, of all things. He used to be in the church choir when he was a little boy."

I smiled. "That's a little hard to picture."

"There's probably a lot about him you don't know."

"Probably," I said. "Each year I get in touch with more of my ignorance. . . . Speaking of grunts, where's our guest?"

"Sleeping in the service porch. I tried keeping him here while I worked, but he kept charging the machines—he was ready to take on the bandsaw when I got him out of here and locked him in."

"Tough love, huh? Did he do his little strangulation routine?"

"Oh, sure," she said. She put her hand around her throat and made a gagging sound. "I yelled at him to be quiet and he stopped."

"Poor guy. He probably thought you were going to be his salvation."

She grinned. "I may be sultry and sensual, but I ain't easy."

I let the dog loose, gave him time to pee outside, and took him into my new office. A chrome-and-glass-topped desk was pushed up against one wall. My papers and books were piled neatly on a black velour couch. The view was fantastic, but after a few minutes I stopped noticing it.

I phoned superior court, got Steve Huff in his chambers, and told him about Evelyn Rodriguez's no-show.

"Maybe she just forgot," he said. "Denial, avoidance, whatever."

"I think there's a good chance she's gone, Steve." I described Roddy Rodriguez's locked yard.

"Sounds like it," he said. "There goes another one."

"Can't say that I blame her. When I saw her two days ago, she really opened up about the girls' problems. They're having plenty of them. And Donald wrote me a letter—no remorse, just tooting his own horn as a good dad."

"Wrote you a *letter*?"

"His lawyer's been calling me, too."

"Any intimidation?"

I hesitated. "No, just nagging."

"Too bad. No law against that . . . no, can't say that I blame her either, Alex—off the record. Do you want to wait and try again, or just write up your report now—document all the crap she told you?"

"What's the difference?"

"The difference is how quickly you want to get paid versus how much lead time you want to give her, if she *has* hightailed it. Once you put it in writing and I receive it, I'm obligated to send it over to Bucklear. Even with reasonable delays he gets it in a couple of weeks or so, then *he* files paper and gets warrants out on her."

"A murderer gets warrants on a grandmother taking her grandkids out of town? Do we file that under 'I for irony' or 'N for nuts'?"

"Do I take that to mean you'll wait?"

"How much lead time can I give her?"

"A reasonable period. Consistent with typical medical-psychological practice."

"Meaning??"

"Meaning what shrinks normally do. Three, four, even five weeks wouldn't chafe any hides—you guys are notorious for being sloppy about your paperwork. You might even stretch it to six or seven—but you never heard that from me. In fact, we never had this talk, did we?"

"Judge who?" I said.

"Attaboy—oops, bailiff's buzzing me, time to be Solomonic again, bye-bye." I put the phone down. The bulldog placed his paws on my knees and tried to get up on my lap. I lifted him and he settled on me like a warm hunk of clay. At *least* thirty pounds.

The Hockney was right in front of me. Great painting. As was the Thomas Hart Benton drawing on the opposite wall—a mural study depicting hypermuscular workmen cheerfully constructing a WPA dam.

I looked at both of them for a while and wondered what Robin and Milo had talked about. The dog stayed as motionless as a little furry Buddha. I rubbed his head and his jowls and he licked my hand. A boy and his dog . . . I realized I hadn't gotten the number for the bulldog club, yet. Almost five p.m. Too late to call the AKC.

I'd do it tomorrow morning.

Denial, avoidance, whatever.

That night I slept fitfully. Friday morning at eight I phoned North Carolina and got an address for the French Bulldog Club of America, in Rahway, New Jersey. A post office box. No phone number was available.

At eight-ten, I called the Rodriguez house. A phone company recording said that line had been disconnected. I pictured Evelyn and the girls barreling over a dirt road in Baja, Rodriguez following in his truck. Or maybe the four of them, wandering through Waikiki with glazed tourists' eyes. If only they knew how much we had in common now . . .

I began unpacking books. At eight thirty-five, the doorbell rang and Milo appeared on one of the TV monitors, tapping a foot and carrying a white bag.

"Breakfast," he said, as I let him in. "I already gave Ms. Castagna hers. God, that woman works— what've you been doing?"

"Getting organized."

"Sleep okay?"

"Great," I lied. "Thanks a lot for setting us up."

He looked around. "How's the office?"

"Perfect."

"Great view, huh?"

"To die for."

We went into the kitchen and he took some onion rolls and two Styrofoam cups of coffee out of the bag.

We sat at a blue granite table. He said, "What's your schedule like today?"

"It's pretty open now that the Wallace thing's on hold. Looks like Grandma decided to take matters into her own hands."

I recounted what I'd found in Sunland.

He said, "They're probably better off. If you feel like taking on a little assignment, I've got one for you."

"What?"

"Go over to the Mental Health Center and talk to Ms. Jean Jeffers. I finally got through to her—she actually called me back last night, which I thought was pretty cool for a bureaucrat. Better attitude than I expected, too. Down to earth. Not that she shouldn't cooperate, after what happened to Becky. I told her we'd come across some harassment crimes—didn't go into specifics—that we had reason to believe might be coming from one of her patients. Someone we also had reason to believe was a buddy of Hewitt's. Mentioning *his* name got her going—she went on about how Becky's murder had traumatized all of them. Still sounds pretty shook up."

He tore an onion roll into three pieces, placed the segments on the table like monte cards, picked one up, and ate it.

"Anyway, I asked her if she knew who Hewitt hung out with and she said no. Then I asked her if I

could look at her patient roster, and she said she
wanted to help but no—the confidentiality thing. So I
threw Tarasoff at her, hoping she didn't know the law
that well. But she did: no specific threat against a specific victim, no Tarasoff obligation. At *that* point, I
played my trump card: told her the department had a
consultant doing some profiling work for us on psycho crimes—a genuine 'pee aitch dee' who respected
confidentiality and would be discreet, and I gave her
your name in case maybe she heard of you. And
guess what, she thought she had. Especially after I
told her you were semi-famous."

"Hoo-hah."

"Hoo-hah to the max. She said she couldn't
promise anything, but she'd be willing to at least talk
to you. Maybe there'd be some way to work something out. The more we talked, the friendlier she got.
My feeling is she wants to help but is afraid of being
burned by more publicity. So be gentle with her."

"No brass knucks," I said. "How much do I tell
her?"

He ate another piece of roll. "As little as possible."

"When can she see me?"

"This afternoon. Here's the number." He took a
scrap of paper out of his pocket, gave it to me, and
stood.

"Where you going?" I said.

"Over the hill. Van Nuys. Try to find out what I
can about who cut up Myra Paprock five years ago."

After he was gone, I called in for messages—still
nothing from Shirley Rosenblatt in New York—then
wrote a letter to the bulldog club informing them I'd
found what might possibly be a member's pet. At
nine-thirty, I phoned Jean Jeffers and was put through
to her secretary, who sounded as if she'd been expect-

ing me. An appointment with Ms. Jeffers was available in an hour if I was free.

I grabbed a roll, put on a tie, and left.

The center was in a block of cheerless, pastel-colored apartments, in a quiet part of West L.A. not far from Santa Monica. An old, working-class district, near an industrial park whose galloping expansion had been choked off by hard times. Constructus interruptus had left its mark all over the neighborhood—half-framed buildings, empty lots dug out for foundations and left as dry sumps, pigeon-specked FOR SALE signs, boarded-up windows on condemned prewar bungalows.

The clinic was the only charming bit of architecture in sight. Its front windows were barred, but boxes filled with begonias hung from the iron. The spot on the sidewalk where Dorsey Hewitt had fallen dead was clean. But for a couple of trash-choked shopping carts in front, it could have been a private sanitarium.

A generous lot next door was two-thirds empty and marked EMPLOYEES ONLY. NO PATIENT PARKING. I decided a consultant qualified as someone's employee, and parked there.

I made my way back to the front of the building, passing the section of wall that had been obsessed upon by the TV camera. A cement cornerstone etched with names of forgotten politicos stated that the building had been dedicated as a veterans clinic in 1919. The door Hewitt had come out of was just to the right, unmarked and locked—two locks, each almost as large as the one sealing Roddy Rodriguez's brickyard.

The main entrance was dead center, through a squat arch leading to a courtyard with an empty fountain. A loggia to the right of the fountain—the path Hewitt would have taken to get to the unmarked door —was sectioned off by thick steel mesh that looked brand-new. An open hallway on the opposite side led me around the fountain to glass-paned doors.

A blue-uniformed guard stood behind the doors, tall, old, black, chewing gum. He looked me over and unlatched one of the doors, then pointed to a metal detector to his left—one of those walk-through airport things. I set it off and had to give the guard my keys before passing silently.

"Go 'head," he said, handing them back.

I walked up to a reception desk. A young black woman sat behind more mesh. "Can I help you?"

"Dr. Delaware for Ms. Jeffers."

"One minute." She got on the phone. Behind her were three other women at desks, typing and talking into receivers. The windows behind them were barred. Through the bars, I saw trucks, cars, and shadows—the gray, graffitied walls of an alley.

I was standing in a small, unfurnished area painted light green and broken only by a single door to the right. Claustrophobic. It reminded me of the sally port at the county jail and I wondered how a paranoid schizophrenic or someone in crisis would handle it. How easy it would be for someone with a muddled psyche to make it from the no-parking lot, through the metal detector, to this holding cell.

The receptionist said, "Okay, she's all the way down at the end," and pressed a button. The door buzzed—not quite as loudly as the one at the pawnshop, but just as obnoxiously—and I opened it and stepped into a very long, cream-colored hall marked by lots of doors. Thick, gray carpeting covered the floor. The light was very bright.

Most of the doors were blank, a few were labeled THERAPY, and even fewer bore slide-in signs with people's names on them. The cream paint smelled fresh; how many coats had it taken to cover up the blood?

The corridor was silent except for my footsteps—the kind of womblike damping that comes only from real soundproofing. As I made my way to the end, a door on the left opened, spilling out people but no noise.

Three people, two women and a man, poorly dressed and shuffling. Not a group; each walked alone. The man was lantern-jawed and stooped, the women heavy and red-faced, with cracked swollen legs and stringy hair. All of them looked down at the carpet as they passed me. They grasped small white pieces of paper, "Rx" stamped at the top.

The room they'd exited was classroom-sized and crowded with another thirty or so people queued up before a metal desk. A young man sat at the desk, talked briefly to each person who stood before him, then filled out a prescription blank and handed it over with a smile. The people in line scuffed forward as automatically as cans on a conveyor belt. Some of them held out their hands in anticipation before they got to the doctor. None of them left without paper, none seemed cheered.

I resumed walking. The door at the end had a slide-in that said JEAN JEFFERS, MSW, LCSW. DIRECTOR.

Inside was a five-by-five secretarial area occupied by a young, full-faced, Asian woman. Her desk was barely big enough to hold a PC and a blotter. The wall behind her was so narrow that a dark, mock wood door almost filled it. A radio on an end table played soft rock almost inaudibly. A nameplate in front of the computer said MARY CHIN.

She said, "Dr. Delaware? Go right in, Jean will see you."

"Thank you."

She began to open the door. A woman caught it

from the other side and pulled it all the way back. Forty-five or so, tall and blond. She wore a crimson shirtdress gathered at the waist by a wide, white belt.

"Doctor? I'm Jean." She held out her hand. Almost as big as mine, lanolin soft. The left one bore a ruby solitaire ring over a broad, gold wedding band.

More white in her teardrop earrings and a mock ivory bracelet around one wrist. A sensible-looking watch encircled the other.

She had a strong frame and carried no extra fat. The belt showed off a firm waist. Her face was long, lightly tanned, with soft, generous features. Only her upper lip had been skimped upon by nature—not much more than a pencil line. Its mate was full and glossed. Dark blue eyes studied me from under black lashes. Gold-framed half-glasses hung from a white cord around her neck. Her hair was frosted almost white at the tips, clipped short in back and layered back at the sides. Pure utility except for a thick, Veronica Lake flap in front. It swooped to the right, almost hiding her right eye. A handsome woman.

She flipped her hair and smiled.

"Thanks for seeing me," I said.

"Of course, doctor. Please have a seat."

Her office was the standard twelve-by-twelve setup, with a real wood desk, two upholstered armchairs, a three-drawer double file, a nearly empty bookcase, and some paintings of seagulls. On the desk were a pen, a memo pad, and a short stack of file folders.

A photo in a standup frame was centered on one of the shelves—she and a nice-looking, heavyset man about her age, the two of them in Hawaiian shirts and bedecked with leis. Social work diplomas made out to Jean Marie LaPorte were propped on another shelf, all from California colleges. I scanned the dates. If she'd graduated college at twenty-two, she was exactly forty-five.

"You're a clinical psychologist, right?" she said, sitting behind the desk.

I took one of the chairs. "Yes."

"You know, when Detective Sturgis mentioned your name I thought I recognized it, though I still can't figure out from where."

She smiled again. I returned it.

She said, "How does a psychologist come to be a police consultant?"

"By accident, really. Several years ago I was treating some children who'd been abused at a day-care center. I ended up testifying in court and getting involved in the legal system. One thing led to another."

"Day-care center—the man who took pictures? The one involved with that horrible molesters' club?"

I nodded.

"Well, that must be where I remember your name from. You were quite a hero, weren't you?"

"Not really. I did my job."

"Well," she said, sitting forward and pushing hair out of her eyes, "I'm sure you're being modest. Child abuse is so—to tell you the truth, I couldn't work with it myself. Which may sound funny considering what we deal with here. But children—" She shook her head. "It would be too hard for me to find any sympathy for the abusers even if they were once victims themselves."

"I know what you mean."

"To me that's the lowest—violating a child's trust. How do you manage to deal with it?"

"It wasn't easy," I said. "I saw myself as the child's ally and tried to do whatever helped."

"Tried? You don't do abuse work anymore?"

"Occasionally, when it comes up as part of a custody case. Mostly I consult the court on trauma and divorce issues."

"Do you do any therapy at all?"

"Not much."

"Me, neither." She sat back. "My main goal in school was to become a therapist, but I can't remember the last time I actually did any real therapy."

She smiled again and shook her head. The wave of hair covered her eyes and she flipped it back—a curiously adolescent mannerism.

"Anyway," she said, "about what Detective Sturgis wants, I just don't know how I can really help. I really need to safeguard our people's confidentiality —despite what happened to Becky." She folded her lips inward, lowered her eyes, and shook her head.

I said, "It must have been terrifying."

"It happened too *quickly* to be terrifying—the *terrifying* part didn't hit me until after it was over—seeing her . . . what he . . . now I really know what they mean by posttraumatic stress. No substitute for direct experience, huh?"

She pressed the skinny upper lip with one finger, as if keeping it still.

"No one knew what he was doing to her. I was right here, going about my business the whole time he was—the treatment rooms are totally sound-proofed. He—" She removed her finger. A white pressure circle dotted her lip, then slowly faded.

"Then I heard noise from the hall," she said. "That horrible screaming—he just kept *screaming*."

" 'Bad love,' " I said.

Her mouth remained open. The blue eyes dulled for a second. "Yes . . . he . . . I went out to Mary's office and she wasn't there, so I opened the door to the hall and saw him. Screaming, waving it—the knife —*splashing* blood, the wall—he saw me—I saw his eyes settle on me—focusing—and he kept screaming.

I slammed the door, shoved Mary's desk up against it, and ran back into my office. Slammed *that* door and blocked *it*. I hid behind my chair the whole time it was . . . it wasn't till later that I found out he'd grabbed Adeline.'' She wiped her eyes. ''I'm sorry, you don't need to hear this.''

''No, no, please.''

She glanced at her message pad. Blank. Picking up the pen, she wrote something on it.

''No, that's it—I've told it so many times . . . no one knows how long he—if she suffered for a long time. That's the one thing I *can* hope. That she didn't. The thought of her trapped in there with him . . .'' She shook her head and touched her temples. ''They soundproofed the rooms back in the sixties, when this place was a Vietnam veterans' counseling center. We sure don't need it.''

''Why's that?''

''Because *no one* does much therapy around here.''

She took a deep breath and slapped her hands lightly on the desk. ''Life goes on, right? Would you like something to drink? We've got a coffee machine in the other wing. I can have Mary go get some.''

''No, thanks.''

''Lucky choice.'' Smile. ''It's actually pretty vile.''

''How come no one does much therapy?'' I said. ''Too disturbed a population?''

''Too disturbed, too poor, too many of them. They need food and shelter and to stop hearing voices. The preferred treatment is Thorazine. And Haldol and lithium and Tegretol and whatever else chases the demons away. Counseling would be a nice luxury, but with our caseload it ends up being a very low priority. Not to mention funding. That's why we don't have any psychologists on our staff, just caseworkers, and most of them are SWAs—assistants. Like Becky."

"On the way in I saw a doctor giving out prescriptions."

"That's right," she said. "It's Friday, isn't it? That's Dr. Wintell, our once-a-week psychiatrist. He's just out of his residency, a real nice kid. But when his practice builds up, he'll be out of here like all the others."

"If no one does therapy, what was Becky doing with Hewitt in the therapy room?"

"I didn't say we never talk to our people, just that we don't do much insight work. Sometimes we get cramped for space and the workers use the treatment rooms to do their paperwork. Basically, all of us use what's on hand. As to what Becky was doing with him, it could have been anything. Giving him a voucher for an SRO hotel, telling him where to get deloused. Then again, maybe she *was* trying to get into his head—she was that kind of person."

"What kind is that?"

"An optimist. Idealistic. Most of us start out that way, don't we?"

I nodded. "Did Hewitt have a history of violence?"

"None that was listed in our files. He'd been arrested just a few weeks before for theft and was due to stand trial—maybe she was counseling him about that. There was *nothing* on paper that would have warned us. And even if he was violent, there's a good chance the information would never have gotten to us, with all the red tape."

She put down her pen and looked at me. Flipped her hair. "The truth is, he was exactly like so many others who come in and out of here—there's still no way to know."

She picked up one of the folders.

"This is his file. The police confiscated it and returned it, so I guess it's not confidential anymore."

Inside were only two sheets, one clipped to each of the covers. The first was an intake form listing Dorsey Hewitt's age as thirty-one and his address as "none." Under REASON FOR REFERRAL someone had written "multiple social problems." Under DIAGNOSIS: "prob. chron. schiz." The rest of the categories—PROGNOSIS, FAMILY SUPPORT, MEDICAL HISTORY, OTHER PSYCH. TREATMENT—had been left blank. Nothing about "bad love."

At the bottom of the form were notations of referral for food stamps. The signature read, "R. Basille, SWA."

The facing page was white and smooth, marked only with the notation, "Will follow as needed, R.B., SWA." The date was eight weeks prior to the murder. I handed the folder back.

"Not much," I said.

She gave a sad smile. "Paperwork wasn't Becky's forte."

"So you have no idea how many times she actually saw him?"

"Guess that doesn't say much for my administrative skills, does it? But I'm not one of those people who believes in riding the staff, checking out every little picayune detail. I try to find the best people I can, motivate them, and give them room to move. Generally it works out. With Becky . . ."

She threw up her hands. "She was a doll, a really sweet person. Not much for rules and regulations, but so what?"

She shook her head. "We'd talked about it—helping her get her paperwork in on time. She promised to try, but to tell the truth, I didn't harbor much hope. And I didn't care. Because she was productive where it counted—getting on the phone all day with agencies and arguing for every last penny for her cases.

She stayed late, did whatever it took to help them. Who knows? Maybe she was going that extra mile for Hewitt."

She picked up the phone. "Mary? Coffee, please. . . . No, just one."

Putting it down, she said, "The *real* horror is that it could happen again. We have a steel corral now, to direct them out onto the street after they get their meds. The county finally sent us a guard and the detector, but you tell me how to predict which of them is going to blow."

"We're not very good prophets under the best of circumstances."

"No, we're not. Hundreds of people file in here each week, for meds and vouchers. We've *got* to let them in. We're the court of last resort. Any of them could be another Hewitt. Even if we wanted to lock them up, we couldn't. The state hospitals that haven't been shut down are filled to capacity—I don't know what your theory is about psychosis, but mine is that most psychotics are born with it—it's biological, like any other illness. But instead of treating them, we demonize them or idealize them, and they get caught in the squeeze between the do-gooders who think they should be allowed to run free and the skinflints who think all they need is to pull themselves up by the bootstraps."

"I know," I said. "When I was in grad school the whole community psych thing was in full bloom— schizophrenia as an alternative lifestyle, liberating patients from the back wards and empowering them to take over their own treatment."

"Empowering." She laughed without opening her mouth.

"I had a professor who was a fanatic on the subject," I said. "Studied the mental health system in Belgium or somewhere and wrote a book on it. He had us do a paper on deinstitutionalization. The more I researched it, the less feasible it seemed. I started to wonder what would happen to psychotics who needed medication and couldn't be counted upon to take it. He handed the paper back with one comment, 'Medication is mind control,' and gave me a C-minus."

"Well, *I* give you an A. Some of *our* patients can't be counted upon to feed themselves, let alone calibrate dosage. In my opinion, deinstitutionalization's the major culprit in the homeless problem. Sure, some street people are working folks who hit the skids, but at least thirty or forty percent are severely mentally debilitated. They belong in hospitals, not under some freeway. And now with all the weird street drugs out there, the old cliché that the mentally ill aren't violent just isn't true anymore. Each year it gets uglier and uglier, Dr. Delaware. I pray there won't be another Hewitt, but I don't count on it."

"Do you try at all to identify which patients are violent?"

"If we have police records, we take them seriously, but like I said, that's rare. We've got to be our own police here. If someone goes around making threats, we call security. But most of them are quiet. Hewitt was. Didn't really relate to anyone else that I'm aware of—that's why we're probably not going to be much help to Detective Sturgis. What exactly is he after, anyway?"

"Apparently, he suspects Hewitt had a friend who may be harassing some people, and he's trying to find out if the friend was a patient here."

"Well, after Sturgis called me I asked some of the other workers if they'd seen Hewitt with anyone, and none of them had. The only one who might have known was Becky."

"Is she the only one who worked with him?"

She nodded.

"How long had she been working here?"

"A little over a year. She got her assistantship from junior college last summer and applied right afterward. One of those second careers—she'd worked as a secretary for a while, decided to go back to school in order to do something socially important—her words."

Her eyes flickered and her mouth set—the lower lip compressing and making her look older.

"Such a sweet girl," she said. She shook her head, then looked at me. "You know—I just thought of something. Hewitt's attorney—the one defending him on that theft thing? *He* might know if Hewitt had any friends. I think I've got his name tucked away somewhere—hold on."

She went to the file, opened the middle drawer, and began flipping. "Just one second, so much junk in here. . . . He called me—the attorney—after Becky's murder. Wanting to know if there was anything he could do. I think he wanted to talk—to get his own guilt off his chest. I didn't have time for . . . ah, here we go."

She pulled out a piece of cardboard stapled with business cards. Working a staple free with her fingernails, she removed a card and gave it to me.

Cheap white paper, green letters.

ANDREW COBURG
Attorney-at-Law
The Human Interest Law Center
1912 Lincoln Avenue
Venice, California

"Human interest law," I said.

"I think it's one of those storefront things."

"Thanks," I said, pocketing the card. "I'll pass it along to Detective Sturgis."

The door opened and Mary came in with the coffee.

Jean Jeffers thanked her and told her to tell someone named Amy that she'd be ready to see her in a minute.

When the door closed, she began stirring her coffee.

"Well," she said, "it was nice talking to you. Sorry I couldn't do more."

"Thanks for your time," I said. "Is there anyone else I could talk to who might be able to help?"

"No one I can think of."

"What about the woman he took hostage?"

"Adeline? Now there's a *really* sad story. She'd transferred over here a month before from a center in South Central because she had high blood pressure and wanted a safer environment."

She threw up her hands again and gave a sour laugh.

"Any particular reason Hewitt grabbed *her*?" I said.

"You mean did she know him?"

"Yes."

She shook her head. The hair flap obscured her eye and she left it there. "Just pure bad luck. She happened to be sitting at a desk in the hall, working, just as he was running out, and he grabbed her."

She walked me to the door. People kept coming out of the psychiatrist's office. She looked at them.

"How can you ever know someone like that, anyway?" she said. "When you get down to it, how can you ever really know anyone?"

12

I decided to drive to Andrew Coburg's office and tender an appeal to his human interest. Getting onto Pico, I drove to Lincoln and headed south into Venice.

The Human Interest Law Center turned out, indeed, to be a storefront—one of three set into an old mustard-colored, one-story building. The brick facade was chipped. Next door was a liquor store advertising screwtop wine on special. The other side was vacant. On the window was painted DELI *** LUNCH & DINNER.

The law office window was papered with wrinkled aluminum foil. An American flag hung over the doorway. Printed on one of the white stripes was KNOW YOUR RIGHTS.

The door was closed but unlocked. As I pushed it open a bell tinkled, but no one came out to greet me. In front of me was a particle-board partition. A black arrow pointed left and handpainted signs said WELCOME! and BIENVENIDOS! A mass of noise—voices, phone rings, clicking typewriter keys—came from the other side.

I followed the arrow around the partition to a

single large room, long and narrow. The walls were gray-white and crowded with bulletin boards and posters, the ceiling a high, dark nest of ductwork, electrical wiring, and stammering fluorescent tubes.

No secretary or receptionist. Eight or nine mismatched desks were spread around the room, each equipped with a black dial phone, a typewriter, and a facing chair. Behind each chair was a U-shaped construction of PVC tubing. White muslin curtains hung from the frame—the kind used for mock privacy in hospitals. Some of the curtains were drawn, others were open. Shoes and cuffs were visible beneath the hems of the drawn drapes.

Young people sat behind the desks, talking into phones or to people in the chairs. The clients were mostly black or Hispanic. Some looked asleep. One of them—an old man of indeterminate race—held a terrier mutt on his lap. A few small children wandered around looking lost.

The desk nearest to me was occupied by a darkhaired man wearing a green plaid suit jacket, white shirt, and bolo tie. He needed a shave, his hair was greased, and his face was as sharp as an icepick. Though the phone receiver was cradled under his chin, he didn't appear to be talking or listening, and his eyes drifted over to me.

"What can I do for you?"

"I'm looking for Andrew Coburg."

"Back there." Making a small, meaningless movement with his head. "But I think he's with someone."

"Which desk?" I said.

He put the phone down, swiveled, and pointed to a station in the center of the room. Drapes drawn. Dirty sneakers and an inch of hairy shin below the hem of the muslin.

"Okay if I wait?"

"Sure. You an attorney?"

"No."

"Sure, wait." He picked up the phone and began dialing laboriously. Someone must have answered, because he said, "Yeah, hi, it's Hank, over at H.I. Yeah, me too—yeah." Laughter. "Listen, what about that *nolo* we talked about? Go and check—yeah, I think so. Yeah."

I stood against the partition and read the posters. One featured a bald eagle on crutches and said HEAL OUR SYSTEM. Another was printed in Spanish—something to do with *immigración* and *liberación*.

The sharp-faced man started talking in lawyer's jargon, jabbing the air with a pen and laughing intermittently. He was still on the phone when the curtains at Andrew Coburg's station parted. An emaciated man wearing a filthy cableknit sweater and cutoff shorts got up. He was bearded and had matted hair, and my chest tightened when I saw him because he could have been Dorsey Hewitt's brother. Then I realized I was seeing the brotherhood of poverty and madness.

He and Coburg shook hands and he left, eyes half closed. As he passed me I backed away from the stench. He passed close to the man named Hank, too, but the lawyer didn't notice, kept talking and laughing.

Coburg was still standing. He wiped his hands on his pants, yawned and stretched. Early thirties, six one, two hundred. Pear shaped, fair haired, arms slightly too short for his long-waisted body. His hair was brass colored, worn full at the sides with no sideburns. He had a soft face, fine features, and rosy cheeks, had probably been a beautiful baby.

He wore a chambray work shirt with the sleeves rolled to the elbows, loosened paisley tie five years too narrow, rumpled khakis, saddle shoes. The laces on one shoe were untied.

Stretching again, he sat, picked up his phone, and began dialing. Most of the other lawyers were on the phone now. The room sounded like a giant switchboard.

I walked over to him. His eyebrows rose as I sat down, but he didn't show any signs of annoyance. Probably used to walk-ins.

He said, "Listen, gotta go," into the phone. "What's that? Fine—I accept that, just as long as we have a clear understanding, okay? What? . . . No, I've got someone here. Okay. Bye. Cheers."

He hung up and said, "Hi, how can I help you?" in a pleasant voice. His tie was clipped with an unusual bit of jewelry: red guitar pick glued to a silver bar.

I told him who I was and that I was trying to locate any friends of Dorsey Hewitt.

"Dorsey. One of my triumphs," he said, all the pleasantness gone. He sat back, crossed his legs. "So what paper do you work for?"

"I'm a psychologist. Just like I said."

He smiled. "Really?"

I smiled back. "Scout's honor."

"And a police consultant, too."

"That's right."

"You don't mind if I see some ID, do you?"

I showed him my psych license, my med school faculty card, and my old LAPD consultant's tag.

"The police," he said, as if he still couldn't believe it. "Is that a problem for you?"

"In what way?"

"Working with the police mentality? All that intolerance—the authoritarianism."

"Not really," I said. "Police officers vary, like anyone else."

"That hasn't been my experience," he said. There was a jar of licorice sticks near his typewriter. He took one and held out the container.

"No, thanks."

"High blood pressure?"

"No."

"Licorice raises it," he said, chewing. "Mine tends to be low. I'm not saying they're intrinsically bad—the police. I'm sure most of them start out as okay human beings. But the job corrupts—too much power, too little accountability."

"I guess the same could be said for doctors and lawyers."

He smiled again. "That's no comfort." The smile stayed on his face, but it began to look out of place. "So. Why does a police consultant need to know anything about Dorsey's *friends*?"

I gave him the same explanation I'd offered Jean Jeffers.

Midway through, his phone rang. He picked it up, said, "What? Okay, sure. . . . Hi, Bill, what is it? What? *What?* You've got to be kidding! No walkie, no talkie—I *mean* it. This is a bullsquat misdemeanor we're talking abou—I don't care what else he's—okay, you do that. Good idea. Go ahead. *Talk* to him and get back to me. Bye."

He put the phone down. "Where were we? Oh, yeah, harassment. What kind?"

"I don't know all the details."

He pulled his head back and squinted. His neck was thick, but soft. His short arms folded over his abdomen and didn't move. "Cops ask you to consult but don't let you in on the details? Typical. *I* wouldn't take the gig."

Not seeing any way out of it, I said, "Someone's been sending people harassing tapes with what may be Hewitt's voice on them—screaming 'bad love'—

the same thing he screamed after he murdered Becky Basille."

Coburg thought for a minute. "So? Someone taped him off the TV. No shortage of strange souls out there. Keeps both of us busy."

"Maybe," I said. "But the police think it's worth looking into."

"Who's getting these tapes?"

"That I don't know."

"Must be someone important for the cops to go to all this trouble."

I shrugged. "You could ask them." I recited Milo's name and number. He didn't bother to write it down.

Taking another licorice stick from the jar, he said, "Tapes. So what's the big deal?"

"The police are wondering if Hewitt might have had a close friend—someone influenced by what he did. Someone with the same dangerous tendencies."

"Influenced?" He looked puzzled. "What, some kind of harassment club? Street people going after the good citizenry?"

"Hewitt wasn't exactly harmless."

He began twisting the licorice stick. "Actually, he was. He was *surprisingly* harmless when he took his medicine. On one of his good days, you might have met him and found him a nice guy."

"Was he off his medicine when he committed the murder?"

"That's what the coroner says. Too much alcohol, not enough Thorazine. Given the biochemistry, he must have stopped eating pills a week or so before."

"Why?"

"Who knows? I doubt it was a conscious decision —'hmm, guess I won't take my meds this morning and let's see how the day goes.' More likely he ran out, tried to get a refill, and ran into such a hassle he gave up. Then, as he got crazier and crazier, he probably forgot all about the pills and why he was taking them in the first place. Happens all the time to people at the bottom. Every detail of daily living's a struggle for them, but they're expected to remember appointments, fill out forms, wait in line, follow a schedule."

"I know," I said. "I've been to the center. Wondered how the patients coped."

"Not well is how they cope. Even when they play by the rules they get turned away—mean old Mr. Recession. Do you have any idea how hard it is for a sick person without money to get help in this city?"

"Sure do," I said. "I spent ten years at Western Pediatric Medical Center."

"Over in Hollywood?"

I nodded.

"Okay," he said, "so you *do* know. Not that I'm glossing over what Dorsey did—that poor girl, every attorney's nightmare, I still lose sleep thinking about it. But he was a victim, too—as sappy and knee-jerk as that sounds. He should have been taken care of, not forced to fend for himself."

"Institutionalized?"

His eyes turned angry. I noticed their color for the first time: very pale brown, almost tan.

"Taken *care* of. Not *jailed*—oh, hell, even jail wouldn't have been bad if that would have meant treatment. But it never does."

"Had he been psychotic for a long time?"

"I don't know. He wasn't someone you just sat down and had a chat with—so tell me your life history, pal. Most of the time he was somewhere else."

"Where was he from, originally?"

"Oklahoma, I think. But he'd been in L.A. for years."

"Living on the street?"

"Since he was a kid."

"Any family?"

"None that I know of."

He took hold of the licorice, touched it to his lip, and used his other hand to caress his tie. Somewhere else, himself.

When he touched his phone I knew he was ready to break off the conversation.

"What kind of music do you play?" I glanced at the guitar-pick clasp.

"What? Oh, this? I just noodle around on week-ends."

"Me, too. I worked my way through college playing guitar."

"Yeah? Guess lots of guys did." He pulled the front end of the tie down and looked at the ceiling. I felt his interest continue to slip.

"What do you do mostly, electric or acoustic?"

"Lately I've been getting into electric." Smile. "So what's this? Gaining rapport with the subject? Got to hand it to you. At least you didn't get into the usual police-prosecutor rap—guilt-tripping me for what Dorsey did, asking me how can I live with myself defending scum."

"That's because I don't have a problem with that," I said. "It's a good system and you're an important part of it—and no, I'm not patronizing you."

He held out his hands. "Whoa."

I smiled.

"Actually, it's an *okay* system," he said. "I'll bet if you met the Founding Fathers, you wouldn't think they were such great guys. Slaveowners, fat cats, and they sure didn't think much of women and kids."

The phone rang again. He took the call while gnawing on the remains of the licorice, talking law-yerese, bartering some defendant's future, never raising his voice.

When he hung up, he said, "We try to make the

system work for the people the Founding Fathers didn't care about."

"Who funds you?"

"Grants, donations—interested in contributing?"

"I'll think about it."

He grinned. "Sure you will. Either way, we'll get by—bad salaries, no expense accounts. That's why most of these people'll be gone by next year—soon as they start thinking home equity and German cars."

"What about you?"

He laughed. "Me? I'm a veteran. Five years and thriving. Because it's a heck of a lot more satisfying than drawing up wills or defending polluters."

He turned serious, looked away from me.

"Sure it gets ugly," he said, as if responding to a question. "What Dorsey did was as ugly as it gets." Eye flicker. "Jesus, what a . . . it was a tragedy. How else can you put it? A goddamn stupid tragedy. I know I couldn't have done anything differently, but it shouldn't have happened—it just stinks, but what can you do when society keeps lowering itself to the brutal denominator? Dorsey'd never shown me any signs of violence. *Nothing*. I was serious when I said you would have liked him. Most of the time he was pleasant—soft-spoken, passive. One of my easier clients, actually. A little paranoid, but it was always low key, he never got aggressive with it."

"What kind of delusions did he have?"

"The usual. Voices in his head telling him to do stuff—cross the street six times one day, drink tomato juice the next—I don't remember exactly."

"Did the voices make him angry?"

"They annoyed him, but no, I wouldn't call it anger. It was as if he accepted the voices as being a part of him. I see that a lot in the long-timers. They're used to it, deal with it. Nothing aggressive or hostile, that's for sure."

"As long as he took his medication."

"I assumed he was taking it because he was always okay with me."

"How well did you know him?"

"I wouldn't call it knowing. I did some basic legal stuff for him."

"When did you first meet him?"

He looked up at the ductwork again. "Let's see . . . it would have to be around a year ago."

"Walk-in?"

"No, he was referred by the court."

"What kind of theft were you defending him on?"

Smile. "Cops didn't tell you?"

"I don't get involved in more than I need to."

"Smart. *Theft* is an overstatement. He lifted a bottle of gin from a liquor store, and a couple of sticks of beef jerky. Did it in plain sight of the clerk and got busted. I'm sure he didn't even mean it. Clerk nearly broke his arm restraining him."

"What defense were you planning?"

"What do you think?"

"Plea bargain."

"What else? He had no prior record other than petty stuff. The way the jails are crowded it would have been a slam-dunk."

He sat up and inserted five fingers into his thick hair. Massaging his scalp, he said, "Gritz."

"Pardon me?"

"It's a name. Gritz."

"As in hominy?"

"With a 'z.' The closest I can come to someone who might be called Dorsey's friend."

"First name or last?"

"Don't know. He came by here a couple of times with Dorsey. Another homeless guy. The only reason I know his name is because I noticed him hanging

around over there"—pointing to the partition—
"asked Dorsey who he was and Dorsey said 'Gritz.'
First thing I said was what you just did: 'As in
hominy?' That went right over Dorsey's head, and I
tried to explain it. Spelled 'grits,' told him what they
were, asked him if it was a last name or a first name.
He said no, it was a *name* and it was spelled with a 'z.'
He spelled it for me. Really slowly—he always talked
slow. 'G-R-I-T-Z.' Like it was profound. For all I know
he was making it up."

"Did he tend to do that?"

"He was schizophrenic—what do you think?"

"Did he ever mention the term 'bad love' to
you?"

He shook his head. "First time I heard about that
was from the police. Asking me why Dorsey had
screamed it—as if I'd know."

Pushing himself away from the desk, he wheeled
back in his chair, then sat up. "And that's about all
she wrote."

"Can you describe this Gritz fellow?"

He thought. "It was a while ago . . . about the
same age as Dorsey—though with street people you
can't really tell. Shorter than Dorsey, I think." He
looked at his watch. "There's a call I've got to make."

I got up and thanked him for his time.

He waved it off and picked up the phone.

"Any idea where this Gritz might be located?" I
said, as he dialed.

"Nope."

"Where did Dorsey hang out?"

"Wherever he could—and I'm not being flip.
When it was warm, he liked to go down by the beach
—Pacific Palisades Park, all up and down the beaches
on PCH. When it cooled down, I was able to get him
into a shelter or an SRO a couple of times, but he

actually preferred sleeping outdoors—lots of times he bunked down in Little Calcutta."

"Where's that?"

"Freeway overpass, West L.A."

"Which freeway?"

"San Diego, just past Sepulveda. Never saw it?"

I shook my head.

He shook his, too, smiled, and put down the phone. "The invisible city . . . there used to be these little hovels there called Komfy Kort—built God knows when, for Mexican workers doing the day-labor pickup thing on Sawtelle."

"Those I remember," I said.

"Did you happen to notice they're not there anymore? City tore them down a few years ago and the street people moved onto the property. Nothing to tear down with *them*, so what could the city do but keep chasing them out? And what with voodoo economics taking hold, *that* became too expensive. So the city let them stay."

"Little Calcutta."

"Yeah, it's a great little suburb—you look like a West Side kind of guy—live anywhere near there?"

"Not that far."

"Go by and take a look, if you can spare the time. See who your neighbors are."

13

I drove east to the overpass Coburg had described. The freeway formed a concrete ceiling over a fenced dirt lot, an arcing canopy of surprising grace supported by columns that would have challenged Samson. The shade it cast was cool and gray. Even with my windows closed I could hear the roar of unseen cars.

The lot was empty and the dirt looked fresh. No tents or bedrolls, no signs of habitation.

I pulled over across the street, in front of a self-storage facility the size of an army base, and idled the Seville.

Little Calcutta. The fresh dirt suggested a bulldozer party. Maybe the city had finally cleared it.

I drove farther, slowly, past Exposition Boulevard. The west side of the street was lined with apartment buildings, the freeway concealed by ivied slopes. A few more empty spots peeked behind the usual chain link. A couple of overturned shopping carts made me stop and peer into the shadows.

Nothing.

I cruised several more blocks, until the freeway twisted out of sight. Then I turned around.

As I neared Exposition again, I spied something shiny and huge—a white-metal mountain, some sort of factory or plant. Giant canisters, duodenal twists of pipe, five-story ladders, valves that hinted at monstrous pressure.

Running parallel to the machine works was a blackened length of railroad track. Bordering the rails was a desert-pale table of sand.

Twenty years in L.A., and I'd never noticed it before.

Invisible city.

I headed toward the tracks, getting close enough to read a small red-and-blue sign on one of the giant towers. AVALON GRAVEL AND ASPHALT.

As I prepared to reverse direction again, I noticed another fenced lot catercorner to the plant—darker, almost blackened by the freeway, blocked from street view by green-gray shrubs. The chain-link fence was obscured by sections of bowed, graffitied plywood, the wood nearly blotted out by the hieroglyphics of rage.

Pulling to the curb, I turned off the engine and got out. The air smelled of dust and spoiled milk. The plant was as still as a mural.

The only other vehicle in sight was the burnt-out chassis of something two-doored, with a crushed roof. My Seville was old and in need of a paint job, but here it looked like a royal coach.

I crossed the empty street over to the plywooded fence and looked through an unblocked section of link. Shapes began forming in the darkness, materializing through the metal diamonds like holograms.

An overturned chair bleeding stuffing and springs.

An empty lineman's spool stripped of wire and cracked down the middle.

Food wrappers. Something green and shredded that might once have been a sleeping bag. And always the overhead roar, constant as breath.

Then movement—something on the ground, shifting, rolling. But it was submerged deeply in the shadows and I couldn't tell if it was human, or even real.

I looked up and down the fence, searching for an entrance to the lot, had to walk a ways until I found it: a square hatch cut into the link, held in place with rusty baling wire.

Prying the wires loose took a while and hurt my fingers. Finally, I bent the flap back, squatted, and passed through, retying one wire from the other side. Making my way across the soft dirt, my nostrils full of shit smell, I dodged chunks of concrete, Styrofoam food containers, lumps of things that didn't bear further inspection. No bottles or cans—probably because they were recyclable and redeemable. Let's hear it for green power.

But nothing green here. Just blacks, grays, browns. Perfect camouflage for a covert world.

A vile smell overcame even the excremental stench. Hearing the buzz of flies, I looked down at a cat's carcass that was so fresh the maggots hadn't yet homesteaded, and gave it a wide berth. Onward, past an old blanket, clumps of newspaper so sodden they looked like printed bread dough . . . no people that I could see, no movement. Where had the movement come from?

I arrived at the spot where I thought the thing had rolled, toward the back of the covered lot, just a few feet from the inner angle of a canted concrete wall.

Standing again, I focused. Waited. Felt my back itch.

Saw it again.

Movement. Hair. Hands. Someone lying rolled up in a sheet—several sheets, a mummy wrap of frayed bed linens. Twitchy movements below.

Lovemaking? No. No room for two people in the swaddle.

I walked toward it slowly, making sure I approached head-on, not wanting to startle.

My shoes kicked something hard. The impact was inaudible over the roar, but the figure in the sheeting sat up.

A young, dark Latina, bare shouldered. Soft shoulders, a large vaccine crater on one arm.

She stared at me, pressing the sheets up to her chest, long hair wild and sticky looking.

Her mouth was open, her face round and plain, scared and baffled.

And humiliated.

The sheet dropped a bit and I saw that she was naked. Something dark and urgent snuffled at her breast—a small head.

A baby. The rest of it concealed by the filthy cotton.

I backed away, smiled, held up my hand in greeting.

The young mother's face was electric with fear.

The baby kept suckling and she placed one hand over its tiny skull.

Near her feet was a small cardboard box. I got down and looked inside. Disposable diapers, new and used. More flies. A can of condensed milk and a rusty opener. A nearly empty bag of potato chips, a pair of rubber sandals, and a pacifier.

The woman tried to nourish her baby while rolling away from me, unraveling more of the sheets and exposing a mottled thigh.

As I started to turn away, the look in her eyes changed from fear to recognition and then to another type of fear.

I whipped around and found myself face-to-face with a man.

A boy, actually, seventeen or eighteen. Also Latin, small and flimsily built, with a fuzz mustache and a sloping chin so weak it seemed part of his skinny neck. His eyes were downslanted and frantic. His mouth hung open; a lot of his teeth were gone. He had on a torn, checked flannel shirt, stretched-out doubleknit pants, and unlaced sneakers. His ankles were black with dirt.

His hands trembled around an iron bar.

I stepped away. He hesitated, then came toward me.

A high sound pierced the freeway din.

The woman screaming.

Startled, the boy looked at her and I moved in, grabbed the bar, and twisted it out of his grip. The inertia threw him backwards onto the ground so easily that I felt like a bully.

He stayed there, looking up at me, shielding his face with one hand, ready to be beaten.

The woman was up, tripping out of the sheets, naked, the baby left squalling on the dirt. Her belly was pendulous and stretchmarked, her breasts limp as a crone's, though she couldn't have been much older than twenty.

I threw the bar as far as I could and held out both hands in what I hoped was a gesture of peace.

The two of them looked at me. Now I felt like a bad parent.

The baby was openmouthed with rage, clawing the air and kicking. I pointed to it.

The woman rushed over and picked it up. Realizing she was naked, she crouched and hung her head.

The chinless boy's hands were still shaking. I tried another smile and his eyes drooped, tugged down by despair.

I took out my wallet, removed a ten, walked over to the woman and held it out to her.

She didn't move.

I put the bill in the cardboard box. Went back to the boy, took out another ten and showed it to him.

More of that same hesitation he'd shown before coming at me with the bar. Then he took a step, biting his lip and teetering like a high-wire artist, and snatched the money.

Holding out yet another bill, I headed for the place where I'd broken through the fence. Checking my back as I trotted through the muck.

After a few steps the boy started following me. I picked up the pace and he tried to catch up, but couldn't. Walking was an effort for him. His mouth was open and his limbs looked rubbery. I wondered when he'd last eaten.

I made it to the flap, untied the wire and walked out to the sidewalk. He came through several moments later, rubbing his eyes.

The light hurt my pupils. He appeared to be in agony.

He finally stopped rubbing. I said, *"Habla inglés?"*

"I'm from Tucson, man," he said, in unaccented English.

His hands were fisted, but the tremor and his small bones mocked his fighter's stance. He started to cough, dry and wheezing. Tried to bring up phlegm and couldn't.

"Didn't mean to scare you," I said.

He was looking at the money. I extended my arm

and he snatched the bill and crammed it under his waistband. The pants were much too big for him and held together with a red plastic belt. One of his sneakers was patched with cellophane tape. As his hand balled up around the bill, I saw that the pinkie of his left hand was missing.

"Gimme more," he said.

I didn't say anything.

"Gimme more. But she won' fuck you, anyway."

"I don't want her to."

He flinched. Thought a moment. "I won', neither."

"I'm not interested in that, either."

He frowned, put a finger inside his mouth and rubbed his gums.

I gave a quick look around, saw no one, and took out a fourth ten.

"Whu'?" he said, yanking his hand free and making a grab for it.

Holding it out of reach, I said, "Is that Little Calcutta?"

"Huh?"

"The place we just were. Is that Little Calcutta?"

"Maybe."

"Maybe?"

"Yeah." He coughed some more, hit his chest with the four-fingered hand.

"How many people live there?"

"I dunno."

"Are there others in there right now? People I didn't see?"

He considered his answer. Shook his head.

"Are there ever others?"

"Sometimes."

"Where are they now?"

"Around." He looked at the money, worked his tongue against his cheek, and came closer.

"She fucks you, it's twenty bucks."

I put the bill in my pocket.

"Hey!" he said, as if I'd cheated at a game.

"I don't want to fuck anyone," I said. "I just want some information. Answer my questions and you'll get paid, okay?"

"Why, man?"

"Because I'm a curious guy."

"Cop?"

"No."

He flexed his shoulders and rubbed his gums some more. When he removed his hand, the fingers were bloody.

"Is the baby yours?" I said.

"Thas what you wanna know?"

"Is it?"

"I dunno."

"It needs to be looked at by a doctor."

"I dunno."

"Is she your woman?"

He smiled. "Sometimes."

"What's your name?"

"Terminator Three." Glaring. Challenging me to mock him.

"Okay," I said. "Are there more people in there?"

"I told you, man. Not now, just at night."

"They come back at night?"

"Yuh."

"Every night?"

He looked at me as if I were stupid. Shook his head slowly. "Some nights—it changes places, I dunno."

"It moves from place to place?"

"Yeah."

Tent City as a concept. Some New Wave journalist would have a ball with it.

"What about a guy named Gritz?"

"Huh?"

"Gritz." I began the description Coburg had given me, and to my surprise he broke in: "Yeah."

"You know him?"

"I seen him."

"Does he live there?"

The hand went back into his mouth. He fiddled, twisted, pulled out a tooth and grinned. The root was inky with decay. He spit blood onto the pavement and wiped his mouth with his sleeve.

"Does Gritz hang out here?"

He didn't hear me, was looking at the tooth, fascinated. I repeated the question. He kept staring, finally dropped the tooth into his pocket.

"Not no more," he said.

"When's the last time you saw him?"

"Dunno."

"Days? Weeks?"

"Dunno."

He reached out to touch the sleeve of my jacket. Fifteen-year-old Harris Tweed. The cuffs were starting to fuzz.

I stepped back.

"Wool?" he said.

"Yeah."

He licked his lips.

"What do you know about Gritz?"

"Nuthin'."

"But you definitely know him?"

"I seen him around."

"When's the last time you saw him around?"

He closed his eyes. Opened them. "A week."

"A week definitely, or a week maybe?"

"I think—I dunno, man."

"Any idea where he is now?"

"To get rich."

"To get rich?"

"Yeah, that's what he said—he was drinking and partying, you know. And singing—sometimes he liked to sing—and he was singing about hey, man, I'm gonna get rich soon. Gonna get me a car and a boat—that kind of shit."

"Did he say how he was going to get rich?"

"Nah." A hint of threat sharpened his eyes. Fatigue wiped it out. He slumped.

"He didn't say how?" I repeated.

"No, man. He wuz partying and singing—he was nuts. That's *it*, man."

"Is Gritz a first name or a last name?"

"*Dunno*, man." He coughed, hit his chest, wheezed, "Fuck."

"If I told you to see a doctor, you'd shine me on, wouldn't you?"

Gap-toothed grin. "You gonna pay me to go?"

"What if you had a disease you could give to her —or the baby?"

"Gimme more money." Holding out a hand again.

"The baby needs to see a doctor."

"Gimme more money."

"Who'd Gritz hang out with?"

"No one."

"No one at all?"

"I dunno, man. Gimme more money."

"What about a guy named Hewitt?"

"Huh?"

"A guy named Dorsey Hewitt? Ever see Gritz with him?"

I described Hewitt. The boy stared—not that much blanker than his general demeanor, but enough to tell me his ignorance was real.

"Hewitt," I repeated.

"Don' know the dude."

"How long have you been hanging out here?"

"Hunerd years." Phlegmy laugh.

"Hewitt killed a woman. It was on the news."

"Don't got cable."

"A social worker named Rebecca Basille—at the Westside Mental Health Center?"

"Yeah, I heard something."

"What?"

Grin. "Music. In my head." He tapped one ear and smiled. "It's like rock and soul, man. The def cool no-fool."

I sighed involuntarily.

He brightened, latching on to my frustration like a buzzard on carrion. "Gimme *money*, man." Cough. *"Gimme."*

"Anything else you want to tell me?"

"Yeah."

Tapping one foot. Waiting for the straight man.

"What?" I said.

"The baby's mine." Smile. His remaining teeth were pink with fresh blood.

"Congratulations."

"Got a cigarette?"

"I don't smoke."

"Then gimme *money*. I aks around for you, man. You come back and I tell you everything I aksed."

I counted what I had in my wallet.

Two twenties and three singles. Gave him all of it. The jacket, too.

14

He scrambled back through the fence and disappeared. I hung around until his footsteps died, then walked back to the car. The air had cooled—sudden shifts were becoming the rule this autumn—and a soft wind from the east was nudging scraps of garbage off the sidewalk.

I gassed up the Seville at a station on Olympic and used the pay phone to get the number of the nearest Social Services office. After being put on hold several times and transferred from bureaucrat to bureaucrat, I managed to reach a supervisor and tell her about the infant living under the freeway.

"Was the baby being mistreated, sir?"

"No."

"Did the baby look malnourished?"

"Actually, no, but—"

"Were there bruises or scars anywhere visible on the baby's body or other signs of abuse?"

"Nothing," I said. "The mother was caring for the baby, but they're living in filthy conditions out there. And the boy who might be the baby's father has a cough that sounds tubercular."

"Was the *baby* coughing?"

"Not yet."

"For a tuberculosis investigation, you'd have to call public health. Ask for a communicable disease officer."

"There's nothing you can do?"

"Doesn't sound like there's anything we should be doing, sir."

"How 'bout getting the baby some shelter?"

"They'd have to ask, sir."

"The baby would?"

"The legal guardians. We don't just go out looking for people."

Click.

The dial tone was as loud as the freeway. I felt nuts. How did the certifiable psychotics handle it?

I wanted to call Robin. Then I realized I hadn't memorized my new phone number, didn't even know the name of the house's owner. I called Milo. He was at his desk and gave me the seven digits, then said, "Before you hang up, I just got through with Myra Paprock's file. She wasn't a therapist. Real estate agent, killed on the job. Showing a house and somebody cut her, robbed her, raped her, and wrote 'bad love' on the wall with her lipstick."

"Oh, Jesus."

"Yeah. In the photos, the lipstick looks like blood."

"Real estate agent," I said. "That's sometimes a second career. Maybe she worked as some kind of therapist first."

"If she did it's not down here in the file, and the Van Nuys guys seem to have done a pretty thorough job. Plus Shipler—the beating victim—wasn't a shrink, either, so I don't see any obvious mental health connection here."

"What did he do?"

"Janitor. Night custodian at Jefferson High. I haven't gotten his file yet, but I had a records clerk over at Central give me the basics."

"Was he killed on the job, too?"

"Nope, in the comfort of his own home."

"Where'd he live?"

"Budlong Avenue—South L.A."

"Black?"

"Yeah."

"What happened to him?"

"Pounded to mush and the house was trashed."

"Robbery?"

"Doubtful. His stereo, TV, and some jewelry were left behind."

"What, then? Someone looking for something?"

"Or someone got really angry. I want to read the whole file—got a call in for it."

"Real estate agent and janitor," I said. "Doesn't make any sense. Any connection between them?"

"Other than 'bad love' on the wall, there doesn't seem to be any. Nothing matches. She was thirty-five, he was sixty-one. He was killed early morning—right after he finished work on the nightshift—and she got it in the middle of the day. She was stabbed, he was clubbed. There were even differences in what the killer used to write 'bad love.' Shipler's was done in molasses from his fridge."

"In both cases the killer was opportunistic—used something of the victim's."

"Weapons, too," he said. "She was killed with a kitchen knife from the house she was showing, Shipler with a fireplace poker that was identified as his. So?"

"I don't know, maybe it indicates some kind of

power thing—dominance over the victims—turning the victims against themselves. Like using my tree branch on the koi. Were there any bondage or S&M overtones to either murder?''

"Paprock's bra was wrapped around her neck, but the coroner said it was done when she was already dead. Far as I can tell there were no sexual overtones at all to Shipler."

"Still," I said, "the message was important. It must mean something to the killer."

"I'm sure it does," he said, without enthusiasm.

"Did Shipler live alone?"

"Yeah, divorced."

"What about Paprock?"

"No match there, either. Married, two kids."

"If nothing was taken from Shipler's house," I said, "what was the assumed motive?"

"A gang thing—there was lots of activity in Shipler's neighborhood, even back then. Lots more, now. Like you said before, a trashed house could mean someone looking for something. Central figured dope. Figured Shipler was involved on some level and 'bad love' was some sort of gangbanger slogan they hadn't heard of yet. They checked it out with the CRASH detail and *they* hadn't heard of it, but new stuff comes up all the time."

"Did Shipler turn out to be involved in gangs or dope?"

"Far as I can tell, he had no record, but plenty of scrotes slip through the cracks. In terms of there being no burglary, Southwest figured it was punks panicking and leaving before they could take anything. Which is consistent with gang wannabees—new recruits out on a virgin adventure."

"An initiation thing?"

"Yeah, they start 'em young. Automatics in the diapers. Speaking of which, I caught my little truant bastards on the Palms robbery—thirteen and fifteen. No doubt they'll get referred for some kind of therapy. Want a referral?''

"No, thanks."

"Cynic."

"Was there gang activity where Paprock was killed?''

"A little, on the fringes. It's mostly working-class tough—north end of Van Nuys. No one made the gang assumption in that one, but maybe if Van Nuys had talked to Southwest, they would have. Neither of them knew about the other case—still don't."

"Going to tell them?" I said.

"First I'm gonna read Shipler's file thoroughly, see what I can pull out of it. Then, yeah, I'll have to tell them, do the old network blah blah. Both cases are real cold—be interesting to see what kind of responses I get. Hopefully the whole thing won't deteriorate into endless memories. Though if 'bad love' shows up anywhere in *Stoumen's* file, we've got interstate blah blah."

"Hear from Seattle, yet?"

"Very briefly. They're sending down records—it'll probably take a week or so. Both detectives on that one are retired and unavailable. Probable translation: burnouts gone fishing. If anything provocative comes up in the file, I'll bug 'em anyway."

"What about the FBI records on other 'bad love' murders?''

"Not yet. *Them* gears grind slowly."

"A real estate agent, a janitor, and 'bad love,' " I said. "I still think it has something to do with that conference. Or de Bosch himself—Paprock and Shipler could have been his patients."

"So why would someone kill them?"

"Maybe it's another patient, mad about something.''

"Then what's *your* connection?"

"I don't know. . . . Nothing makes sense, dammit."

"You learn anything from Jeffers?"

"No one at the center remembers Hewitt having any friends. But she referred me to Hewitt's lawyer and he gave me a name and possible address." I described my encounter with the people under the freeway.

"Gritz," he said. "As in hominy."

"With a 'z.' Could be a first name or a last, or just a nickname."

"I'll run it through."

"The kid I spoke to said he's been gone about a week. He also said Gritz was talking and singing about getting rich."

"Singing?"

"That's what he said."

"Oh those romantic hoboes, strumming around the campfire."

"Maybe Gritz had some kind of job lined up, or maybe it's baloney. The kid could very well have been putting me on. For what it's worth, he said he'd ask around, I should come back later."

"Getting rich," he said. "*Everyone* talks and sings about it. That Calcutta place might be the dregs, but it's still L.A."

"True," I said. "But wouldn't it be interesting if Gritz really did expect to get paid for something—like killing my koi, and other nasties."

"Hitman on a fish? So who's doing the hiring?"

"The anonymous bad guy—I know, it's a ridiculous idea."

"At this point nothing's ridiculous, Alex, but if someone was looking to hire a nighttime skulker, would they choose a homeless nutcase?"

"True. . . . Maybe what Gritz was hired for was

to scream on tape—to imitate Hewitt because he knew what Hewitt sounded like."

"Imitate?" he said. "Those voice tracks sounded identical to me, Alex. Though we may never be able to verify it. I talked to the voiceprint guy over at the sheriff's, and screams *are* useless, legally. In order to make a match that can be used in court, you need two samples, minimum of twenty words on each and the exact same phrases. Even then, it gets challenged a lot and thrown out."

"What about for nonadmissible comparison?"

"Matching screams is still an iffy business. It's words that have unique characteristics. I asked the sheriff to give a listen anyway. He said he's backlogged but would try to get to it eventually. . . . Why would someone want to imitate Hewitt?"

"I don't know—I can't help but think the tape's part of a ritual. Something ceremonial that means something only to the killer."

"What about the kid on the tape?"

"Could be a homeless kid—someone from Little Calcutta or some place like it. Living down there could explain the robot quality of the voice—despair. You should have seen it, Milo. The boy's teeth were rotting, he had a tubercular cough. The girl was naked, wrapped up in a sheet, trying to feed the baby. If I'd offered enough money, I probably could have *bought* the baby."

"I've seen it," he said softly.

"I know you have. I have too. It's all around. But I haven't really let it register for a while."

"What're you gonna do, solve everyone's problems? Plenty of your own to deal with, for the time being. You get names on the freeway people?"

"Not the girl. *He* calls himself Terminator Three."

He laughed. "No one else down there besides them and the baby?"

"No one I could see, and I was flashing ten-dollar bills."

"Real smart, Alex."

"I watched my back."

"Yeah."

"The kid said the place fills up at night. I could go back after dark and see if anyone else knows Gritz."

"You're really in the mood to get your throat cut, aren't you?"

"If I had a macho cop with me I'd be safe, right?"

"Don't count on it. . . . Yeah, okay, it's probably a waste of time, but that makes me feel *right* at home."

Robin was still working in the garage, hunched over her bench, wielding shiny sharp things that resembled dental picks. Her hair was tied up and her goggles were lodged in her curls. Under her overalls, her T-shirt was tightened by perspiration. She said, "Hi, doll," as her hands continued to move. The dog was at her feet and he stood and licked my hand as I looked over Robin's shoulder.

A tiny rectangle of abalone was clamped to a padded section of the bench. The edges were beveled and the corners were inlaid with bits of ivory and gold wire. She'd traced the shell with minuscule curlicue shapes, cut out some of them, and was in the process of excising another.

"Beautiful," I said. "Fretboard inlay?"

"Uh-huh. Thanks." She blew away dust and cleaned the edge of a pick with a fingernail.

"You do root canal, too?"

She laughed and hunched lower. The tools clicked as she carved out a speck of shell. "Kind of baroque for my taste, but it's for a stockbroker who wants a showpiece for his wall."

She worked some more, finally put the tools down, wiped her forehead, and wiggled her fingers. "Enough for one day, I'm cramping up."

"Everything okay?" I rubbed her neck.

"Nice and quiet. How about you?"

"Not bad."

I kissed her. The wind got stronger and drier, ruffling the cypress trees and shooting a cold stream through the open garage. Robin unclamped the abalone, and put it in her pocket. Her arms were goosebumped. I put mine around them and the two of us headed for the house. By the time we got to the door, the wind was whipping the trees and stirring the dust, causing the bulldog to blink and sniff.

"Santa Ana?" she said.

"Too cold. Probably the tail end of something arctic."

"Brr," she said, unlocking the door. "Leave your jacket in the car?"

I shook my head. We went inside.

"You were wearing one, weren't you?" she said, rubbing her hands together. "That baggy brown tweed."

Artist's eye.

"Yup."

"Did you lose it?"

"Not exactly."

"Not exactly?"

"I gave it away."

She laughed. "You what?"

"No big deal. It was fraying."

"Who'd you give it to?"

I told her about Little Calcutta. She listened with her hands on her hips, shaking her head, and went into the kitchen to wash her hands. When she came back, her head was still moving from side to side.

"I know, I know," I said. "It was a bleeding-heart reflex, but they really were pitiful—it was a cheap old thing, anyway."

"You wore it the first time we went out. I never liked it."

"You didn't?"

"Nope. Too philosophy prof."

"Why didn't you tell me?"

She shrugged. "It wasn't that important."

"Snoring, poor taste in haberdashery. What else don't you like that you haven't informed me about?"

"Nothing. Now that you've ditched the coat, you're perfect."

She ruffled my hair, walked to the French doors, and looked out at the mountains. They were shimmering, denuded in patches, where the foliage was brushed back like blow-dried hair. The pool water was choppy, the surface gritty with leaves and dirt.

Robin loosened her hair. I hung back and kept looking at her.

Perfect female statuary, rock-still against the turbulence.

She unsnapped one overall strap, then the other, letting the baggy denim collapse around her feet, and stood there in T-shirt and panties.

Half turning, hands on hips, she looked back at me. "How 'bout giving *me* something, big boy?" she said, in a Mae West voice.

The dog grumbled. Robin cracked up. "Quiet, you! You're wrecking my timing."

"*Now* it feels like a home," she said, snuggling under the covers. "Though I do prefer our little love nest, be it ever so humble. So what'd you find out today?"

My second summation of the day. I did it quickly, adding what Milo'd told me about the murders and leaving out the gross pathology. Even sanitized, it was bad, and she turned quiet.

I rubbed her lower back, allowing my hand to linger on swells and dimples. Her body loosened, but only for a moment.

"You're sure you've never heard of those other two people?" she said, stilling my hand.

"I'm sure. And there doesn't even seem to be any connection between the two of *them*. The woman was a white real estate agent, the man a black janitor. He was twenty-six years older, they lived on opposite ends of the city, were killed in different ways. Nothing in common but 'bad love.' Maybe they were patients of de Bosch."

"They couldn't be old patients of *yours*?"

"No way," I said. "I've been through every one of my case files. To be honest, I don't see the patient angle as too likely, period. If someone has a hangup with de Bosch, why go after the people he treated?"

"What about group therapy, Alex? Things can get rough in groups, can't they? People lashing out at one another? Maybe someone got dumped on badly and never forgot it."

"I guess it's possible," I said, sitting up. "A good therapist always tries to keep a handle on the group's emotional climate, but things can get out of control. And sometimes there's no way to know someone's feeling victimized. Once, at the hospital, I had to calm down the father of a kid with a bone tumor who brought a loaded pistol onto the ward. When I finally got him to open up, it came out that he'd been boiling for weeks. But there was no warning at all—till then he'd been a really easygoing guy."

"There you go," she said. "So maybe some patient of de Bosch's sat there and took it and never told anyone. Finally, years later, he decided to get even."

"But what kind of therapy group would bring together a real estate agent from the valley and a black janitor?"

"I don't know—maybe *they* weren't the patients, maybe their kids were. A parents' group for problem kids—de Bosch was basically a *child* therapist, wasn't he?"

I nodded, trying to imagine it. "Shipler was a lot older than Paprock—I suppose she could have been a young mother and he an old father."

We heard scratching and thumping at the door. I got up and opened it and the dog bounded in. He headed straight for Robin's side of the bed, stood on his hind legs, put his paws on the mattress, and began snorting. She lifted him up and he rewarded her with lusty licks.

"Settle down," she said. "Uh-oh—look, he's getting excited."

"Without testicles, yet. See the effect you have on men?"

"But of *course*." She batted her lashes at me, turned back to the dog, and finally got him to lie still by kneading the folds of flesh around his jowls. He lapsed into sleep with an ease that I envied. But when I leaned over to kiss her, he opened his eyes, snuffled, and insinuated himself between us, curling atop the covers and licking his paws.

I said, "Maybe Milo can get hold of Paprock's and Shipler's medical histories, see if de Bosch's name or the Corrective School appears on them. Sometimes people conceal psych treatment, but with the cost, it's more likely there's some kind of insurance record. I'll ask him when I see him tonight."

"What's tonight?"

"We were planning on going back to the freeway, try to talk to more of the homeless people in order to get a handle on this Gritz character."

"Is it safe going back there?"

"I'll have Milo with me. Whether or not it's productive remains to be seen."

"All right," she said uneasily. "If you want it to be productive, why don't you stop at a market and get those people some food?"

"Good idea. You're full of them today, aren't you?"

"Motivation," she said. She turned serious, reached up and held my face in both of her hands. "I want this to be over. Please take care of yourself."

"Promise." We managed to maintain a convoluted embrace despite the dog.

I fell asleep, smelling perfume and kibble. When I woke up my stomach was sour and my feet were sore. Inhaling and letting out the air, I sat up and cleared my eyes.

"What is it?" Robin mumbled, her back to me.

"Just thinking."

"About what?" She rolled over and faced me.

"Someone in a therapy group, getting wounded and keeping it inside all these years."

She touched my face.

"What the hell do *I* have to do with it?" I said. "Am I just a name on a damned brochure, or did I hurt someone without ever knowing it?"

15

I heard the unhealthy-sounding engine from inside the house. Milo's Fiat, reduced to a squat little toy on the monitor.

I went outside. The wind had stopped. The car expelled a plume of smoke, then convulsed. It didn't look as if it would survive the evening.

"Figured it would blend in where we're going," he said, getting out. He carried a large, white plastic bag and was wearing work clothes. The bag smelled of garlic and meat.

"More food?" I said.

"Sandwiches—Italian. Just consider me your official LAPD delivery boy."

Robin was back in the garage, working under a funnel of fluorescence. The dog was there, too, and he charged us, heading straight for the bag.

Milo lifted it out of reach. "Sit. Stay—better yet, go away."

The dog snorted once, turned his back on us, and sank to his haunches.

Milo said, "Well, one out of three ain't bad." He

waved at Robin. She raised a hand and put down her tools.

"She looks right at home," he said. "How 'bout you, Nick Danger?"

"I'm fine. Anything on Gritz in the records?"

Before he could answer, Robin came over.

"He's brought us dinner," I said.

"What a prince." She kissed his cheek. "Are you hungry right now?"

"Not really," he said, touching his gut and looking down at the ground. "Had a little appetizer while I waited."

"Good for you," she said. "Growing boy."

"Growing the wrong way."

"You're fine, Milo. You've got *presence*." She patted his shoulder. From the way her fingers were flexing I knew she was eager to get back to her bench. I was itchy, too, thinking of the freeway people. The dog continued to sulk.

"How 'bout you, hon?" she said to me. The dog came over, thinking—or pretending—it was meant for him.

"I can wait."

"Me, too. So let me stick this in the fridge and when you guys get back, we'll chow down."

"Sounds good." Milo gave her the bag. The dog tried to lick it and she said, "Relax, I've got a Milk-Bone for you."

Above the roofline, the sky was black and empty. Lights from the houses across the canyon seemed a continent away.

"You'll be okay?" I said.

"I'll be fine. Go." She gave me a quick kiss and a small shove.

Milo and I headed for the Fiat. The dog watched us drive away.

*   *   *

The sound of the gate clanking shut made me feel better about leaving her up there. Milo coasted to Benedict, shifted to first, then upward, squeezing as much speed as possible out of the little car. Shifting roughly, big hands nearly covering the top of the steering wheel. As we headed south, I said, "Anything on Gritz?"

"One possible citation—thank God it's an unusual name. Lyle Edward, male white, thirty-four years old, five six, one thirty, I forget the color of his eyes."

"Coburg said he was shorter than Hewitt."

He nodded. "Bunch of drunk and disorderlies from back when we still bothered with those, possession of narcotics, couple of shoplifting busts, nothing heavy."

"When did he come to L.A.?"

"First arrest was fourteen years ago. The computer gives him no known address, no parole officer, either. He got probation for some of his naughties, lived at county jail for the others, and paid his debt in full."

"Any mention of mental illness?"

"There wouldn't be unless he was classified as a mentally disordered sex offender or committed some other kind of violent psycho crime."

"I'll call Jean Jeffers Monday, see if I can find out if he ever got treated at the center."

"Meanwhile, we can talk to the offrampers, for what it's worth. All he is is a name, so far."

"Robin suggested we should bring them food. Increase the rapport."

He shrugged. "Why not. There's a minimarket over on Olympic."

We drove a bit more. He frowned and rubbed his face with one hand.

"Something the matter?" I said.

"Nah . . . just the usual. Justice got raped again —my truant scumbags. The old lady died this afternoon."

"I'm sorry. Does that make it murder?"

He pumped his gas pedal leg. "It makes it *shit*. She had badly clogged arteries and a big tumor growing in her colon. Autopsy said it was just a matter of time. That, her age, and the fact that the kids never actually touched her means the DA's office doesn't want to bother to prove it was an unnatural death. Once they hospitalized her, she was never well enough to get even a deathbed declaration, and without her testimony, there's not much of a case against the little bastards even for robbery. So they probably get a stern lecture and walk. Wanna make a bet by the time they start shaving, someone else'll be dead?"

He got to Sunset and joined the smooth, fast traffic flowing west from Beverly Hills. Amid the Teutonic tanks and cigarillo sports jobs, the Fiat looked like a mistake. A Mercedes cut in front of us and Milo swore viciously.

I said, "You could give him a ticket."

"Don't tempt me."

A mile later, I said, "Robin came up with a possible link between Paprock and Shipler. Both could have been in group therapy with de Bosch. Treatment for themselves, or some kind of parent's group to talk about problem kids. The killer could also have been in the group, gotten treated roughly—or thought he had —and developed a grudge."

"Group therapy . . ."

"Some kind of common problem—what else would draw two people from such different backgrounds to de Bosch?"

"Interesting . . . but if it was a parent's group, de Bosch didn't run it. He died in eighty, and Paprock's kids are six and seven years old now. So they weren't alive when he was. In fact, at the time Myra died, they were only babies. So what kind of problems could they have had?"

"Maybe it was a child-rearing program. Or some kind of chronic illness support group. And are you sure Paprock was only married once?"

"According to her file she was."

"Okay," I said. "So maybe *Katarina* was the therapist. Or someone else at the school—maybe the killer believes in collective guilt. Or it could have been an *adult* treatment group. Child therapists don't always limit themselves to kids."

"Fine. But now we're back to the same old question: what's *your* link?"

"Has to be the conference. The killer's gotten severely paranoid—let his rage get out of control. To him, anyone associated with de Bosch is guilty, and where better to start than a bunch of therapists paying public homage to the old man? Maybe Stoumen's hit-and-run was no accident."

"What? Major-league mass murder? The killer's going after patients *and* therapists?"

"I don't know—I'm just grasping."

He heard the frustration in my voice. "It's okay, keep grasping. Doesn't cost the taxpayers a dime. For all I know we're dealing with something so crazy it'll never make sense."

We rode for a while. Then he said, "De Bosch's clinic was private, expensive. How could a janitor like Shipler afford getting treatment there?"

"Sometimes private clinics treat a few hardship cases. Or maybe Shipler had good health insurance through the school system. What about Paprock? Did she have money?"

"Nothing huge, as far as I can tell. Husband worked as a car salesman."

"Can you get hold of their insurance records?"

"If they had any, and haven't been destroyed."

I thought of two motherless grade-school children and said, "How old, exactly, were Paprock's children at the time of her murder?"

"Don't remember exactly—little."

"Who raised them?"

"I assume the husband."

"Is he still in town?"

"Don't know that either, yet."

"If he is, maybe he'll be willing to talk about her, tell us if she was ever a therapy patient at de Bosch's clinic."

He hooked a finger toward the rear seat. "Got the file right there. Check out the address."

I swung around toward the darkened seat and saw a file box.

"Right on top," he said. "The brown one."

Colors were indistinguishable in the darkness, but I reached over, groped around, and came up with a folder. Opening it, I squinted.

"There's a penlight in the glove compartment."

I tried to open the compartment, but it was stuck. Milo leaned across and slammed it with his fist. The door dropped open and papers slid to the floor. I stuffed them back in and finally found the light. Its skinny beam fell on a page of crime-scene photos stapled to the right-hand page. Lots of pink and red. Writing on a wall: a closeup of "bad love" in big, red block letters that matched the blood on the floor . . . neat lettering . . . a bloody thing below.

I turned to the facing page. The name of Myra Paprock's widower was midway through the intake data.

"Ralph Martin Paprock," I said. "Valley Vista Cadillac. The home address is in North Hollywood."

"I'll run it through DMV, see if he's still around."

I said, "I need to keep looking for the other conference people to warn them."

"Sure, but if you can't tell them who and why, what does that leave? 'Dear Sir or Madam, this is to inform you you might be bludgeoned, stabbed, or run over by an unidentified, revenge-crazed psycho?'"

"Maybe one of them can tell me the who and why. And I know I'd have liked to have been warned. The problem is finding them. None of them are working or living where they were at the time of the conference. And the woman I thought might be Rosenblatt's wife hasn't returned any of my calls."

Another stretch of silence.

"You're wondering," he said, "if they've been visited, too."

"It did cross my mind. Katarina's not been listed in the APA directory for five years. She could have just stopped paying dues, but it doesn't seem like her to just drop out of psychology and close up the school. She was ambitious, very much taken with carrying on her father's work."

"Well," he said, "it should be easy enough to check tax rolls and Social Security records on all of them, find out who's breathing and who ain't."

He reached Hilgard and turned left, passing the campus of the university where I'd jumped through academic hoops for so many years.

"So many people gone," I said. "Now the Wallace girls. It's as if everyone's folding up their tents and escaping."

"Hey," he said, "maybe they know something we don't."

*   *   *

The strip-mall at Olympic and Westwood was dark except for the flagrant white glare from the minimart. The store was quiet, with a turbaned Pakistani drinking Gatorade behind the counter.

We stocked up on overpriced bread, canned soup, lunch meat, cereal, and milk. The Pakistani eyed us unpleasantly as he tallied up the total. He wore a company shirt printed repetitively with the name of the mart's parent company in lawn green. The nametag pinned to his breast pocket was blank.

Milo reached for his wallet. I got mine out first and handed the clerk cash. He continued to look unhappy.

"Whatsamatter?" said Milo. "Too much cholesterol in our diet?"

The clerk pursed his lips and glanced up at the video camera above the door. The machine's cyclops eye was sweeping the store slowly. The screen below filled with milky gray images.

We followed his gaze to the dairy case. An unkempt man stood in front of it, not moving, staring at cartons of Half-and-Half. I hadn't noticed him while shopping and wondered where he'd come from.

Milo eyed him for a long moment, then turned back to the clerk.

"Yeah, police work's strenuous," he said in a loud voice. "Got to shovel in those calories in order to catch the bad guys."

He laughed even louder. It sounded almost mad.

The man at the dairy case twitched and half turned. He glared at us for a second, then returned to studying the cream.

He was gaunt and hairy, wearing a dirt-blackened army jacket, jeans, and beach sandals. His hands shook and one clouded eye had to be blind.

Another member of Dorsey Hewitt's extended family.

He slapped the back of his neck with one hand, turned again, tried to match Milo's stare.

Milo gave a salute. "Evening, pal."

The man didn't move for a second. Then he shoved his hands into his pockets and left the store, sandals slapping the vinyl floor.

The clerk watched him go. The cash register gave a computer burp and expelled a receipt. The clerk tore off the tape and dropped it into one of the half-dozen bags we'd filled.

"Got a box for all this?" said Milo.

"No, sir," said the clerk.

"What about in back?"

Shrug.

We carried the food out. The gaunt man was at the far end of the lot, kicking asphalt and walking from store to store, staring at black glass.

"Hey," Milo called out. No response. He repeated it, pulled a cereal variety pack out of one of the bags and waved it over his head.

The man straightened, looked toward us, but didn't approach. Milo walked ten feet from him and underhanded the cereal.

The man shot his arms out, missed the catch, sank to his knees, and retrieved it. Milo was heading back to the car and didn't see the look on the man's face. Confusion, distrust, then a spark of gratitude that fizzled just short of ignition.

The gaunt man hobbled off into the darkness, fingers ripping at the plastic wrapping, sprinkling cereal onto the pavement.

Milo said, "Let's get the hell out of here." We got into the Fiat and he drove around toward the back of the mall where three dumpsters sat. Several empty cartons were piled up loosely against the bins, most of them torn beyond utility. We finally found a couple that looked and smelled relatively clean, put the bags in them, and stashed the food in back of the car, next to Myra Paprock's homicide file.

A sliver of moon was barely visible behind a cloud-veil, and the sky looked dirty. The freeway was a stain topped with light and noise. After we rounded Exposition, Little Calcutta continued to elude us—the darkness and the plywood barrier concealed the lot totally. But the place on the sidewalk where I'd talked to Terminator Three was just within the light of an ailing street lamp and I was able to point it out to Milo.

We got out and found gaps in the plywood. Through them, blue tongues quivered—thin, gaseous alcohol flames.

"Sterno," I said.

Milo said, "Frugal gourmets."

I took him to the spot along the fence where I'd unhinged the makeshift hatch a few hours before. Extra wires had been added since then, rusty and rough, wound too tightly to unravel by hand.

Milo took a Swiss army knife out of his trouser pocket and flipped out a tiny pliers-like tool. Twisting and snipping, he managed to free the hatch.

We went back to the car, took out the boxes of groceries, and stepped through. Blue lights began extinguishing, as if we'd brought a hard wind.

Milo reached into his trousers again and pulled out the penlight I'd used in the car. I'd replaced it in the glove compartment and hadn't seen him pocket it.

He removed something from one of the grocery bags and shined the light on it. Plastic-wrapped bologna slices.

He held it up and shouted, "Food!"

Barely audible over the freeway. Fires continued to go out.

Training his beam more directly on the bologna, he waved the meat back and forth. The package and the hand that held it seemed suspended in midair, a special effect.

When nothing happened for several more seconds, he placed the meat on the ground, making sure to keep the penlight trained on it, then removed more groceries from his bag and spread them out on the dirt. Walking backward, toward the hatch, he created a snaky trail of food that led out to the sidewalk.

"Goddamn Hansel and Gretel," he muttered, then he slipped back out.

I followed him. He was standing against the Fiat, had emptied one bag and crumpled it and was tossing it from hand to hand.

As we stood there and waited, cars rocketed overhead and the concrete hummed. Milo lit up a bad panatela and blew short-lived smoke rings.

A few minutes later, he stubbed out his cigar and jammed it between his fingers. Walking back to the hatch, he stuck his head through, didn't move for a second, then beckoned me to follow him through.

We stopped just a few feet from the hatch and he aimed the penlight upward, highlighting movement about fifteen feet up.

Frantic, choppy, a scramble of arms.

Squinting, I managed to make out human forms. Down on their knees, scooping and snatching, just as the man at the minimart had done.

Within seconds they were gone and the food had vanished. Milo cupped his hands around his mouth and shouted over the freeway: "Lots more, folks."

Nothing.

He clicked his light off and we retreated to the other side of the fence again.

It seemed like a game—a futile one. But he looked at ease.

He began emptying another bag, placing food on the streetlit patch of sidewalk, just out of reach of the hatch. Then he returned to the car, sat on the rear deck causing the springs to groan, and relit his cigar.

Luring and trapping—*enjoying* the hunt.

More time passed. Milo's eyes kept shifting to the fence, then leaving it. His expression didn't change, the cigar tilted as he bit down on it.

Then he stayed on the fence.

A large, dark hand was reaching out, straining to grab a loaf of white bread.

Milo went over and kicked the package away and the hand drew back.

"Sorry," said Milo. "No grain without pain."

He took his badge out and shoved it at the hatch.

"Just talk, that's it," he said.

Nothing.

Sighing, he picked up the bread, tossed it through the hatch. Picking up a can of soup, he wiggled it.

"Make it a balanced meal, pal."

A moment later, a pair of unlaced sneakers appeared in the opening. Above them, the frayed cuffs of greasy-looking plaid pants and the bottom seam of an army blanket.

The head above the cloth remained unseen, shielded by darkness.

Milo held the soup can between thumb and forefinger. New Orleans Gourmet Gumbo.

"Lots more where this came from," he said. "Just for answering a few questions, no hassles."

One plaid leg angled forward through the opening. A sneaker hit the pavement, then the other.

A man emerged into the streetlight, wincing.

He had the blanket wrapped around him to the knees, covering his head like a monk's cowl and shrouding most of his face.

What showed of the skin was black and grainy. The man took an awkward step, as if testing the integrity of the sidewalk, and the blanket dropped a bit. His skull was big and half bald, above a long, bony face that looked caved in. His beard was a kinky gray rash, his skin cracked and caked. Fifty or sixty or seventy. A battered nose so flat it almost merged with his crushed cheeks, spreading like melted tar. His eyes squinted and watered and didn't stop moving.

He had the white bread in his hand and was looking at the soup.

Milo tried to give it to him.

The man hesitated, working his jaws. His eyes were quieter now.

"Know what a gift horse is?" said Milo.

The man swallowed. Drawing his blanket around himself, he squeezed the bread so hard the loaf turned into a figure eight.

I went over to him and said, "We just want to talk, that's it."

He looked into my eyes. His were jaundiced and clogged with blood vessels, but something shone through—maybe intelligence, maybe just suspicion. He smelled of vomit and alcohol belch and breath mints, and his lips were as loose as a mastiff's. I worked hard at standing my ground.

Milo came up behind me and covered some of the stench with cigar smoke. He put the soup up against the man's chest. The man looked at it and finally took it, but continued to stare at me.

"You are not police." His voice was surprisingly clear. "You are definitely not police."

"True," I said. "But he is."

The man glanced at Milo and smiled. Rubbing the part of the blanket that covered his abdomen, he shoved both hands under it, secreting the bread and the soup.

"A few questions,, friend," said Milo. "Simple stuff."

"Nothing in life is simple," said the man.

Milo hooked a thumb at the bags on the side-walk. "A philosopher. There's enough there to feed you and your friends—have a nice little party."

The man shook his head. "It could be poison."

"Why the hell would it be poison?"

Smile. "Why not? The world's poison. A while back someone gave someone a present and it was full of poison and someone died."

"Where'd this happen?"

"Mars."

"Seriously."

"Venus."

"Okay," said Milo, blowing smoke. "Suit your-self, we'll ask our questions elsewhere."

The man licked his lips. "Go ahead. I've got the virus, makes no difference to me."

"The virus, huh?" said Milo.

"Don't believe me, you can kiss me."

The man flicked his tongue. The blanket fell to his shoulders. Underneath, he wore a greasy Bush-Quayle T-shirt. His neck and shoulders were emaci-ated.

"I'll pass," said Milo.

The man laughed. "Bet you will—now what? Gonna beat it *out* of me?"

"Beat what out of you?"

"Whatever you want. You've got the power."

"Nah," said Milo. "This is the new LAPD. We're New Age sensitive guys."

The man laughed. His breath was hot and emetic. "Bearshit. You'll always be savages—got to be to keep order."

Milo said, "Have a nice day," and began to turn.

"What do you want to know, anyway?"

"Anything about a citizen named Lyle Edward Gritz," said Milo. "You know him?"

"Like a brother."

"That so?"

"Yup," said the man. "Unfortunately, this day and age, families deteriorating and all, that means not well at all."

Milo looked over at the hatch. "He in there now?"

"Nope."

"See him recently?"

"Nope."

"But he did hang out here."

"From time to time."

"When was the last time?"

The man ignored the question and began staring at me again.

"What *are* you?" he said. "Some kind of journalist riding along?"

"He's a doctor," said Milo.

"Oh yeah?" Smile. "Got any penicillin? Things get pretty infectious down here. Amoxicillin, erythromycin, tetracycline—anything to zap those little cocci boogers?"

I said, "I'm a psychologist."

"Ooh," said the man, as if wounded. He closed his eyes and shook his head. When he opened them they were dry and focused. "Then you're not worth a damn to me—pardon my linguistics."

"Gritz," said Milo. "Can you tell me anything about him?"

The man appeared to be contemplating. "White trash, juicehead, low IQ. But able-bodied. He had no excuse ending up down here. Not that I do—you probably think I was some kind of white collar overachiever, don't you? 'Cause I'm black and I know grammar."

Smiling.

I smiled back.

"Wrong," he said. "I collected *garbage*. Professionally. City of Compton. Good pay, you wear your gloves, it's fine, terrific benefits. My mistake was leaving and starting my own business. Vinyl flooring. I did good work, had six people working for me. Did fine until business slumped and I let the dope comfort me."

He produced one arm from under the blanket. Raised it and let the sleeve fall back from a bony forearm. The underside of the limb was knotted with scars and abscesses, keloidal and bunched, raw in spots.

"This is a fresh one," he said, eyeing a scab near his wrist. "Got off just before sundown. I waive my rights, why don't you take me in, give me a bunk for the night?"

"Not my thing," said Milo.

"Not your thing?" The man laughed. "What are you, some kind of liberal?"

Milo looked at him and smoked.

The man put his arm back. "Well, at least get me a *real* doctor, so I can get hold of some methadone."

"What about the county?"

"County ran out. Can't even get antibiotics from the county."

"Well," said Milo, "I can give you a lift to an emergency room if you want."

The man laughed again, scornfully. "For what? Wait around all night with gunshots and heart attacks? I've got no active diagnosis—just the virus, no symptoms yet. So all they'll do is keep me waiting. Jail's better—they process you faster."

"Here," said Milo, dipping into his pocket for his wallet. He took out some bills and handed them to the man. "Find a room, keep the change."

The man gave a warm, broad smile and tucked the money under his blanket. "That's real nice, Mr. Policeman. You made this po', unfortunate, homeless individual's evening."

Milo said, "Was Gritz into dope, too?"

"Just juice. Like I said, white trash. Him and his hillbilly singing."

"He liked to sing?"

"All the time, this yodely white-trash voice. Wanted to be Elvis."

"Any talent?"

The man shrugged.

"Did he ever get violent with anyone?"

"Not that I saw."

"What else can you tell me about him?"

"Not much. Sticks to himself—we all do. This is Little Calcutta, not some hippie commune."

"He ever hang out with anyone?"

"Not that I saw."

"How about Dorsey Hewitt?"

The man's lips pursed. "Hewitt, Hewitt . . . the one that did that caseworker?"

"You knew him?"

"No, I read the paper—when that fool did that, I was worried. Backlash. Citizens coming down here and taking it out on all us po' unfortunates."

"You never met Hewitt?"

"Nope."

"Don't know if he and Gritz were buddies?"

"How would I know that if I never met him?"

"Someone told us Gritz talked about getting rich."

"Sure, he always did, the fool. Gonna cut a record. Gonna be the next Elvis. Pour a bottle down his gullet and he was number one on the charts."

The man turned to me. "What do you think my diagnosis is?"

"Don't know you well enough," I said.

"They—the interns over at County—said I had an affective disease—severe mood swings. Then they cut off my methadone."

He clicked his teeth together and waited for me to comment. When I didn't, he said, "Supposedly I was using stuff to self-medicate—being my own psychiatrist." He laughed. "Bearshit. I used it to be *happy*."

Milo said, "Back on track: what else do you know about Gritz?"

"That's it." Smile. "Do I still get to keep the money?"

"Is Terminator Three still here?" I said.

"Who?"

"A kid from Arizona. Missing pinkie, bad cough. He has a girlfriend and a baby."

"Oh yeah, Wayne. He's calling himself *that*, now?" Laughter. "Nah, they all packed up this afternoon. Like I said, people come and go—speaking of which . . ."

He hooded himself with the blanket and, keeping his eyes on us, began edging toward the fence.

"What about your room for the night?" said Milo.

The man stopped and looked back. "Nah, I'll camp out tonight. Fresh air." Grin.

Milo laughed a little bit with him, then eyed the food. "What about all this?"

The man scrutinized the groceries. "Yeah, I'll take some of that Gatorade. The Pepsi, too."

He picked up the beverages and stashed them under the blanket.

"That's it?" said Milo.

"On a diet," said the man. "You want, you can bring the rest of it inside. I'm sure someone'll take it off your hands."

*   *   *

The hooded man led us through the darkness, walking unsteadily but without hesitation, like a well-practiced blind man.

Milo and I stumbled and fought to keep our balance, hauling boxes with only the skimpy guidance of the penlight beam.

As we progressed, I sensed human presence—the heat of fear. Then the petrol sweetness of Sterno.

Urine. Shit. Tobacco. Mildew.

The ammonia of fresh semen.

The hooded man stopped and pointed to the ground.

We put the boxes down and a blue flame ignited. Then another.

The concrete wall came into focus, in front of it bedrolls, piles of newspaper. Bodies and faces blue-lit by the flames.

"Suppertime, chillun'," shouted the man, over the noise of the freeway. Then he was gone.

More lights.

Ten or so people appeared, faceless, sexless, huddled like storm victims.

Milo took something out of the box and held it out. A hand reached out and snatched it. More people collected around us, blue tinted, rabbity, open-mouthed with expectation.

Milo leaned forward, moving his mouth around his cigar. What he said made some of the people bolt. Others stayed to listen, and a few talked back.

He distributed more food. I joined in, feeling hands brush against mine. Finally our boxes were empty and we stood, alone.

Milo swung the penlight around the lot, exposing cloth heaps, lean-tos, people eating.

The hooded black man, sitting with his back up

against the freeway wall, plaid legs splayed. One naked arm stretched out over a skinny thigh, bound at the biceps by a coil of something elastic.

A beautiful smile on his face, a needle buried deep in his flesh.

Milo snapped his head away and lowered the beam.

"C'mon," he said, loud enough for me to hear.

He headed west rather than back toward Beverly Hills, saying, "Well, that was a big goddamn zero."

"None of them had anything to say?"

"The consensus, for what it's worth, is that Lyle Gritz hasn't been seen for a week or two and that it's no big deal, he drifts in and out. He did, indeed, mouth off a bit about getting rich before he split, but they've all heard that before."

"The next Elvis."

He nodded. "Music fantasies, not fish murder. I pressed for details and one of them claimed to have seen him get into someone's car a week or so ago—across the street, over at the cement yard. But that same person seemed rather addled and had absolutely no clue as to make, model, color, or any other distinguishing details. And I'm not sure he didn't just say it because I was pushing. I'll see if Gritz's name shows up on any recent arrest files. You can ask Jeffers if he was ever a patient at the center. If he was, maybe you can get her to point you in any direction he may have gone. But even if we do find him, I'm not convinced it means a damn thing. Now you up for a little rest-stop? I'm still smelling that hellhole."

He drove to a cocktail lounge on Wilshire, in the drab part of Santa Monica. Neon highball glass above a quilted door. I'd never been there, but the way he pulled into the parking lot told me he knew it well.

Inside, the place wasn't much brighter than the overpass. We washed our hands in the men's room and took stools at the bar. The decor was red vinyl and nicotine. The resident rummies seemed to be elderly and listless. A few looked dead asleep. The jukebox helped things along with low-volume Vic Damone.

Milo scooped up a handful of bar nuts and fed his face. Ordered a double Chivas and didn't comment when I asked for a Coke.

"Where's the phone?" I said.

He pointed to a corner.

I called Robin. "How's it going?"

"Not bad," she said. "The other man in my life and I are cuddled up watching a sitcom."

"Funny?"

"I don't think so, and he's not laughing—just drooling. Any progress?"

"Not really, but we did give away lots of food."

"Well," she said, "good deeds don't hurt. Coming home?"

"Milo wanted to stop for a drink. Depending on his mood, I may need to drive him home. Go ahead and eat without us."

"Okay. . . . I'll leave a light in the window and a bone in your dish."

16

Though Milo seemed coherent by the time we reached Benedict Canyon, I suggested he sack out in one of the bedrooms, and he agreed without protest. When I awoke Saturday morning at seven, he was gone and the bed he'd slept in was in perfect order.

At nine, my pond maintenance people called to confirm they'd be moving the fish at two p.m.

Robin and I had breakfast, then I drove to the biomed library.

I looked up Wilbert Harrison in the psychiatric section of the *Directory of Medical Specialists*. His most recent listing was ten years old—an address on Signal Street in Ojai, no phone number. I copied it down and read his bio.

Medical education at Columbia University and the Menninger Clinic, a fellowship in social anthropology at UC Santa Barbara and a clinical appointment at the de Bosch Institute and Corrective School.

The anthro training was interesting, suggesting interests that stretched beyond private practice. But he'd had no academic appointments and his fields of specialty were psychoanalysis and the treatment of impaired physicians and health professionals. His birthdate made him sixty-five. Old enough to have retired—the move to Ojai from Beverly Hills and the lack of a phone listing implied a yearning for the quiet life.

I flipped forward to the R's and found Harvey Rosenblatt's citation, complete with the NYU affiliation and an office on East Sixty-fifth Street in Manhattan. Same address as the Shirley I'd been trying to reach. Had she ignored my call because they were no longer together—divorced? Or something worse?

I read on. Rosenblatt had graduated from NYU, done his clinical training at Bellevue, the Robert Evanston Hale Psychoanalytic Institute in Manhattan, and Southwick Hospital in England. Fields of specialty, psychoanalysis and psychoanalytic psychotherapy. Fifty-eight years old.

He was listed in the next volume of the directory, too. I worked my way forward in time, until his name no longer appeared.

Four years ago.

Right between the Paprock and Shipler murders.

You're wondering if they've been visited, too.

One way to check: like most house organs, the *Journal of the American Medical Association* ran obituaries each month. I went up to the stacks and retrieved bound copies, four and five years old for Rosenblatt, ten and eleven for Harrison.

There were no notices on either psychiatrist. But maybe they hadn't bothered to join the AMA.

I consulted the *American Journal of Psychiatry*. Nothing there, either. Perhaps neither man had been a member of the specialty guild.

Bound copies of the *American Psychological Association Directory* were just a few aisles over. The five-

year-old listing on Katarina de Bosch that I'd found in
my volume at home was indeed her last.

No death notice on her, either.

So maybe I was working myself up for nothing.

I thought of another possible way to locate addresses—bylines in scientific publications. The *Index
Medicus* and *Psychological Abstracts* revealed that Katarina had coauthored a couple of articles with her father, but nothing since his death. One of them had to
do with child rearing and contained a reference to
"bad love":

> The process of mother-child bonding forms
> the foundation for all intimate relationships,
> and disruptions in this process plant the
> seed of psychopathology in later life. Good
> love—the nurturant, altruistic, psychosocial
> "suckling" by the mother/parenting figure,
> contributes to the child's sense of security
> and, hence, molds his ability to form stable
> attachments. Bad love—the abuse of parental
> authority—creates   cynicism,   alienation,
> hostility, and, in the worst cases, violent act-
> ing-out that is the child's attempt to seek ret-
> ribution from the breast that has failed him.

Retribution. The abuse of parental authority.
Someone had been failed. Someone was seeking revenge.

I checked for articles by Harrison and Rosenblatt.
Neither had published a word.

No great surprise, most practitioners never get
into print. But it still seemed odd that I couldn't locate
any of them.

One therapist to go: the social worker, Mitchell
Lerner.

He'd been last counted a member in good standing of the national social work organization six years ago. I made a note of his office address on Laurel Canyon and the accompanying phone number. BA from Cal State Northridge, MSW from Berkeley, clinical training at San Francisco General Hospital, followed by two years as a staff social worker at the Corrective School.

Another disciple. Under specialties he'd listed family therapy and substance abuse.

Not hoping for much, I took the stairs back up to the stacks and pulled out six- and seven-year-old bound volumes of the social work journal.

No obits on him either, but a paragraph headed "Suspensions" just below the death notices in a December issue caught my eye. A list followed. Thirteen clinical social workers dropped by the organization because of ethics violations. Dead center among the names, "Lerner, Mitchell A."

No details were given about his or any of the others' sins. The State Board of Behavioral Science Examiners was closed for the weekend, so I jotted down the date he'd been expelled and made a note to call first thing Monday morning.

Figuring I'd learned as much as I could from books, I left the library. Back at the house on Benedict, Robin was working and the dog looked bored. He followed me into the house and slavered as I fixed myself a sandwich. I did some paperwork and shared my lunch with him, and he tagged along as I walked outside to the Seville.

"Where to?" said Robin.

"The house. I want to make sure the fish get transferred okay."

She gave a doubtful look but said nothing.

"There'll be plenty of people around," I said.

She nodded and looked over at the car. The dog was pawing the front bumper. It made her smile.

"Someone's in a traveling mood. Why don't you take him along?"

"Sure, but pond drainage isn't his thing—the water phobia."

"Why don't you try some therapy with him?"

"Why not?" I said. "This could be the start of a whole new career."

The four-man crew had arrived early, and when I got there the pond was half empty, the waterfall switched off, and the fish transferred to aerated, blue vats that sat in the bed of a pickup truck. Workers uprooted plants and bagged them, shoveled gravel, and checked the air lines to the vats.

I checked in with the crew boss, a skinny brown kid with blond Rasta locks and a dyed white chin beard. The dog kept his distance, but followed me as I went up to the terrace to pick up two days' worth of mail.

Lots of stuff, most of it routine. The exception was a long white envelope.

Cheap paper that I'd seen before.

SHERMAN BUCKLEAR, ATTORNEY-AT-LAW above a return address in Simi Valley.

Inside was a letter informing me that Petitioner Donald Dell Wallace had good reason to believe that I had knowledge of the whereabouts of said petitioner's legal offspring, Chondra Nicolette Wallace and Tiffani Starr Wallace and was demanding that I pass along said information to said petitioner's attorney, without delay, so that said petitioner's legal rights would not be abridged.

The rest consisted of threats in legalese. I put the letter back in the envelope and pocketed it. The dog was scratching at the front door.

"Nostalgic already?" I unlocked the door and he

ran ahead of me, straight into the kitchen. Straight to the refrigerator.

Milo's spiritual son.

Scratch, scratch, pant, pant.

I realized that, in all the haste of moving, I'd forgotten to remove the perishables from the fridge.

I did a quick visual survey of the shelves, spilled out milk and dumped cheese that had turned and fruit that was beginning to brown. Putting the unspoiled food in a bag, I thought of the people under the freeway.

Some meatloaf remained in a plastic container. It smelled okay and the dog looked as if he'd seen the messiah.

"Okay, okay." I put it in a bowl and set it down before him, bagged the good fruits and vegetables and brought them down to the car.

The pond crew was finishing up. The koi in the truck all seemed to be swimming fine.

The crew boss said, "Okay, we've got the sump running, it'll take another hour or so to drain off. You want us to wait, we can, but you're paying us by the hour, so you can stick around and turn it off yourself."

"No problem," I said, glancing at the truck. "Take care of them."

"Sure. When do you think you'll be wanting 'em back?"

"Don't know yet."

"Some kind of long vacation?"

"Something like that."

"Cool." He handed me a bill and got behind the wheel of the truck. A moment later, they were gone and all I heard was the slow gurgle of draining water.

I sat down on the bank of what was now a muddy hole, waiting and watching the level drop. The heat and the quiet combined to lull me, and I wasn't sure how long I'd been there when someone said, "Hey."

I jerked up, groggily.

A man stood in the gateway, holding a tire iron.

Late twenties or early thirties, heavy growth of dark stubble, thick black Fu Manchu that drooped to his chin.

He had on greasy jeans and Wellington boots with chains, a black T-shirt under a heavy black leather vest. Black, thinning hair, gold hoop earring, steel chains around his neck. Big tattooed arms. Big, hard belly, bowlegs. Maybe six one, two hundred.

Red-rimmed eyes.

At Sunny's Sun Valley, next door to Rodriguez's masonry yard, he'd been wearing a black cap that said CAT.

The muscular guy at the bar who hadn't said much.

He whistled once and came closer. Let one hand drop from the iron. Lowered the metal, swung it parallel to his leg in a slow, small arc and came a few steps closer. Looked at my face. His wore a slow, lazy smile of recognition.

"Retaining wall, huh?"

"What do you want?"

"Donald's kids, man." Deep slurry voice. He sounded as if he'd come straight from the bar.

"They're not here."

"Where, man?"

"I don't know."

The iron arc widened.

I said, "Why would I know?"

"You were lookin' for the little brown brother, man. Maybe you found him."

"I didn't."

"Maybe you *did*, man." Stepping forward. Just a few feet away, now. Lots of missing teeth. Mustache clogged with dandruff. An angry pus pimple had erupted under his left eye. The tattoos were badly done, a green-blue riot of female torsos, bloody blades, and Gothic lettering.

I said, "I already got a letter from Wallace's lawyer—"

"Fuck *that*." He came within swinging range, smelling like the bottom of a clothes hamper that needed emptying.

I backed up. Not much room to maneuver. Behind me was shrubbery—hedges and the maple tree whose branch had been used to skewer the koi.

"You're not helping Donald Dell," I said. "This won't look good for him."

"Who gives a fuck, man? You're off the case."

He swung the iron listlessly, pointing downward and hitting the dirt. Looking at the pond just for a second, then back at me. I searched the area for possible weapons.

Slim pickings: oversized polyethylene bags left behind by the pond crew. Lengths of rubber hosing. A couple of sheets of scummy filter screen. Maybe the koi net. Six feet of stout oak handle below a steel-mesh cup—but it was out of reach.

"Since when?" I said.

"*What?*"

"Since when am I off the case?"

"Since we said so, man."

"The Iron Priests?"

"Where're the kids, man?"

"I told you. I don't know."

He shook his head and advanced. "Don't get hurt over it, man. It's just a job, what the fuck."

"You like fish?" I said.

"Huh?"

"Fish. Finny creatures. Seafood. Piscinoids."

"Hey, ma—"

"You like to sneak around, spearing 'em? Breaking branches off trees and doing the old rotisserie bit?"

"*What?*"

"You've been here before, haven't you? Sportfishing carp, you sick fuck."

Confusion tugged at his face, zipping it up into something peevish and tight and offering a hint of what he'd look like on the off-chance he made it to old age. Then anger took its place—a brattish resentment—and he lifted the iron and took a poke at my middle.

I danced away.

"Hey," he said, annoyed. He jabbed again, missed. Sloshed, but not enough to stagger, and there was force in his movements. "Here, chickie chick." He laughed.

I kept moving away from his blows, managed to get up on the rock rim of the pond. The stones were slick with algae and I used my arms for balance. That made him laugh some more. He shouted, came after me, clumsy and slow. Caught up in the game as if it were what he'd come for.

He began making barnyard clucks.

I split my focus between the iron and his eyes. Readying myself for the chance to use surprise and his own weight against him. If I missed, my hand would get shattered.

"Boom, boom, boom," he said. "Chickie-chick."

"C'mon, stupid," I said.

His face puffed up and reddened. Two-handing the iron, he made a sudden swing for my knees.

I jumped back, stumbled, pitched forward onto the pond rim, breaking my fall with my palms.

The iron landed on rock and clanged. He raised it high over his head.

The next sounds came from behind him.

Deep bark.

Angry snorts.

He wheeled toward them, holding the iron in front of his own chest in instinctive defense. Just in time to see the bulldog racing toward him, a little black bullet, its teeth bared in a pearly grimace.

Just in time for me to spring to my feet and throw my arms around his front.

Not enough force to knock him over, but I got my hands on the ends of the iron and slammed it hard into his rib cage. Something cracked.

He said, "Ohh," sounding curiously girlish. Buckled. Bent.

The dog was on him now, fixing his teeth on denim leg, shaking his head from side to side, growling and spraying spit.

The man's back was pushing against me. I pressed up on the iron, sharply, forcing it under his chin. Got it against his Adam's apple and pulled in steadily until he made gagging noises and started to loosen his grip.

I held on. Finally, he dropped his arms and let his full weight fall against me. Struggling to remain on my feet, I let him sink to the ground, hoping I hadn't destroyed his larynx but not torturing myself over it.

The dog stayed on him, grunting and eating denim.

The man sank to the dirt. I felt for a pulse. Nice and steady, and he was already starting to move and groan.

I looked for something to bind him. The polyethylene bags. Telling the dog, "Stay," I ran to get them. I tied them together, managed to fashion two thick, plastic ropes and used one to secure his hands behind his back, the other his legs.

The dog had stepped back to watch me, head cocked. I said, "You did great, Spike, but you don't get to eat this one. How about sirloin instead—it's higher grade."

The man opened his eyes. Tried to speak but produced only a retching cough. The front of his neck was swollen, and a deep blue bruise that matched his tattooes was starting to blossom.

The dog padded over to him.

The man's eyes sparked. He turned his head away and grimaced in pain.

I said, "Stay, Spike. No blood."

The dog looked up at me with soft eyes that I hoped wouldn't betray him.

The man coughed and choked.

The dog's nostrils opened and shut. Saliva dripped from his maw and he growled.

"Good boy, Spike," I said. "Watch him for a sec, and if he gives you any problems, you're allowed to rip out his throat for an appetizer."

17

"What an idiot," said Milo, putting his notepad away. "His name's Hurley Keffler and he's got a sheet, but not much of one. More of a bad guy wannabee. We found his bike parked down the road. He claims he wasn't stalking you, got here just as the pond people drove away and decided to have a talk."

"Just one of those impulsive weekend jaunts, huh?"

"Yeah."

We were up on the landing, watching the police cars drive away. The dog watched, too, sticking his flat face through the slats of the railing, ears pricked.

"I found a letter from the Wallaces' lawyer in my mailbox," I said. "He wanted to know where the girls were and threatened me with legal action if I didn't tell him. Looks like the Priests decided not to wait."

"It might not be an official Priest mission," he said. "Just Keffler having a few too many and deciding to improvise. His dinky record, he's probably low man in the gang, trying to impress the hairy brothers."

"What are you booking him on?"

"ADW, trespassing, DUI if his blood alcohol's high enough to prove he drove over here soused. If the Priests go his bail, he'll probably be out within a few days. I'll have a talk with them, tell them to lock him in the house. What a clown."

He chuckled. "Bet your little chokehold didn't do much for his powers of comprehension, either. What'd you use, one of those karate things I'm always ribbing you about?"

"Actually," I said, bending and patting the dog's muscular neck, "*he* gets the credit. Pulled a sneak attack from the back that allowed me to jump Keffler. Plus he overcame his water phobia—ran right up to the pond."

"No kidding?" Smile. "Okay, I'll put him up for sainthood." He bent, too, and rubbed the dog behind the ears. "Congrats, St. Doggus, you're a K-9 hero."

The driver of one of the black-and-whites looked up at us and Milo waved him on.

"Good boy," I said to the dog.

"Seeing as he's saved your kneecaps, Alex, don't you think he deserves a real name? My vote's still for Rover."

"When I was trying to intimidate Keffler, I called him Spike."

"Very manly."

"Only problem is," I said, "he's already got a name—someone's bound to come get him. What a drag. I'm getting kind of attached to him."

"What?" He elbowed my ribs, gently. "We're afraid of getting hurt, so we don't reach out for intimacy? Give him a goddamn name, Alex. *Empower* him so he can fulfill his dogly potential."

I laughed and rubbed the dog some more. He panted and put his head against my leg.

"Keffler's not the one who killed the koi," I said. "When I mentioned it, he fuzzed over completely."

"Probably," he said. "That tree branch was too subtle for the Priests. They would have taken out all the fish and mashed 'em up, maybe eaten them and left the bones."

"Back to our 'bad love' fiend," I said. "Anything new on Lyle Gritz?"

"Not yet."

"I was over at the library this morning, checking out the professional directories. No current listings on Rosenblatt or Katarina de Bosch. Harrison moved to Ojai and has no phone number, which sounds like retirement—and the social worker, Lerner, was suspended from the social work organization for an ethics violation."

"What kind of violation?"

"The directory didn't say."

"What's it usually mean? Sleeping with a patient?"

"That's the most common, but it could also be financial shenanigans, betrayal of confidentiality, or a personal problem, like drug or alcohol addiction."

He rested his arms on the top of the railing. The squad cars were gone now. My pond was a dry hole and the sump pump was sucking air. I went down to the garden, dog at my heels, and turned it off.

When I got back, Milo said, "If Lerner was a bad boy, *he* could have done something that pissed off a patient."

"Sure," I said. "I looked up de Bosch's writings on 'bad love.' Specifically, it refers to abuse of parental authority leading to alienation, cynicism, and, in extreme cases, violence. De Bosch actually used the term 'retribution.' But, pardon the whining, I still don't know what the hell *I* could have done."

"Why don't you try to get in touch with Harrison

in Ojai, see if he has any idea what's going on? If his number's unlisted, I can get it for you."

"Okay," I said. "And Harrison may be a good source for another reason. When therapists are suspended, they're usually required to get therapy. One of Harrison's specialties was treating impaired therapists. Wouldn't it be interesting if he treated Lerner? It's not that farfetched—Lerner turning to someone he knew. Get me that number right now and I'll call."

He went to his car and got on the radio. Returned ten minutes later and said, "No listing at all, even though the address is still on the tax roles. Can you spare the time for a little drive? Ojai's nice this time of year. Cute little shops, antiques, whatever. Take the lovely Miss C for a cruise up the coast, combine business with pleasure."

"Get out of town for a while?"

He shrugged.

"Okay," I said. "And Ojai's close to Santa Barbara—I can extend my trip. De Bosch's school is defunct, but it might be interesting to see if any of the neighbors remember it. Maybe there was some kind of scandal, something that closed it down and left someone with a long-term grudge."

"Sure, snoop around. If Robin can stand it, who am I to try and stop you?"

He slapped my back. "I'm off."

"Where to?"

"A little more research on Paprock and Shipler."

"Anything new?"

"Nope. I'm planning to drop in on Paprock's husband tomorrow. He's still a car salesman at the Cadillac place, and Sunday's a good day for those guys."

"I'll go with you."

"Thought you were cruising to Ojai."

"Monday," I said. "Monday's a good day for psychologists."

"Oh, yeah? Why's that?"

"Blue day for everyone else. We get to concentrate on other people's problems and forget our own."

I went back into the house and looked through the freezer. In our haste to move, we hadn't emptied it, and there were several steaks in the top compartment. I took out a choice-cut rib eye and put it in the oven to broil. The dog's eyes were glued to my every move. As the aroma of broiling meat filled the kitchen, his nose started to go crazy and he got down on the floor in a supplicatory posture.

"Restrain the caballos," I said. "All good things come to those who salivate."

I petted him and called my service for messages. Only one, from Jean Jeffers. The clinic director had called at eleven a.m. leaving an 818 return number.

"Did she say what it was about?" I asked the operator.

"No, just to call her, doctor."

I did and got an answering tape with a friendly-sounding male voice backgrounded by Neil Diamond. I was starting to leave a message when Jean's voice broke in.

"Hi, thanks for calling back."

"Hi, what's up?"

I thought I heard her sigh. "I've got some . . . I think it would be best if we met personally."

"Something about Hewitt?"

"Somethi—I'm sorry, I'd rather just talk about it in person, if you don't mind."

"Sure. Where and when would you like to meet?"

"Tomorrow would be okay for me."

"Tomorrow's fine."

"Great," she said. "Where do you live?"

"West L.A."

"I'm in Studio City, but I don't mind coming over the hill on the weekend."

"I can come out to the valley."

"No, actually, I like to come out when it's not for work. Never get a chance to enjoy the city. Whereabouts in West L.A.?"

"Near Beverly Hills."

"Okay . . . how about Amanda's, it's a little place on Beverly Drive."

"What time?"

"Say one p.m.?"

"One it is."

Nervous laughter. "I know this must seem strange coming out of the blue, but maybe . . . oh, let's just talk about it tomorrow."

I gave the dog a few bites of steak, wrapped the rest in plastic, and pocketed it. Then we drove to the pet store, where I let him sniff around the food bags. He lingered at some stuff that claimed to be scientifically formulated. Organic ingredients. Twice the cost of any of the others.

"You earned it," I said, and I purchased ten pounds along with several packets of assorted canine snacks.

Going home, he munched happily on a bacon-flavored pretzel.

"*Bon appetit*, Spike," I said. "Your real name's probably something like Pierre de Cordon Bleu."

Back at the house on Benedict Canyon, I found Robin reading in the living room. I told her what had happened with Hurley Keffler and she listened, quiet

and resigned, as if I were a delinquent child with no hope of rehabilitation.

"What a good friend you turned out to be," she said to the dog. He jumped up on the couch and put his head in her lap.

"So what are they going to do with him—this Keffler?"

"He'll be in jail for a while."

"How long's a while?"

"Probably not long. His gang's likely to make his bail."

"And then?"

"And then he'll be out, but he won't know this address."

"Okay."

"Want to take a drive up to Ojai and Santa Barbara, next couple of days?"

"Business or pleasure?"

"Both." I told her about Lerner and Harrison, my wanting to speak to the Corrective School's neighbors.

"Love to, but I really shouldn't, Alex. Too much work down here."

"Sure?"

"I am, hon. Sorry." She touched my face. "There's so much piled up, and even though I've got all my gear set up, it feels different here—I'm working slower, need to get back on the track."

"I'm really putting you through it, aren't I?"

"No," she said, smiling and mussing my hair. "You're the one being put through."

The smile lingered and grew into a soft laugh.

"What's funny?" I said.

"The way men think. As if our going through some stress together would be putting me *through* it. I'm worried about you, but I'm glad to be here with

you—to be part of it. Putting me *through* it means something totally different."

"Such as?"

"Constantly diminishing me—condescending to me, dismissing my opinions. Anything that would make me question my worth. Do those kinds of things to a woman and she may stay with you, but she'll never think the same of you."

"Oh."

"Oh," she said, laughing and hugging me. "Pretty profound, huh? Are you mad at me for not wanting to go to Ojai?"

"No, just disappointed."

"You go anyway. Promise to be careful?"

"I promise."

"Good," she said. "That's important."

18

We had dinner at an Indian place near Beverly Hills'
eastern border with L.A., washing the meal down
with clove tea and driving home feeling good. Robin
went to run a bath and I phoned Milo at home and
told him about Jean's call.

"She has something to tell me but wouldn't elaborate over the phone—sounded nervous. My guess is
she found something about Hewitt that scares her.
I'm meeting her at one, and I'll ask her about Gritz.
When were you planning to see Ralph Paprock?"

"Right around then."

"Care to make it earlier?"

"Dealership won't be open. I suppose we could
catch him just as he comes in."

"I'll pick you up."

Sunday morning I drove to West Hollywood.
Milo's and Rick's place was a small, perfectly kept
Spanish house at the end of one of those short, ob-
scure streets that hide in the grotesque shadow of the

Design Center's blue-green mass. Cedars-Sinai was within walking distance. Sometimes Rick jogged to work. Today, he hadn't: the white Porsche was gone.

Milo was waiting outside. The small front lawn had been replaced by ground cover and the flowers were blooming bright orange.

He saw me looking at it and said, "Drought resistant," as he got into the car. "That 'environmental designer' I told you about. Guy would upholster the world in cactus if he could."

I took Laurel Canyon up into the Valley, passing stilt-box houses and postmodern cabins, the decaying Palladian estate where Houdini had done tricks for Jean Harlow. A governor had once lived right around there. None of the magic had rubbed off.

At Ventura, I turned left and traveled two miles to Valley Vista Cadillac. The showroom was fronted by twenty-foot slabs of plate glass and bordered by a huge outdoor lot. Banners were strung on high-tension wire. The lights were off, but morning sun managed to get in and bounce off the sparkling bodies of brand-new coupes and sedans. The cars out on the lot were blinding.

A trim black man in a well-cut navy suit stood next to a smoke-gray Seville. When he saw us get out of my seventy-nine, he went over to the front door and unlocked it, even though business hours hadn't begun. When Milo and I stepped in, his hand was out and his smile was blooming brighter than Milo's lawn.

He had a perfectly trimmed pencil mustache and a pin-collar shirt as white as an avalanche. Off to the side of the showroom, beyond the cars, was a warren of cubicles, and I could hear someone talking on the phone. The cars were spotless and perfectly detailed. The whole place smelled of leather and rubber and conspicuous consumption. My car had smelled that way once, even though I'd bought it used. Someone had told me the fragrance came in aerosol cans.

"That's a classic you've got," said the man, looking through the window.

"Been good to me," I said.

"Keep it and garage it, that's what I'd do. One of these days you'll see it appreciate, like money in the bank. Meanwhile, you can be driving something new for every day. Good lines this year, don't you think?"

"Very nice."

"Got those foreign deals beat hands down. Get folks in to actually test drive, they see that. You a lawyer?"

"Psychologist."

He gave an uncertain smile and I found a business card in my hand.

John Allbright
Sales Executive

"Got a real good suspension this year, too," he said. "With all due respect to your classic, I think you'll find it a whole other world, drive-wise. Great sound system, too, if you go for the Bose option and—"

"We're looking for Ralph Paprock," said Milo.

Allbright looked at him. Squinted. Put his hand to his mouth and compressed his smile manually.

"Ralph," he said. "Sure. Ralph's over there."

Pointing to the cubicles, he walked away fast, ending up in a glass corner, where he lit up a cigarette and stared out at the lot.

The first two compartments were empty. Ralph Paprock sat behind a desk in the third. He was in his late forties, narrow and tan, with sparse gray-blond hair on top and a bit more of it on the sides, combed over his ears. His double-breasted suit was the same cut as Allbright's, olive green, just a bit too bright. His shirt was cream with a long-point collar, his tie crowded with parrots and palm trees.

He was hunched over some papers. The tip of his tongue protruded from the corner of his narrow mouth. The pen in his right hand tapped his blotter very fast. His nails were shiny.

When Milo cleared his throat, the tongue zipped in and an eager grin took hold of Paprock's face. Despite the smile, his face was tired, the muscles loose and droopy. His eyes were small and amber. The suit gave them a khaki tint.

"Gentlemen. How can I help you?"

Milo said, "Mr. Paprock, I'm Detective Sturgis, Los Angeles police," and handed him a card.

The look that took hold of the salesman next— *What are you hitting me with this time?*—made me feel lousy. We had nothing to offer him and plenty to take.

He put his pen down.

I caught a side view of a photo on his desk, propped up next to a mug printed with the Cadillac crest. Two round-faced, fair-haired children. The younger one, a girl, was smiling, but the boy seemed to be on the verge of tears. Behind them hovered a woman of around seventy with butterfly glasses and cold-waved white hair. She resembled Paprock, but she had a stronger jaw.

Milo said, "Sorry to bother you, Mr. Paprock, but we've come across another homicide that might be related to your wife's and wondered if we could ask you a few questions."

"Another—a *new* one?" said Paprock. "I didn't see anything on the news."

"Not exactly, sir. This crime occurred three years ago—"

"Three years ago? Three *years* and you've just come *across* it? Did you finally get him?"

"No, sir."

"Jesus." Paprock's hands were flat on the desk and his forehead had erupted in sweat. He wiped it with the back of one hand. "Just what I need to start off the week."

There were two chairs facing his desk. He stared at them but didn't say anything else.

Milo motioned me into the office and closed the door behind us. There was very little standing room. Paprock held a hand out to the chairs and we sat. A certificate behind the desk said he'd been a prizewinning salesman. The date was three summers ago.

"Who's the other victim?" he said.

"A man named Rodney Shipler."

"A man?"

"Yes, sir."

"A man—I don't understand."

"You don't recognize the name?"

"No. And if it was a man, what makes you think it has anything to do with my Myra?"

"The words 'bad love' were written at the crime scene."

" 'Bad love,' " said Paprock. "I used to dream about that. Make up different meanings for it. But still . . ."

He closed his eyes, opened them, took a bottle out of his desk drawer. Enteric aspirin. Popping a couple of tablets, he dropped the bottle into his breast pocket, behind the colored handkerchief.

"What kind of meanings?" said Milo.

Paprock looked at him. "Crazy stuff—trying to figure out what the hell it meant. I don't remember. What's the difference?"

He began moving his hands around, stirring the air very quickly, as if searching for something to grab. "Was there any—some sign of—was this Shipler . . . what I'm getting at is, was there something sexual?"

"No, sir."

Paprock said, " 'Cause that's what *they* told me they thought it might mean. The first cops. Some psychotic thing—using—sex in a bad way, some sort of sex nut. A pervert *bragging* about what he did—bad love."

Nothing like that had been in Myra Paprock's file.

Milo nodded.

"A man," said Paprock. "So what are you *telling* me? The first cops had it all *wrong*? They went and looked for the *wrong* thing?"

"We don't really know much at all at this point, sir. Just that someone wrote 'bad love' at the scene of Mr. Shipler's homicide."

"Shipler." Paprock squinted. "You're opening the whole thing up again, 'cause of him?"

"We're taking a look at the facts, Mr. Paprock."

Paprock closed his eyes, opened them, and took a deep breath. "My Myra was taken *apart*. I had to identify her. To you that kind of thing's probably old hat, but . . ." Shake of the head.

"It's never old hat, sir."

Paprock gave him a doubtful look. "After I did it —identified her—it took me a long time to be able to remember her the way she used to be . . . even now . . . the first cops said whoever—did those things to her, did them after she was dead." Alarm brightened his eyes. "They were right about *that*, weren't they?"

"Yes, sir."

Paprock's hands gripped the edge of his desk and he wheeled forward. "Tell me the truth, detective —I *mean* it. I don't want to think of her suffering, but if—no, forget it, don't tell me a damn thing, I don't *want* to know."

"She didn't suffer, sir. The only thing new is Mr. Shipler's murder."

More sweat. Another wipe.

"Afterwards," said Paprock. "After I identified her—I had to go tell my kids. The older one, anyway —the little one was just a baby. Actually, the older one wasn't much more than a baby, either, but he was asking for her, I had to tell him something."

He knocked the knuckles of both hands together. Shook his head, tapped the desk.

"It took a helluva long time to get it set in my mind—what had happened. When I went to tell my boy, all I could think of was what I'd seen in the morgue—imagining her . . . and here he is asking for Mommy. 'Mommy, Mommy'—he was two and a half. I told him Mommy got sick and went to sleep forever. When his sister got old enough, I gave *him* the job of telling *her*. They're great kids, my mother's been helping me take care of them, she's close to eighty and they don't give her any problems. So who needs to change that? Who needs Myra's name in the papers and digging it all up? There was a time, finding out who did it was *all* that mattered to me, but I got over that. What's the difference, anyway? She's not coming back, right?"

I nodded. Milo didn't move.

Paprock touched his brow and opened his eyes wide, as if exercising the lids.

"That it?" he said.

"Just a few questions about your wife's background," said Milo.

"Her *background*?"

"Her work background, Mr. Paprock. Before she became a real estate agent, did she do anything else?"

"Why?"

"Just collecting facts, sir."

"She worked for a bank, okay? What kind of work did this Shipler do?"

"He was a janitor. What bank did she work for?"

"Trust Federal, over in Encino. She was a loan officer—that's how I met her. We used to channel our car loans through there and one day I went down there on a big fleet sale and she was at the loan desk."

Milo took out his notepad and wrote.

"She would have probably made vice president," said Paprock. "She was smart. But she wanted to work for herself, had enough of bureaucracies. So she studied for her broker's license at night, then quit. Was doing real well, lots of sales . . ."

He looked off to one side, fixing his gaze on a poster. Two perfect-looking, tennis-clad people getting into a turquoise Coupe de Ville with diamond-bright wire wheels. Behind the car, the marble-and-glass facade of a resort hotel. Crystal chandelier. Perfect-looking doorman smiling at them.

"Bureaucracies," said Milo. "Did she deal with any others before the bank?"

"Yeah," said Paprock, still turned away. "She taught school—but that was before I met her."

"Here in L.A.?"

"No, up near Santa Barbara—Goleta."

"Goleta," said Milo. "Do you remember the name of the school?"

Paprock faced us again. "Some public school— why? What does her work have to do with any-thing?"

"Maybe nothing, sir, but please bear with me. Did she ever teach in L.A.?"

"Not to my knowledge. By the time she moved down here, she was fed up with teaching."

"Why's that?"

"The whole situation—kids not interested in learning, lousy pay—what's to like about it?"

"A public school," I said.

"Yeah."

Milo said, "What subjects did she teach?"

"All of them, I guess. She taught fifth grade, or maybe it was fourth, I dunno. In elementary school, you teach all the subjects, right? We never really had any detailed discussions about it."

"Did she teach anywhere before Goleta?" said Milo.

"Not as far as I know. I think that was her first job out of school."

"When would that be?"

"Let's see, she graduated at twenty-two, she'd be forty this May." He winced. "So that would have been, what, eighteen years ago. I think she taught maybe four or five years, then she switched to banking."

He looked at the poster again and wiped his forehead.

Milo closed his pad. The sound made Paprock jump. His eyes met Milo's. Milo gave as gentle a smile as I'd ever seen him muster. "Thanks for your time, Mr. Paprock. Is there anything else you want to tell us?"

"Sure," said Paprock. "I want to tell you to find the filthy fuck who killed my wife and put me in a room with him." He rubbed his eyes. Made two fists and opened them and gave a sick smile. "Fat chance."

Milo and I stood. A second later, Paprock rose, too. He was medium-sized, slightly round-backed, almost dainty.

He patted his chest, removed the aspirin bottle from his breast pocket and passed it from hand to hand. Walking around the desk, he pushed the door open and held it for us. No sign of John Allbright or anyone else. Paprock walked us through the showroom, touching the flanks of a gold Eldorado in passing.

"Whyncha buy a car, as long as you're here?" he said. Then he colored through his tan and stopped.

Milo held out his hand.

Paprock shook it, then mine.

We thanked him again for his time.

"Look," he said, "what I said before—about not wanting to know? That was bullshit. I still think about her. I got married again, it lasted three months, my kids hated the bitch. Myra was . . . special. The kids, someday they're gonna have to know. I'll handle it. I can handle it. You find something, you tell me, okay? You find *anything*, you tell me."

I headed for Coldwater Canyon and the drive back to the city.

"Public school near Santa Barbara," I said. "Lousy pay, so maybe she moonlighted at a local private place."

"A reasonable assumption," said Milo. He lowered the Seville's passenger window, lit up a bad cigar, and blew smoke out at the hot valley air. The city was digging up Ventura Boulevard and sawhorses blocked one lane. Bad traffic usually made Milo curse. This time he kept quiet, puffing and thinking.

I said, "Shipler was a school janitor. Maybe he worked at de Bosch's school, too. That could be our connection: they were both staffers, not patients."

"Twenty years ago. . . . Wonder how long the school district keeps records. I'll check, see if Shipler transferred down from Santa Barbara."

"More reasons for me to drive up there," I said.

"When are you doing it?"

"Tomorrow. Robin can't make it—all for the best. Between trying to find remnants of the school and looking for Wilbert Harrison in Ojai, it won't be a pleasure trip."

"Those other guys—the therapists at the symposium—they worked at the school, too, right?"

"Harrison and Lerner did. But not Rosenblatt—he trained with de Bosch in England. I'm not sure about Stoumen, but he was a contemporary of de Bosch, and Katarina asked him to speak, so there was probably some kind of relationship."

"So, one way or the other, it all boils down to de Bosch. . . . Anyone seen as being close to him is fair game for this nut. . . . Bad love—destroying a kid's sense of trust, huh?"

"That's the concept."

I reached Coldwater and started the climb. He drew on his cigar and said, "Paprock was right about his wife. You saw the pictures—she *was* taken apart."

"Poor guy," I said. "Walking wounded."

"What I told him, about her being dead when she was raped? True. But she suffered, Alex. Sixty-four stab wounds and plenty of them landed before she died. That kind of revenge—rage? Someone must have gotten fucked up big-time."

19

I made it to Beverly Hills with five minutes to spare for my one o'clock with Jean Jeffers. Parking was a problem and I had to use a city lot two blocks down from Amanda's, waiting at the curb as a contemplative valet decided whether or not to put up the FULL sign.

He finally let me in, and I arrived at the restaurant five minutes late. The place was jammed and it reeked of Parmesan cheese. A hostess was calling out names from a clipboarded list and walking the chosen across a deliberately cracked white marble floor. The tables were marble, too, and a gray faux-marble treatment had been given to the walls. The crypt look, nice and cold, but the room was hot with impatience and I had to elbow my way through a cranky crowd.

I looked around and saw Jean already seated at a table near the back, next to the south wall of the restaurant. She waved. The man next to her looked at me but didn't move.

I recalled him as the heavyset fellow from the photo in her office, a little heavier, a little grayer. In the picture, he and Jean had been wearing leis and matching Hawaiian shirts. Today, they'd kept the Bobbsey twins thing going with a white linen dress for her, white linen shirt for him, and matching yellow golf sweaters.

I waved back and went over. They had half-empty coffee cups in front of them and pieces of buttered olive bread on their bread plates. The man had an executive haircut and an executive face. Great shave, sunburnt neck, blue eyes, the skin around them slightly bagged.

Jean rose a little as I sat down. He didn't, though his expression was friendly enough.

"This is my husband, Dick Jeffers. Dick, Dr. Alex Delaware."

"Doctor."

"Mr. Jeffers."

He smiled as he shot out his arm. "Dick."

"Alex."

"Fair enough."

I sat down across from them. Both their yellow sweaters had crossed tennis-racquet logos. His bore a small, gold Masonic pin.

"Well," said Jean, "some crowd. Hope the food's good."

"Beverly Hills," said her husband. "The good life."

She smiled at him, looked down at her lap. A large, white purse sat there and one of her arms was around it.

Dick Jeffers said, "Guess I'll be going, Jeanie. Nice to meet you, doctor."

"Same here."

"Okay, honey," said Jean.

Cheek pecks, then Jeffers stood. He seemed to lose balance for a second, caught himself by resting one palm on the table. Jean looked away from him as he straightened. He shoved the chair back with the rear of his thighs and gave me a wink. Then he walked off, limping noticeably.

Jean said, "He has one leg, just got a brand new prosthesis and it's taking a while getting used to." It sounded like something she'd said many times before.

I said, "That can be tough. Years ago, I worked with children with missing limbs."

"Did you?" she said. "Well, Dick lost his in an auto accident."

Pain in her eyes. I said, "Recently?"

"Oh, no, several years ago. Before anyone really appreciated the value of seat belts. He was driving a convertible, was unbelted, got hit from behind and thrown out. Another car ran over his leg."

"Terrible."

"Thank God he wasn't killed. I met him when he was in rehab. I was doing a rotation at Rancho Los Amigos and he was there for a couple of months. He made a great adjustment to his appliance—always had until it started bothering him a few months ago. He'll get used to the new one. He's a good guy, very determined."

I smiled.

"So," she said, "how are you?"

"Fine. And intrigued."

"By?"

"Your call."

"Oh." The sheet of hair fell over her eye. She let it stay there. "Well, I didn't mean to be overly dramatic, it's just—" She looked around. "Why don't we order first, and then we can talk about it."

We read the menu. Someone in the kitchen had a thing for balsamic vinegar.

When she said, "Well, I know what *I* want," I waved over a waiter. Asian kid, around nineteen, with a waist-length ponytail and ten stud earrings rimming the outer cartilage of his left ear. It hurt to look at him and I stared at the table as Jean ordered an *insalata* something or other. I asked for linguine marinara and an iced tea. Ruined Ear came back quickly with the drink and a refill of her coffee.

When he left, she said, "So you live pretty close to here?"

"Not far."

"For a while Dick and I thought about moving over the hill, but then prices started to go crazy."

"They've slid quite a bit recently."

"Not enough." She smiled. "Not that I'm complaining. Dick's an aerospace engineer and he does well, but you never know when the government's going to cancel a project. The place we've got in Studio City is really pretty nice." She looked at her watch. "He's probably over at Rudnicks now. He likes to shop there for sweaters."

"He's not having lunch?"

"What I need to talk to you about is confidential. Dick understands that. So why did I bring him with me, right? To be honest, it's because I'm still shaky. Still haven't gotten used to being alone."

"I don't blame you."

"Don't you think I should be past it by now?"

"I probably wouldn't be."

"That's a very nice thing to say."

"It's the truth."

Another smile. She reached over and touched my hand, just for a second. Then back to her coffee cup.

"I'm *sleeping* a little better," she said, "but still far from perfect. In the beginning I'd be up all night, heart pounding away, nauseated. Now I can *get* to sleep, but sometimes I still wake up all in a knot. Sometimes the thought of going to work makes me just want to crawl back in bed. Dick works in Westchester near the airport, so sometimes we take one car and he drops me off and picks me up. I guess I've become pretty dependent on him."

She gave a small smile. The unspoken message: *for a change.*

"Meanwhile, I'm telling the staff and the patients there's nothing to worry about. Nothing like consistency."

Ear brought the food.

"This looks yum," she said, pushing her fork around in her salad bowl. But she didn't eat, and one arm stayed around her purse.

I tried a little linguine. Memories of school lunch.

She nibbled on a piece of lettuce. Dabbed at her mouth. Looked around. Unsnapped the purse.

"You have to promise me to keep this absolutely confidential," she said. "At least where you got it from, okay?"

"Does it relate to Hewitt?"

"In a way. Mostly—it's nothing that can help Detective Sturgis—not that I can see, anyway. I shouldn't even be showing it to you. But people are being harassed and I know what it's like to feel besieged. So if this does lead anywhere, please keep me out of it—please?"

"All right," I said.

"Thank you." She inhaled, shoved her hand into the purse, and drew out a legal-sized envelope. White, clean, unmarked. She held on to it. The paper made her nails look especially red.

"Remember how sketchy Becky's notes on Hewitt were?" she said. "How I made excuses for her, saying she'd been a good therapist but not big on paperwork? Well, it bothered me more than I let on. Even for Becky that was cursory—I guess I just didn't want to deal with anything related to her murder. But after you left, I kept thinking about it and went look-

ing to see if she'd taken any other notes that had
somehow been misfiled. With all the upheaval right
after, housekeeping wasn't exactly a high priority. I
didn't find anything, so I asked Mary, my secretary.
She said all Becky's active charts had been distributed
to other caseworkers, but it was possible some of her
inactive files might have ended up in our storage
room. So she and I took some time on Friday and
looked around for a few hours, and sure enough,
stuck in a corner was a box with Becky's initials on it
—'RB.' Who knows how it got there. Inside was junk
that had been removed from her desk—pens, paper
clips, whatever. Underneath all that, was this.''

Her hand shook slightly as she handed me the
envelope.

I removed the contents. Three sheets of horizon-
tal-ruled chart paper, slightly grimy and bearing deep
fold marks, each partially filled with typed notations.
The first was dated six months ago:

Saw DH today. Still hearing vces, but meds
seem to hlp. Still dealing w strss of strt-life.
Came in with G, both strssd.

> BB, SWA

Three weeks later:

D lots better. Snstv, too. Just meds, or me?
Ha ha. Maybe some hope?

> BB, SWA

Then:

D showing feelngs, more and more. Tlking
lots, too. Very good! Yeah, thrpy! Success!
But keep limits.

> BB, SWA

D cohrnt—hr brshed, totally clean! But still late. Talk re childhd, etc. Some p-c, but approp. G there, waiting. A bit hostl? Jealous? Follow.

BB

D a diff prsn. Open, vrbal, affectnt. Still late. A bit more p-c. Approp? Set lmts? Talk to JJ? Wrth the progrss? Yes!

BB

D late, but less—15 min. Some anx. Hrng vcs? Denies, says strss, alchl—drnkng with G. Talked re G, re rel bet D and G. Some anx, defens, but also opn-mind. More p-c, but ok, relieves anx. O.K.

BB

D looking hppy. Vry vrbl, no angr, no hrng vcs. G not there. Conflct bet G and D? P-c, tried to kss, no hostil when I say no. Good! Approp soc sklls! Rah rah!

BB

The final note was dated three weeks before Becky's murder:

D early—positv change! Yeah! G waits in hall. Definit hostil. Rel bet D and G straind? Re me? D's growth a stress on G? More p-c. Kss, but quick. Much affectn. Talk re this. Boundaries, lmts, etc. D a little down, but dealt w it, approp.

BB

'' 'P-c,' '' I said, putting the papers down. ''Physical contact,'' she said, miserably. ''I went

over and over it and it's the only thing that makes
sense."

I reread the notes. "I think you're right."

"Hewitt was getting attached to her. Progres-
sively more physical."

She shuddered. "Look at the last one. She let him
kiss her. She must have totally lost control of the situation. I had no idea—she never told me."

"She obviously thought of telling you—'talk to
JJ?' "

"But she didn't follow through. Look what she
wrote right after that."

I read out loud: " 'Worth the progress? Yes!'
Sounds like she convinced herself she was helping
him."

"She convinced herself she knew what she was
doing." She shook her head and looked down at the
table. "My God."

"Beginner's euphoria," I said.

"She was such a sweet thing—so naive. I should
have kept a closer eye on her. Maybe if I had, it
could've been prevented." She pushed her salad
away. Her hair hung in a sheet. Her head rested in her
hands and I heard her sigh.

I said, "Hewitt was psychotic, Jean. Who knows
what set him off."

She looked up. "Letting him *kiss* her sure didn't
help! She talks about setting limits, but he probably
saw it as rejection, what with his paranoia!"

She'd allowed her voice to climb. The man at the
next table looked up from his cappuccino. Jean smiled
at him, picked up her napkin, and wiped her face.

I scanned the notes again. *Yeah, therapy! Rah rah!*

She held out her hand. "I need them back."

I gave her the papers and she slipped them back
in the envelope.

I said, "What are you going to do with them?"

"Destroy them. Can you just imagine what the media would do with it? Blaming Becky, turning the whole thing into something sleazy? Please, Alex, keep it to yourself. I don't want to see Becky victimized a second time." She flipped her hair again. "Also, to be perfectly honest, I don't want to be blamed for not supervising her."

"It took guts for you to show it to me," I said.

"Guts?" She laughed softly. "Stupidity, maybe, but for some reason I trust you—I don't even know why I did show it to you—getting it off my chest, I guess."

She put the envelope in her purse and shook her head again.

"How could she have let it *happen*? She talks about *him* trying to touch her and kiss her, but what I got between the lines was her developing some sort of feelings for *him*. All that *p-cing*, as if it was a cute little game. Don't you agree?"

"Fondness for him definitely comes across," I said. "Whether or not it was sexual, I don't know."

"Even if it was plain *affection*, it was irrational. The man was psychotic, couldn't even keep himself *clean*. And this *G* person she keeps mentioning, I still have no idea who *that* is. Probably Hewitt's girlfriend —some other psychotic he met on the street and dragged in with him. Becky was getting herself involved in a love triangle with *psychotics*, for God's sake. How could she? She was naive, but she was bright—how could she have shown such poor judgment?"

"She probably didn't think she was doing anything wrong, Jean. Otherwise, why would she have kept notes?"

"But if she thought what she was doing was okay, why not keep those notes right in Hewitt's chart?"

"Good point," I said.

"It's a mess. I should have supervised her more closely. I should have been more in touch. . . . I just can't understand how she could have let him get that close to her."

"Countertransference," I said. "Happens all the time."

"With someone like that?"

"Prison therapists get attached to convicts. Who knows what causes attraction?"

"*I* should have known."

"No sense blaming yourself. No matter how closely you supervise someone, you can't be with them twenty-four hours a day. She was trained, Jean. It was up to her to tell you."

"I *tried* to supervise her. I made appointments, but she broke more than she kept. Still, I could have clamped down further—I should've. If I'd had any *idea* . . . she never gave a *hint*. Always had a smile on her face, like one of those kids who works at Disneyland."

"She *was* happy," I said. "She thought she was curing him."

"Yup. What a mess . . . I probably showed it to you because you were sympathetic and I'm still so uptight over what happened . . . I thought I could talk to you."

"You can."

"I appreciate that," she said wearily, "but let's be honest. What good will more talking do? Becky's dead and I'm going to have to live with the fact that I might have been able to prevent it."

"I don't see it that way. You did all you could."

"You're sweet." She looked at my hand, as if ready to touch it again. But she didn't move and her eyes shifted to her salad.

"Happy lunch," she said glumly.

"Jean, it's possible the notes might be relevant to Detective Sturgis."

"How?"

" 'G' may not be a woman."

"You *know* who it is?" This time her hand did move. Covering mine, taking hold of my fingers. Ice cold.

"That lawyer whose card you gave me—Andrew Coburg? I went over to see him and he told me Hewitt had a friend named Gritz. Lyle Edward Gritz."

No reaction.

I said, "Gritz is a heavy drinker, and he has a criminal record. He and Hewitt hung out together, and now no one can find him. A week or two ago, Gritz told some street people he expected to get rich, then he disappeared."

"Get rich? How?"

"He didn't say, though in the past he'd talked about becoming a recording star. For all I know, it was drunk talk and has nothing to do with Becky. But if 'G' does refer to him, it indicates tension between him and Becky."

"Gritz," she said. "I assumed G was a woman. Are you saying Hewitt and this Gritz had something homosexual going on and Becky stepped in the middle of it? Oh, God, it just keeps getting worse, doesn't it?"

"Maybe there was nothing sexual between Gritz and Hewitt. Just a close friendship that Becky intruded upon."

"Maybe . . ." She pulled out the envelope, removed the notes, ran her finger down the page, and read. "Yes, I see what you mean. Once you think of G as a man you don't have to see it that way at all. Just friendship. . . . But whatever the reason, Becky felt G was hostile to her."

"She was getting between them," I said. "The

whole therapy process was challenging whatever Hewitt had with Gritz. How did Becky phrase it in that last note?"

"Let me see—here it is: 'Relationship between D and G strained. Me? D's growth?' Yes, I see what you mean. Then right after that, she mentions another p-c —the session where he actually kissed her. . . . You know, you could read this and feel almost as if she was seducing him." She crumpled the notes. "God, what a travesty—why are you interested in this Gritz? You think he could be the one harassing people?"

"It's possible."

"Why? What else has he done criminally?"

"I'm not sure of the details, but the harassment involved the words 'bad love'—"

"What Hewitt screamed . . . Does that actually *mean* something? What's going *on*?"

Her fingers had become laced with mine. I looked at them and she pulled away and fooled with her hair. The flap covered one eye. The exposed one was alive with fear.

I said, "I don't know, Jean. But given the notes, I have to wonder if Gritz played a role in getting Hewitt to murder Becky."

"Played a *role*? How?"

"By working on Hewitt's paranoia—telling Hewitt things about Becky. If he was a close friend, he'd know which buttons to push."

"Oh, God," she said. "And now he's missing . . . it's not over, is it?"

"Maybe it is. This is all conjecture, Jean. But finding Gritz would help clear it up. Any chance he was a patient at the center?"

"The name doesn't ring a bell . . . bad love . . . I thought Hewitt was just raving, now you're saying maybe he was reacting to something that had gone on between him and Becky? That he killed her because she rejected him."

"Could be," I said. "I found a reference to 'bad love' in the psych literature. It's a term coined by a psychoanalyst named Andres de Bosch."

She stared at me, nodded slowly. "I think I've heard of him. What did he say about it?"

"He used it to describe poor child rearing—a parent betraying a child's trust. Building up faith and then destroying it. In extreme cases, he theorized, it could lead to violence. If you consider the therapist-patient relationship similar to child rearing, the same theory could be applied to cases of transference gone really bad. Hewitt may have heard about 'bad love' somewhere—probably from another therapist or even from Gritz. When he felt Becky had rejected him, he fell apart, became a betrayed child—and lashed out violently."

"Betrayed child?" she said. "You're saying his killing her was a *tantrum*?"

"A tantrum heated to the boiling point by Hewitt's delusions. And by his failure to take his medication. Who knows, Gritz may have convinced him not to take it."

"Gritz," she said. "How do you spell it?"

I told her. "Be good to know if he was one of your patients."

"I'll comb the files first thing tomorrow, take that damned storage room *apart* if I have to. If he's anywhere in there, I'll call you right away. We need to know for our own safety."

"I'll be out of town tomorrow. You can leave a message with my service."

"All day tomorrow?" A touch of panic in her voice.

I nodded. "Santa Barbara and back."

"I love Santa Barbara. It's gorgeous. Taking some vacation time?"

"De Bosch used to have a clinic and a school up there. I'm going to try and find out if Hewitt or Gritz were ever patients."

"I'll let you know if he was ours. Call me back, okay? Let me know what you find."

"Sure."

She looked at her salad again. "I can't eat."

I waved Ear over and got the bill.

She said, "No, I invited *you*," and tried to take it, but she didn't put up much of a fight and I ended up paying.

She stashed the notes in her purse and glanced at her watch. "Dick's not coming back for another half an hour."

"I can wait."

"No, I won't keep you. But I wouldn't mind some fresh air. I'll walk you to your car."

Just outside the restaurant she paused to button her sweater and smooth her hair. The first time, the buttons were out of line and she had to redo them.

We walked to the city lot without speaking. She looked in shop windows but seemed uninterested in the wares they displayed. Waiting until I'd redeemed the keys from the attendant, she accompanied me to the Seville.

"Thanks," I said, shaking her hand. I opened the driver's door.

She said, "What I said before still stands, right? About keeping all this quiet?"

"Of course."

"It's nothing Detective Sturgis could ever use, anyway," she said. "Legally speaking—what does it really prove?"

"Just that people are fallible."

"Oh, boy, are they."

I got into the car. She leaned in through the window.

"You're more than just a consultant on this, aren't you?"

"What makes you say that?"

"Your passion. Consultants don't go this far."

I smiled. "I take my work seriously."

She moved her head back, as if I'd blown garlic in her face.

"So do I," she said. "Sometimes I wish I didn't."

20

Monday morning at nine, I set out for Ojai, taking the 405 to the 101 and making it to the strawberry fields of Camarillo in less than an hour. Migrant workers stooped in the stubby, green rows. The crop became blue cabbage and the air turned bitter. Kissy-face billboards boosted housing developments and home equity loans.

Just past the Ventura County Fairgrounds, I turned onto 33 north, speeding by an oil refinery that resembled a giant junkyard. Another few miles of trailer parks and mower rental sheds and things got pretty: two lanes draped by eucalyptus, black mountains off to the northwest, the peaks flesh colored where the sun hit.

The town of Ojai was a quarter of an hour farther, announced by a bike and equestrian trail, orange groves, and signs directing the motorist to the Ojai Palm Spa, the Humanos Theosophic Institute, Marmalade Hot Springs. To the south were the clean, green slopes of a country club. The cars were good-looking and so were the people.

Ojai proper was quiet and slow moving, with one traffic light. The main drag was Ojai Avenue, lined with the kind of low-rise, neo-Spanish architecture that usually means tight zoning laws. Unrestricted parking, plenty of spaces. Tans and smiles, natural fibers and good posture.

On the left side of the avenue, a colonnaded, tile-roofed building was filled with storefronts. Native American art and antiques, body wraps and herbal facials, a Little Olde Tea Shoppe. Across the street was an old theater, freshly adobed. Playing tonight: *Leningrad Cowboys*.

I had my Ventura County Thomas Guide on the passenger seat, but I didn't need it. Signal was a couple of intersections up, and 800 north meant a left turn.

Big trees and small houses, residential lots alternating with olive groves. A drainage ditch paved with fieldstones ran alongside the left side of the street, spanned every few yards by one-stride foot bridges. Wilbert Harrison's address was near the top, one of the last houses before open fields took over.

It was a shingle-roofed wooden cottage painted an odd purplish-red and nearly hidden behind unruly snarls of agave cactus. The purple was vivid and it shone through the agave's sawtooth leaves like a wound. Atop a steep dirt driveway, a Chevy station wagon was parked up against a single garage. Four stone steps led up to the front porch. The screen door was shut, but the wooden one behind it was wide open.

I knocked on the frame while looking into a small, dark living room, plank floored and crowded with old furniture, shawls, throw pillows, an upright piano. A bay window was lined with dusty bottles.

Chamber music came from another room.

I knocked louder.

"One minute." The music turned off and a man appeared from a doorway to the right.

Short. Chubby as in his old picture and white haired. He had on a polyester jumpsuit the same purplish-red as the house. Some of the furniture was upholstered that color, too.

He opened the screen door and gave me a curious but friendly look. His eyes were gray, but they picked up magenta accents from his surroundings. There was a softness to his face, but no weakness.

"Dr. Harrison?"

"Yes, I'm Bert Harrison." His voice was a clear baritone. The jumpsuit was zipped in the front and had large, floppy lapels. Short-sleeved, it exposed white, freckled arms. His face was freckled, too, and I noticed reddish-blond tints in his white hair. He wore a pinkie ring set with a violet cabochon, and a bolo tie with leather thongs held together by a big, shapeless purple rock. Sandals on his feet, no socks.

"My name is Alex Delaware. I'm a clinical psychologist from Los Angeles and I wondered if I could talk to you about Andres de Bosch and 'bad love.'"

The eyes didn't change shape or hue, but they became more focused.

He said, "I know you. We've met somewhere."

"Nineteen seventy-nine," I said. "There was a conference at Western Pediatric Medical Center on de Bosch's work. You presented a paper and I was a co-chair, but we never actually met."

"Yes," he said, smiling. "You were there as the hospital's representative, but your heart wasn't in it."

"You remember that?"

"Distinctly. The entire conference had that flavor —ambivalence all around. You were very young— you wore a beard then, didn't you?"

"Yes," I said, amazed.

"The beginnings of old age," he said, still smiling. "Distant memories become clearer, but I can't remember where I put my keys."

"I'm still impressed, doctor."

"I remember the beard vividly, perhaps because I have trouble growing one. And your voice. Full of stress. Just as it is right now. Well, come in, let's take care of it. Coffee or tea?"

There was a small kitchen beyond the living room and a door that led to a single bedroom. The little I could see of the sleeping chamber was purple and book-lined.

The kitchen table was birch, not more than four feet long. The counters were old white tile trimmed with purple-red bullnoses.

He fixed instant coffee for both of us and we sat. The scale of the table put us close together, elbows nearly touching.

"In answer to your unasked question," he said, whitening his coffee with lots of cream, then adding three spoonfuls of sugar, "it's the only color I can see. A rare genetic condition. Everything else in my world is gray, so I do what I can to brighten it."

"Makes sense," I said.

"Now that that's out of the way, tell me what's on your mind concerning Andres and 'bad love'—that was the title of the conference, wasn't it."

"Yes. You don't seem surprised that I just popped in."

"Oh, I am. But I like surprises—anything that breaks up routine has the ability to freshen our lives."

"This may not be a pleasant surprise, Dr. Harrison. You may be in danger."

His expression didn't change. "How so?"

I told him about the "bad love" tape, my revenge

theory, the possible links to Dorsey Hewitt and Lyle Gritz.

"And you think one of these men may have been a former patient of Andres's?"

"It's possible. Hewitt was thirty-three when he died, and Gritz is a year older, so either of them could have been his patient as a child. Hewitt killed one psychotherapist, perhaps under Gritz's influence, and Gritz is still out there, possibly still trying to even scores."

"What would he be trying to avenge?"

"Some kind of mistreatment—by de Bosch himself or a disciple. Something had happened at the school."

No response.

I said, "Real or imagined. Hewitt was a paranoid schizophrenic. I don't know Gritz's diagnosis, but he may be delusional, as well. The two of them could have influenced each other's pathology."

"Symbiotic psychosis?"

"Or at least shared delusions—playing on each other's paranoia."

He blinked hard. "Tapes, calls . . . no, I haven't experienced anything like that. And the name of this person who giggled over the phone was Silk?"

I nodded.

"Hmm. And what role do you think the conference played?"

"It may have triggered something—I really don't know, but it's my only link to de Bosch. I felt an obligation to tell you because one of the other speakers—Dr. Stoumen—was killed last year, and I haven't been able to loca—"

"Grant?" he said, leaning forward close enough for me to smell the mint on his breath. "I heard he died in an auto accident."

"A hit-and-run accident. While attending a conference. He stepped off the curb and was knocked down by a car. It was never solved, Dr. Harrison. The police put it down to Dr. Stoumen's old age—poor vision, faulty hearing."

"A conference," he said. "Poor Grant—he was a nice man."

"Did he ever work at the school?"

"He did occasional consultations. Coming up summers for a week or two, combining vacation with business. Hit-and-run . . ." He shook his head.

"And as I was saying, I can't locate any of the other speakers or co-chairs."

"You've located me."

"You're the only one, Dr. Harrison."

"Bert, please. Just out of curiosity, how did you find me?"

"From the *Directory of Medical Specialists.*"

"Oh. I suppose I forgot to cancel it." He looked troubled.

"I didn't want to impose on your privacy, but—"

"No, no, that's fine. You're here for my own good . . . and, to tell the truth, I welcome visitors. After thirty years in practice, it's nice to talk to people rather than just listen."

"Do you know where any of the others are? Katarina de Bosch, Mitchell Lerner, Harvey Rosenblatt."

"Katarina is just up the coast, in Santa Barbara."

"She's still there?"

"I haven't heard that she's moved."

"Do you have her address?"

"And her phone number. Here, let me call it for you."

He reached over, pulled a crimson rotary phone from the counter, and put it on the table. As he dialed I wrote down the number on the phone. Then he held the receiver to his ear for a while, before putting it down.

"No answer," he said.

"When's the last time you saw her?"

He thought. "I suppose about a year or so. By coincidence. I was in a bookstore in Santa Barbara and ran into her, browsing."

"Psychology?"

He smiled. "No, fiction, actually. She was in the science-fiction section. Would you like her address?"

"Please."

He wrote it down and gave it to me. Shoreline Drive.

"The ocean side," he said, "just up from the marina."

I remembered the slide Katarina had shown. Blue skies behind a wheelchair. The ocean.

"Did she live there with her father?" I said.

"Since the two of them came to California."

"She was very attached to him, wasn't she?"

"She worshiped him." He continued to look preoccupied.

"Did she ever marry?"

He shook his head.

"When did the school close?" I said.

"Not long after Andres died—eighty-one, I believe."

"Katarina didn't want to keep it going?"

He put his hands around his coffee cup. He had hammer thumbs and his other digits were short. "You'd have to ask her about that."

"Does she do any kind of psychological work now?"

"Not to my knowledge."

"Early retirement?"

He shrugged and drank. Put his cup down and touched the stone of his bolo tie. Something bothering him.

I said, "I only met her twice, but I don't see her as someone with hobbies, Bert."

He smiled. "You encountered the force of her personality."

"She was the reason I was at the conference against my will. She pulled strings with the chief of staff."

"That was Katarina," he said. "Life as target practice: set your sights, aim, and shoot. She pressured me to speak, too."

"You were reluctant?"

"Yes, but let's get back to Grant for a moment. Hit-and-run isn't really the same as premeditated murder."

"Maybe I'm wrong, but I still can't find anyone who was up on that dais."

He grabbed the cup with both hands. "I can tell you about Mitch—Mitchell Lerner. He's dead. Also the result of an accident. Hiking. Down in Mexico—Acapulco. He fell from a high cliff."

"When?"

"Two years ago."

One year before Stoumen, one year after Rodney Shipler. Fill in the gaps. . . .

". . . the time," he was saying, "I had no reason to assume it was anything but an accident. Especially in view of it being a fall."

"Why's that?"

He worked his jaws and his hands went flat on the table. His mouth twisted a couple of times. Anxiety and something else—dentures.

"Mitchell had occasional balance problems," he said.

"Alcohol?"

He stared at me.

"I know about his suspension," I said.

"I'm sorry, I can't talk any more about him."

"Meaning he was your patient—your bio mentioned your specialties. Impaired therapists."

Silence that served as affirmation. Then he said, "He was trying to ease his way back into work. The trip to Mexico was part of that. He was attending a conference there."

He put his finger in his mouth and fooled with his bridgework.

"Well," he said, smiling, "I don't go to conferences anymore, so maybe I'm safe."

"Does the name Myra Paprock mean anything to you?"

He shook his head. "Who is she?"

"A woman who was murdered five years ago. The words 'bad love' were scrawled at the murder scene in her lipstick. And the police have found one other killing where the phrase was written. A man named Rodney Shipler, beaten to death *three* years ago."

"No," he said, "I don't know him, either. Are they therapists?"

"No."

"Then what would they have to do with the conference?"

"Nothing that I know of, but maybe they had something to do with de Bosch. Myra Paprock was working as a real estate agent at the time, but before that she was a teacher in Goleta. Maybe she moonlighted at the Corrective School. This was before she married, so her surname would have been something other than Paprock."

"Myra," he said, rubbing his lip. "There *was* a Myra who taught there when I was consulting. A young woman, just out of college . . . blond, pretty . . . a little . . ." He closed his eyes. "Myra . . . Myra . . . what was her name—Myra *Evans*, I think. Yes, I'm pretty sure that's what it was.

Myra Evans. And now you're saying she was murdered . . ."

"What else were you going to say about her, Bert?"

"Excuse me?"

"You just said she was blond, pretty, and something else."

"Nothing, really," he said. "I just remembered her as being a little hard. Nothing pathologic—the dogmatism of youth."

"Was she rough on the kids?"

"Abusive? I never saw it. It wasn't that kind of place—Andres's force of personality was enough to maintain a certain level of . . . order."

"What was Myra's method for maintaining order?"

"Lots of rules. One of those everything-by-the-rules types. No shades of gray."

"Was Dr. Stoumen like that too?"

"Grant was . . . orthodox. He liked his rules. But he was an extremely gentle person, somewhat shy."

"And Lerner?"

"Anything but rigid. *Lack* of discipline was his problem."

"Harvey Rosenblatt?"

"Don't know him at all. Never met him before the conference."

"So you never saw Myra Evans come down too hard on a child?"

"No . . . I barely remember her—these are just impressions, they may be faulty."

"I doubt it."

He moved his jaws from side to side. "All these murders. You actually think . . ." Shaking his head.

I said, "How important was the concept of 'bad love' to de Bosch's philosophy?"

"I'd say it was fairly central," he said. "Andres was very concerned with justice—he saw achieving consistency in our world as a prime motive. Saw many symptoms as attempts to accomplish that."

"The search for order."

Nod. "And good love."

"When did you become disillusioned about him?"

He looked pained.

I held my gaze and said, "You said Katarina pressured you to speak at the symposium. Why would a faithful student have to be pressured?"

He got up, turned his back on me, and rested his palms on the counter. A little man in ridiculous clothing, trying to bring color to his world.

"I really wasn't that close to him," he said. "After I began my anthropology studies, I wasn't around much." Taking a couple of steps, he wiped the counter with one stubby hand.

"Your own search for consistency?"

He stiffened but didn't turn.

"Racism," he said. "I heard Andres making remarks."

"About who?"

"Blacks, Mexicans."

"Were there black and Mexican children at the school?"

"Yes, but he didn't malign them. It was the workers—hired laborers. There was acreage behind the school. Andres hired people down on lower State Street to come clear the weeds every month or so."

"What did you hear him say about them?"

"The usual garbage—that they were lazy, stupid. Genetically inferior. He called the blacks one half-step up from apes, said the Mexicans weren't much better."

"He said this to your face?"

Hesitation. "No. To Katarina. I overheard it."

I said, "She didn't disagree with him, did she?"

He turned around. "She *never* disagreed with him."

"How did you happen to overhear their conversation?"

"I wasn't eavesdropping," he said. "That would almost have been better. I walked in on the middle of the conversation and Andres didn't bother to interrupt himself. That really troubled me—the fact that he thought I would laugh along with it. And it wasn't just once—I heard him say those things several times. Almost taunting me. I didn't respond. He was my teacher and I became a worm."

He returned to his chair, slumping a bit.

I said, "Did Katarina respond at all to his remarks?"

"She laughed. . . . I was disgusted. Lord knows I'm no paragon of virtue, I've done my share of pretending to listen to patients when my mind was elsewhere. Pretending to care. Been married five times, never longer than twenty-six months. When I finally achieved enough insight to realize I should stop making women's lives miserable, I opted for the solitary life. Drew plenty of blood along the way, so I don't put myself up on any moral pedestal. But I *have* always prided myself on tolerance—I'm sure part of it is personal. I was born with multiple anomalies. Other things besides the lack of color vision."

He looked away, as if considering his choices. Held out his short fingers and waved them. Pointing at his mouth, he said, "I'm completely edentulous. Born without adult teeth. My right foot has three toes, the left one is clubbed. I'm unable to sire children and one of my kidneys atrophied when I was three. Most of my childhood was spent in bed due to severe skin rashes and a hole in the ventricular septum of my heart. So I guess I'm a little sensitive to discrimination. But I didn't speak up, just left the school."

I nodded. "Did de Bosch's intolerance come out in other ways?"

"No, that's the thing. On a day-to-day basis, he was extremely liberal. *Publicly*, he was liberal—took in minority patients, most of them charity cases, and seemed to treat them as well as the others. And in his writings, he was *brilliantly* tolerant. Have you ever read his essay on the Nazis?"

"No."

"Brilliant," he repeated. "He composed it while fighting in the French Resistance. Taking the bastards' own pseudo-theories of racial superiority and throwing it all back in their faces with good, sound science. That was one of the things that attracted me to him when I was a resident. The *combination* of social conscience and psychoanalysis. Too many analysts live in a twelve-foot-square world—the office as universe, rich people on the couch, summers in Vienna. I wanted more."

"Is that why you studied anthropology?"

"I wanted to learn about other cultures. And Andres supported me in that. Told me it would make me a better therapist. He *was* a great mentor, Alex. That's why it was so crushing to hear him sneer at those field hands—like seeing one's father in a disgusting light. I swallowed it in silence several times. Finally, I resigned and left town."

"For Beverly Hills?"

"I did a year of research in Chile, then caved in and returned to my own twelve-foot-square world."

"Did you tell him why you were leaving?"

"No, just that I was unhappy, but he understood." He shook his head. "He was an intimidating man. I was a coward."

"It had to take force of personality to dominate Katarina."

"Oh, yes, and he did dominate her . . . after I returned from Chile, he called me just once. We had a frosty conversation, and that was that."

"But Katarina wanted you at the conference anyway."

"She wanted me because I was part of his past—the glory years. By then he was a vegetable and she was *resurrecting* him. She brought me pictures of him in his wheelchair. 'You abandoned him once, Bert. Don't do it again.' Guilt's a great motivator."

He looked away. Worked his jaws.

"I don't see any obvious tie-in," I said, "but Rodney Shipler, the man who was beaten to death, was black. At the time of his murder, he was a school janitor in L.A. Do you have any memory of him at all?"

"No, that name isn't familiar." He looked back at me. Edgy—guilty?

"What is it, Bert?"

"What's what?"

"Something's on your mind." I smiled. "Your face is full of stress."

He smiled back and sighed. "Something came into my mind. Your Mr. Silk. Probably irrelevant."

"Something about Lerner?"

"No, no, this is something that happened after the 'bad love' conference—soon after, a couple of days, I believe." He closed his eyes and rubbed his forehead, as if coaxing forth memories.

"Yes, it was two or three days," he said, working his jaws again. "I received a call in my office. After hours. I was on my way out and I picked up the phone before the answering service could get to it. A man was on the other end, very agitated, very angry. A young man—or at least he sounded young. He said he'd sat through my speech at the conference and wanted to make an appointment. Wanted to go into long-term psychoanalysis with me. But the way he said it—hostile, almost sarcastic—brought my guard up, and I asked him what kinds of problems he was experiencing. He said there were many—too many to go into over the phone and that my speech had reminded him of them. I asked him how, but he wouldn't say. His voice was *saturated* with stress—real suffering. He demanded to know if I was going to help him. I said, of course, I'd stay late and see him right away."

"You considered it a crisis?"

"At the least, a borderline crisis—there was real pain in his voice. An ego highly at risk. And," he smiled, "I had no pressing engagements other than dinner with one of my wives—the third one, I think. You can see why I was such a poor matrimonial prospect. . . . Anyway, to my surprise, he said no, right now wasn't a good time for him, but he could come in the next evening. Standoffish, all of a sudden. As if *I'd* come on too strong for *him.* I was a bit taken aback, but you know patients—the resistance, the ambivalence."

I nodded.

He said, "So we made an appointment for the following afternoon. But he never showed up. The phone number he'd given me was out of order and he wasn't listed in any local phone books. I thought it odd, but after all, odd is our business, isn't it? I thought about it for a while, then I forgot about it. Until today. His being at the conference . . . all that anger." Shrug. "I don't know."

"Was his name Silk?"

"This is the part I hesitate about, Alex. He never became my patient, formally, but in a sense he was.

Because he asked for help and I counseled him over the phone—or at least I attempted to."

"There was no formal treatment, Bert. I don't see any problem, legally."

"That's not the point. Morally, it's an issue—moral issues transcend the law." He slapped his own wrist and smiled. "Gawd, doesn't that sound self-righteous."

"There *is* a moral issue," I said. "But weigh it against the alternatives. Two definite murders. Three if you include Grant Stoumen. Maybe four, if someone pushed Mitchell Lerner off that cliff. Myra Paprock was raped, as well. Taken apart physically. She left two small children. I just met her husband. He still hasn't healed."

"You're quite good at guilt yourself, young man."

"Whatever works, Bert. How's that for a moral stance?"

He smiled. "No doubt you're a practical therapist. . . . No his name wasn't Silk. Another type of fabric. That's what made me think of it. Merino." He spelled it out.

"First name?"

"He didn't give one. Called himself 'Mister.' Mr. Merino. It sounded pretentious in someone so young. Awful insecurity."

"Can you pinpoint his age?"

"Twenties—early twenties would be my guess. He had a young man's impetuousness. Poor impulse control to call like that and make demands. But he was stressed, and stress causes regression, so maybe he was older."

"When was the Corrective School established?"

"Nineteen sixty-two."

"So if he was in his twenties in seventy-nine, he

could easily have been a patient. Or one of the field hands—Merino's an Hispanic name."

"Or someone with no connection to the school at all," he said. "What if he was just someone with deep-seated problems who sat in on the conference and reacted to it for one reason or another?"

"Could be," I said, calculating silently: Dorsey Hewitt would have been around eighteen in 1979. Lyle Gritz, a year older.

"All right," I said, "thanks for telling me, and I won't give out the information unless it's essential. Is there anything else you remember that might help?"

"No, I don't think so. Thank *you*. For warning me."

He looked around his small house with longing. I knew the feeling.

"Do you have a place to go?" I said.

Nod. "There are always places. New adventures."

He walked me to my car. The heat had turned up a bit and the air was thick with honeybees.

"Off to Santa Barbara now?" he said.

"Yes."

"Give Katarina my best when you see her. The easiest way is Highway 150. Pick it up just out of town and take it all the way. It's no more than a half-hour drive."

"Thanks."

We shook hands.

"One more thing, Bert?"

"Yes?"

"Mitchell Lerner's problems. Could they have resulted in any way from his work at the school—or did they *cause* problems there?"

"I don't know," he said. "He never spoke about the school. He was a *very* closed person—highly defensive."

"So you did ask him about it?"

"I asked him about every element of his past. He refused to talk about anything but his drinking. And even then, just in terms of getting rid of a bad habit. In his own work, he despised behaviorism, but when it came to his therapy, he wanted to be reconditioned. Overnight. Something short term and discreet—hypnosis, whatever."

"You're an analyst. Why did he come to you?"

"Safety of the familiar." He smiled. "And I've been known to be pragmatic from time to time."

"If he was so resistant, why'd he bother to go into therapy in the first place?"

"As a condition of his probation. The social work ethics committee demanded it, because it had affected his work—missed appointments, failure to submit insurance forms so his patients could recover. I'm afraid he acted the same way as a patient. Not showing up, very unreliable."

"How long did you see him?"

"Obviously, not long enough."

21

There seemed little doubt that Myra Evans and Myra Paprock were the same person. And that her murder and the deaths of others were related to de Bosch and his school.

Silk. Merino.

The conference putting someone in touch with his problems . . . some sort of trauma.

Bad love.

Taken apart.

A child's voice chanting.

I felt a sudden stab of panic about leaving Robin alone, stopped in the center of Ojai, and called her from a pay phone. No answer. The Benedict number had been channeled through my answering service, and on the fifth ring an operator picked up.

I asked her if Robin had left word where she was going.

"No, she didn't, doctor. Would you like your messages?"

"Please."

"Just one, actually, from a Mr. Sturgis. He called

to say Van Nuys will be getting to your tape soon—
got a broken stereo, Dr. Delaware?"

"Nothing that simple," I said.

"Well, you know how it is, doctor. They keep
making things more complicated so people have to
feel stupid."

I picked up 150 a few miles out of town and
headed northwest on two curving lanes. Lake Casitas
meandered parallel to the highway, massive and gray
under a listless sun. The land side was mostly avocado groves, gold tipped with new growth. Halfway
to Santa Barbara, the road reconnected with 101 and I
traveled the last twelve miles at freeway speed.

I kept thinking about what Harrison had told me
about de Bosch's racism and wondered what I'd tell
Katarina when I found her, how I'd approach her.

I got off the highway without an answer, bought
gas, and called the number Harrison had given me.
No answer. Deciding to delay confrontation for a
while, I looked through my Thomas Guide for the site
where the Corrective School had once been. Near the
border with Montecito, several miles closer than
Shoreline Drive—an omen.

It turned out to be a straight, shady street lined
with gated properties. The eucalyptus here grew
huge, but the trees looked dried out, almost des-
iccated. Despite the fire risk, shake roofs were in
abundance. So were Mercedes.

The exact address corresponded to a new-looking
tract behind high stone walls. A sign advertised six
custom homes. What I could see of them was massive
and cream colored.

Across the way was a pink and brown Tudor
mansion with a sign out in front that said THE BANCROFT
SCHOOL. A semicircular gravel drive girdled the build-

ing. A black Lincoln was parked under a spreading live oak.

A man got out of the car. Midsixties—old enough to remember. I drove across the road, pulled up next to his driver's side, and lowered my window.

His expression wasn't friendly. He was big and powerful looking, dressed in tweeds and a light blue sweater vest despite the heat, and he had very white, very straight hair and knocked-about features. A leather briefcase—an old one with a brass clasp—dangled from one hand. The leather had been freshly oiled—I could smell it. Several pens were clasped to his breast pocket. He looked the Seville over with narrow, dark eyes, then had a go at my face.

"Excuse me," I said, "was the Corrective School once across the street?"

Scowl. "That's right." He turned to leave.

"How long has it been gone?"

"Quite a while. Why?"

"I just had a few questions about it."

He put his briefcase down and peered into the car. "Are you an . . . alumnus?"

"No."

He looked relieved.

"Do alumni come back frequently?" I said.

"No, not frequently, but . . . you do know what kind of school it was."

"Troubled children."

"A bad lot. We were never happy with it—we were here first, you know. My father broke ground thirty years before *they* came."

"Really."

"We were here before most of the houses. This was all agricultural back then."

"Did the students from the Corrective School cause problems?"

"And what's your interest in that?"

"I'm a psychologist," I said, and gave him a card. "I'm doing some consulting to the Los Angeles Police Department, and there's some evidence one of the alumni is involved in something unpleasant."

"Something unpleasant. Well, that's not much of a surprise, is it?" He scowled again. His eyebrows were bushy, low-set, and still dark, giving him a look of perpetual annoyance. "What kind of unpleasantness?"

"I'm sorry but I can't go into detail—is it Mr. Bancroft?"

"It certainly is." He produced a card of his own, white, heavy stock, a heraldic shield in one corner.

The Bancroft School
Est. 1933 by Col. C. H. Bancroft (Ret.)

"Building Scholarship and Character"

Condon H. Bancroft, Jr., B.A., M.A., Headmaster

"By unpleasant do you mean criminal?" he said.

"It's possible."

He gave a knowing nod.

I said, "Why did the place close down?"

"He died—the Frenchman—and no one was left to run it. It's an art, education."

"Didn't he have a daughter?"

His eyebrows arched. "She offered me the place, but I turned her down. Error on my part—I should have done it for the land alone. Now they've come and built *those*." He cast a glare at the stone wall.

"They?"

"Some sort of foreign group. Asians, of course. She offered me all of it, lock, stock. But she wanted an outlandish amount of money and refused to negotiate. For *them*, money's no object."

"She's still here in town, isn't she?"

"She's in Santa *Barbara*," he said.

I wondered where he thought he was, then I answered my own question: Montecito wannabee.

"This unpleasantness," he said. "It isn't anything that would—*impinge* upon my school, is it? I don't want publicity, the police traipsing around."

"Did de Bosch's students ever impinge?"

"No, because I made sure they didn't. For all practical purposes, this property line was as impermeable as the Berlin Wall." He drew a line in the gravel with the toe of one wingtip. "Some of them had been to reform school. Fire setters, bullies, truants —all sorts of miscreants."

"Must have been difficult being this close."

"No, it wasn't *difficult*," he reprimanded. "If they chanced to wander, I sent them hopping right back."

"So you never had any problems?"

"Noise was a problem. There was always too much noise. The only *untoward* thing occurred after they were gone. One of them showed up and made quite a nuisance of himself." Smile. "His condition didn't speak well of the Frenchman's methods."

"What condition was that?"

"A *tramp*," he said. "Unwashed, uncombed, high on drugs—his eyes had that look."

"How do you know he was an alumnus?"

"Because he told me he was. Said it in those words: 'I'm an alumnus.' As if that should have impressed me."

"How long ago was this?"

"Quite a while—let's see, I was interviewing the Crummer boy. The youngest one, and he applied around . . . ten years ago."

"And how old was this tramp?"

"Twenties. A real churl. He barged right into my office, past my secretary. I was interviewing young Crummer and his parents—a fine family, the elder boys had attended Bancroft quite successfully. The scene *he* created dissuaded them from sending the youngest lad here."

"What did he want?"

"*Where* was the school? *What* had happened to it? Raising his voice and creating a scene—poor Mrs. Crummer. I thought I'd have to call the police, but I was finally able to convince him to leave by telling him the Frenchman was long dead."

"That satisfied him?"

The eyebrows dipped. "I don't know *what* it did to him but he left. Lucky for him—I'd had my fill." A big fist shook. "He was insane—*must* have been on drugs."

"Can you describe him?"

"Dirty, uncombed—what's the difference? And he didn't have a car, he walked away on foot—I watched him. Probably on his way to the highway. God help anyone who picked him up."

He watched me leave, too, standing with his arms folded across his chest as I drove away. I realized I hadn't heard or seen any children at his school.

Bullies and fire setters. A tramp in his twenties.

Trying to dig up the past.

The same man who'd called Harrison?

Merino.

Silk. A thing for fabrics.

Hewitt and Gritz, two tramps who would have been in their twenties back then.

Myra Paprock was killed five years ago. Two years after that, Shipler. Then Lerner. Then Stoumen. Was Rosenblatt still alive?

Katarina was, just a few miles up this beautiful road. That gave us something in common.   .

I was ready to talk to her.

*   *   *

Cabrillo Boulevard swept up past the ocean, cleansed of the weekend tourist swarm and the bad sidewalk art. The wharf looked depopulated and its far end disappeared in a bank of fog. A few cyclists pumped in the bike lane and joggers and speed walkers chased immortality. I passed the big new hotels that commandeered the prime ocean views and the motels that followed them like afterthoughts. Passed a small seafood place where Robin and I had eaten shrimp and drunk beer. People were eating there now, laughing, tan.

Santa Barbara was a beautiful place, but sometimes it spooked me. Too much psychic space between the haves and the have-nots and not enough geography. A walk up State Street took you from welfare hotels and mean bars to custom jewelers, custom tailors, and two-bucks-a-scoop ice cream. The fringes of Isla Vista and Goleta were as hard as any inner city, but Montecito was still a place where people ate cake. Sometimes the tension seemed murderous.

I pictured Andres de Bosch trolling lower State for day laborers. His daughter listening and laughing as he dehumanized those he'd found. . . .

Cabrillo climbed higher and emptied of pedestrians, and I caught an eyeful of endless Pacific. Sailboats were out in force at the marina, most of them floundering as they searched for a tailwind. Nearer to the horizon, fishing scows sat, still as artist's models. The boulevard flattened once again, turned into Shoreline and got residential. I began checking the numbers on the curb.

Most of the houses were fifties rancheros, several of them in renovation. I remembered the neighborhood as well planted. Today, lots of the plants were gone, and the ones that remained looked discouraged.

The drought had come hard to this town kissed by salt water.

The lawns were suffering the most, most of them dead or dying. A few were vivid green—too green.

Spray paint.

Santa Barbara, trying to free itself from dependence on Sierra snowpack, had declared mandatory rationing long before L.A. Now the town was returning to desert, but the addiction to emerald was hard to shake.

I reached Katarina's house. Older than its neighbors and considerably smaller, a pale blue, English country cottage with two turrets, a slate roof that needed mending, and a big dirt expanse in front. A privet hedge rimmed the plot, uneven, and picked apart in spots. What had once been a rose garden was now a collection of trellised sticks.

An old-fashioned wire-link gate was fastened across an asphalt driveway, but as I pulled up I could see it was unlocked. I got out and pushed it open and walked up the drive. The asphalt was old and cracked, stretching a hundred feet to the tail end of a small, Japanese car.

Drapes whited all the windows of the house. The front door was paneled oak, its varnish bubbling, a NEIGHBORHOOD WATCH sticker affixed just below the lion's head knocker. Below that was another one, bearing the name of an alarm company.

I rang the bell. Waited. Did it again. Waited some more. Used the lion. Nothing.

No one was around. I could hear the ocean.

I went around the side, past the little white car and a high-peaked garage with sagging swivel doors left half open. The backyard was twice the size of the front plot and denuded. The borders with its neighbors were obscured by thick plantings of dead citrus and dead avocado. On the ground were shapeless patches of lifeless shrubbery. Even the weeds were struggling.

But a couple of giant pines toward the back had survived nicely, their roots deep enough to tap into groundwater. Their trunks yearned for the ragged cliff that overlooked the beach. Through their boughs, the ocean was gray lacquer. The property was at least a hundred feet up, but the tide was a drum roll, loud enough to block out every other sound.

I looked at the rear of the house. Buttoned up and curtained. Near the cliff was an old redwood table and two chairs, guano specked and faded to ash. But half of the table was covered with a white tablecloth, and on the cloth were a cup and saucer and a plate.

I walked over. Coffee dregs in the cup, crumbs on the plate, and an orange smear that looked like ossified marmalade.

The ocean grumbled and seabirds shrieked in response. I walked to the edge of the cliff. To the spot where Katarina had photographed her father, slumped in his wheelchair.

Dry dirt. No fence, easy fall. I peered over and a splinter of vertigo pierced my chest. When it subsided, I looked over again. The hillside was gouged with erosion—giant fingermarks that traced a dead drop down to the rocky beach.

The gulls screamed again—a reprimand that reminded me I was trespassing.

The coffee and crumbs said Katarina was in town. Probably gone out for an errand.

I could wait here, but the more efficient thing would be to call Milo and catch him up on Becky Basille's notes, Harrison, and Bancroft.

As I started to leave, I passed the garage once again and saw the rear end of another car, parked in front of the little white sedan. Bigger and darker—black. The distinctive vertical slash taillights of a Buick Electra. Same car I'd seen at the front of the hospital, in seventy-nine.

Something near the rear tire.

Fingers. White and thin. A hand, the top speckled by an eczematous rash.

No, another kind of speckling.

Darker than eczema.

She was lying on the cement floor, faceup, parallel to the Buick, nearly concealed under the chassis. The other hand was over her head, palm exposed, gouged with deep cuts. Tendons looped from some of the wounds, limp as tired elastic bands.

Defense cuts.

She had on a pink housedress under a white terry cloth robe. The robe was splayed open and the dress was pushed up past her waist, nearly reaching her chin. Her feet were bare, the soles grimed by garage dirt. Her eyeglasses were a few feet away, one of the sidepieces twisted nearly off, one of the lenses cracked.

Her neck was cut, too, but most of the damage had been done to her abdomen. It was black and red —ripped apart, a jumble of viscera—but oddly bloated.

The vertigo returned. I wheeled around, then checked my back. I faced the body again and felt myself grow weirdly calm. Time slowed and an internal rush and roar filled my head, as if the ocean had been transplanted there.

Something missing. Where was the inevitable message?

I forced myself to look for red letters.

Searching for two words . . . nothing. Nothing in the garage but the car and Katarina and a small metal workbench off to one side, backed by a pegboard panel.

A workbench like Robin's, but cluttered with

paint cans, tools, gluepots, jars of shellac. Hanging from the pegboard, hooks bearing hammers, gouges, chisels—one of the chisel hooks empty.

A knife on the table, its blade glazed red.

Birchwood handle. Wide tapered blade. Everything glazed . . . the bench stained, but no words, just a spatter of stains.

Old paint blotches. New ones. All mixed in with the telltale red-brown.

Dribs and droplets but no proclamation.

Something white underneath the handle of the killing tool.

A scrap of paper. Not white—almost white, beige. A nice, classy shade of ecru.

Business card.

Confident-looking brown letters said:

SDI, Inc.
9817 Wilshire Boulevard
Suite 1233
Beverly Hills, CA 90212

Something else.

In the upper right.

Tiny.

Hand printed by ballpoint.

Printed neatly, the characters identical to the lettering on my tape package.

So much pressure on the pen that the stiff paper had been torn through in spots.

BL!

22

I ran down the driveway, threw myself into the car, and sped down to the marina. There was a pay phone on the boat moorings, near some trash cans. The stench was welcome.

I tried Robin again. Still no answer.

A detective at West L.A. Robbery-Homicide said, "He's not in."

"It's an emergency."

"Sorry, don't know where he is."

"Maybe he's out in his car," I said. "Could you try radioing him?"

His voice hardened: "Who is this?"

"Assistant Chief Murchison," I said without thinking, marveling at the ease of the lie.

Second of silence. Something that might have been a gulp. "One moment, sir."

Thirty seconds later: "Sturgis."

"It's me, Milo—"

Pause.

"Alex," I said.

"You palmed yourself off as *Murchison*?"

"Katarina's dead. I just found her body." I gave him the details, describing the crime scene in a rapid word storm. The card with the "bad love" message.

"Same printing as the package the tape came in."

"SDI," he said.

"It's right there in Beverly Hills. Maybe he chose to use it for the message for a reason."

"SDI . . . sure as hell not the Strategic Defense Initiative."

"Could you check on Robin? I know the place is secure, but the killer's picking up speed, and the idea of her being alone up there . . . I tried calling her twice, but she's not in."

"Probably went out to do some shopping, but I'll stop by."

"Thanks. What do I do now? I haven't even called the local police yet."

"Where are you?"

"Pay phone, a few minutes from the house."

"Okay, go back there. Stay away from the actual crime scene and just wait. I'll call Santa Barbara PD, tell 'em you're kosher, then I'll head up there myself —what time is it?—three-thirty . . . I should be there by six, the latest."

I waited near the cliff, as far from the garage as I could be. Staring at the ocean, inhaling brine, and trying to make sense of things.

Two young uniforms showed up first. One stayed with the body and the other took a superficial report from me—name, rank, serial number, time and place —listening courteously and just a bit suspiciously.

Twenty minutes later, a pair of detectives arrived. One was a woman named Sarah Grayson, tall, slim, attractive, in her forties. Her eyes were slightly slanted, colored an even brown. They moved slowly but frequently. Taking things in. Reserving judgment.

Her partner was a big, heavy man named Steen, with a bushy dark mustache and not much hair on top. He went straight into the garage and left me to Grayson.

Somehow we'd ended up back near the cliff edge. I told her tape recorder everything I knew, and she listened without interruption. Then she pointed at the water and said, "There's a seal flipping around out there."

I followed her arm and made out a small black dot, ten breaststrokes from the tideline, cutting a perpendicular line through the breakwaters.

"Or a sea lion," she said. "Those are the ones with the ears, right?"

I shrugged.

"Let's go over it again, doctor."

When I finished, she said, "So you were looking for Dr. de Bosch to warn her about this revenge nut?"

"That, and I wanted to find out if she could tell me anything about why he's *out* for revenge."

"And you think it has something to do with this school?"

"She and her father ran it. It's the only thing I can come up with."

"What was the exact name of the school?" she said.

"The de Bosch Institute and Corrective School. It closed in eighty-one."

"And you thought she'd know what happened because she was the owner's daughter."

I nodded and looked at the rear of the house. "There could be records in there. Therapy notes, something about an incident that traumatized one of the students enough to set him off years later."

"What kind of students went to this school?"

"Emotionally disturbed. Mr. Bancroft, the owner of the school across the street, described them as anti-social—fire setters, truants, and other miscreants."

She smiled. "I know Mr. Bancroft. So when do you think this traumatic episode might have occurred?"

"Some time before nineteen seventy-nine."

"Because of that conference?"

"That's right."

She thought for a while. "And how long was the school around?"

"From nineteen sixty-two to eighty-one."

"Well, that's verifiable," she said, more to herself than to me. "Maybe if there was a trauma we'll have a record of it. Assuming something happened."

"What do you mean?"

"You just told me you think this guy's crazy, doctor—this supposed avenger." She kept her eyes on me and turned one of her earrings. "So maybe he cooked it all up in his head."

"Maybe, but being psychotic doesn't mean being totally delusional—most psychotics have periods of lucidity. And psychotics can be traumatized, too. Plus, he might not even be psychotic. Just extremely disturbed."

She smiled again. "You sound like an expert witness. Cautious."

"I've been to court."

"I know—Detective Sturgis told me. And I discussed you with Judge Stephen Huff, too, just to play it safe."

"You know Steve?"

"Know him well. I used to work juvenile down in L.A. Steve was handling that kind of thing, back then. I know Milo, too. You keep good company, doctor."

She looked at the house. "This victim down in

L.A.—Ms. Paprock. You think she taught at the school?"

"Yes. Under the name of Evans. Myra Evans. Her day job was with the public school system in Goleta. There might still be records of that. And the male victim, Rodney Shipler, worked as a school janitor in L.A., so he may have had a similar job up here."

"Shipler," she said, still looking at the house. "Whereabouts in L.A. do you practice?"

"Westside."

"Child counseling?"

"I do mostly forensic work now. Custody evaluations, injury cases."

"Custody—*that* can get mean." She turned her earring again. "Well, we'll go and look around in the house soon as the tech team and the coroner come and okay it."

She gazed at the ocean some more, brought her eyes back to the redwood table, and lingered on the coffee cup.

"Having her breakfast," she said. "The dregs still haven't solidified, so my guess is this is from this morning."

I nodded. "That's why I thought she was home. But if she was eating out here and he surprised her, wouldn't the house be open? Look how sealed up it looks. And why didn't anyone hear her scream?"

Holding up a finger, she slung her purse over her shoulder and went to the garage. She and Steen came out a few minutes later. He was holding a metal tape measure and a camera, listening to her and nodding.

She took something out of her purse. Surgical gloves. After shaking them out, she donned them and tried a rear door. It opened. She stuck her head inside for a moment, then drew it back.

Another conference with Steen.

Back to me.

"What's in there?" I said.

"Total mess," she said, wrinkling her nose.

"Another body?"

"Not that I can see so far. . . . Look, doctor, it's going to take a long time to get things sorted out here. Why don't you just try to relax until Detective Sturgis gets here? Sorry you can't sit on these chairs, but if you don't mind the grass, get yourself a place over on that side." Indicating the south end of the yard. "I already checked it for footprints and it's okay—ah, look, there's another sea lion. It's real pretty up here, isn't it?"

Milo made it by five forty-eight. I'd staked out a position in a corner of the yard, and he walked straight to it after talking to Grayson.

"Robin was still out when I checked," he said. "Her truck and her purse were gone and so was the dog, and she'd written down something on the fridge pad about salad, so she probably went shopping. I saw absolutely nothing wrong. Don't worry."

"Maybe she should stay with you."

"Why?"

"I'm not safe to be around."

He looked at me. "Okay, sure, if it helps your peace of mind. But we'll *keep* you safe."

He put a hand on my shoulder for a moment, then entered the garage and stayed there for twenty minutes or so. The coroner had come and gone and so had the body, and the technicians were still working, dusting and peeking and making casts. I watched them until Milo came out.

"Let's go," he said.

"Where?"

"Out of here."

"They don't need me anymore?"

"Did you tell Sally everything you know?"

"Yup."

"Then let's go."

We left, passing the garage. Steen was on his knees by a chalk body outline, talking into a tape recorder. Sarah Grayson was standing near him, writing in a notepad. She saw me and waved, then returned to her work.

"Nice lady," I said, as we walked away.

"She was one of Central Juvey's best investigators, used to be married to one of the watch commanders—real asshole, mean drunk. Rumor had it he was rough on her and the kids."

"Physically rough?"

He shrugged. "I never saw bruises, but he had a vicious temper. Finally, they got divorced, and a couple of months later he came over to her place, raising a ruckus, and ended up shooting himself in the foot and losing a toe." Smile. "Whole big investigation. Afterward, Sally moved up here and the asshole retired on disability and packed out to Idaho."

"In the foot," I said. "Not exactly a marksman."

He smiled again. "Actually, he was a crack shot, had once been a range instructor. A lot of people found it hard to believe he'd done it to himself, but you know how it is with chronic alcohol abuse. All that loss of *muscle* control. No telling."

We reached the street. Santa Barbara police cars were parked at the curb, sandwiching the Seville. Neighbors were pressing up against the crime scene tape, and a TV van was driving up. I looked in vain for Milo's Fiat or an unmarked.

"Where's your car?"

"Back in L.A. I took a chopper."

"To where?"

"The airport."

"How'd you get here from there?"

"Santa Barb uniform picked me up."

"Status," I said. "Hoo-hah."

"Yeah," he said. "Sally used to live in Mar Vista. I was the detective on her ex's toe job."

"Oh."

"Yeah. Oh. Now *you* drive me. Let's split before the press leeches start sucking."

I headed down Cabrillo. He said, "Are you too wiped out or grossed out to eat?"

"I haven't eaten since breakfast. I can probably hold something down, or at least watch you."

"Voyeur—this looks okay, pull in." He pointed to a small seafood place tucked next to one of the beach motels. Inside was a scattering of oilcloth-draped tables with abalone-shell ashtrays, sawdust floors, netted walls, a live bar, and a self-order counter. The special of the day was salmon and chips. Both Milo and I ordered it, took a number, and sat down at a window table. We tried to look through the traffic at the water. A young waitress inquired if we wanted anything to drink, brought us two beers, and left us alone.

I called Robin again, using a phone at the back, next to a cigarette machine. Still out. When I got back to the table, Milo was wiping foam from his upper lip.

"Katarina was pregnant," he said. "Coroner actually found the fetus hanging out of her."

"God," I said, remembering the mess and the bloated abdomen. "How far along was she?"

"Five to six months. Coroner could tell it was a boy."

I tried to push aside my revulsion. "Harrison

said she never married and she lived alone. Who could the father have been?"

"Probably some med student with a Mensa membership. SDI stands for Seminal Depository and Inventory."

"A sperm bank?"

"This particular one claims to screen its donors for both brains and brawn."

"Designer babies," I said. "Yeah, I can see Katarina going for something like that. Artificial insemination would give her total control over the child rearing, no emotional entanglements. . . . At five months she'd probably be showing. That's why the killer concentrated on her belly—focused his anger there. Wiping out de Bosch's line."

He frowned.

I said, "Maybe the sperm bank's card was chosen for the message for that same reason. The way it was pinned under the murder weapon was deliberate—setting the scene. It's all a big ritual for him."

The waitress brought the food. A look at our faces erased the smile on hers.

I said, "He's trying to obliterate everything associated with de Bosch. And once again, he used a weapon he found on hand. Turning the victim against herself—insult *and* injury. Trying to reverse what he thinks was done to him. But he must have brought another weapon with him, to intimidate her."

"His fists could have been all he needed for that. Lots of bruises around her eyes."

"Did he hit her hard enough to knock her out?"

"Hard to tell without an autopsy, but Sally said the coroner didn't think so."

"If she was conscious, why didn't anyone hear her scream?"

"Sometimes people don't scream," he said. "Lots of times they freeze and can't get a sound out. Or the head blows could have stunned her. Even if she did scream, it might not have helped. Neighbors on both sides are away, and the ocean blocks out lots of sound to begin with."

"What about other neighbors? Didn't anyone see someone enter the property?"

"No one's come forward yet. Sally and Steen are gonna do a door-to-door canvass."

"Sally said the house was a mess. Did she mean poor housekeeping or a toss?"

"A toss. There was overturned furniture, ripped upholstery."

"Rage," I said. "Or he could have been looking for old school records. Something that might incriminate him."

"Getting rid of the evidence? He's been bumping off people for years, why start covering now?"

"Maybe he's getting more nervous."

"My experience is just the opposite," he said. "Killers acquire a taste for it, enjoy it more and more and get careless."

"Hope he did get careless and you find something in there."

"It'll take a couple of days to do a thorough workover."

"From the outside, the place looked sealed up. If I hadn't seen the breakfast dishes, I would have assumed Katarina was out of town. The killer must have closed the drapes after he killed her, then tossed in peace."

"Like you said, it's a ritual, something he sets up carefully."

"So, we're not dealing with a raving psychotic. Everything that's happened is too calculated for a schizophrenic: traveling around to conventions, simulating accidents. Skewering my fish. Taping Hewitt screaming. Stalking, delaying gratification for years.

This is calculated cruelty, Milo. Some kind of psycho-path. Becky's notes mean we have to look at Gritz carefully. If he's Silk-Merino, his street-bum-alkie thing may be a disguise. The perfect disguise, when you think about it, Milo. The homeless are every-where, part of the scenery. To most of us they all look alike. I remember seeing a guy at Coburg's office. He looked so similar to Hewitt it startled me. All Bancroft really remembered about his intruder, besides age, was dirt and hair."

He thought. "How many years ago did Bancroft say this guy barged in?"

"Around ten. The guy was in his twenties, so he'd be in his thirties now, which would fit Gritz. Bert Harrison's Mr. Merino fits that time frame, too. Both Merino and Bancroft's tramp were agitated. Merino talked about the conference putting him in touch with his problems. A few years later, the tramp returned to his old school, causing a scene, trying to dig up his past. So it could be the same guy, or maybe there are lots of Corrective School alumni wandering around, trying to put their lives together. Whatever the case, something *happened* there, Milo. Bancroft called the school's students miscreants and fire setters. He de-nied there'd been any major problems that he couldn't handle, but he could have been lying."

"Well," he said, "local records can be checked, and Sally'll be talking to Bancroft again, see if she can get more details."

"Good luck to her. He doesn't suffer the middle class lightly."

He smiled and lifted his glass. "That's okay. Sally doesn't suffer assholes lightly."

He drank some beer but didn't touch his food. I looked at mine. It appeared well prepared but had all the appeal of fried lint.

I said, "Myra Paprock taught school here during

the late sixties to the midseventies, so that's probably the time frame we're looking at. Lyle Gritz would have been around ten or eleven. Harrison remembers Myra as being young and very dogmatic. So maybe she got heavy-handed with discipline. Something a child could perceive as bad love. Shipler could have worked there, too, as a janitor. Got involved, somehow, in whatever happened. And most of the conference speakers were on staff then, too. I've got the exact dates in my notes back home. Let's finish up here, get back to L.A., and check."

"You check," he said. "I'll be staying up here for a day or two, working with Sally and Bill Steen. Leave messages at her desk." He gave me a business card.

I said, "The killer's been accelerating his pace. One year between victims, now only a few months between Stoumen and Katarina."

"Unless there are other victims we don't know about."

"True. I still can't find Harvey Rosenblatt, and his wife hasn't returned my call. Maybe she's a widow who just doesn't want to deal with it. But I've got to keep trying. If Rosenblatt's alive, I need to warn him —need to warn Harrison, too. Let me call him right now and tell him about Katarina."

I returned to the pay phone and dialed Ojai while reading the warning label on the cigarette machine. No answer, no tape. I hoped it was because Harrison's self-preservation instincts were sharp. The little man would make an easy, crimson target.

When I returned to the table, Milo still hadn't eaten.

"Gone," I said. "Maybe hiding already. He said he had somewhere to go."

"I'll ask an Ojai cop to stop by. What about Becky Basille? How do you fit her into this? Hewitt screaming 'bad love,' the killer taping Hewitt?"

"Maybe Hewitt was a Corrective School alumnus, too. Or maybe the killer indoctrinated Hewitt about bad love. If G is our guy, Becky's notes imply a close relationship of some kind between him and Hewitt. If I'm right about the killer not being psychotic, he'd have been the more put-together partner —the dominant one. Able to push Hewitt's buttons, feed Hewitt's paranoia, get him off his medication, and turn him against his therapist. Because of *his* hatred of therapists. Plus, he had another reason to hate Becky: Hewitt was getting attached to her."

Milo began cutting salmon with his fork. Stopped and ran his hand over his face. "I'm still looking for Mr. Gritz. Pulled his complete sheet and it's all minor league."

"He told the Calcutta folks he was going to get rich. Could there be some kind of profit motive to these murders?"

"Maybe he was just bragging. Psychopaths do that." He looked at his food and shoved his plate away. "Who'm I kidding?"

"The kid on the tape," I said. "Any record of Gritz having children?"

He shook his head.

"The chant," I said. " 'Bad love, bad love, don't give me the bad love.' *Sounds* like something an abused kid might say. Having a child recite it could be part of the ritual. Reliving the past, using de Bosch's own terminology. God only knows what else he's done, trying to work through his pain."

He took out his wallet, pulled out cash, and put it on the table. Tried to catch the waitress's attention, but her back was to us.

"Milo," I said, "Becky might still be a link. She could have talked to someone about Hewitt and G."

"Like who?"

"A relative, a friend. Did she have a boyfriend?"

"You're saying she broke confidentiality?"

"She was a beginner, and we already know she wasn't that careful."

"Don't know about any boyfriend," he said. "But why would she not tell Jeffers, then go and gab to a layperson?"

"Because telling Jeffers would have meant getting pulled off Hewitt's case. And she could have talked without feeling she was breaching confidentiality. Leaving out names. But she might have said something to someone that can give us a lead."

"The only member of her family I ever met was her mother, and that was just once, to listen to her cry."

"A mother can be a confidante."

He looked at me. "After that picnic with Paprock's husband, you'd be willing to do another exhumation?"

"What else do we have going?"

He pushed food around his plate. "She was a nice person—the mother. What approach would you take with her?"

"Straight and narrow. Hewitt had a friend who may be involved in other killings. Someone whose name starts with G. Did Becky ever talk about him?"

He caught the waitress's eye and waved her over. She smiled and held up a finger, finished reciting the specials to a couple across the room.

"She lives near Park LaBrea," he said. "Near the art museum. Ramona or Rowena, something like that. I think she's in the book. Though she may have unlisted it after the murder. If she did, call me at Sally's and I'll get it for you."

He looked at our untouched plates, took a toothpick from a can on the table, and poked at his incisors.

"Got your message about the sheriff," I said. "When does he plan to get to the tape?"

"Next couple of days, unless some emergency comes up. Don't know what it'll accomplish, but at least we'll feel scientific."

"Speaking of science," I said, "any estimates yet about when Katarina was killed?"

"Coroner's initial guess is anywhere from eight to twenty hours before you found her."

"Eight's more likely. The coffee dregs were still moist. If I'd gotten there a little earlier I might have—"

"Gotten hurt yourself." He leaned forward. "Forget the rescue fantasies, Alex."

My head hurt and so did my eyes. I rubbed them and drank water.

The waitress came over and looked at our uneaten meals.

"Is something wrong?"

"No," said Milo. "Something just came up and we've gotta run."

"I can doggy-bag it for you."

"No, that's okay." He handed her the cash.

She frowned. "Oka-ay, I'll be back with your change, sir."

"Keep it."

Her smile was as wide as the beach. "*Thank* you, sir—we're offering a complimentary custard dessert, today."

Milo patted his gut. "Maybe another time."

"You're sure, sir? They're real good." She touched his arm, briefly. "*Really.*"

"Okay," he said, "you twisted my arm. Pack a couple to go."

"Right away, sir."

She ran off and came back seconds later with a paper bag printed with the face of a happy-looking hound and the words FOR BOWSER. Milo carried it and we left the restaurant and headed for the Seville. As I got in the car, I realized he wasn't with me and I turned back to see him standing over a skinny, barechested kid of around eighteen. The kid was sitting on the breezeway in front of the motel and holding a shirt-cardboard sign that said, WILL WORK FOR FOOD. His tan was intense, his cheeks were sunken, and his hair was a greasy umbrella.

Milo gave him the bag. The kid said something. Milo looked angry, but he reached into his wallet and handed the kid something green.

Then he got in the passenger seat and growled: "Take me to work."

23

The scene in the garage stayed with me during the drive back to L.A. Bad traffic just past Thousand Oaks had me sitting still, Katarina's mangled body filling my head. I listened to the Seville idle, thought about pain and vengeance and Robin all alone up on Benedict Canyon. Mr. Silk, whoever he was, had won a partial victory.

Things finally got moving again. I escaped 101, made it to 405 and had a clear sail to Sunset. I was heading up Benedict shortly after nine-thirty when I noticed two red dots floating ahead of me.

Brake lights. A car stopped.

It seemed to be paused right in front of the narrow road that led to my adopted home, though from this distance, I couldn't be sure. I put on speed, but before I got there, the lights dimmed and the car was gone, traveling too fast for me to catch up.

Probably nothing, but I was stumbling along the thin line between paranoia and caution and my heart was pounding. I waited. Everything stayed silent. I drove up to the white gate, slipped the cardkey in the slot, and raced up the cypress-lined driveway.

The house was lit from within, the garage shut. I approached the front door, wet with sweat, turned the key, and stepped inside, chest bursting.

Robin was stretched out on a sofa reading a design magazine. The bulldog was wedged between her legs, head nestled in her lap, trapdoor mouth open and snoring.

"Beauty and the Beast," I said, but my voice was weak.

She looked up, smiled, and held out her hand. The dog opened one eye, then let the lid drop.

"Been shopping all afternoon?" I said, taking off my jacket. "I tried calling a bunch of times."

"Uh-huh," she said. "Lots of errands. . . . What's the matter, Alex?"

I told her what I'd found on Shoreline Drive.

"Oh, no!" She propped herself on her elbows. The dog grumbled awake, but he stayed down. "You came so close to walking in on it."

I sat down. As she squeezed my hand, I recounted what I'd found and what I'd learned from Bert Harrison and Condon Bancroft. She listened with her fingers at her mouth.

"Whoever's behind this is relentless," I said. "I want you to move somewhere else temporarily."

She sat up completely. "*What?*"

"Just for a while. I'm not safe to be around."

"We moved so you *would* be, Alex. How could anyone know you're here?"

Thinking of the brake lights, I said, "I'm sure no one does, but I just want to be careful. I spoke to Milo. You can move into his place. Just till things ease up."

"It's not necessary, Alex."

The dog was completely awake now, shifting his glance from Robin to me, his brow wrinkles deeper.

The confusion and fear of a kid watching his parents fight.

"Just temporarily," I said.

"*Temporarily?* If this person's done everything you think he has, he waits years! So what kind of temporary are we talking about here?"

I had no answer.

She said, "No. No way, Alex, I won't leave you. To hell with him—he can't do that to us."

"Robin, she was pregnant. I saw what he did to her."

"No," she said, eyes brimming. "Please. I don't want to hear about it."

"Okay," I said.

She pitched forward as if falling and grabbed my shoulders with both hands. Pulling me closer, she held on tight, as if still off balance. Her cheek was up against mine and her breath was in my ear, hot and quick.

"It's okay," I said. "We'll work it out."

She squeezed me. "Oh, Alex, let's just move to another planet."

The dog jumped from the couch to the floor, sat down and stared at us. Whistling noises came from his compressed nostrils, but his eyes were clear and active, almost human.

"Hey, Spike," I said, reaching over. "He been good?"

"The best."

The affection in her voice made his ears go up. He trotted up to the edge of the couch and rested his flews on her knee. She caressed his head and he lifted his chin and gave her palm a long, wet tongue swipe.

"You could take *him* with you," I said. "You'd have *constant* masculine attention."

"Put it out of your mind, Alex." Her nails dug into my back. "We probably won't have him much longer, anyway. I got a call this morning from a group called French Bulldog Rescue. Very sweet lady over in Burbank—you wrote to the national club and they forwarded it to her. She's putting out feelers, says these little guys are almost never intentionally abandoned, so it's just a matter of time before the owners call to claim him."

"No one's reported him missing so far?"

"No, but don't get your hopes up. She's got a pretty good communication network, seems pretty sure she'll find his owner. She offered to come by and take him off our hands, but I said we'd care for him in the meantime."

The dog was looking up at me expectantly. I rested my hand on his head and he made a low, satisfied noise.

Robin said, "Now I know how foster parents feel." She grabbed a handful of soft chin and kissed it. Her shorts had rolled high on her thighs and she tugged them down. "Have you had dinner yet?"

"No."

"I bought stuff—chilies rellenos, enchiladas. Even got a six-pack of Corona, so we could pretend we were party animals. It's a little late now to start a whole feast, but I can put something together if you're hungry."

"Don't bother, I'll make a sandwich."

"No, *let* me, Alex. I need something to do with my hands. Afterward we can get in bed with the crossword and some really bad TV and who knows what else."

"Who knows?" I said, drawing her to me.

We turned off the lights around midnight. I fell away easily, but I woke up feeling as if I'd been drained of body fluids.

I endured breakfast, feeding the dog bits of scrambled egg and making conversation with Robin until the two of them went to the garage.

As soon as I was alone, I called Dr. Shirley Rosenblatt in Manhattan and got the same taped message. I repeated my pitch, told her it was more urgent than ever, and asked her to get in touch as soon as possible. When no callback had come in by the time I'd finished showering, shaving, and dressing, I phoned Jean Jeffers. She was out for the day—some kind of meeting downtown—and hadn't left word with her secretary about Lyle Gritz. Remembering her eagerness to look for him, I figured she'd come up empty.

Information had no listing for a Ramona or Rowena Basille, but there was a "Basille, R." on 618 South Hauser Street. Right near Park LaBrea.

An older woman's voice answered, "Hello."

"Mrs. Basille?"

"This is Rolanda, who're you?" Scratchy timbre, the midwestern tones I'd grown up with.

"My name's Alex Delaware. I'm a psychologist, consulting to the Los Angeles Police Department—"

"Yes?" Rise in pitch.

"Sorry to be bothering you—"

"What is it? What's happened?"

"Nothing, Mrs. Basille. I was just wondering if I could ask you a few questions."

"About Becky?"

"About someone Becky might have known."

"Who?"

"A friend of Dorsey Hewitt's."

The name made her groan. "What friend? Who? I don't understand."

"A man named Lyle Gritz—"

"What about him? What's going on?"

"Have you ever heard of him?"

"No, never. What's this got to do with Rebecca?"

"Nothing directly, Mrs. Basille, but Gritz may have been involved in some other crimes. He may also have used the names Silk or Merino."

"What kind of crimes? Murders?"

"Yes."

"I don't understand. Why's a psychologist calling —that's what you said you were, right? Psychologist, psychiatrist?"

"Psychologist."

"If there's murders involved, why aren't the police calling?"

"It's not an official investigation, yet."

Pause. "Okay, who are you, buster? Some sleazy tabloid writer? I've already been through that, and let me tell you what you can—"

"I'm not a reporter," I said. "I'm who I said I was, Mrs. Basille. If you'd like to verify it, you can call Detective Milo Sturgis at West L.A. detectives. He gave me your name—"

"Sturgis," she said.

"He handled the investigation of Becky's case."

"Which one was that—oh yeah, the big one . . . yeah, he tried to be nice. But where does he come off giving you my name? What are you doing, some kind of psychological *study*? Want to make me a guinea pig?"

"No, nothing like that—"

"What, then?"

There seemed no choice. "My involvement's a lot more personal, Mrs. Basille. I'm a potential victim."

"A vic—of who, this Gritch?"

"Gritz. Lyle Edward Gritz. Or Silk or—"

"Never heard of any of those."

"There's evidence he's been murdering psychotherapists—several of them over a five-year period."

"Oh, no."

"The latest occurred yesterday, in Santa Barbara. A woman named Katarina de Bosch."

"Yester—oh, goodness." Her voice changed—lower, softer, still perplexed. "And now you think he's out for *you*?"

"Yes."

"Why?"

"He may have a thing against psychotherapists. He leaves a message at the crime scene. The words 'bad love'—"

"That's the same thing that scum yelled out!"

"That's why we think there may be a connection. Last week, I received a tape with someone chanting 'bad love.' As well as a sample of Hewitt screaming. Shortly after that, I got a crank phone call, then someone snuck onto my property and did damage."

"What are you *saying*? That Rebecca was *part* of something?"

"I really don't know, Mrs. Basille."

"But maybe that's what it *was*? Someone *else* was involved in my Becky's . . ."

A loud bang percussed in my ear. A few seconds later: "Dropped the phone, you still there?"

"Yes."

"So what're you saying? This Gritz could have been involved in hurting my baby?"

"I wish I could tell you, Mrs. Basille. Gritz and Hewitt were friends, so it's possible Gritz had some influence on Hewitt. But there's no evidence—"

"Bad *love*," she said. "No one was ever able to explain to me what it meant."

"It's a psychological term coined by Katarina de Bosch's father—Dr. Andres de Bosch."

"Debauch?"

"De Bosch. He was a psychologist who ran a remedial school up in Santa Barbara."

No reaction.

I said, "Lyle Gritz may have been a patient there. For all I know, Hewitt may have been also. Did Rebecca ever mention anything related to any of this?"

"No . . . God in heaven . . . I think I'm going to be sick."

"I'm truly sorry, Mrs.—"

"What'd you say your name was?"

"Alex Delaware."

"Give me your phone number."

I did.

"Okay," she said, "I'm calling that Sturgis right now and checking you out."

"He's in Santa Barbara. You can reach him at the police department there." I fished around, retrieved Sarah Grayson's card, and read off the number.

She hung up without comment.

Ten minutes later, my service put her through.

"He wasn't in," she said, "but I spoke to a woman cop who said you're for real. So, okay, I'm sorry for what you're going through—once you been through it you get sorry a *lot* for other people. Okay, what can I do for you?"

"I was just wondering if Becky ever talked about her work. Said anything that might help find Gritz and clear this up."

"Talked? Yeah, she talked. She loved her . . . hold on . . . my stomach . . . hold on, I thought I was okay, but now I feel like I have to throw up again —let me go do that, and then I'll call you back—no, forget that, I hate the phone. Phone rings now, my heart starts going like it's going to explode—you want to come down and see me it's okay. Let me see what you look like, I hate the phone."

"How about I come to your house?"

"Sure—no, forget it. The place is depressing. I never was a homemaker, now I don't do a darn thing. Why don't you meet me over in Hancock Park? Not the neighborhood, the actual park—know where it is?''

"Over by the tar pits."

"Yeah, meet me on the Sixth Street side, behind the museums. There's a shady area, some benches. What're you gonna wear?"

"Jeans and a white shirt."

"Fine. I'll be wearing—no, this is wrinkled, gotta change it—I'll be wearing a . . . green blouse. Green with a white collar. Just look for an ugly old woman with a green blouse and a crappy disposition."

The blouse was grass green. She was sitting under a thatch of mismatched trees, on a bench facing the rolling lawn that separated the County Art Museum from the dinosaur depository George Page had built with Mission Pack money. At the end of the lawn the tar pits were an oily black sump behind wrought iron pickets. Through the fence, plaster mastodons reared and glared at the traffic on Wilshire Boulevard. Tar leaked through the entire park, seeping up in random spots, and I just missed stepping in a bubbling pool as I made my way toward Rolanda Basille.

Her back was to Sixth Street, but I had a three-quarter view of her body. Around sixty-five. Her collar was a snowy Peter Pan job, her slacks olive wool, much too heavy for the weather. She had hair dyed as black as the tar, cut in a flapper bob with eyebrow-length bangs. Her face was crinkled and small. Arthritic hands curled in her lap. Red tennis shoes covered her feet, over white socks, folded over once. A big, green plastic purse hung from her shoulder. If she weighed a hundred pounds, it was after Thanksgiving dinner.

The ground was covered with dry leaves and I

made noise as I approached. She kept gazing out at the lawn and didn't look back. Children were playing there, mobile dots on an emerald screen, but I wasn't sure she saw them.

The random trees had been trimmed to form a canopy, and the shadows they cast were absolute. Several other benches were scattered nearby, most of them empty. A black man slept on one, a paper bag next to his head. Two women of Rolanda Basille's approximate age sat on another, strumming guitars and singing.

I walked in front of her.

She barely looked up, then slapped the bench.

I sat down. Music drifted over from the two guitarists. Some sort of folk song, a foreign language.

"The Stepne sisters," she said, sticking out her tongue. "They're here all the time. They stink. Did you ever see a picture of my daughter?"

"Just in the paper."

"That wasn't a flattering one." She opened the big purse, searched for a while, and took out a medium-sized envelope. Withdrawing three color photographs, she handed them to me.

Professional portraits, passable quality. Rebecca Basille sitting in a white wicker chair, posed three different ways in front of a mountain-stream backdrop, wearing a powder-blue dress and pearls. Big smile. Terrific teeth. Very pretty; soft, curvy build, soft arms, a trifle heavy. The dress was low-cut and showed some cleavage. Her brown hair was shiny and long and iron-curled at the ends, her eyes full of humor and just a bit of apprehension, as if she'd been sitting for a long time and had doubts about the outcome.

"Very lovely," I said.

"She was beautiful," said Rolanda. "Inside and out."

She held out her hand and I returned the photos. After she'd replaced them in the purse, she said, "I just wanted you to see the person she was, though even these don't do it. She didn't like having her picture taken—used to be chubby when she was little. Her face was always gorgeous."

I nodded.

She said, "There was a wounded bird within five miles, Becky'd find it and bring it home. Shoeboxes and cotton balls and eyedroppers. She tried to save anything—*bugs*—those little gray curly things?"

"Potato bugs?"

"Those. Moths, ladybugs, whatever, she'd save 'em. When she was *real* little she went through this stage of not wanting anyone to cut the lawn because she thought it hurt the grass."

She tried to smile, but her lips got away from her and began trembling. She covered them with one hand.

"You see what I'm saying?" she said, finally.

"I do."

"She never changed. In school, she went straight for the outcasts—anyone who was different, or hurting—the retarded kids, harelips, you name it. Sometimes I think she was *attracted* to hurt."

Another forage in the purse. She found red-framed sunglasses and put them on. Given the ambient shade, they must have blacked out the world.

I said, "I can see why she went into social work."

"Exactly. I always figured she would do something like that, always told her nursing or social work would be perfect for her. But of course when you tell them, they do something else. So it took her a while to know what she wanted. She didn't want to go to college, did some waitressing, some file clerking, secretarial. My other kids were different. Real driven. Got a boy practicing orthopedic medicine in Reno, and my older girl works in a bank in St. Louis—assistant vice president."

"Was Becky the youngest?"

She nodded. "Nine years between her and Kathy, eleven between her and Carl. She was—I was forty-one when I had her, and her father was five years older than me. He walked out on us right after she was born. Left me high and dry with three kids. Sugar diabetic, and he refused to stop drinking. He started losing feeling in his feet, then the eyes started going. Finally, they began cutting pieces off of him and he decided with no toes and one arm it was time to be a swinging bachelor—crazy, huh?"

She shook her head.

"He moved to Tahoe, didn't last long after that," she said. "Becky was two when he died. We hadn't heard from him all that time, suddenly the government started sending me his veteran's benefits. . . . You think that's what made her so vulnerable? No—what do you people call it?—father role model?"

"How was Becky vulnerable?" I said.

"Too trusting." She touched her collar, smoothed out an invisible wrinkle. "She went straight for the losers. Believed every cock-and-bull story."

"What kind of losers?"

"More wounded birds. Guys she thought she could fix. She wanted to fix the world."

Her hands began to shake and she shoved them under her purse. The Stepne sisters were singing louder. She said: "Shut up."

"Did the losers mistreat her?"

"Losers," she said, as if she hadn't heard. "The great poet with no poems to show for it, living off welfare. Bunch of musicians, so-called. Not men. Little boys. I nagged her all the time, all the dead-ends she was choosing. In the end, none of that mattered a whit, did it?"

She lifted her sunglasses and wiped an eye with one finger. Putting the shades back, she said, "You don't need to hear this, you've got your own problems."

I saw faint reflections of myself in her black lenses, distorted and tense.

"You seem like a nice young fellow, listening to me go on like this. Ever save any bugs yourself?"

"Maybe a couple of times."

She smiled. "Bet it was more than a couple. Bet you punched those holes in the top of the jars so the bugs could breathe, right? Bet your mother loved that, too, all those creepy things in the house."

I laughed.

"I'm right, aren't I? *I* should be a psychologist."

"It does bring back certain memories," I said.

"Sure," she said. "Out to save the world, all of you. You married?"

"No."

"A fellow like you, same attitude as my Becky, you would have been okay for her. You could have saved the world together. But to be honest, she probably wouldn't have gone for you—no offense, you're just too . . . put-together. That's a compliment, believe me." She patted my knee. Frowned. "I'm sorry for what you're going through. And be sure to take good care of yourself. Something happens to you, your mother's going to die, over and over. You'll be gone but she'll be left dying every *day*—understand?"

The hand on my knee clawed.

I nodded.

"Something happens to you, your mother's going to lie in bed and think about you, over and over and over. Wondering how much you suffered. Wondering what you were *thinking* when it happened to you— *why* it happened to her kid and not someone else's. Do you understand what I'm saying?"

"I do."

"So be careful."

"That's why I'm here," I said. "To protect myself."

She whipped off the sunglasses. Her eyes were so raw the whites looked brown. "Gritz—no, she never said a word about anyone named that. Or Silk or Merino."

"Did she ever talk about Hewitt?"

"No, not really." She seemed to be deliberating. I didn't move or speak.

The raw eyes moistened. "She mentioned him once—maybe a week or two before. Said she was treating this really crazy person and thought she was helping him. She said it respectfully—this poor, sick fellow that she really wanted to help. Schizophrenic, whatever—hearing voices. No one else had been able to help him, but she thought she could. He was starting to trust her."

She spat on the ground.

"She mentioned him by name?"

"No. She made a point of not talking about any of them by name. Big point of following the rules."

Remembering Becky's sketchy notes and lack of follow-through with Jean, I said, "A real stickler, huh?"

"That was Becky. Back when she was in grade school, her teachers always said they wished they had a classroom full of Beckys. Even with her loser boyfriends, she always stayed on the straight and narrow, not using drugs, nothing. That's why they wouldn't . . ."

She shook her head. Put her glasses back on and showed me the back of her head. Between thin strands of dyed hair, her neck was liver-spotted and loose-skinned.

I said, "Why they wouldn't what?"

No answer for a moment.

Then: "They wouldn't stick with her—*they* always left *her*. Can you beat that? The ones who were going to get divorced, always went back to their wives. The ones who were on the wagon, always fell off. And left *her*. She was *ten* times the human being any of them were, but *they* always walked out on *her*, can you beat that?"

"They were the unstable ones," I said.

"Exactly. Dead-end losers. What she needed was someone with high standards, but she wasn't attracted to that—only the broken ones."

"Was she in a relationship at the time she died?"

"I don't know—probably. The last time I saw her —couple of days before she stopped by to give me some laundry—I asked her how her social life was and she refused to talk about it. What that usually meant was she was involved with someone she knew I'd nag her about. I got upset with her—we didn't talk much. How was I supposed to know it was the last time and I should have enjoyed every minute I had with her?"

Her shoulders bowed and quivered.

I touched one of them and she sat up suddenly.

"Enough of this—I hate this moping around. That's why I quit that survivor's group your friend Sturgis recommended. Too much self-pity. Meanwhile, I haven't done a damn thing for you."

My head was full of assumptions and guesses. Learning of Becky's attraction to losers had firmed up the suspicions left by her notes. I smiled and said, "It's been good talking to you."

"Good talking to you, too. Do I get a bill?"

"No, the first hour's free."

"Well, look at that. Handsome, a Caddy, and a sense of humor to boot—you do pretty well, don't you? Financially."

"I do okay."

"Modesty—bet you do better than okay. That's what I wanted for Becky. Security. I told her, what are you wasting your time for, doing dirty work for the county? Finish up your degree, get some kind of license, open up an office in Beverly Hills and treat fat people or those women who starve themselves. Make some *money*. No crime in that, right? But she wouldn't hear of it, wanted to do *important* work. With people who were really *needy*."

She shook her head.

"Saving the bugs," she said, almost inaudibly. "She thought she was dealing with those potato thingies, but a scorpion got into the jar."

24

Her description of Becky as a stickler for the rules didn't fit with Jean Jeffers' recollections. A mother's vision could be overly rosy, but she'd been frank about Becky's chronic attraction to losers.

Had Becky finally been attracted to the ultimate loser? How loose had things gotten between her and Hewitt?

And what twisted dynamic bound the two of them to G?

Bad love.

Blaming the victim bothered me, but revenge seemed to be the fuel that powered the killer's engine, and I had to wonder if Becky had been a target of something other than random psychosis.

I drove home straining to make sense of it. No strange vehicles within a hundred yards of the gate, and last night's anxiety seemed silly. Robin was working, looking preoccupied and content, and the dog was chewing a nylon bone.

"Milo just called from Santa Barbara," she said. "The number's on the kitchen counter."

I went into the house, found an 805 exchange that wasn't Sally Grayson's, and punched it. A voice answered, "Records."

"Dr. Delaware returning Detective Sturgis's call."

"One minute."

I waited five.

"Sturgis."

"Hi. Just got through talking to Becky's mother. Becky never mentioned anyone by name, but she did talk about helping a poor unfortunate psychotic who could very well have been Hewitt."

"No mention of Gritz?"

"Nor of Silk or Merino. One thing that was interesting, though: she said Becky liked to mend broken wings and had a penchant for losers—guys who involved her in dead-end relationships. If you think of Hewitt as the ultimate loser, it supports what we suspected about things getting unprofessional between them. Having said all that, I don't know that it *leads* us anywhere."

"Well, we're not doing much better here. No school records at Katarina's house, so either she never kept them or the killer made off with them. We do have confirmation that Myra Evans was Myra Paprock, but it's a no-go on Rodney Shipler. His tax records show him working for the L.A. Unified School District for thirty years—right after he got out of the Army. Never up here—and I verified it with the S.B. district. No connection at all to the de Bosch school."

"What about summer vacations?" I said. "School personnel sometimes take part-time jobs during the off-season."

"Summers he worked in L.A."

"How long was he in the Army?"

"Fifteen years—staff sergeant, most of it over in the Philippines. Honorable discharge, no blots on his record."

"He made somebody mad."

"It doesn't look like it was someone at the school. In fact, we can't find any records of *anything* fishy happening out at the school. No fires or felonies or anything anybody would want to avenge, Alex. Just a few complaints about noise from Bancroft and one vehicular accident that did occur when Myra Evans was teaching there—May of seventy-three—but it was clearly an accident. One of the students stole a school truck and took a joyride. Made it up to the Riviera district and spun off a mountain road. He died, Santa Barbara PD investigated, found no foul play."

"How old was the student?"

"Fifteen."

"Vehicular accident off a mountain road," I said. "Grant Stoumen was hit by a car and Mitchell Lerner was pushed off a mountain."

"That's a little abstract, Alex."

"Maybe not, if matching things—achieving consistency—is part of the killer's fantasy."

Pause. "You'd know more about that than I would, but why focus on the school when we've got a victim with no connection to it? No obvious connection to de Bosch, period."

"Shipler could have been connected to the symposium."

"How? A janitor with a side interest in psychology, or did he sweep up afterward?"

"Maybe it's the race angle somehow. Shipler was black and de Bosch was a covert bigot."

"Why would someone pissed off about *racism* beat a *black* man to death?"

"I don't know . . . but I'm sure de Bosch is at the core of this. The school, the conference—all of it. Merino told Harrison the conference set off something in him—maybe it was seeing de Bosch lauded publicly, when he knew the truth to be otherwise."

"Maybe, but so far the school's got a clean record."

"Bancroft seemed to think it was a hotbed of anti-social behavior."

"Bancroft isn't your most reliable witness. Sally says he's been known to hit the bottle pretty hard, and his world view's somewhat to the right of the Klan. Compared to his old man, he's a pussycat. The two of them had a special thing for de Bosch because de Bosch overbid Bancroft Senior for the land the school was built on. When de Bosch broke ground in sixty-two, they tried to mobilize the neighbors against it—disturbed kids running amok. But no one went along with it because the Bancrofts had alienated everyone over the years."

"The neighbors didn't mind a school for problem kids?"

"There were some worries, but the lot being vacant bothered them more. Vagrants used to come off the highway, light fires, toss trash, make a mess. Bancroft Senior had dickered with the owner for years, making offers, withdrawing them. De Bosch's school was an improvement as far as the neighborhood was concerned. Real quiet, no problems."

"Except for a fifteen-year-old kid in a stolen truck."

"One incident in twenty years, Alex. Considering that de Bosch dealt with emotionally disturbed kids, wouldn't you say that's pretty good?"

"I'd say it's excellent," I said. "Exemplary. And one way to keep things so tidy is through firm discipline. *Very* firm discipline."

He sighed. "Sure, it's possible. But if de Bosch was running a torture chamber, wouldn't there be complaints?"

"Five dead people is a complaint."

"Okay. But if you want a hostility motive, look at

Bancroft. He had a *hard-on* for de Bosch for over twenty years. But that doesn't mean he ran around the country murdering everyone associated with him."

"Maybe he *should* be looked into."

"He will be," he said wearily. "He's *being* looked into. Meanwhile, you be careful and sit tight. I'm sorry, Alex, I wish the goddamn pieces had fit together neatly, but it's turning out to be messy."

"Just like real life," I said. "Anything new on Katarina?"

"Coroner still can't decide if she was conscious or unconscious after those blows to the face. Her baby was, indeed, a twenty-two-week-old normal male, Caucasian. I called the sperm bank, they wouldn't even verify she was a customer. Sally and I can probably pry some information loose, eventually. Meanwhile, is Robin coming to us? Rick says no problem except for Rover—excuse me, Spike. Dog allergy. But if Robin really wants to take the pooch with her, he can put himself on antihistamines."

"He won't need to," I said. "Robin insists on staying with me."

"Must be your charm . . . well, don't sweat it, I'm sure you're safe."

"Hope so." I told him about the brake lights the previous night.

"Just lights, nothing funny?"

"Just lights. And then the car drove off."

"What time was this?"

"Nine forty-five or so."

"Any other cars around?"

"Quite a few."

"Sounds like nothing. If you see anything funny, call Beverly Hills PD—they protect their citizenry."

"I will. Thanks for everything. . . . The kid who went off the mountain, did he have a name?"

"Still on that, huh?" He gave a small laugh. "His name was Delmar Parker and he originally came from New Orleans."

"What was he being treated for at the school?"

"Don't know, there's no complete police report, because the case was closed and filed. We're working from summary cards at the coroner's office and lucky to find *them*. . . . Let's see . . . name, date, age, cause of death—multiple traumas and internal injuries—place of birth, N'Awleens . . . parent or guardian—here it is—the mother . . . Marie A. Parker."

"Any address?"

"No. Why? You want to dig up *another* one?"

"No," I said. "I don't *want* to dig up anything, believe me. I'm just grasping, Milo."

Silence. "Okay, I'll try, but don't count on it. It was a long time ago. People move. People die."

I pretended everything was normal. Robin and I ate lunch out by the pool. The sky was clear and beautiful, bracing itself for a smog cloud heading over from the east.

Lifestyles of the rich and fearful.

Terror and anger still gnawed at my spine, but I thought of the people under the freeway and knew I had it damned good.

The phone rang. My service operator said, "There's a long-distance call for you, Dr. Delaware. From New York, a Mr. Rosenblatt."

"Mister, not doctor?"

"Mister's what he said."

"Okay," I said. "Put him on."

She did, but no one answered my hello. A few seconds later a young woman with an all-business voice clicked in and said, "Schechter, Mohl, and Trimmer. Who are you holding for?"

"Mr. Rosenblatt."

"One moment."

A few seconds later a young voice said, "This is Mr. Rosenblatt."

"This is Dr. Delaware."

Throat clear. "Dr. Delaware, my name is Joshua Rosenblatt, I'm a practicing attorney here in New York and I'm calling to ask you to stop phoning my mother, Dr. Shirley Rosenblatt."

"I've been phoning because I was concerned about your father—"

"Then you have nothing to be concerned about."

"He's all right?"

Silence.

I said, "Is he all right?"

"No. I wouldn't say that." Pause. "My father's deceased."

I felt myself deflate. "I'm sorry."

"Be that as it may, Dr. Delaware—"

"When did it happen? Was it four years ago?"

Long silence. Throat clear. "I really don't want to get into this, doctor."

"Was it made to look like an accident?" I said. "Some kind of fall? Something to do with a vehicle? Were the words 'bad love' left anywhere at his death scene?"

"Doctor," he began, but his voice broke on the second syllable and he blurted: "We've been through enough, already. At this point, there's no need to rake it up."

"I'm in danger," I said. "Maybe from the same person who killed your father."

"What!"

"I called because I was trying to *warn* your father and I'm so sorry it's too late. I only met him once, but I liked him. He seemed like a really decent guy."

Long pause. "When did you meet him?" he said, softly.

"In nineteen seventy-nine, here in Los Angeles. He and I co-chaired a mental health symposium called 'Good Love/Bad Love, Strategies in a Changing World.' A tribute to a teacher of your father's named Andres de Bosch."

No response.

"Mr. Rosenblatt?"

"None of this makes any sense."

"You were with him on that trip," I said. "Don't you remember?"

"I went on lots of trips with my father."

"I know," I said. "He told me. He talked about you quite a bit. Said you were his youngest. You liked hot dogs and video games—he wanted to take you to Disneyland, but the park closed early in the fall, so I suggested he take you to the Santa Monica pier. Did you go?"

"Hot dogs." His voice sounded weak. "So what? What's the point?"

"I think that trip had something to do with his death."

"No, no, that's crazy—no. Back in seventy-nine?"

"Some kind of long-term revenge plot," I said. "Something to do with Andres de Bosch. The person who murdered your father has killed other people. At least five others, maybe more."

I gave him names, dates, places.

He said, "I don't know any of those people. This is crazy. This is really insane."

"Yes, it is, but it's all true. And I may be next. I need to talk to your mother. The killer may have presented himself to your father as a patient—lured him that way. If she's still got your father's old appointment books, it could—"

"No, she has nothing. Leave her out of this."

"My life's at stake. Why won't your mother just talk to me? Why'd she have you call me instead of calling herself?"

"Because she can't," he said angrily. "Can't talk to anyone. She had a stroke a month ago and her speech was severely affected. It just came back a few weeks ago, but she's still weak."

"I'm sorry, but—"

"Listen, I'm sorry, too. For what *you're* going through. But at this point, I just don't see what I can do for you."

"Your mother's talking now."

"Yes, but she's weak. Really weak. And to have her talk about my father. . . . She just started rehab and she's making progress, Dr. Delaware. I can't have her interrogated."

"You never told her I called?"

"I'm taking care of her. It calls for decisions."

"I understand," I said. "But I don't want to interrogate her, I just want to talk to her. A few questions. At her pace—I can fly out to New York, if that'll help, and do it face-to-face. As many sessions as she needs. Go as slowly as she needs."

"You'd *do* that? Fly out here?"

"What choice do I have?"

I heard him blow out breath. "Even so," he said. "Her talking about Dad—no, it's too risky. I'm sorry, but I have to hold firm."

"I'll work with her doctors, Mr. Rosenblatt. Clear my questions with them and with you. I've done hospital work for years. I understand illness and recovery."

"What makes you think she knows anything that could help you?"

"At this point she's my last hope, Mr. Rosenblatt. The creep who's after me is picking up his pace. He murdered someone in Santa Barbara yesterday—de

Bosch's daughter. She was pregnant. He cut her up, made it a point to go after the fetus."

"Oh, God."

"He's stalking me," I said. "To tell the truth, I'd be safer in New York than here. One way or the other, I may come out."

Another exhalation. "I doubt she can help you, but I'll ask."

"I really apprecia—"

"Don't thank me yet. I'm not promising anything. And fax your credentials to me, so I can check them out. Include two verifiable references."

"No problem," I said. "And if your mother won't speak to me, please ask her if she knows anything about the term 'bad love.' And did your father report anything unusual about the nineteen seventy-nine conference. You can also throw out some names: Lyle Gritz, Dorsey Hewitt, Silk, Merino."

"Who're they?"

"Hewitt's a definite killer—murdered a therapist out here and was shot by the police. Gritz was his friend, may have been an accomplice. He may also be the one who killed your father. Silk and Merino are possible aliases."

"Fake names?" he said. "This is so bizarre."

"One more thing," I said. "There's an LAPD detective working the case out here, named Milo Sturgis. I'm going to inform him of your father's murder and he'll be contacting the New York police and asking for records."

"That won't help you," he said. "Believe me."

25

Milo was no longer at Records, and Sally Grayson's number was picked up by a male detective who hadn't seen her all morning and had no idea who Milo was. I left a message, and wondered why Joshua Rosenblatt had been so sure the police couldn't help.

My offer to go to New York had been impulsive —probably an escape reflex—but maybe something would come out of my talk with Shirley Rosenblatt.

I'd leave as soon as possible; Robin would *have* to move out now.

I looked out at the pool, still as a slab of turquoise. A few leaves floated on top.

Who cleaned it? How often?

I didn't know much about this place.

Didn't know when I'd be able to leave it.

I got up, ready to drive into Beverly Hills to find a fax service. Just as I put my wallet in my pants pocket, the phone rang and my service operator said, "A Mr. Bucklear wants to talk to you, doctor."

"Put him on."

Click.

"Doctor? Sherman Bucklear."

"Hello."

"Have you received my correspondence?"

"Yes, I have."

"I haven't received any reply, doctor."

"Didn't know there was anything to reply to."

"I have reason to believe you have knowledge of the whereabouts—"

"I don't."

"Can you prove that?"

"Do I have to?"

Pause. "Doctor, we can go about this civilly or things can get complicated."

"Complicate away, Sherman."

"Now, wait a sec—"

I hung up. It felt great to be petty. Before I could put down the phone, the service patched in again with a call from New York.

"Dr. Delaware? Josh Rosenblatt, again. My mother's willing to talk to you but I've got to warn you, she can't handle much—just a few minutes at a time. I haven't discussed any details with her. All she knows is you knew my father and think he was murdered. She may have nothing to tell you. You may end up wasting your time."

"I'll take the chance. When would you like me there?"

"What's today? Tuesday . . . Friday's bad and she needs her weekends for total bedrest—Thursday, I guess."

"If I can catch a flight tonight, how about tomorrow?"

"Tomorrow . . . I guess so. But it'll have to be in the afternoon. Mornings she has her therapy, then she naps. Come to my office first—500 Fifth Avenue. Schechter, Mohl, and Trimmer. The thirty-third floor. Have you faxed me your credentials yet?"

"Just on my way out to do it."

"Good, because that'll be a prerequisite. Send me something with a picture, too. If everything checks out, I'll see you, say, two-thirty."

I found a quick-print place on Cañon Drive and faxed my documents to New York. Returning home, I postponed telling Robin and called an airline, booking myself a ten p.m. flight out of LAX. I asked the ticket agent about hotels.

She said, "Midtown? I really don't know, sir, but you might try the Middleton. The executives from our company stay there, but it's expensive. Of course, everything in New York is unless you want a real dive."

I thanked her and phoned the hotel. A very bored-sounding man took my credit card number, then grudgingly agreed to give me a single room for two hundred and twenty dollars a night. When he quoted the price, he suppressed a yawn.

I told Robin about Rosenblatt first.

She shook her head, took hold of my hand.

"Four years ago," I said. "Another gap filled in."

"How'd he die?"

"The son didn't go into any details. But if the killer's being consistent, it was probably something to do with a car or a fall."

"All those people. My God." Pressing my hand up against her cheek, she closed her eyes. The smell of glue hung in the garage, along with coffee and dust and the sound of the dog's breathing.

I felt him nosing up against my leg. Looked down at his wide, flat face. He blinked a couple of times and licked my hand.

I told Robin of my plan to fly east and offered to have her come with me.

She said, "There'd be no point to it, would there?"

"It's not going to be a vacation, just more digging up people's misery. I'm starting to feel like a ghoul."

She looked off, at her tools and her molds.

"Only time I've been in New York was a family trip. We went all the way up to Niagara Falls, Mom and Dad squabbling the whole time."

"I haven't been there, myself, since grad school."

She nodded, touched my biceps, rubbed it. "You have to go—things are getting uglier and uglier here. When are you leaving?"

"I was thinking tonight."

"I'll take you to the airport. When will you be coming home, so I can pick you up?"

"Depends on what I find—probably within a day or two."

"Do you have a place to stay?"

"I found a hotel."

"A hotel," she said. "You, alone in some room . . ." She shook her head.

"Could you please stay with Milo and Rick while I'm gone? I know it's disruptive and unnecessary, but I'd have a lot more peace of mind."

She touched my face again. "You haven't had much of that lately, have you? Sure, why not."

I tried a couple more times to reach Milo without success. Wanting to get Robin settled as soon as possible, I phoned his house. Rick was there and I told him we'd be coming over.

"We'll take good care of her, Alex. I'm really sorry for all this crap you've been going through. I'm sure the big guy will get to the bottom of it."

"I'm sure he will, too. Will the dog be a problem?"

"No, I don't think so. Milo tells me he's pretty cute."

"Milo never expressed any affection for him in my presence."

"Does that surprise you?"

"No," I said.

He laughed.

"Are you badly allergic, Rick?"

"Don't know, never had a dog. But don't worry, I'll pick up some Seldane in the ER, or write myself a scrip. Speaking of which, I have to head over to Cedars pretty soon. When were you planning on coming?"

"This evening. Any idea when Milo'll be back?"

"Your guess is as good as mine. . . . Tell you what, I'll leave a key in back of the house. There're two sago palms growing up against the rear wall— you haven't been here since we relandscaped, have you?"

"Just to pick up Milo."

"Came out great, our water consumption's way down . . . the sago palms—do you know what they are?"

"Squat things with leaves that look like fan blades?"

"Exactly. I'll leave the key under the branches of the smaller one—the one on the right. Milo would kill me if he knew." More laughter. "We have a new alarm code, too—he changes it every couple of months."

He rattled off five numbers. I copied them down and thanked him again.

"Pleasure," he said. "This should be fun, we've never had a pet."

*   *   *

I packed my carry-on and Robin packed hers. We took the dog for a walk around the property and played with him, and finally he got sleepy. We left him resting and drove into town for an early dinner, taking Robin's truck. Cholesterol palace on South Beverly Drive: thick steaks and home-fried potatoes served in lumberjack portions at prices no lumberjack could afford. The food looked great and smelled great, and my taste buds told me it probably tasted great, too. But somewhere along the line the circuitry between my tongue and my brain fizzed and I found myself chewing mechanically, forcing meat down a dry, tight throat.

At seven, we cleaned the house on Benedict, picked up the dog, locked up, and drove over to West Hollywood. The key was where Rick had said it would be, placed on the ground precisely at the middle of the palm's corrugated trunk. The rest of the yard was desert-pale and composed, drought-tolerant plants spread expertly around the tiny space. The walls were higher and topped with ragged stone.

Inside, the place was different, too: whitewashed hardwood floors, big leather chairs, glass tables, gray fabric walls. The guest room was pine. An old iron bed was freshly made and turned down. A single white rose rested on the pillow and a bar of Swiss chocolate was on a dish on the nightstand.

"How sweet," said Robin, picking up the flower and twirling it. She looked around. "This is like a great little inn."

Sheets of newspaper were spread on the floor next to the bed. On them were a white ceramic bowl filled with water, a plastic-wrapped hunk of cheddar cheese, and a shirt cardboard lettered in fountain pen, in Rick's perfect, surgeon's hand: POOCH'S CORNER.

The dog went straight for the cheese—nosing it and having trouble with the concept of see-through plastic. I unwrapped it and fed it to him in bits.

We let him explore the yard for a while, then went back inside. "Every time I come here, they've done something else," Robin said.

"*They?* I don't think so, Rob."

"True. You know, sometimes I have trouble imagining Milo living here."

"I bet he loves it. Refuge from all the ugliness, someone else to worry about the details for a change."

"You're probably right—we can all use a refuge, can't we?"

At eight, she drove me to LAX. The place had been rebuilt a few years ago, for the Olympics, and was a lot more manageable, but incoming arteries were still clogged and we waited to enter the departure lanes.

The whole city had been freshened up for the games, more energy and creativity mustered during one summer than the brain-dead mayor and the piss-and-moan city council had come up with in two decades. Now they were back to their old apathy-and-sleaze routine, and the city was rotting wherever the rich didn't live.

Robin pulled up to the curb. The dog couldn't enter the terminal, so we said our good-byes right there, and feeling lost and edgy, I entered the building.

The main hall was a painfully bright temple of transition. People looked either bone weary or jumpy. Security clearance was slow because the westerngarbed man in front of me kept setting off the metal detector. Finally, someone figured out it was due to the metal shanks in his snakeskin boots, and we started moving again.

I made it to the gate by nine-fifteen. Got my boarding pass, waited a half hour, then stood in line and finally got to my seat. The plane began taxiing at ten-ten, then stopped. We sat on the runway for a while and finally lifted off. A couple of thousand feet up, L.A. was still a giant circuit board. Then a cloud bank. Then darkness.

I slept on and off for most of the flight, woke varnished in sweat.

Kennedy was crowded and hostile. I lugged my carry-on past the hordes at the baggage carousels and picked up a cab at the curb. The car smelled of boiled cabbage and was plastered with no-smoking signs in English, Spanish, and Japanese. The driver had an unpronounceable name and he wore a blue tank top and a white ski hat. The hat was rolled triple so the edge created a brim. It resembled a soft bowler.

I said, "The Middleton Hotel, on West Fifty-second Street."

He grunted something and drove off, very slowly. The little I saw of Queens from the highway was low-rise and old, bricks and chrome and graffiti. But when we got on the Queensboro Bridge, the water was calm and lovely and the skyline of Manhattan loomed with threat and promise.

The Middleton was twenty stories of black granite sandwiched between office buildings that dwarfed it. The doorman looked ready for retirement and the lobby was shabby, elegant, and empty.

My room was on the tenth floor, small as a death row cell, filled with colonial furniture and sealed by blackout drapes. Clean and well ordered, but it smelled of mildew and roach killer. A dead quail-hunt print hung over the bed. The air-conditioner was a heavy-metal instrument. Street noise made it up this far with little loss of volume.

No rose on my pillow.

Unpacking, I changed into shorts and a T-shirt, ordered a three-dollar English muffin and five-dollar eggs, then punched the operator's 0 and asked for a wakeup call at one. The food came surprisingly quickly and, even more amazing, was tasty.

When I finished, I put the tray on a glass-topped bureau, pulled back the covers, and got into bed. The TV remote was bolted to the nightstand. A cardboard guide listed thirty or so cable stations. The last choice was an early morning public access show featuring a dull, pudgy nude man interviewing dull, nude women. He had narrow, womanish shoulders and a very hairy body.

"Okay, Velvet," he said, leering. "So . . . what do you do for, uh . . . fun?"

A painfully thin blond with a beak nose and frizzy hair touched a nipple and said, "Macramé."

I switched off the set.

Lights out. The blackout drapes did their job well.

My heart was as dark as the room.

26

I beat the wakeup call by more than an hour. After showering, shaving, and dressing, I drew open the drapes on a view of the red-brick building across the street. Men in white shirts and ties were framed in its windows, sitting at desks, talking into phones, and stabbing the air with pens. Down below, the streets were clogged with double-parked cars. Horns blatted. Someone was using a compression drill. Even through the sealed windows I could smell the city.

I phoned Robin at just past nine L.A. time. We told each other we were fine and chatted for a while before she put Milo on.

"Talk about bicoastal," he said. "Expedition or escape?"

"Bit of both, I guess. Thanks for taking care of the lady and the tramp."

"Pleasure. Got a little more info on Mr. Gritz. Traced him to a small town in Georgia and just got finished talking to the police chief. Seems Lyle was a weird kid. Acted goofy, walked funny, mumbled a lot, didn't have any friends. Out of school more than he was in, never learned to read properly or speak clearly. His home life was predictably bad, too. No father on the scene, and he and his mother lived in a trailer on the outskirts of town. He started drinking, slid straight into trouble. Shoplifting, theft, vandalism. Once in a while he'd get into a fight with someone bigger and stronger than himself and come out the loser. Chief said he locked him up plenty, but he didn't seem to care, jail was as good as his home, or better. He used to sit in his cell and rock and talk to himself, as if he was in his own world."

"Sounds more like the early signs of schizophrenia than a developing psychopath," I said. "Onset during adolescence fits the schizophrenic pattern, too. What *doesn't* fit is the kind of calculated thing we're dealing with. Does this sound like a guy who could blend in at medical conferences? Delay gratification long enough to plot murders years in advance?"

"Not really. But maybe he changed when he grew up, got smoother."

"Mr. Silk," I said.

"Maybe he's a good faker. Always was. Faked looking nuts, even back then—psychopaths do that all the time, right?"

"They do," I said. "But did this police chief sound like someone easily fooled?"

"No. He said the kid was nuts but had one thing going for him. Musical talent. Taught himself to play guitar and mandolin and banjo and a bunch of other instruments."

"The next Elvis."

"Yeah. And for a while people thought he might actually make something of himself. Then one day, he just left town and no one heard from him again."

"How long ago was this?"

"Nineteen-seventy."

"So he was only twelve. Any idea why he left?"

"Chief had just busted him for drunk and disorderly again, gave him the usual lecture, then added a few bucks for him to get some new clothes and a haircut. Figured maybe if the kid looked better he'd act better. Lyle walked out of the police station and headed straight for the train depot. Police chief later found he used the money to buy a one-way ticket to Atlanta."

"Twelve years old," I said. "He could have kept traveling and ended up in Santa Barbara, been taken in by de Bosch as a charity case—de Bosch liked to put forth the humanitarian image, publicly."

"Wish I could get hold of school records. No one seems to have any. Not the city or the county."

"What about federal? If de Bosch applied for government funding for the charity cases, there might be some kind of documentation."

"Don't know how long those agencies hold on to their records, but I'll check. So far I'm drawing a blank on this bastard. First time he shows up in California is an arrest nine years ago. No NCIC record prior to that, so that's over a decade between his leaving Georgia and the beginnings of his West Coast life of crime. If he got busted for petty stuff in other small towns, it might very well not have been entered into the national computer. But still, you'd expect something. He's a bad egg, where the hell was he all that time?"

"How about in a mental institution?" I said. "Twelve years old, out on his own. God knows what could have happened to him out on the street. He might have suffered a mental breakdown and got put away. Or, if he was at the school the same time as Delmar Parker, maybe he observed Delmar's death and broke down over that."

"Big assumption, he and Delmar knowing each other."

"It is, but there are some factors that might point in that direction: he and Delmar were around the same age, both were Southern boys a long way from home. Maybe Gritz finally made a friend. Maybe he even had something to do with Delmar stealing the truck. If he did and escaped death but saw Delmar die, that could have pulled the rug out from under him, psychologically."

"So now he's blaming the school and de Bosch and everyone associated with it? Sure, why not? I just wish we could push it past theory. Place Gritz in Santa Barbara, let alone the school, let alone knowing the Parker kid, et cetera, et cetera."

"Any luck finding Parker's mother?"

"She doesn't live in New Orleans, and I haven't been able to find any other relatives. So where does this Silk-Merino thing come in? Why would a Southern boy pick himself a Latino alias?"

"Merino's a type of wool," I said. "Or a sheep—the flock following the shepherd, and getting misled?"

"Baaa," he said. "When are you planning to see Rosenblatt's kid?"

"Couple of hours."

"Good luck. And don't worry, everything here's cool. Ms. Castagna lends a nice touch to the place, maybe we'll keep her."

"No, I don't think so."

"Sure," he said, chuckling. "Why not? Woman's touch and all that. Hell, we can keep the beast, too. Put up a picket fence around the lawn. One big happy family."

New York was as clear as an etching, all corners and windows, vanishing rooflines, skinny strips of blue sky.

I walked to the law firm, heading south on Fifth Avenue, swept along in the midtown tide, comforted, somehow, by the forced intimacy.

The shop windows were as glossy as diamonds. People wearing business faces hurtled toward the next obligation. Three-card monte players shouted invitations, took quick profit, then vaporized into the crowd. Street vendors hawked silly toys, cheap watches, tourist maps, and paperback books stripped of their covers. The homeless squatted in doorways, leaned against buildings. Bearing crudely lettered signs and paper cups, their hands out, their eyes leeched of expectation. So many more of them than in L.A. but yet they seemed to belong, part of the city's rhythm.

Five Hundred Fifth Avenue was a six-hundred-foot limestone tower, the lobby an arena of marble and granite. I arrived with an hour to spare and walked back outside, wondering what to do with the time. I bought a hot dog from a pushcart, ate it watching the throng. Then I spotted the main branch of the public library, just across Forty-second Street, and made my way up the broad, stone stairs.

After a bit of asking and wandering, I located the periodicals room. The hour went fast as I checked four-year-old New York newspapers for obituaries on Harvey Rosenblatt. Nothing.

I thought of the psychiatrist's kind, open manner. The loving way he'd spoken about his wife and children.

A teenaged boy who'd liked hot dogs. The taste of mine was still on my lips, sour and warm.

My thoughts shifted to a twelve-year-old, leaving town on a one-way ticket to Atlanta.

Life had sneak attacked both of them, but Josh Rosenblatt had been much more heavily armed for the ambush. I left to see how well he'd survived.

* * *

Schechter, Mohl, and Trimmer's decorator had gone for Tradition: carved, riff-oak panels with laundry-sharp creases, layers of heavy moldings, voluptuous plaster work, wool rugs over herringbone floors. The receptionist's desk was a huge, walnut antique. The receptionist was pure contemporary: midtwenties, white-blonde, *Vogue* face, hair tied back tight enough to pucker her hairline, breasts sharp enough to make an embrace dangerous.

She checked a ledger and said, "Have a seat and Mr. Rosenblatt will be right with you."

I waited twenty minutes until the door to the inner offices opened and a tall, good-looking young man stepped into the reception area.

I knew he was twenty-seven, but he looked like a college student. His face was long and grave under dark, wavy hair, nose narrow and full, his chin strong and dimpled. He wore a pinstriped charcoal suit, white tab shirt, and red and pearl tie. Pearl pocket handkerchief, quadruple pointed, tassled black loafers, gold Phi Beta Kappa pin in his lapel. Intense brown eyes and a golf tan. If law started to bore him, he could always pose for the Brooks Brothers catalogue.

"Dr. Delaware, Josh Rosenblatt."

No smile. One arm out. Bone-crusher handshake.

I followed him through a quarter acre of secretaries, file cabinets, and computers to a broad wall of doors. His was just off to the left. His name in brass, on polished oak.

His office wasn't much bigger than my hotel cubicle, but one wall was glass and it offered a falcon's lair view of the city. On the wall were two degrees from Columbia, his Phi Beta Kappa certificate, and a lacrosse stick mounted diagonally. A gym bag sat in one corner. Documents were piled up everywhere, including on one of the straight-backed side chairs facing the desk. I took the empty chair. He removed his jacket and tossed it on the desk. Very broad shoulders, powerful chest, outsize hands.

He sat down amid the clutter, shuffled papers while studying me.

"What kind of law do you practice?" I said.

"Business."

"Do you litigate?"

"Only when I need to get a taxi—no, I'm one of the behind-the-scenes guys. Mole in a suit."

He drummed the desk with his palm a few times. Kept staring at me. Put his hands down flat.

"Same face as your picture," he said. "I'd expected someone older—closer to . . . Dad's age."

"I appreciate your taking the time. Having someone you love murdered—"

"He wasn't murdered," he said, almost barking. "Not officially, anyway. *Officially*, he committed *suicide*, though the rabbi filed it as an accident so he could be buried with his parents."

"Suicide?"

"You met my dad—did he seem like an unhappy person?"

"On the contrary."

"Damn *right* on the contrary." His face reddened. "He *loved* life—really knew how to have fun. We used to kid him that he never really grew up. That's what made him a good psychiatrist. He was such a happy guy, other psychiatrists used to make *jokes* about it. Harvey Rosenblatt, the only well-adjusted shrink in New York."

He got up, looked down on me.

"He was *never* depressed—the least moody person I ever met. And he was a great father. Never played shrink with us at home. Just a dad. He played ball with me even though he was no good at it. Couldn't change a lightbulb, but no matter what he was doing, he'd put it aside to listen to you. And we knew it—all three of us. We saw what other fathers were like and we *appreciated* him. We never believed he killed himself, but they kept saying it, the goddamn police. 'The evidence is clear.' Over and over, like a broken record."

He cursed and slapped the desk. "They're a bureaucracy just like everything else in this city. They went from point A to point B, found C and said, good night, time to punch the clock and go home. So we hired a private investigator—someone the firm had used—and all *he* did was go over the same territory the police had covered, say the same damn thing. So I guess I should be happy you're here, telling me we weren't nuts."

"How did they say it happened?" I said. "A car crash or some kind of fall?"

He pulled his head back as if avoiding a punch. Glared at me. Began loosening his tie, then thought better of it and tugged it up against his throat, even tighter. Picking up his jacket, he flipped it over his shoulder.

"Let's get the hell out of here."

"You in shape?" he said, looking me up and down.

"Decent."

"Twenty blocks do you in?"

I shook my head.

He pressed forward into the throng, heading uptown. I jogged to catch up, watching him manipulate the sidewalk like an Indy driver, swaying into openings, stepping off the curb when that was the fastest way to go. Swinging his arms and looking straight ahead, sharp-eyed, watchful, self-defensive. I started to notice lots of other people with that same look. Thousands of people running the urban gauntlet.

I expected him to stop at Sixty-fifth Street, but he kept going to Sixty-seventh. Turning east, he led me up two blocks and stopped in front of a red-brick building, eight floors high, plain and flat, set between two ornate graystones. On the ground floor were medical offices. The town house on the right housed a French restaurant with a long black awning lettered in gold at street level. A couple of limousines were parked at the curb.

He pointed upward. "That's where it happened. An apartment on the top floor, and yeah, they said he jumped."

"Whose apartment was it?"

He kept staring up. Then down at the pavement. Directly in front of us, a dermatologist's window was fronted by a boxful of geraniums. Josh seemed to study the flowers. When he faced me, pain had immobilized his face.

"It's my mother's story," he said.

Shirley and Harvey Rosenblatt had worked where they lived, in a narrow brownstone with a gated entry. Three stories, more geraniums, a maple with an iron trunk guard surviving at the curb.

Josh produced a ring of keys and used one key to open the gate. The lobby ceiling was coffered walnut, the floor was covered in tiny black-and-white hexagonal tiles backed by etched glass double doors and a brass elevator. The walls were freshly painted beige. A potted palm stood in one corner. Another was occupied by a Louis XIV chair.

Three brass mailboxes were bolted to the north wall. Number 1 said, ROSENBLATT. Josh unlocked it and drew out a stack of envelopes before unlatching the glass doors. Behind it was a smaller vestibule, dark paneled and gloomy. Soup and powdered-cleanser smells. Two more walnut doors, one unmarked, with a mezuzah nailed to the post, the other bearing a brass plaque that said SHIRLEY M. ROSENBLATT, PH.D., P.C. The faint outline of where another sign had been glued was visible just above.

Josh unlocked the plain one and held it open for me. I stepped into a narrow entry hall lined with framed Daumier prints. To my left was a bentwood hall tree from which hung a single raincoat.

A gray tabby cat came from nowhere and padded toward us on the parquet floor.

Josh stepped in front of me and said, "Hey, Leo."

The cat stopped, arched its tail, relaxed it, and walked up to him. He dropped his hand. The cat's tongue darted. When it saw me, its yellow eyes slitted.

Josh said, "It's okay, Leo. I guess." He scooped up the cat, held it to his chest, and told me, "This way."

The hall emptied into a small sitting room. To the right was a dining room furnished with mock Chippendale, to the left a tiny kitchen, white and spotless. Though the shades were up on every window, the view was a brownstone six feet away, leaving the entire apartment dark and denlike. Simple furniture, not much of it. Some paintings, nothing flashy or expensive. Everything perfectly in place. I knew one way Josh had rebelled.

Beyond the sitting room was another living area, slightly larger, more casual. TV, easy chairs, a spinet piano, three walls of bookshelves filled with hardbacks and family photos. The fourth was bisected by an arched door that Josh opened.

"Hello?" Josh said, sticking his head through.

The cat fussed and he let it down. It studied me, finally disappeared behind a sofa.

The sound of another door opening. Josh stepped back as a black woman in a white nurse's uniform came out. In her forties, she had a round face, a stocky but shapely figure, and bright eyes.

"Hello, Mr. Rosenblatt." West Indian accent.

"Selena," he said, taking her hand. "How is she?"

"Everything is *perfect*. She had a generous breakfast and a nice long nap. Robbie was here at ten, and they did almost the full hour of exercise."

"Good. Is she up now?"

"Yes." The nurse's eyes shifted to me. "She's been waiting for you."

"This is Dr. Delaware."

"Hello, doctor. Selena Limberton."

"Hello." We shook hands. Josh said, "Have you had your lunch break yet?"

"No," said the nurse.

"Now would be a good time."

They talked a bit more, about medicines and exercises, and I studied the family portraits, settling on one that showed Harvey Rosenblatt in a dark three-piece suit, beaming in the midst of his brood. Josh around eighteen, with long, unruly hair, a fuzzy mustache, and black-rimmed eyeglasses. Next to him, a beautiful girl with a long, graceful face and sculpted cheekbones, maybe two or three years older. The same dark eyes as her brother. The oldest child was a young man in his midtwenties who resembled Josh, but thick necked and heavier, with cruder features, curly hair, and a full, dark beard that mimicked his father's.

Shirley Rosenblatt was tiny, fair, and blue-eyed, her blond hair cut very short, her smile full but frail even in health. Her shoulders weren't much wider than those of a child. It was hard to imagine her birth-ing the robust trio.

Mrs. Limberton said, "All righty, then, I'll be back in an hour—where's Leo?"

Josh looked around.

I said, "I think he's hiding behind the couch."

The nurse went over, bent, and lifted the cat. His body was limp. Nuzzling him, she said, "I'll bring you back some chicken if you behave." The cat blinked. She set him down on the couch and he curled up, eyes open and watchful.

Josh said, "Did you feed the fish?"

She smiled. "Yes. Everything's taken care of. Now you don't worry yourself about any more de-tails, she's going to be fine. Nice meeting you, doctor. Bye-bye."

The door closed. Josh frowned.

"Don't worry?" he said. "I went to school to learn how to worry."

27

Another small room, this one yellow, the windows misted by lace curtains.

Shirley Rosenblatt looked better than I had expected, propped up in a hospital bed and covered to the waist with a white comforter. Her hair was still blond, though dyed lighter, and she'd grown it out a little. Her delicate face had remained pretty.

A wicker bed tray was pushed into one corner. To one side of the bed was a cane chair and a pine dresser topped by perfume bottles. Opposite that stood a large saltwater aquarium on a teakwood base. The water bubbled silently. Gorgeous fish glided through a miniature coral reef.

Josh kissed his mother's forehead. She smiled and took hold of his hand. Her fingers barely stretched the width. The comforter dropped a couple of inches. She was wearing a flannel nightgown, buttoned to the neck and fastened with a bow. On her nightstand was a collection of pill bottles, a stack of magazines, and a coil-spring hand-grip exerciser.

Josh held onto her hand. She smiled up at him, then turned the smile on me. Gentle blue eyes. None of her children had gotten them.

Josh said, "Here's the mail. Want me to open it?"

She shook her head and reached out. He put the stack on her lap, but she left it there and continued to look at me.

"This is Dr. Delaware," he said.

I said, "Alex Delaware." But I didn't hold out my hand because I didn't want to dislodge his. "Thanks for seeing me, Dr. Rosenblatt."

"Shirley." Her voice was very weak and talking seemed a great effort, but the word came out clearly. She blinked a couple of times. Her right shoulder was lower than her left and her right eyelid bagged a bit.

She kissed Joshua's hand. Slowly, she said, "You can go, hon."

He looked at me, then back at her. "Sure?"

Nod.

"Okay, but I'm coming back in half an hour. I already let Mrs. Limberton go to lunch and I don't want you alone for too long."

"It's okay. She doesn't eat long."

"I'll make sure she stays all afternoon until I get here—probably not before seven-thirty. I have paperwork. Is that okay, or do you want to eat earlier?"

"Seven-thirty is fine, honey."

"Chinese?"

She nodded and smiled, let go of his hand.

"I can also get Thai if you want," he said. "That place on Fifty-sixth."

"Anything," she said. "As long as it's with you." She reached up with both hands and he bent for a hug.

After he straightened, she said, "Bye, sweets."

"Bye. Take care of yourself."

One final look at me, and then he was gone.

She pushed a button and propped herself up higher. Took a breath and said, "I'm blessed. Working with kids . . . my own turned out great."

"I'm sure it wasn't an accident."

She shrugged. The higher shoulder made it all the way through the gesture. "I don't know . . . so much is chance."

She pointed to the cane chair.

I pulled it up close and sat down.

"You're a child therapist, too?"

I nodded.

She took a long time to touch her lip. Another while to tap her brow. "I think I've seen your name on articles . . . anxiety?"

"Years ago."

"Nice to meet you." Her voice faded. I leaned closer.

"Stroke," she said and tried to shrug again.

I said, "Josh told me."

She looked surprised, then amused. "He hasn't told many people. Protecting me. Sweet. All my kids are. But Josh lives at home, we see more of each other . . ."

"Where are the others?"

"Sarah's in Boston. Teaches pediatrics at Tufts. David's a biologist at the National Cancer Institute in Washington."

"Three for three," I said.

She smiled and looked at the fish tank. "Batting a thousand . . . Harvey liked baseball. You only met him once?"

"Yes." I told her where and when.

"Harvey," she said, savoring the word, "was the nicest man I've ever known. *My* mother used to say don't marry for looks or money, both can disappear fast, so marry for nice."

"Good advice."

"Are you married?"

"Not yet."

"Do you have someone?"

"Yes. And she's very nice."

"Good." She began laughing. Very little sound came out, but her face was animated. Managing to raise one hand, she touched her chest. "Forget the Ph.D. I'm just a Jewish mother."

"Maybe the two aren't all that different."

"No. They are. Therapists don't judge, right? Or at least we pretend we don't. Mothers are always judging."

She tried to lift an envelope from the mail stack. Got hold of a corner and fumbled.

"Tell me," she said, letting go, "about my husband."

I began, including the other murders but leaving out the savagery. When I reached the part about "bad love" and my revenge theory, her eyes started blinking rapidly and I was afraid I'd caused some sort of stress reaction. But when I paused, she said, "Go on," and as I did, she seemed to sit up straighter and taller, and a cool, analytic light sharpened her eyes.

The therapist in her driving out the patient.

I'd been there. Now I was on the couch, opening myself up to this tiny, crippled woman.

When I was finished, she looked at the dresser and said, "Open that middle drawer and take out the file."

I found a black-and-white marbled box with a snap latch resting atop neatly folded sweaters. As I started to hand it to her, she said, "Open it."

I sat down beside her and unlatched the box. Inside were documents, a thick sheaf of them. On top was Harvey Rosenblatt's medical license.

"Go on," she said.

I began leafing. Psychiatric board certification. Internship and residency papers. A certificate from the Robert Evanston Hale Psychoanalytic Institute in Manhattan. Another from Southwick Hospital. A six-year-old letter from the dean of the NYU medical school reaffirming Rosenblatt's appointment as associate clinical professor of psychiatry. An honorable discharge from the Navy, where he'd served as a flight surgeon aboard an aircraft carrier. A couple of life insurance policies, one issued by the American Psychiatric Association. So he had been a member—the absence of an obituary was probably due to shame about suicide. As I came to his last will and testament, Shirley Rosenblatt looked away.

Death certificate. Burial forms.

I heard her say, "Should be next."

Next was a stapled collection of photocopied sheets. The face sheet was white. Handwritten on it was "Investig. Info."

I removed it from the box. She sank back against the pillows and I saw that she was breathing hard. When I began to read, she closed her eyes.

Page two was a police report. The writer was one Detective Salvatore J. Giordano, 19th Precinct, Borough of Manhattan, City of New York. In his

> opinion, and supported by subsequently entered Medical Examiner's Report, Case #1453331, Deceased Victim Rosenblatt, H. A., white male, age 59, expired as the consequence of a rapid downward descent from diagrammed window B, master bedroom, of said address on E. 67 St., and subsequent extreme bodily contact with pavement in front of said address.

> Descent process was most probably self-induced, as D. Victim's blood alcohol was not elevated and there is no lab evidence of

drug-induced accident and no signs of co-
erced egress enforced on Deceased Victim on
the part of another as well as no skidmarks
on the carpeting of said address or defense
marks on window sills, and, in summary, no
evidence of the presence of any other individual at said address. Of further note is the
presence of Drinking Glass A (see diagram)
and Apparatus B (see diagram) conforming
to method operandus of the "East Side Burglar."

An aerial diagram at the bottom of the page illus-
trated the locations of doors, windows, and furniture
in the room where Harvey Rosenblatt had spent his
last moments.

A bed, two nightstands, two dressers—one
marked "Low," the other "High"—a television set,
something marked "antique," and a magazine rack.
On one of the nightstands were written "Glass A"
and "Apparatus B (lockpicks, files, and keys)." Ar-
rows marked the window from which the psychiatrist
had leaped.

The next paragraph identified the apartment as
an eighth-floor, five-room unit in a co-op building. At
the time of Rosenblatt's jump, the owners and sole
occupants, Mr. and Mrs. Malcolm J. Rulerad, he a
banker, she an attorney, were away in Europe on a
three-week vacation. Neither had ever met

deceased Victim Rosenblatt and both wit-
nesses state unequivocally that they have no
idea how D.V. gained ingress to said domicile. However, the burglary apparatus recovered from a bathroom of said domicile
indicates Breaking and Entering, and the fact
that the day doorman, Mr. William P.

O'Donnell, states he never saw D. Victim enter the building's main lobby, indicates a stealthy ingress by D. Victim. Furthermore, Drinking Glass A, subsequently identified by Mrs. Rulerad as coming from her kitchen, was full of a dark liquid, subsequently identified as Diet Pepsi-Cola, a drink favored by Mrs. M. Rulerad, and this is in conformity with the method operandus of three prior B and E burglaries within a six-block radius, previously attributed to the "East Side Burglar," in which soft drinks were displayed in a partially drunk status. Though D. Victim's wife denies a criminal history on the part of D. Victim, who she says was a psychiatrist, physical evidence indicates a "secret life" on the part of D. Victim and a possible motive: guilt over said secret life due to D. Victim being a psychiatrist and outward "solid citizen" and finally coming to grips with this unrespectable secret.

Next came a half page follow-up by Detective Giordano, dated a week later:

Case #1453331, Rosenblatt, H. Requested permission from D. Victim's wife to search home premises on E. 65 St. due to search for evidence related to D. Victim's death. Said search effected 4/17/85 at 3:23 P.M. to 5:17 P.M. in company of Det. B. Wildebrandt and Officer J. McGovern. Home and office premises of D. Victim searched in presence of D. Victim's wife, Shirley Rosenblatt. No contraband from previous "East Side Burglaries" found. Permission requested to read D. Victim's psychiatric files for possible patient/fence connection, refused by S. Rosenblatt. Will consult with Chief of Dets. A. M. Talisiani.

The following page was typed on a different machine and signed by Detective Lewis S. Jackson, 19th Precinct. The date was four weeks later.

Conf. on Det. Giordano's case, #1453331, H. A. Rosenblatt. Det. Giordano on med. leave. D. Victim's wife, Shirley Rosenblatt, and son, Joshua Rosenblatt, requested meeting to review case. Wanting "progress" report. Met with them at Pcnct. Told of disposition. Very angry, said they were "deceived" as to purpose of home search. Son stated he is an attorney, knows "people." He and mother convinced hom., not sui. Stated D.V. not depressed, never depressed, not "criminal." Further stated "there was some sort of setup." Further stated D.V. had talked to wife, prior to death, about "upsetting case that could be related to what happened to my dad," but when asked for details, said he didn't know because D.V. was psychiatrist and kept secrets because of "ethics." When told nothing more could be done based on available evidence, son became even more irate and threatened to "go above you to get some action." Conversation reported to Chief of Dets. A. M. Talisiani.

The final two pages consisted of a letter on heavy white bond, dated one and a half months later.

COMSAC INVESTIGATIVE SERVICES
513 Fifth Avenue
Suite 3463
New York, NY 10110

June 30, 1985

Dr. Shirley Rosenblatt
c/o J. Rosenblatt, Esq.
Schechter, Mohl, and Trimmer
500 Fifth Avenue
Suite 3300

New York, NY 10110

Dear Dr. Rosenblatt:

Pursuant to your request, we have reviewed data and materials relevant to the unfortunate death of your husband, including but not limited to detailed inspection of all case reports, forensic reports, and laboratory analyses. We have also interviewed police personnel involved in this case.

Personal inspection of the premises where aforesaid unfortunate death took place was not fully accomplished because the owners of the apartment in question, Mr. and Mrs. Malcolm J. Rulerad, did not grant permission to our staff to enter and inspect. However, we do feel that we have accrued enough data with which to evaluate your case and we regret to inform you that we see no reason to doubt the conclusions of the police department in this matter. Furthermore, in view of the specific details of this case, we do not advise any further investigation into this matter.

Please feel free to get in touch if there are any questions concerning this matter.

Respectfully yours,
Robert D. Sugrue
Senior Investigator and Supervisor

INVOICE FOR SERVICES RENDERED

*Twenty-two (22) hours at
Sixty-Five (65) Dollars per Hour: $1430.00*

*Minus 10% Professional Discount to
Schechter, Mohl, and Trimmer, Attys: $1287.00*

Please Remit This Sum

I put down the file.

Shirley Rosenblatt's eyes were wide open and moist.

"The second death," she said. "Like killing him again." Shake of head. "Four years . . . but it's still —that's why Josh is so angry. No resolution. Now, you come . . ."

"I'm—"

"No." She managed to place a finger over her mouth. Dropped it and smiled. "Good. The truth outs."

Wider smile, a different meaning behind it.

"Harvey as a burglar," she said. "It's almost funny. And I'm not in prolonged denial. I lived with him for thirty-one years."

Sounding resolute, but she looked to me for confirmation, anyway.

I nodded.

She shook her head. "So how did he get in that apartment, right? That's what they kept asking me, and I didn't know what to tell them."

"He was lured there," I said. "Probably under the guise of a patient call. Someone he thought he could help."

"Harvey," she said softly. She closed her eyes. Opened them. "The police kept saying suicide. Over and over. . . . Because Harvey was a psychiatrist, one of them—the chief of detectives—Talisiani—told me everyone knew psychiatrists had a high suicide rate. Then he told me to consider myself lucky that they weren't pursuing it further. That if they did, everything would come out."

" 'In view of the specific details of this case,' " I said.

"That's the private one, right? Comsac. At least the police were a lot more . . . direct. Talisiani told me if we made waves Harvey's name would be dragged through the slime. The whole family would be permanently coated with 'slime.' He seemed *offended* that we didn't want him to close the case. As if we were criminals. Everyone made us feel that way . . . and now you're coming and telling me we were right."

She managed to press her palms together. "Thank you."

She slumped back on the pillow and breathed hard through dry lips. Tears filled her eyes, overflowed, and began draining down her cheeks. I wiped them with a tissue. Her lower body still hadn't moved.

"I'm so sad," she whispered. "Thinking about it, again . . . picturing it. But I'm glad you've come. You've . . . validated me—us. I'm only sorry you have to go through this pain. You really think it's something to do with Andres?"

"I do."

"Harvey never said anything."

I said, "The upsetting case Josh told Detective Jackson about—"

"A few weeks before . . ." Two deep breaths. "We were lunching, Harvey and I. We had lunch almost every day. He was upset. He was rarely upset —such an even man . . . he said it was a case. A patient he'd just talked to, he'd found it very disillusioning."

She turned toward me and her face was quaking.

"Disillusioned about Andres?" I said.

"He didn't mention Andres's name . . . didn't give me any details."

"Nothing at all?"

"Harvey and I never talked about cases. We made that rule right at the beginning of our marriage . . . two therapists . . . it's so easy to slip. You tell yourself it's . . . okay, it's professional consultation. And then you let loose more details than you need to. And then names slip out . . . and then you're talking about patients to your therapist friends at cocktail parties." She shook her head. "Rules are best."

"But Harvey must have told you something to make you suspect a connection to his death."

"No," she said sadly. "We really didn't suspect . . . we were just . . . grasping. Looking for anything out of the ordinary. So the police would see Harvey didn't . . . the whole thing was so . . . psychotic. Harvey in a stranger's apartment."

Remembered shame colored her face.

I said, "The owners of the apartment—the Rulerads. Harvey didn't know them?"

"They were mean people. Cold. I called the wife and begged her to let the private detective in to look. I even apologized—for what I don't know. She told me I was lucky she wasn't suing me for Harvey's break-in and hung up."

She closed her eyes for a long time and didn't move. I wondered if she'd fallen asleep.

Then she said, "Harvey was so affected . . . by this patient. *That's* what made me suspect. Cases never got to him. To be disillusioned . . . Andres? It doesn't make sense."

"De Bosch was his teacher, wasn't he? If Harvey

learned something terrible about him, that could have disillusioned him."

Slow, sad nod.

I said, "How close was their relationship?"

"Teacher and student close. Harvey admired Andres, though he thought he was a little · . . . authoritarian."

"Authoritarian in what way?"

"Dogmatic—when he was convinced he was right. Harvey thought it ironic, since Andres had fought so hard against the Nazis . . . wrote so passionately for democracy . . . yet his personal style could be so . . ."

"Dictatorial?"

"At times. But Harvey still admired him. For who he was, what he'd done. Saving those French children from the Vichy government, his work on child development. And he *was* a good teacher. Once in a while I sat in on seminars. Andres holding court —like a don. He could talk for hours and keep you interested . . . lots of jokes. Tying everything in with punchlines. Sometimes he brought children in from the wards. He had a gift—they opened up to him."

"What about Katarina?" I said. "Harvey told me she sat in, too."

"She did . . . just a child, herself—a teenager, but she spoke up as if she was a peer. And now she's . . . and those other people—how can this be!"

"Sometimes authoritarianism can go too far," I said.

Her cheeks shook. Then her mouth turned up in a tiny, disturbing smile. "Yes, I suppose nothing's what it seems, is it? Patients have been telling me that for thirty years and I've been nodding and saying, yes, I know . . . I really didn't know . . ."

"Did you ever go back into Harvey's files? To try to figure which patient had upset him?"

Long stare. Guilty nod.

"He kept tapes," she said. "He didn't like writing —arthritis—so he taped. I wouldn't let the police listen to them . . . protecting the patients. But later, I began playing them for myself . . . I gave myself an excuse. For their own good—I was responsible for them, until they found another permanent therapist. Had to call them, to notify them . . . so I needed to know them." Downcast eyes. "Flimsy . . . I listened anyway. Months of sessions, Harvey's voice . . . sometimes I couldn't stand it. But there was nothing that would have disillusioned him. All his patients were like old friends. He hadn't taken on any new ones for two years."

"None at all?"

She shook her head. "Harvey was an old-fashioned analyst. The couch, free association, long-term, intensive work. The same fifteen people, three to five times a week."

"Even an old patient might have told him something disillusioning."

"No," she said, "there was nothing like that in any of the sessions. And none of his old patients brought him to harm. They all loved him."

"What did you do with the tapes?"

Rather than answer, she said, "He was gentle, accepting. He helped those people. They were all crushed."

"Did you pick any of them up as patients?"

"No . . . I was in no shape to work. Not for a long time. Even my own patients . . ." She attempted another shrug. "Things fell apart for a while . . . so many people let down. That's why I didn't pursue his death. For my kids and for his patients—his extended family. For me. I couldn't have us dragged through the slime. Do you understand?"

"Of course." I asked her again what she'd done with the tapes.

"I destroyed them," she said, as if hearing the question for the first time. "Smashed the cassettes with a hammer . . . one by one . . . what a mess . . . threw it all away." She smiled. "Catharsis?"

I said, "Did Harvey attend any conventions just before his death? Any psychiatric meetings or seminars on child welfare?"

"No. Why?"

"Because professional meetings may set the killer off. Two of the other therapists were murdered at conventions. And the de Bosch symposium where I met Harvey may have triggered the killings in the first place."

"No," she said. "No, he didn't attend anything. He'd sworn off conventions. Sworn off academia. Gave up his appointment at NYU so he could concentrate on his patients and his family and getting in shape—his father had died young of a heart attack. Harvey had reached that age, confronted his own mortality. He was starting to work out. Trimming the fat from his diet and his life—that's a quote. . . . He said he wanted to be around for me and the kids for a long, long time."

Grimacing, she lifted her hand, with effort, and let it drop upon mine. Her palm was soft and cold. Her eyes aimed at the fish tank and stayed there.

"Is there anything else you can tell me?" I said. "Anything at all?"

She thought for a long time. "No . . . I'm sorry, I wish there was."

"Thanks for seeing me," I said. Her hand weighed a ton.

"Please let me know," she said, keeping it there. "Whatever you find."

"I will."

"How long will you be in New York?"

"I think I'll try to head back this evening."

"If you need a place to stay, you're welcome here . . . if you don't mind a pull-out couch."

"That's very kind," I said, "but I need to be getting back."

"Your nice woman?"

"And my home." Whatever that meant.

Grimacing, she exerted barely tangible pressure upon my hand. Giving *me* comfort.

We heard the door close, then footsteps. Josh came in, holding Leo, the cat. He looked at our hands and his eyebrows dipped.

"You okay?" he said to his mother.

"Yes, honey. Dr. Delaware's been helpful. It's good you brought him."

"Helpful how?"

"He validated us . . . about Dad."

"Great," said Josh, putting the cat down. "Meanwhile, you're not getting enough rest."

Her lower lip dropped.

"Enough exertion, Mom," he said. "*Please.* You have to rest."

"I'm okay, honey. Really."

I felt a small tug atop my hand, not much more than a muscle twitch. Lifting her hand and placing it on the bedcovers, I stood.

Josh walked around the other side of the bed and began straightening the covers. "You *really* need to rest, Mom. The doctor said rest is the most important thing."

"I know . . . I'm sorry . . . I will, Josh."

"Good."

She made a gulping sound. Tears clouded the gentle blue eyes.

"Oh, Mom," he cried out, sounding ten years old.

"It's okay, honey."

"No, no, I'm being an asshole, I'm sorry, it's been a really tough day."

"Tell me about it, baby."

"Believe me, you don't want to hear it."

"Yes, I do. Tell me."

He sat down next to her. I slipped out the door and saw myself out of the apartment.

28

I reserved a seat on the next flight back to L.A., threw clothes in my bag, and told Milo and Rick's message machine my arrival time. Checking out of the Middleton, I flagged a taxi to Kennedy.

A fire on Queens Boulevard slowed things down and it took an hour and three quarters to reach the airport. When I got to the check-in counter, I learned my flight had been delayed for thirty-five minutes. Pay TVs were attached to some of the seats, and travelers stared at their screens as if some kind of truth was being broadcast.

I found a terminal lounge that looked half decent and downed a leathery corned beef sandwich and a club soda while eavesdropping on a group of salesmen. Their truths were simple: the economy sucked and women didn't know what the hell they wanted.

I returned to the departure area, found a free TV, and fed it quarters. A local station was broadcasting the news and that seemed about as good as it was going to get.

Potholes in the Bronx. Condom handouts in the

public schools. The mayor fighting with the city council as the city accrued crushing debt. That made me feel right at home.

A few more local stories, and then the anchorwoman said, "Nationally, government statistics show a decline in consumer spending, and a Senate subcommittee is investigating charges of influence peddling by another of the President's sons. And in California, officials at Folsom Prison report that a lockdown has apparently been successful in averting riots in the wake of what is believed to have been a racially motivated double murder at that maximum-security facility. Early this morning, two inmates, both believed to have been associates of a white supremacist gang, were stabbed to death by unknown inmates suspected of belonging to the Nuestra Raza, a Mexican gang. The dead men, identified as Rennard Russell Haupt and Donald Dell Wallace, were both serving sentences for murder. A prison investigation into the killings continues . . ."

Nuestra Raza. NR forever. The tattoos on Roddy Rodriguez's hands. . . .

I thought of Rodriguez's masonry yard, shut down, cleaned out, and padlocked. The flight from the house on McVine prepared well in advance.

Evelyn had entertained me in her backyard, as her husband's homeboys honed their shanks.

Making an appointment for Wednesday, then going into the house with her husband and changing it to Thursday.

Twenty-four more hours for getaway.

Hurley Keffler's debacle at my house made sense now, as did Sherman Bucklear's nagging. Prison rumblings had probably told the Iron Priests what was brewing. Locating Rodriguez might have forestalled the hit or, if the deed had already been done, given the Priests instant payback.

Payback.

The same old stupid cycle of violence.

Burglary tools and a quick shove out a eight-story window.

A corpse on a garage floor, a little boy baby never to be.

Two little girls on the run.

Were Chondra and Tiffani in some Mexican border town, being tutored in Fugitive 1A with more care than they'd ever been taught to read or write?

Or maybe Evelyn had taken them somewhere they could blend in. On the surface. But, suckled on violence, they'd always be different. Unable to understand why, years later, they gravitated toward cruel, violent men.

Static dripped out of the speakers—a barely comprehensible voice announcing something about boarding. I got up and took my place in line. Six thousand miles in less than twenty-four hours. My mind and my legs ached. I wondered if Shirley Rosenblatt would ever be able to walk again.

Soon, I'd be three time zones away from her problems and a lot closer to my own.

The flight got in just before midnight. The terminal was deserted and Robin was waiting outside the automatic doors.

"You look exhausted," she said, as we walked to her truck.

"I've felt perkier."

"Well, I've got some news that might perk you up. Milo called just before I left to pick you up. Something about the tape. I was just out the door and he was running, too, but he says he learned something important."

"The sheriff who was working on it must have picked up something. Where's Milo now?"

"Out on some assignment. He said he'd be home when we got there."

"Which home?"

The question threw her. "Oh—Milo's house. He and Rick took really good care of us. And home is where the heart is, right?"

I slept in the car. We pulled up at Milo's house at twelve-forty. He was waiting in the living room, wearing a gray polo shirt and jeans. A cup of coffee was in front of him, next to a portable tape recorder. The dog snored at his feet, but woke up when we came in, gave out a few desultory licks, then collapsed again.

"Welcome home, boys and girls."

I put my bags down. "Did you hear about Donald Dell?"

Milo nodded.

"What?" said Robin.

I told her.

She said, "Oh . . ."

Milo said, "Nuestra Raza. Could be the father-in-law."

"That's what I figured. It's probably why Evelyn postponed her appointment with me. Rodriguez told her they had to leave Wednesday. And why Hurley Keffler hassled me—where is he?"

"Still in. I found a few traffic warrants and had one of the jailers lose his paperwork—just another few days, but every little bit helps."

Robin said, "It never ends."

"It's all right," I said. "There's no reason for the Priests to bother us."

"True," said Milo, too quickly. "They and the

Raza boys will be concentrating on each other now.
That's their main game: my turn to die, your turn to
die."

"Lovely," said Robin.

"I had some Foothill guys drop in on them after
Keffler's bust," he said, "but I'll see if I can arrange
another visit. Don't worry about them, Rob. Really.
They're the least of our problems."

"As opposed to?"

He looked at the tape recorder.

We sat down. He punched a button.

The child's voice came on.

> Bad love bad love.
> Don't give me the bad love.

I looked at him. He held up a finger.

> Bad love bad love.
> Don't give me the bad love . . .

Same flat tones, but this time the voice was that
of a man.

Ordinary, middle-pitched, male voice. Nothing
remarkable about the accent or the timbre.

The child's voice transformed—some kind of
electronic manipulation?

Something familiar about the voice . . . but I
couldn't place it.

Someone I'd met a long time ago? In 1979?

The room was silent, except for the dog's breathing.

Milo turned the recorder off and looked at me.
"Ring any bells?"

I said, "There's something about it, but I don't
know what it is."

"The kid's voice was phony. What you just heard might be the real bad guy. No bells, huh?"

"Let me hear it again."

Rewind. Play.

"Again," I said.

This time, I listened with my eyes closed, squinting so hard the lids felt welded together.

Listening to someone who hated me.

Nothing registered.

Robin and Milo studied my face as if it were some great wonder. My head hurt badly.

"No," I said. "I still can't pinpoint it—I can't even be sure I've actually heard it."

Robin touched my shoulder. Milo's face was blank, but his eyes showed disappointment.

I glanced at the recorder and nodded.

He rewound again.

This time the voice seemed even more distant—as if my memory was spiraling away from me. As if I'd missed my chance.

"Goddammit," I said. The dog's eyes opened. He trotted over to me and nuzzled my hand. I rubbed his head, looked at Milo. "One more time."

Robin said, "You're tired. Why don't we try again in the morning?"

"Just once more," I said.

Rewind. Play.

The voice.

Completely foreign now. Mocking me.

I buried my face in my hands. Robin's hands on my neck were an abstract comfort—I appreciated the sentiment but couldn't relax.

"What did you mean *might* be the bad guy?" I asked Milo.

"Sheriff's scientific guess. He tuned it down from the kid's voice using a preset frequency."

"How can he be sure the kid's voice was altered in the first place?"

"Because his machines told him so. He came across it by accident—working on the screams—which, incidentally, he's ninety-nine percent positive are Hewitt's. Then he got to the kid chanting and something bothered him about it—the evenness of the voice."

"The robot quality," I said.

"Yeah. But he didn't assume brainwashing or anything else psychological. He's a techno-dude, so he analyzed the sound waves and saw something fishy with the cycle-to-cycle amplitude—the changes in pitch within each sound wave. Real human voices shimmer and jitter. This didn't, so he knew the tape had been messed with electronically, probably using a pitch shifter. It's a gizmo that samples a sound and changes the frequency. Tune up, you've got Alvin and the Chipmunks; tune down, you're James Earl Jones."

"Hi-tech bad guy," I said.

"Not really. The basic machines are pretty cheap. People attach them to phones—women living alone wanting to sound like Joe Testosterone. They're also used for recording music—creating automatic harmonies. A singer lays down a vocal track, then creates a harmony and overdubs it, instant Everly Brothers."

"Sure," said Robin. "Shifters are used all the time. I've seen them interfaced with amps so guitarists can do multiple tracks."

"Lyle Gritz," I said. "The next Elvis. . . . How'd the sheriff know which frequency to tune down to?"

"He assumed we were dealing with a male bad guy using a relatively cheap shifter because nowadays the better machines *can* be programmed to include jitter. The cheap ones usually come with two, maybe three standard settings: tune up to kid, tune down to adult, sometimes there's an intermediate set-

ting for adult female. By computing the pitch difference, he worked backwards and tuned down. But if
our guy's some sort of acoustics nut with fancy equipment, there may be other things he's done to alter his
voice and what you heard may be nowhere near his
real voice."

"It may not even be his voice that he altered. He
could have shifted someone else's."

"That, too. But you think you might have heard
him before."

"That was my first impression. But I don't know.
I don't trust my judgment anymore."

"Well," he said, "at least we know there's no actual kid involved."

"Thank God for that. Okay, leave the tape with
me. I'll work with it tomorrow, see if anything clicks."

"The screams being Hewitt, what does 'ninety-
nine percent' mean?"

"It means the sheriff'll get up on the stand and
testify it's highly probable to the best of his professional knowledge. Only trouble is, we need to get
someone on trial first."

"So I was right, this isn't some homeless guy.
He'd need a place to keep his equipment."

He shrugged. "Maybe he's got a secret den somewhere and that's where he's hiding out right now. I
had talks about Gritz with detectives at other substations. If the scrote's still lurking around, we'll hook
him."

"He is," I said. "He hasn't completed his homework."

I told Milo what I'd learned in New York.

He said, "Pseudo-burglary? Sounds hokey."

"New York cops didn't think so. It matched some
previous break-ins in the neighborhood: jimmied
locks, people on vacation, a glass of soda left on the

bedroom nightstand. Soda from the victim's kitchen. Sound familiar?''

"Were any of the other burglaries in the papers?"

"I don't know."

"If they were, all we've probably got is a copycat. If they weren't, maybe our killer has a burglary sideline. Why don't you get a hold of some four-year-old papers and find out. I'll phone New York and see if Gritz's name or Silk-Merino's shows up on their blotters around the time of Rosenblatt's fall."

"He's been pretty careful about keeping his nose clean so far."

"It doesn't have to be a major felony, Alex. Son of Sam got busted on a parking ticket. Lots of cases get solved that way, the stupid stuff."

"Okay," I said. "I'll hit the library soon as it opens."

He picked up his cup and drank. "So what's Rosenblatt's motive for jumping supposed to have been?"

"Guilt. Coming to grips with his secret criminal identity."

He scowled. "What, he's standing there, about to glom jewelry, and he suddenly gets a guilt flash? Sounds like horseshit to me."

"The family thought so, too, but the New York police seemed convinced. They told the widow if she pressed the issue, everyone's name would be dragged through the slime. A private investigator she hired told her the same thing, more tactfully."

I gave him names and he jotted them down.

Looking into his coffee, he said, "You want, there's still some in the pot."

"No, thanks."

Robin said, "Another fall—just like the other two."

"Delmar Parker's run off the mountain," I said.

"That has to be the connection. The killer was trauma-tized in a major way and is trying to get even. We've got to find out more about the accident."

Milo said, "I still haven't had any luck locating Delmar's mother. And none of the Santa Barbara pa-pers covered the crash."

"Out of all those Corrective School alumni," I said, "someone's got to know."

"Still no files, anywhere. Sally and the gang pried up Katarina's floorboards. And we can't find any records, yet, of de Bosch applying for government funds."

Over the rim of his cup, his face was heavy and beat. He ran his hand over it.

"It bothers me," he said. "Rosenblatt—an experi-enced psychiatrist—meeting someone in a strange apartment like that."

"He was experienced, but he had a soft heart. The killer could have lured him there with a cry for help."

"That's not exactly standard operating shrink procedure, is it? Was Rosenblatt some kind of avant-garde guy, believed in on-the-scene treatment?"

"His wife said he was an orthodox analyst."

"Those guys *never* leave the office, right? Need their couches and their little notebooks."

"True, but she also said he'd been very upset by something that had happened in a session recently. Disillusioned. It's a reasonable bet it had something to do with de Bosch. Something that shook him up enough to meet the killer out of the office. He could have believed he was going to the killer's home—the killer could have given him a good rationale for meet-ing there. Like a disability that kept him homebound —maybe even bedridden. The window Rosenblatt went out of was in a bedroom."

"Phony cripple," he said, nodding. "Then Rosenblatt goes to the window and the bad guy jumps up, shoves him out . . . very cold. And the wife had no idea what disillusioned him enough to make a house call?''

''She tried to find out. Broke her own rules and listened to his therapy tapes. But there was nothing out of the ordinary in them.''

''This disillusioning thing definitely happened during a session?''

''That's what he told her.''

''So maybe the session where he died wasn't the first with the killer. So why wasn't the first session on tape?''

''Maybe Rosenblatt didn't take his recorder with him. Or the patient requested no taping. Rosenblatt would have complied. Or maybe the session was re-corded and the tape got destroyed.''

''A stranger's bedroom—that has almost a sexual flavor to it, don't you think?''

I nodded. ''The ritual.''

''Who owned the place?''

''A couple named Rulerad. They said they'd never heard of Harvey Rosenblatt. Shirley said they were pretty hostile to her. Refused access to the pri-vate detective and threatened to sue her.''

''Can't really blame them, can you? Come home and find out someone broke into your place and used it for a swan dive. Was Rosenblatt the type to be a soft touch for a sob story?''

''Definitely. He probably got the same kind of call Bert Harrison did and responded to it. And died because of it.''

Milo said, ''So why did the killer keep his ap-pointment with Rosenblatt but not with Harrison? Why, now that I'm thinking about it, was Harrison let off the hook completely? *He* worked for de Bosch, *he* spoke at that goddamn conference, too. So how come everyone else in that boat is sunk or sinking and *he's* on shore drinking piña coladas?"

"I don't know."

"I mean, that's funny, don't you think, Alex? That break in the pattern—maybe I should learn a little more about Harrison."

"Maybe," I said, feeling sick. "Wouldn't *that* be something. There I was, sitting across the table from him—trying to protect him . . . he treated Mitch Lerner. He knew where Katarina lived . . . hard to believe. He seemed like such a sweet guy."

"Any idea where he's gone?"

I shook my head. "But he's not exactly unobtrusive with those purple clothes."

"Purple clothes?" said Robin.

"He says it's the only color he can see."

"Another weird one," said Milo. "What is it about your profession?"

"Ask the killer," I said. "He's got strong opinions on the subject."

29

We spent the night at Milo's. After he left for work, I stayed and listened to the tape another dozen times.

The chanting man sounded like an accountant tallying up a sum.

That maddening hint of familiarity, but nothing jelled.

We returned to Benedict Canyon, where Robin took the dog to the garage and I called in for messages. One from Jean Jeffers—*No record of Mr. G*—and a request to phone Judge Stephen Huff.

I reached him in his chambers.

"Hi, Alex. I assume you heard."

"Is there anything I should know other than what's been on the news?"

"They're pretty positive who did it, but can't prove it yet. Two Mexican gang members—they're figuring some kind of drug war."

"That's probably it," I said.

"Well, that's one way to settle a case. Any word from the grandmother?"

"Not a one."

"Better off—the kids, I mean. Away from all of this—don't you think?"

"Depends on what environment they've been placed into."

"Oh, sure. Absolutely. Well, thanks for your help. Onward toward justice."

Several more tries at the tape, then I left for the Beverly Hills library.

I scoured four- and five-year-old editions of New York dailies all morning, reading very slowly and carefully, but finding no record of any "East Side Burglar."

No great surprise: the 19th Precinct serviced a high-priced zip code, and its inhabitants probably despised getting their names anywhere in the paper other than the society pages. The people who *owned* the papers and broadcast the news probably lived in the 19th. The rest of the city would know exactly what they wanted it to.

Lack of coverage still didn't mean Rosenblatt's killer had committed the earlier break-ins. Local residents might be aware of the burglaries, and a local could know who was on vacation and for how long. But the idea of a 19th Precinct resident owning burglary tools and robbing from his neighbors seemed less than likely. So Mr. Silk probably had burgled before. Ritualistically.

The same attempt to use what was at hand, to master and dominate the victim.

Bad love.

Myra Evans Paprock.

Rodney Shipler.

Katarina.

Only at those three scenes had the words been left behind.

Three bloody, undisguised murders. No attempt made to present them as anything else.

Stoumen, Lerner, and Rosenblatt, on the other hand, had been dispatched as phony accidents.

Two classes of victims . . . two kinds of revenge?

Butchery for the laypeople, falls for the therapists.

But *Katarina* had been a therapist . . .

Then I realized that at the time of Mr. Silk's trauma—sometime before seventy-nine, probably closer to seventy-three, the year Delmar Parker had gone off the mountain—she hadn't yet graduated. In her early twenties, still a grad student.

Two patterns . . . part of some elaborate ragelust fantasy that a sane mind could never hope to understand?

And where did Becky Basille fit in?

Two killers . . .

I remembered the clean, bustling street where Harvey Rosenblatt had landed: French restaurants, flower boxes, and limos.

How long had it taken the poor man to realize what the swift, sharp shove at the small of his back meant?

I hoped he hadn't. Hoped, against logic, that he'd felt nothing but the Icarus-pleasure of pure flight.

A fall, always a fall.

Delmar Parker. Had to be.

Avenging an abused child?

Surely if de Bosch had been abusive, someone would remember.

Why hadn't anyone spoken out after all these years?

But no big puzzle there: without proof, who would believe them? And why rake up the dirt around a dead man's grave if it meant stirring up one's own childhood demons?

Still, *someone* had to know what happened to the boy in the stolen truck, and why it had set off a killer.

I sat there for a long time, staring at tiny, microfilmed words.

Corrective School alumni . . . how to get hold of them. Then I thought of one. Someone I'd never met, a name I'd never even learned.

A problem child whose treatment had given Katarina the leash to put around my neck.

I returned the microfilm spools and rushed to the pay phones in the library's lobby, trying to figure out who to call.

Western Pediatric, the late seventies . . .

The hospital had undergone a massive financial and professional overhaul during the past year. So many people gone.

But one notable one had returned.

Reuben Eagle had been chief resident when I'd started as a staff psychologist. He'd taken a professorship at the U's med school, a gifted teacher, specializing in medical education. The new Western Peds board had just wooed him back as general pediatrics division head. I'd just seen his picture in the hospital newsletter: the same tortoiseshell spectacles, the light brown hair thinner, grayer, the lean, ruddy outdoorsman's face adorned by a trimmed, graying beard.

His secretary said he was out on the wards and I asked her to page him. He answered a few moments later, saying, "Rube Eagle," in a soft, pleasant voice.

"Rube, it's Alex Delaware."

"Alex—wow, this is a surprise."

"How're things going?"

"Not bad, how about you?"

"Hanging in. Listen, Rube, I need a small favor. I'm trying to locate one of Henry Bork's daughters and I was wondering if you had any idea how to reach her."

"Which daughter? Henry and Mo had a bunch—three or four, I think."

"The youngest. She had learning problems, was sent to a remedial school in Santa Barbara around seventy-six or seventy-seven. She'd be around twenty-eight or twenty-nine now."

"That would have to be Meredith," he said. "*Her* I remember because one year Henry had the interns' party at his house and she was there—very good-looking, a real flirt. I thought she was older and ended up talking to her. Then someone warned me and I split fast."

"Warned you about her age?"

"That and her problems. Supposedly a wild kid. I remember hearing something about institutionalization. Apparently she really put Henry and Mo through it—did you know he died?"

"Yes," I said.

"Ben Wardley, too. And Milt Chenier . . . how come you're looking for Meredith?"

"Long story, Rube. It has to do with the school she was sent to."

"What about it?"

"Things may have happened there."

"Happened? *Another* mess?" He sounded more sad than surprised.

"It's possible."

"Anything I should know about?"

"Not unless you had something to do with the school—the Corrective School, founded by a psychologist named Andres de Bosch."

"Nope," he said. "Well, I hope you clear it up.

And as far as Meredith's concerned, I think she still lives in L.A. Something to do with the film business."

"Is her name still Bork?"

"Hmm, don't know—if you'd like I can call Mo and find out. She's still pretty involved with the hospital—I can tell her I'm putting a mailing list together or something."

"I'd really appreciate that, Rube."

"Stay on the line, I'll see if I can get her."

I waited for fifteen minutes with the speaker to my mouth. Pretending to look busy each time someone came by to use the phone. Finally, Rube came back on the line.

"Alex?"

"Still here."

"Yes, Meredith's in L.A. She has her own public relations firm. I don't know if she ever married, but she still goes by Bork."

He gave me the address and phone number and I thanked him again.

"Sure bet . . . another mess. Too bad. How'd you get involved, Alex? Through a patient?"

"No," I said. "Someone sent me a message."

Bork and Hoffman Public Relations, 8845 Wilshire Boulevard, Suite 304.

The eastern edge of Beverly Hills. A five-minute ride from the library.

The receptionist said, "Ms. Bork is on another line."

"I'll hold."

"And what was the name again?"

"Dr. Alex Delaware. I worked with her father at Western Pediatric Medical Center."

"One moment, sir."

A few minutes later: "Sir? Ms. Bork will be right with you."

Then, a smoky female voice: "Meredith Bork."

I introduced myself.

She said, "I specialize in the entertainment industries, doctor—movies, theater. We do a few doctors when they write books. Have you written a book?"

"No—"

"Just want to beef up your practice, a little press exposure? Good idea in today's economy, but it's not our thing. Sorry. I'll be happy to give you the name of someone who does medical publicity, though—"

"Thanks, but I'm not looking for a publicist."

"Oh?"

"Ms. Bork, I'm sorry to bother you, but what I'm after is some information about Andres de Bosch and the Corrective School, in Santa Barbara."

Silence.

"Ms. Bork?"

"This is for *real*?"

"Some suspicions have come up about mistreatment at the school. Things that happened during the early seventies. An accident involving a boy named Delmar Parker."

No answer.

"May, nineteen seventy-three," I said. "Delmar Parker went off a mountain road and died. Do you remember hearing anything about him? Or anything about mistreatment?"

"This is too much," she said. "Why the fuck is this any of *your* business?"

"I work as a consultant to the police."

"The *police* are investigating the school?"

"They're doing a preliminary investigation."

Harsh laughter. "You're putting me on."

"No." I gave her Milo as a reference.

She said, "Okay, so? What makes you think I even went to this school?"

"I worked at Western Pediatric Medical Center when your father was chief of staff and—"

"Word got around. Oh, I'll just bet it did. Jesus."

"Ms. Bork, I'm really sorry—"

"I'll just bet it did . . . the Corrective School." Another angry laugh. "Finally."

Silence.

"After all these years. What a trip . . . the Corrective School. For bad little children in need of correction. Yeah, I was corrected, all right. I was corrected up the ying-yang."

"Were you mistreated?"

"Mistreated?" Peals of laughter so loud I backed away from the receiver. "How delicately put, doctor. Are you a delicate man? One of those sensitive guys really tuned in to people's feelings?"

"I try."

"Well, goody for you—I'm sorry, this *is* serious, isn't it. My problem—always was. Not taking things seriously. Not being *mature*. Being mature's a drag, isn't it, doc? I fucking refuse. That's why I work in entertainment. Nobody in entertainment's grown up. Why do *you* do what *you* do?"

"Fame and fortune," I said.

She laughed, harder and louder. "Psychologists, psychiatrists, I've known a shitload of them . . . how do I know you're for real—hey, this isn't some gag, is it? Did *Ron* put you up to this?"

"Who's Ron?"

"Another sensitive guy."

"Don't know him."

"I'll bet."

"I'd be happy to show you credentials."

"Sure, slip them through the phone."

"Want me to fax them?"

"Nah . . . what's the diff? So what do you really want?"

"Just to talk to you a bit about the school."

"Good old school. School days, cruel days . . . hold on . . ." Click. Silence. Click. "Where are you calling from?"

"Not far from your office."

"What, the pay phone downstairs, like in the movies?"

"Mile away. I can be there in five minutes."

"How convenient. No, I don't want to bring my personal shit into the office. Meet me at Cafe Mocha in an hour, or forget it. Know where it is?"

"No."

"Wilshire near Crescent Heights. Tacky little strip mall on the . . . southeast corner. Great coffee, people pretending to be *artistes*. I'll be in a booth near the back. If you're late, I won't wait around."

The restaurant was a narrow storefront blocked by blue gingham curtains. Pine tables and booths, half of them empty. Sacks of coffee stood on the floor near the entrance, listing like melting snowmen. A few desperate-looking types sat far from one another, poring over screenplays.

Meredith Bork was in the last booth, her back to the wall, a mug in her left hand. A big, beautiful, dark-haired woman sitting high and straight. The moment I walked in, her eyes were on me and they didn't waver as I approached.

Her hair was true black and shiny, brushed straight back from her head and worn loose around her shoulders. Her face was olive tinted like Robin's, just a bit rounder than oval, with wide, full lips, a straight, narrow nose, and a perfect chin. Perfect cheekbones, too, below huge gray-blue eyes. Silver-

blue nail polish to match her silk blouse. Two buttons
undone, freckled chest, an inch ·of cleavage. Strong,
square shoulders, lots of bracelets around surprisingly slender wrists. Lots of gold, all over. Even in the
weak light, she sparkled.

She said, "Great. You're cute. I allow you to sit."

She put the mug down next to a plate bearing an
oversized muffin.

"Fiber," she said. "The religion of the nineties."

A waitress came over and informed me the coffee
of the day was Ethiopian. I said that was fine and
received my own mug.

"Ethiopian," said Meredith Bork. "They're starving over there, aren't they? But they're exporting designer beans? Don't you think that's weird?"

"Someone always does okay," I said. "No matter
how bad things get."

"How true, how true." She smiled. "I like this
guy. Perfect mixture of sincerity and cynicism. *Lots* of
women love it, right? You probably use it to get laid,
then get bored and leave them weeping, right?"

I laughed involuntarily. "No."

"No, you don't get *laid*, or no, you don't get
bored?"

"No, I'm not into conning women."

"Gay?"

"No."

"What's your problem, then?"

"Are we discussing that?"

"Why not?" Giant smile. Capped teeth. "You
want to discuss *my* problems, jocko, fair is fair."

I raised my cup to my lips.

"How's the java?" she said. "Those starving Ethi-
opians know how to grow 'em?"

"Very good."

"I'm *so* veddy glad. Mine's Colombian. My regular fix. I keep hoping there'll be a packaging error and I'll get a little snort mixed in with the grind."

She rubbed her nose and winked, leaned forward, and showed more chest. A black lace bra cut into soft, freckled flesh. She wore a perfume I'd never smelled before. Lots of grass, lots of flowers, a bit of her own perspiration.

She giggled. "No, I'm just joshing you, Mr.—sorry, *Doctor* No Con. I know how touchy you healer types are about that. Daddy always had a *bovine* when someone called him mister."

"Alex is fine."

"Alex. The Great. *Are* you great? Wanna *fuck and suck*?"

Before my mouth could close, she said, "But seriously, folks."

Her smile was still on high beam and her breasts were still pushing forward. But she'd reddened and the muscles beneath one of the lovely cheekbones were twitching.

She said, "What a tasteless thing to say, right? Stupid, too, in the virus era. So let's forget about stripping off my *clothes* and concentrate on stripping my *psyche*, right?"

"Meredith—"

"That's the name, don't wear it out." Her hand brushed against the mug and a few droplets of coffee spilled on the table.

"Shit," she said, grabbing a napkin and blotting. "Now you've *really* got me spazzing."

"We don't need to talk about you, personally," I said. "Just about the school."

"Not talk about *me*? That's my favorite *topic*, Alex, the sincere shrink. I've spent Godknowshowmuch money talking to your ilk about *me*. They all pretended to be utterly fascinated, least you can do is fake it, too."

I sat back and smiled.

"I don't *like* you," she said. "Way too agreeable. Can you get a hard-on on demand—no, scratch that, no more dirty talk. This is going to be a platonic, asexual, antiseptic discussion . . . the Corrective School. How I spent my summer vacation by Meredith Spill-the-Coffee Bork."

"Were you there for only one summer?"

"It was enough, believe me."

The waitress came over and asked if we wanted anything else.

"No, dear, we're in love, we don't need anything else," said Meredith, waving her away. A wine list was propped between the salt and pepper shakers. She pulled it out and studied it. Moving her lips. Tiny droplets had formed over them. Her smooth, brown brow puckered.

She put the list down and wiped the sweat from her mouth.

"Caught me," she said. "Dyslexic. Not illiterate —I probably know more about what's going on than your average asshole senator. But it takes effort—little tricks so the words make sense." Another huge smile. "That's why I like to work with Hollywood assholes. *None* of them read."

"Is the dyslexia why you went to the Corrective School?"

"I didn't *go, Alex.* I was sent. And no, that wasn't the official reason. The official reason was I was *acting out.* One of you guys' quaint little terms for being a naughty girl—do you want to know how?"

"If you'd like to tell me."

"Of course I would, I'm an exhibitionist. No, scratch that. What's it your business?" She moistened her lips and smiled. "Suffice it to say I learned about cocks when I was much too young to appreciate them." She held out her mug to me, as if it were a microphone. "And why was that, Contestant Number One? Why, for the washer-dryer and the trip to Hawaii, did a sweet young thing from Sierra Madre besmirch herself?"

I didn't speak.

"Buzz," she said. "Sorry, Number One, that's not quick enough. The correct answer is: poor self-esteem. Twentieth-century root of all evil, right? I was fourteen and could barely read, so instead, I learned to give dynamite blow jobs."

I looked down at my coffee.

"Oh, look, I've *embarrassed* him—don't worry, I'm okay. Damn proud of my blow jobs. You work with what you've got." Her grin was huge but hard to gauge.

"One fateful morning, Mommy discovered strange, yucky stains on my junior high prom dress. Mommy consulted with learned Doctor Daddy and the two of them threw a joint shit-fit. The day school ended I was shipped off to the wild and woolly hills of Santa Barbara. Little brown uniforms, ugly shoes, girls' bunks separated from the boys' bunks by a scuzzy vegetable garden. Dr. Botch stroking his little goatee and telling us this could turn out to be the best summer we ever had."

She hid her mouth behind her mug, broke off a piece of muffin, and let it crumble between her fingers.

"I couldn't read, so they sent me to Buchenwald-on-the-Pacific. There's juvenile justice for you."

"Did de Bosch ever diagnose your dyslexia?" I said.

"You kidding? All he did was throw this Freudian shit at me: I was frustrated because Mommy had Daddy and I wanted him. So I was trying to be a woman, rather than a girl—acting *out*—in order to *displace* her."

She laughed. "Believe me, I *knew* what I wanted, and it wasn't *Daddy*. It was lean, young, well-hung bodies and James Dean faces. And I had the power to get it all back then. I believed in myself until Botch botched me up."

All at once her face changed, loosening and paling. She put the mug down hard, shook her hair like a wet puppy, and rubbed her temples.

"What did he do to you?" I said.

"Tore my soul out," she said glibly. But as she spoke she brought strands of hair forward and hid her face.

Long silence.

"Shit," she said finally. "This is harder than I thought it would be. How did he mess me up? Subtly. Nothing he could go to jail for, darling. So tell your police pals to go back to giving parking tickets, you'll never pin him. Besides, he must be ancient by now. Who's going to drag a poor old fart into court?"

"He's dead."

The hair fell away. Her eyes were very still. "Oh . . . well, that's okay by me, pal. Was it long and painful, by any chance?"

"He killed himself. He'd been sick for a while. Multiple strokes."

"Killed himself how?"

"Pills."

"When?"

"Nineteen-eighty."

The eyes tightened. "Eighty? So what's all this b.s. about an investigation?"

Her arm shot forward and she grabbed my wrist. Big, *strong* woman. "Fess up, psych-man: Who are you and what's all this really about?"

A few heads turned. She let go of my arm.

I pulled out ID, showed it to her, and said, "I've told you the truth, and what it's about is revenge."

I summarized the "bad love" murders, throwing out names of victims.

When I finished, she was smiling.

"Well, I'm sorry for those others, but . . ."

"But what?"

"Bad love," she said. "Turning his own crap against him. I like that."

"Bad love was something he *did*?"

"Oh, yeah," she said, through clenched jaws. "Bad love meant you were a worthless piece of shit who deserved to be mistreated. Bad *love* for bad little *children*—like psychological acupuncture, these tiny little needles, jabbing, twisting."

Her wrists rotated. Jewelry flashed. "But no scars. No, we didn't want to leave any marks on the beautiful little children."

"What did he actually do?"

"He *bounced* us. Good love one day, bad love the next. Publicly—when we were all together, in the lunch room, at an assembly—he was Joe Jolly. When visitors came, too. Joe Jolly. Laughing, telling jokes, lots of jokes. Tousling our hair, joining in our games— he was old but athletic. Used to like to play tether ball. When someone hurt their hand on the knob, he'd make a big show of cuddling them and kissing the boo-boo. Mister Compassionate—*Doctor* Compassionate. Telling us we were the most beautiful children in the world, the school was the most beautiful school, the teachers the most beautiful teachers. The goddamn *vegetable* garden was beautiful, even though the stuff we planted always came out stringy and we had to eat it anyway. We were one big happy, global family, a real sixties kind of thing—sometimes he even wore these puka shells around his neck, over his pukey tie."

"That was good love," I said.

She nodded and gave a small, ugly laugh. "One

big family—but if you got on his bad side—if you acted *out*, then he gave you a *private* session. And all of a sudden you weren't beautiful anymore, all of a sudden the world turned *real* ugly.''

She sniffed and used her napkin to wipe her nose. Thinking of her Colombian coffee comment, I wondered if she'd fortified herself for our appointment. She cut me off midthought:

''Don't worry, it's not nasal candy, it's plain old emotion. And the emotion I feel for that bastard, even with his being dead, is pure hatred. Isn't that amazing —after all these years? I'm surprising *myself* with how much I hate him. Because he *made* me hate *myself*—it took years to get out from under his fucking bad love.''

''The private sessions,'' I said.

''*Real* private . . . he hit me where it counted. I didn't need anyone tearing down my self-esteem—I was already fucked up enough, not able to read at thirteen. Everyone blaming me, me blaming myself . . . my sisters were all A students. I got D's. I was a premature baby. Difficult labor. Must have affected my brain—the dyslexia, my other prob—''

She threw up her hands and fluttered her fingers.

''So now it's out,'' she said, smiling. ''I have yet *another* problem. Want a shot at that diagnosis, Contestant Number One?''

I shook my head.

''Not a gambler? Oh, well, there's no reason I should be ashamed, it's all chemistry—that was my point, wasn't it? Bipolar affective disorder. Your basic, garden variety manic-depressive maniac. You tell people you're manic and they say, oh yeah, I'm feeling really manic, too. And you say, no, no, no, this is different. This is *real*, my little pretties.''

''Are you on lithium?''

Nod. ''Unless the work piles up and I need the

extra push. I finally found a psychiatrist who knew what the hell he was doing. All the others were ignorant assholes like Dr. Botch. Analyzing me, blaming me. Botch nearly convinced me I *did* want to fuck Daddy. He *totally* convinced me I was *bad*."

"With bad love?"

She stood suddenly and snatched up her purse. She was six feet tall, with a tiny waist, narrow hips, and long legs under a charcoal-colored silk miniskirt. The skirt had ridden up, revealing sleek thigh. If she realized it, she didn't choose to fix it.

"He's worried I'm leaving." She laughed. "Mellow out, son. Just going to pee."

She made an abrupt about-face and sashayed toward the rear of the restaurant. A few moments later, I got up and verified that the restrooms were back there, and the only exit a grimy gray door with a bar across it marked EMERGENCY.

She returned a few minutes later, hair fluffed, eyes puffy but freshly shadowed. Sitting down, she nudged my shin with a toe and gave a weak smile. Waving for the waitress, she got a refill and drank half the cup, taking long, silent swallows.

Looking ready to choke. My therapeutic impulse was to pat her hand. I resisted it.

"Bad love," she said softly. "Little rooms. Little locked cells. Bare bulbs—or sometimes he'd just light a candle. Candles *we* made in crafts. *Beautiful* candles —actually they were ugly pieces of shit, with this really disgusting scent. Nothing in the cell but two chairs. He'd sit opposite you, your knees almost touching. Nothing between you. Then he'd stare at you for a long time. A *long* time. Then he'd start talking in this low, relaxed voice—like it was just a chat, like it was just two people having a nice, civil conversation. And at first you'd think you were getting away easy, he'd sound so pleasant. Smiling, playing with that stupid little beard or his puka shells."

She said, "Shit," and drank coffee.

"What did he talk about?"

"He'd start off lecturing about human nature. How everyone had good parts of their character and bad parts and the difference between the successful people and the unsuccessful people was which part you used. And that we kids were there because we were using too much bad part and not enough good part. Because we'd gotten warped somehow—*damaged* was the way he put it—from wanting to sleep with our mommies and our daddies. But how everyone else at the school was now doing great. *Everyone except you, young lady, is controlling their impulses and learning to use the good part. They are going to be okay. They deserve good love and are going to have happy lives.*"

She closed her eyes. Took a deep breath. Funneled her lips into a pinhole and blew air out through it.

"Then he'd stop. To let it all sink in. And stare some more. And get even closer. His breath always stank of cabbage . . . the room was so small the smell filled it—*he* filled it. He wasn't a big man, but in there he was *huge.* You felt like an ant, about to be crushed—like the room was running out of air and you were going to strangle . . . the way he stared—his eyes were like drills. And the look—when you got the bad love. After the soft talk was through. This hatred—letting you know you were scum.

" '*You*,' he'd say. And then he'd repeat it. '*You*, *you, you.*' And then it would start—*you* were the only one who wasn't doing good. *You* couldn't control your impulses, *you* weren't trying—*you* were acting just like an animal. A dirty, filthy animal—a *vermin* animal. That was a favorite of his. Vermin animals—

in his creepy Inspector Clouseau accent. *Vermeen aneemals*. Then he'd start calling you other names. Fool, idiot, weakling, moron, savage, excrement. No curse words, just one insult after another, sometimes in French. Saying them so quietly you could barely hear them. But you had to hear them because there was nothing else to hear in that room. Just the wax dripping, sometimes a plumbing pipe would rumble, but mostly it was silent. You *had* to listen."

A lost look came into her eyes. She shifted as far from me as the booth would allow. When she spoke again, her voice was even softer, but deeper, almost masculine.

"You are acting like vermin animal, young lady. You are going to live like vermin animal and you will end up dying like vermin animal. And then he'd go into these detailed descriptions of how vermin lived and died and how no one loved them and gave them good love because they didn't deserve it and how the only thing they deserved was bad love and filth and humiliation."

She reached for her mug. Her hand shook and she braced it with the other one before raising the coffee to her lips.

"He'd keep going like that. Don't ask me how long because I don't know—it felt like years. *Chanting.* Over and over and over. You *will* get the bad love, you *will* get the bad love . . . pain, and suffering and loneliness that would never end—prison, where people will rape you and cut you and tie you up so you can't move. Horrible diseases you will get—he'd go into the symptoms. Talk about the loneliness, how you'd always be alone. Like a corpse left out in the desert to dry. Like a piece of dirt on some cold, distant planet—he was full of analogies, Dr. B. was, *playing* loneliness like an instrument. *Your life will be as empty and dark as this room we are sitting in, young lady.*

*Your entire future will be desolate. No good love from any-
one—no good love, just bad love, filth, and degradation.
Because that is what bad children deserve. A cold, lonely
world for children who act like vermin animals.* Then he'd
show photos. Dead bodies, concentration camp stuff.
This is how you will end up!"

She shifted closer.

"He'd just *chant* it," she said, touching my cuff.
"Like some priest . . . throwing out these images.
Not giving you a chance to speak. He made you feel
you were the only bad person in a beautiful world—a
shit smear on silk. And you believed him. You believed everyone was changing for the better, learning
to control themselves. Everyone was on his side, you
were the *only* piece of shit."

"Cutting you off," I said, "so you wouldn't con-
fide in the other kids."

"It worked; I never confided in anyone. Later,
when I was out of there—*years* later—I realized it was
stupid, I couldn't have been the only one. I'd seen
other kids go into the rooms—it seems so ridiculously
logical now. But back then, I couldn't—he kept focusing me in on *myself.* On the bad parts of me. The *vermin animal* parts."

"You were isolated right from the beginning.
New environment, new routine."

"Exactly!" she said, squeezing my arm. "I was
scared *shitless.* My parents never told me where we
were going, just shoved me in the car and tossed in a
suitcase. The whole ride up there, they wouldn't
speak to me. When we got there, they drove through
the gates, dumped me in the office, left me there and
drove away. Later I found out that's what he in-
structed them to do. Have a happy summer, Meredith . . ."

Her eyes got wet. "I'd just repeated seventh
grade. Finally faked enough to barely pass and was

looking forward to a vacation. I thought summer would be the beach and Lake Arrowhead—we had a cabin, always went there as a family. They dumped me and went without me . . . no apologies, no explanation. I thought I'd died and gone to hell—sitting in that office, all those brown uniforms, no one talking to me. Then *he* came out, smiling like a clown, saying, what a pretty girl you are, telling me to come with him, *he'd* be taking care of me. I thought: what a jerk, no problem putting it over on him. The first time I stepped out of line, he let it pass. The second time, he pulled me into a room and bad-loved me. I walked out of there in a semi-coma . . . blitzed, wasted—it's hard to explain, but it was almost like dying. Like bad dope—I felt I was on a rocky island in the middle of a storm. This crazy, black, roaring sea, with sharks all around . . . no escape, him working on my bad parts—chewing me *up*!''

"What a nightmare," I said.

"The first week I hardly slept or ate. Lost ten pounds. The worst part was that you believed him. He had a way of taking over your head—like he was sitting in your skull, scraping away at your brain. You really felt you were shit and belonged in hell."

"None of the kids *ever* talked to each other?"

"Maybe some did, I didn't. Maybe I could've, I don't know—I sure didn't *feel* I could. Everyone walking around smiling, saying how great Dr. B. was. Such a *beautiful* guy. You found yourself saying it, too, mouthing along without thinking, like one of those dumb camp songs. There was this—this *feverish* atmosphere to the place. Grinning idiots. Like a cult. You felt if you spoke out against him, someone would pour poison Kool-Aid down your throat."

"Was physical punishment ever part of bad love?"

"Once in a while—usually a slap, a pinch, noth-

ing that hurt too much. It was mostly the humiliation
—the surprise. When he *wanted* to hurt you, he'd
poke you in the elbow or the shoulder. Flick his finger
on the bone. He knew all the spots . . . nothing that
would leave a scar, not that anyone would have believed us, anyway. Who were we? Truants, fuckups,
rejects. Even *now*, would I be credible? Four abortions,
Valium, Librium, Thorazine, Elavil, lithium? All the
other things I've done? Wouldn't some lawyer dig
that up and put *me* on trial? Wouldn't I be a piece of
shit all over again?"

"Probably."

Her smile was rich with disgust. "I'm *jazzed* that
he's dead—doubly jazzed he did it to himself—his
turn for humiliation."

She looked up at the ceiling.

"What is it?" I said.

"Killing himself—do you think he could have felt
some guilt?"

"With what you've told me, it's hard to imagine."

"Yeah. You're probably right . . . yeah, he
slapped me plenty of times, but the pain was *welcome*.
'Cause when he was getting *physical*, he wasn't *talking*. His voice. His *words*. He could reach into your
center and squeeze the life out of you . . . did you
know he used to write columns in magazines—hu-
mane child rearing? People sent in problems and he'd
offer fucking *solutions*?"

I sighed.

"Yes," she said. "My sad, sad story—such pa-
thos." Looking around the restaurant, she cupped one
ear. "Any daytime-serial people listening? Got a
bitchin' script for you."

"You never told anyone?"

"Not until you, dear." Smile. "Aren't you flat-
tered? All those shrinks and you're the *very* first—

why, you've deflowered me—busted my psychological *cherry*!''

"Interesting way to put it."

"But fitting, right? Therapy's just like fucking—you open yourself up to a stranger and hope for the best."

I said, "You said you saw other kids going into the rooms. Were they taken by other people, or just de Bosch?"

"Mostly by him, sometimes by that creepy daughter of his. *I* always got personal attention from the big cheese—Daddy's social position and all that."

"Katarina was involved in treatment? When exactly were you there?"

"Seventy-six."

"She was only twenty-three. Still a student."

Shrug. "Everyone treated her as if she was a shrink. What she was was a real *bitch*. Walking around with this smug look on her face—Daddy was the king and she was the princess. Now there's one dutiful daughter who really *did* want to fuck Papa."

"Did you have any direct dealings with her?"

"Other than a sneer in the hall? No."

"What about other staffers? Did you see any of them doing private sessions?"

"No."

"None of those names I mentioned rang a bell?"

She gave a pained look. "It all blurs—I've been through changes, my whole *life* until a few years ago is a blur."

"Can I go over those names again?"

"Sure, why not." She picked up her cup and drank.

"Grant Stoumen."

Headshake.

"Mitchell Lerner."

"Maybe . . . that one's a little familiar, but I have no face to go with it."

I gave her some time to think.

She said, "Nope."

"Harvey Rosenblatt."

"Uh-uh."

"Wilbert Harrison."

"No."

"He's a little man who wears purple all the time."

"Does he ride a pink elephant?" Grin.

"Myra Evans."

Eyeblink. Frown.

I repeated the name.

"You used another name before," she said. "Myra something hyphenated."

"Evans-Paprock—Paprock was her married name."

"Evans." Another smile, not at all happy. "Myra Evans—Myra the Bitch. She was a teacher, right? A little blond with a tight butt and an attitude—am I right?"

I nodded.

"Yeah," she said. "Myra the Bitch. She was assigned to tread where others had failed. Like teaching *moi* how to read. She kept drilling me, harassing me, forcing me to do stupid exercises that didn't do a fucking bit of good because the words stayed all scrambled. When I got something wrong, she'd clap her hands together and say *no* in this loud voice. Like training a dog. Telling me I was stupid, a moron, not paying attention—she used to clamp her hands on my face and force me to look into her eyes."

She placed her hands on my cheeks and pressed them together, hard. Her palms were wet and her mouth was parted. She brought me forward and I thought she might kiss me. Instead, she said, "Pay attention! Listen, you moron!" in a grating voice.

I suppressed the impulse to twist free. That instant of confinement drove my empathy up another notch.

"Pay *attention*! Stop *wandering*, stupid! This is *important*! You need to *learn* this! If you don't pay *attention*, you can't *learn*!"

She squeezed harder. Let go. Smiled again. "Breath mints—that was her smell. Isn't it funny how you remember the smells? Mints, but her breath was still shitty. She thought she was hot. Kinda young, little miniskirts, big boobs . . . maybe she was letting Dr. B. slip it to her."

"Why do you say that?"

"Because of the way she acted around him. Looks. Following him around. She reported directly to him. One thing you could count on, after a difficult session with Miss Bitch, you'd soon be seeing Dr. Botch for candles and needle twisting. So she got murdered, huh?"

"Very nastily."

"Too bad." She pouted, then smiled. "See, I can be a hypocrite, too. It's called acting, I work with people who do it for a living—we all do, actually, don't we?"

"What about Rodney Shipler? Does that name mean anything to you?"

"Nope."

"Delmar Parker—the boy I told you about over the phone."

"Yeah, the truck. That's how I knew you were for real. He was before my time."

"May seventy-three. You heard about it?"

"I heard about it from *Botch*. Boy, did I."

"During a bad love session?"

Nod. "The wages of sin. I'd committed some ma-

jor felony—I think it was not wearing underwear, or
something. Or maybe he caught me with a boy—I
don't remember. He said I was a *vermeen aneemal* and
stupid, then gave me this whole spiel about a *vermeen
aneemal* boy who'd received the ultimate punishment
for *his* stupidity. 'Death, young lady. Death.' "

"What did he say happened?"

"The kid stole a truck, ran it off the road, and got
killed. Proof positive of what happened to *vermeen
aneemal* moron children. Botch had a good time with it
—making fun of the kid, laughing a lot, as if it were
just a big joke. *'Do you comprehend, you bad, styupid
girl? A boy so styupid, he steals a truck even though he
doesn't know how to drive? Ha ha ha. A boy so styupid he
virtually choreographs his own death? Ha ha ha.'* "

"He used that word? 'Choreograph'?"

"Yes," she said, looking surprised. "I believe he
actually did."

"What else did he say about the accident?"

"Disgusting details—that was part of bad love.
Grossing you out. He had a ball with this one. How
they didn't find the boy right away and when they
did there were maggots in his mouth and crawling in
and out of his eyes—*'He is being eaten by maggots, my
dear Meredith. Feasted upon. Consumed. And the animals
have feasted upon him, too. Chewed away most of his face
—it is a real mess—just like your character, styupid Meredith. You are not listening, you are not concentrating, you
bad, styupid girl. We are trying to mold you into something decent but you refuse to cooperate. Think, Meredith.
Think of that styupid boy. The bad love he received from the
maggots. That is what happens when vermeen aneemals
don't change their ways.'* "

She gave a hard, dry laugh and dabbed her nose
again.

"That might not be an exact quote, but it's pretty
damn close. He also got into this whole racist rap—

said the kid in the truck was black. 'A *savage*, Meredith. A jungle *native*. Why would you want to imitate the savages when there's a world of *civilization* out there?' On top of everything else, he's a racist, too. Even without the rap, you could tell. The looks he gave the minority kids."

"Were there a lot of minority kids?"

She shook her head. "Just a few. Tokens, probably—part of the public image. In public he was Mr. Liberal—pictures of Martin Luther King and Gandhi and the Kennedys all over the place. Like I said, it's all acting—the world is a fucking stage."

She placed her hands flat on the table, looking ready to get up again.

"A couple more names," I said. "Silk."

Headshake.

"Merino."

"What is this, a fabric show? Uh-uh."

"Lyle Gritz?"

"Grits and toast," she said. "Nope. How many people have gotten bumped off, anyway?"

"Lots. I'm on the list, too."

Her eyes rounded. "You? Why?"

"I co-chaired a symposium on de Bosch's work. At Western Peds."

"Why?" she said coldly. "Were you a fan?"

"No. Actually, your father requested it of me."

"Requested it, huh? What approach did he take? Squeezing your balls or kissing your ass?"

"Squeezing. He did it as a favor to Katarina."

"Symposium, huh? Gee thanks, *Dad*. The man tortures me, so you throw him a party—when did this take place?"

"Seventy-nine."

She thought. "Seventy-nine—I was in Boston in seventy-nine. Catholic girls' school, even though we weren't Catholic . . . a symposium." She laughed.

"You never told your parents anything that happened at the Corrective School?"

"Nothing—I was too numb, and they wouldn't have listened, anyway. After that summer, I didn't talk to anyone, just went along, like some robot. They handed Botch a naughty *acting-out* girl and got back this compliant little zombie. They thought it was a miracle *cure*. Years later, they were still saying it was the best decision they ever made. I'd just stare at them, want to kill them, keep my feelings all inside."

The pale eyes were wet.

"How long did you stay that way?" I said softly.

"I don't know—months, years—like I said, it blurs. All I know is it took a real long time to get back to my true self, get smart enough to mess around and cover my tracks. No sticky stains on the clothes."

She licked her lips and grinned. A tear dripped down one cheek. She wiped it away angrily.

"When I was eighteen, I told them 'fuck you' and left—ran away with a guy who came to unclog the toilet."

"Sounds like you've done pretty well since."

"How kind of you to say so, dear—oh yeah, it's been a blast. PR's a bullshit business, so I'm perfect for it. Throwing parties, setting up promos. Feeding rumors to the idiot press. Well, the show must go on. Ciao. It was real, stud."

She stood and nearly ran out of the restaurant.

I put money on the table and followed her, caught up as she was getting into a red Mustang convertible. The car looked new, but there were dings and dents all along the driver's side.

"Uh-uh, no more," she said, starting the engine. "You get a quickie mind-fuck for your ten bucks, and that's it."

"Just wanted to thank you," I said.

"Polite, too," she said. "I *really* don't like you."

30

Robin said, "Bad love. The hypocrisy."

"The bastard coins a phrase to describe poor child rearing, but has his own private meaning for it."

"Victimizing little kids." Her hands tightened around the handle of a wood rasp. The blade caught on a piece of rosewood, and she pulled it free and put it down.

"And," I said, "if this woman's experience was typical, the victimization was perfectly legal. De Bosch didn't sexually molest anyone, and none of the physical things he did would fall under any child-abuse statutes but Sweden's."

"Not the poking and slapping?"

"No bruises, no case, and usually you need deep wounds and broken bones to get anywhere legally. Corporal punishment's still allowed in many schools. Back then, it was accepted procedure. And there's never been any law against mind control or psychological abuse—how can you pin down the criteria? Basically, de Bosch behaved like a really rotten parent, and that's no crime."

She shook her head. "And no one ever said anything."

"Maybe some of the children did, but I doubt anyone believed them. These were problem kids. Their credibility was low and their parents were angry. In some cases de Bosch was probably the court of last resort. This woman came back to her family traumatized but perfectly compliant. They never suspected the summer at the school was anything but successful."

"Some success."

"We're talking ultrahigh levels of parental frustration, Rob. Even if what de Bosch did had come to light and some parents had pulled their kids out, I'll bet you others would have rushed to enroll theirs. De Bosch's victims never had any legal recourse. Now, one of them's evening the score his own way."

"The same old chain," she said. "Victims and victimizers."

"The thing that bothers me, though, is why the killer didn't strike out against de Bosch, only the disciples. Unless de Bosch died before the killer was old enough—or assertive enough—to put together a revenge plot."

"Or crazy enough."

"That, too. If I'm right about the killer being directly traumatized by Delmar Parker's accident, we're talking about someone who was a student at the school in 1973. De Bosch died seven years later, so the killer may still have been a kid. Felons that young rarely commit carefully planned crimes. They're more into impulsive stuff. Another thing that could have stopped him from getting de Bosch was being locked up. Jail or a mental institution. That fits with our Mr. Gritz—the ten years unaccounted for between his leaving Georgia and getting arrested here."

"More frustration," she said.

"Exactly. Not being able to punish de Bosch directly could have heated him up even further. The first murder occurred five years ago. Myra Paprock. Maybe that was the year he was released. Myra would have been a good target for him. A trusted disciple, dictatorial."

"Makes sense," she said, looking down at her workbench and arranging some files, "if de Bosch really killed himself. But what if he was murdered and made to look like a suicide?"

"I don't think so," I said. "His death was too peaceful—overdose of medication. Why would the killer butcher subordinates and allow the boss to get off so easy? And a ritual approach—one that fulfilled a psychological need—would have meant leaving the best for last, not starting with de Bosch first and working backwards."

"Best for last," she said, in a tremulous voice. "So where do you fit in?"

"The only thing I can think of is that damned symposium."

She started to switch off her tools. The dog tagged after her, stopping each time she did, looking up, as if seeking approval.

"Alex," she said, removing her apron, "if de Bosch did commit suicide, do you think it could have been due to remorse? It doesn't mean much, but it would be nice to think of him having some self-doubts."

"The woman asked me the same thing. I'd have liked to say yes—she'd have loved to *hear* it, but she wouldn't have bought it. The man she described didn't sound very conscience laden. My guess is his motivation was just what the papers printed: despondence over ill health. The slides his daughter flashed at the symposium showed a physical wreck."

"A wrecker," she said.

"Yeah. Who knows how many kids he messed up over the years?"

The dog heard the tension in my voice and cocked his head. I petted him and said, "So who's the higher life-form, anyway, bub?"

Robin picked up a broom and began to sweep wood shavings.

"Any other calls?" I said, holding the dustpan for her.

"Uh-uh." She finished and wiped her hands. We stepped out of the garage and she pulled down the door. The mountains across the canyon were clear and greening. Drought-starved shoots, trying for another season.

All at once the big, low house seemed more foreign than ever. We went inside. The furniture looked strange.

In the bedroom, Robin unbuttoned her work shirt and I unsnapped her bra and cupped her breasts. They were warm and heavy in my palms and as I touched her, she arched her back. Then she stepped away from me and crossed her arms over her chest.

"Let's get out of here, Alex—out of the city."

"Sure," I said, looking over at the dog, head-butting the bedcovers. "Do we take him with us?"

"I'm not talking summer vacation, just dinner. Somewhere far enough to feel *different*. He'll be fine. We'll leave food and water, the air-conditioning on, give him a couple of chew-bones."

"Okay, where would you like to go?"

Her smile was barren. "Normally I'd say Santa Barbara."

I forced myself to laugh. "How about the other direction—Laguna Beach?"

"Laguna would be peachy." She came over and placed my hands on her hips. "Remember that place with the ocean view?"

"Yeah," I said. "Calamari and pictures of weeping clowns—wonder if it's still in business?"

"If it isn't, there'll be someplace else. The main thing is we get away."

We left at seven-thirty, to avoid the freeway jam, taking the truck because the gas tank was fuller. I drove, enjoying the height and the heft and the power. A tape Robin had picked up at McCabe's was in the deck: a teenager named Allison Krause, singing bluegrass in a voice as sweet and clear as first love and running off fiddle solos that had the wondrous ease of the prodigy.

I hadn't called Milo to tell him about Meredith.

Another scumbag, he'd say, world-weary. Then he'd rub his face . . .

I thought of the man on the tape, chanting like a child, reliving his past. . . .

Bad thoughts intruding.

I felt Robin tighten up. Her fingers had been tapping my thigh in time with the music, now they stopped. I squeezed them. Strummed the fingertips, let my hand wander to her small, hard waist as the truck roared in the fast lane.

She had on black leotards under a short denim skirt. Her hair was tied up, showing off her neck, smooth as cream. A man with a functioning brain would have thanked God for sitting next to her.

I pressed my cheek against hers. Let my shoulders drop and bobbed my head to the music. Not fooling her, but she knew I was trying and she put her hand high on my thigh.

A babe and a truck and the open road.

By the time I reached Long Beach, it started to feel real.

*   *   *

Laguna was quieter and darker than I remembered, the art fair over, nearly all the tourist traps and galleries closed.

The place with the squid and clowns was no longer in business; a karaoke bar had taken its place—people getting slogged on margaritas and pretending to be Righteous Brothers. The painful sounds made their way to the sidewalk.

We found a pleasant-looking cafe farther up the street, ate huge, cold salads, decent swordfish, and excellent Chilean sea bass with french fries and coleslaw, and drank a bit of wine, then strong black coffee.

Walking it off, we went far enough past the commercial zone to get an ocean glimpse of our own. The water was a thousand miles of black beyond a white thread of sand. The waves rolled drunkenly, sending up ice chips of spray and an occasional roar that sounded like applause. We held hands so tightly our fingers ached, grabbed at each other, and kissed until our tongues throbbed.

Barely enough light to see Robin's dark eyes, narrowing.

She bit my lower lip and I knew some of it was passion, the rest, anger. I kissed her behind her ear and we embraced for a long time, then we returned to the truck and drove north, out of town.

"Don't get on the freeway," she said. "Drive awhile."

I got onto Laguna Canyon Road, went for several miles, and made a random turn onto an unmarked strip that corkscrewed up into the mountains.

No talk or music. Her hands on me as she cried out her tension. We passed a pottery studio, its wooden sign barely lit by a dusty bulb. A glimpse of chicken-wire fencing. A couple of horse ranches, an unmarked shack. Then nothing for a long time and the road dead-ended at brush.

Crickets and shadows, the ocean nowhere in sight.

I put the truck in reverse. Robin stopped me and turned off the engine.

We locked eyes and kissed, fumbling with each other's clothing.

Stripped completely naked, we held each other, shivering, knitting our limbs. Breathing into one another, fighting for oblivion.

The ride back was slow and silent, and I managed to keep reality at bay till we got off the freeway. Robin slept, as she had since we'd crossed the L.A. county line, low in the seat, half smiling.

It was one forty-two in the morning and Sunset was nearly bare of cars. The familiar eastward cruise was solitary and peaceful. As I approached the Beverly Glen intersection, I prepared to shoot through the green light. Then wailing sirens sounded from somewhere I couldn't pinpoint, surrounding me, growing louder.

I slowed and stopped. Robin was startled, sitting up just as flashing red lights popped out from around the bend and the sirens became unbearable. A hook-and-ladder came at us from the east, bearing down; for an instant I felt trapped. Then the fire engine made a sharp right turn, northward, onto the Glen, followed closely by another fire truck, then another smaller unit. A cherry-topped sedan brought up the rear as the sirens tapered off to a distant whistle.

Robin was clutching the armrest. Her eyes were gigantic, as if the lids had been stapled back.

We looked at each other.

I turned left and followed the shrieking caravan.

*   *   *

A hundred yards in I could smell it. A pot left too long on the stove, overlaid with gasoline.

I put on speed, just able to see the fire car's taillights. Hoping the company would continue on up, toward Mulholland and beyond. But they hooked west.

Up an old bridle path that led up to a solitary property.

Robin held her head and moaned as I floored the truck. Coming to my street, I sped up the slope. The road was blocked by the newly arrived fire trucks and I had to pull over and park.

Work lights were scattered about, highlighting the firefighters' yellow hats. Lots of movement, but the night blocked out the details.

Robin and I jumped out and began running up the hill. The burnt stench was stronger now, the sky a black, camouflaging host for the plumes of dark smoke that shot upward in greasy gray spirals. I could feel the fire—the caustic heat—better than I could see it. My body was drenched with sweat. I was cold to the marrow.

The firefighters were uncoiling hoses and shouting, too busy to notice us.

What had once been my pond gate was charcoal. The carport had collapsed and the entire right side of my house was smoldering. The back of the building was haloed in orange. Tongues of fire licked the sky. Sparks jumped and died, wood crackled and crashed.

A tall firefighter handed a hose to another man and pulled off his gloves. He saw us and came forward, gesturing us back.

We walked toward him.

"It's our house," I said.

The look of pity on his face cut me deeply. He

was black, with a big jaw and wide, dark mustache. "Sorry, folks—we're working hard on it, got here as quick as we could from the Mulholland substation. Reinforcements just came in from Beverly Hills."

Robin said, "Is it all gone?"

He removed his hat and wiped his forehead, exhaling. "It wasn't as of a few minutes ago, ma'am, and we've controlled it—you should start to see that smoke turn white real soon."

"How bad is it?"

He hesitated. "To be frank, ma'am, you've suffered some serious structural damage all along the rear. What with the drought and all that wood siding —your roof's half gone, must have been pretty dry up there. What was it, ceramic tile?"

"Some sort of tile," I said. "It came with the house, I don't know."

"Those old roofs . . . give thanks it wasn't wood shingle, that would have been like a pile of kindling."

Robin was looking at him but she wasn't listening to him. He bit his lip, started to place a hand on her shoulder, but stopped himself. Putting his glove back on, he turned to me.

"If the wind doesn't do squirrely things, we should be able to save some of it. Get you in there soon as possible to start taking a look."

Robin started to cry.

The fireman said, "I'm real sorry, ma'am—if you need a blanket, we've got some in the truck."

"No," she said. "What happened?"

"Don't know exactly, yet—why don't you talk to the captain—that gentleman over there? Captain Gillespie. He should be able to help you."

After pointing to a medium-sized man up near the carport, he ran off. We made our way to the captain. His back was to us and I tapped him on the shoulder. He turned quickly, looking ready to snap. One look at us shut his mouth. He was in his fifties and had a deeply scored face that was almost a perfect square.

Tugging at his chin strap: "Owners?"

Two nods.

"Sorry, folks—out for the night?"

More nods. I felt encased in sand. Movement was an ordeal.

"Well, we've been at it for about half an hour, and I think we got to it relatively fast after ignition. Luckily, someone driving up the Glen smelled it and phoned it in on cellular. We've got most of the really hot spots out. Look for white smoke soon, Mr.—?"

"Alex Delaware. This is Robin Castagna."

"Ron Gillespie, Mr. Delaware. Are you the legal owners or tenants?"

"Owners."

Another pitying look. A whooshing sound came from the house. He glanced over his shoulder, then looked back.

"We should be able to save at least half of it, but our water does some damage, too." He looked back again. Something creased his brow. "One minute." Jogging over to a group of new arrivals, he pointed at my flaming roof and spread his arms like a preacher.

When he came back, he said, "You folks want something to drink? C'mon, let's get away from the heat."

We followed him down the road a bit. The house was still in sight. Some of the smoke had startened to lighten, pluming upward like an earthborn cloud.

He pulled a canteen out of his jacket and held it out to us.

Robin shook her head.

I said, "No, thanks."

Gillespie opened the bottle and drank. Screwing

the cap back on, he said, "Do you know of anyone who'd want to do this to you?"

"Why?"

He stared at me. "Usually, people say no."

"There is someone," I said. "I don't know who—it's a long story—there's a police detective you can talk to."

I gave him Milo's name and he wrote it down.

"I'd better call him now," he said. "Our arson investigators will be in on it too. This is an obvious intentional, we've got three discrete points of origin and we found a gasoline can out back that's probably the accelerant—looks like the bastard didn't even try to hide it."

"No," I said. "He wouldn't want to do that."

He stared at me again. I looked back without focusing.

Gillespie said, "I'll go call that detective now."

31

Milo spent a few seconds of silent comfort with us, then he huddled with Gillespie.

The fire went out, sending off columns of white smoke. Some time after—I still don't know how long—Robin and I were able to tour the damage, accompanied by a fireman with a flashlight who looked out for our safety but hung back, diplomatically, as we stumbled and cursed in the dark.

The garden and the rear half of the house were a total loss, the air still hot and bitter. The front rooms were sodden and putrid, ash filled, already moldering. I ran my hand along scorched furniture, fingered hot dust, looked at ruined art and decimated keepsakes, TV and stereo equipment that had blistered and burst. After a while it got too difficult. I pulled the paintings and prints that looked intact off the wall and made a neat stack. Short stack. My Bellows boxing print seemed to have come out okay, but the frame was blackened around the edges.

Robin was across the living room when I said, "I've got to get out of here."

She gave a dull nod—more of a bow. We carried the art out and took it to the truck.

Beyond the vehicles, Milo and Gillespie were still conferring and a third man had joined them—young, chubby, balding, with bristly red hair. He held a pad and his writing hand was busy.

"Drew Seaver," he said, holding out the other one. "Fire Department arson investigator. Detective Sturgis has been filling me in—sounds like you've really been through it. I'll have some questions for you, but they can wait a couple of days."

Milo told him, "I'll get you whatever you need."

"Fine," said Seaver. "What's your insurance situation, doctor?"

As if cued, Captain Gillespie said, "Better be getting back—good luck, folks."

When he was gone, Seaver repeated his insurance question.

I said, "I never really checked the details. I'm up to date on my premiums."

"Well, that's good. Those insurance guys are real sonofa's, believe me. Dot your 'i' wrong and they'll find a way not to pay you. You need any help with justification, just have 'em call me."

He handed me his card. "That and a statement from Detective Sturgis should handle it."

"What needs to be handled?" said Robin. "What do we need to justify?"

Seaver picked at his chin. His lips were thick, pink, and soft looking, with a natural turndown that made him look sad.

"Arson fires tend to be self-generated, Mrs. Delaware. In lots of cases, anyway. Like I said, insurance companies'll do anything not to pay up. First thing they're going to be assuming is you're behind this."

"Then fuck 'em," said Milo. To us: "Don't sweat it, I'll handle it."

Seaver said, "Okay . . . well, better be looking around some more." Cracking a brief smile, he left.

Milo's hair was ragged, his eyes electric. He had on a shirt and tie, but the tie was crooked and his collar was loosened. In the darkness his acne-scarred face looked like moonscape. His hand moved over it rapidly and repeatedly—almost ticlike.

"It's okay," said Robin.

"No, no," he said. "Uh-uh, don't comfort me—you're the victims—goddamn protect and serve—some protection. I know it sounds like a crock but we *are* gonna get him—one fucking way or the other, he's history. We'll get free of this."

The three of us walked back to the truck. Milo's unmarked was parked behind it. None of us looked back.

The firefighters' lights were going out, one by one, as some of the trucks pulled away. Sunrise was several hours away. Without the bulbs and the flames, the night seemed hollow, just a thin membrane holding back the void.

"Wanna go back with me?" said Milo.

"No," I said. "I can handle it."

Robin stood on tiptoes and kissed his cheek.

"I found out what de Bosch's sin was," I said. I told him of Meredith Bork's experience.

"You stab me, I stab you," he said. "No fucking excuse."

"Can we be sure this wasn't the Iron Priests?"

"We can't be sure of anything," he said furiously. "But a thousand to one it's not them. No offense, but you're just not important enough to them—they want Raza blood. No, this was our bad love buddy—remember Bancroft's comment about firesetters at the school?"

"You told me there was no record of any fires there."

"Yeah . . . the kids behaved themselves there. It's when they graduated that the problems started."

I drove, but I felt as if I was being towed. Each segment of white line diminished me. Across the cab of the truck, Robin wept, unable to stop, finally surrendering to deep, wracking sobs.

I was beyond tears.

Just as I crossed into Beverly Hills, she took a sucking breath and pressed fisted hands together.

"Oh, well," she said, "I always wanted to redecorate."

I must have laughed, because my throat hurt and I heard two voices chuckling hysterically.

"What style should we choose?" I said. "Phoenix Rococo?"

Benedict Canyon appeared. Red light. I stopped. My eyes felt acid washed.

"It was a crummy little place anyway," she said. "No, it *wasn't*, it was a *beautiful* little place—oh, Alex!"

I pulled her to me. Her body felt heavy but boneless.

Green light. My brain said go, but my foot was slow to follow. Trying not to think of everything I'd lost—and everything yet to lose—I managed to complete the left turn and began a solitary crawl up Benedict.

Home temporary home.

The dog would run out to greet us. I felt inadequate for the role of animal buddy. For anything.

I drove up to the white gate. It took a long time to find the card key, even longer to slip it in the slot. Moving the truck up the drive, I counted cypress trees in an effort to settle my mind on something.

I parked next to the Seville and we got out.

The dog didn't rush out to greet us.

I fumbled with the key to the front door. Turned it. As I walked through the door, something cold and hard pressed against my left temple and a hand reached around and clapped me hard on the right side of my head.

Immobilizing my skull.

"Hello, doctor," said a voice from a chant. "Welcome to Bad Love."

32

He said, "Don't move or speak, pardon the cliché."

The pressure on my temple was intense. Strong fingers dug into my cheek.

"Good," he said. "Obedient. You must have been a good student."

Dig.

"*Were* you?"

"I was okay."

"Such modesty—you were a lot *better* than okay. Your fourth-grade teacher, Mrs. Lyndon, said you were one of the best students she ever had—do you remember Mrs. Lyndon?"

Squeeze and shake.

"Yes."

"She remembers you . . . such a *good* little boy . . . keep being good: hands on head."

As my fingers touched my hair, the lights went on.

One of the couches was out of place, pushed closer to the coffee table. There were drinks and plates on the coffee table. A glass of something brown. The bag of taco chips Robin had bought a couple of days ago was open, crumbs scattered on the table.

Making himself comfortable.

Knowing we'd be gone for a while but would come back, nowhere else to go.

Because he'd used the fire to flush me out. Used the time to prepare the scene.

The ritual.

Choreographing death.

Firesetters and felons . . .

I considered how to get at him. Felt the pressure, saw only dark sleeve. Where was Robin?

"Forward march," he said, but he continued to hold me still.

Footsteps on marble. Someone walked into my line of sight, holding Robin the same way.

Tall. Bulky black sweater. Baggy black slacks. Black ski mask with eye holes. Shiny eyes, the color indeterminate at this distance. He towered over Robin, gripping her face and forcing her eyes up at the ceiling. Her neck was stretched, exposed.

I gave an involuntary start, and the hand gripped my head harder.

Imprisoning it.

I knew where they'd learned that.

Bumping and scratching from the back of the house. The dog tied out there, behind drapes that had been drawn over the French doors.

Something else at Robin's head besides a hand. Automatic pistol, small, chrome plated.

Bump, scratch.

The voice behind me laughed.

"Great attack dog . . . some tight security you've got here. Alarm system with an obvious home run, one snip and bye-bye. Fancy electric gate a dwarf could climb over, and a cute little closed-circuit TV to announce your arrival."

More laughter. The tall man with Robin didn't move or make a sound.

Two types of killing. Two killers. . . .

My captor said, "Okay, campers."

The tall man shifted his free hand from Robin's face to the small of her back and began propelling her down the hallway toward the bedrooms.

Swinging his hips. Effeminate.

Walking the way Robin walked.

A woman? A tall woman with strong shoulders . . .

I'd talked to a tall, angry woman this afternoon.

A Corrective School alumna with plenty of reason to hate.

I really don't like you.

I'd called Meredith out of the blue, yet she'd been willing to talk to me—too eager.

And she had a special reason to feel rage over the Western Peds symposium.

Thanks, Dad.

I'd just stare at them, want to kill them, keep my feelings all inside.

Alone with Robin, now. Her appetites and anger . . .

"Forward march, fool." The gun stayed in place as the hand moved from my face. No more pressure, but his touch lingered like phantom pain.

A sharp prod to my kidneys as he shoved me farther into the room. Onto a couch. As I bounced, my hands left my head.

His foot met my shin and pain burned through my leg.

"Back up—up, up, up!"

I complied, waiting to be tied or restrained.

But he let me stay there, hands on head, and sat down facing me, just out of reach.

I saw the gun first. Another automatic—bigger

than Meredith's. Dull black, a dark wooden grip. Freshly oiled; I could smell it.

He looked tall too. Long waist, and long legs that he planted firmly on the marble. A little narrow in the shoulders. Arms a bit short. Navy blue sweatshirt with a designer logo. Black jeans, black leather, high-top athletic shoes that looked spanking new.

The chic thing to wear for homicide—the avenger reads *GQ*.

His mask had a mouth cutout. A sharklike smile filled the hole.

The dog scratched some more.

Under the mask, his forehead moved.

He crossed his legs, keeping the big black gun a couple of feet from the center of my chest. Breathing fast, but his arm was stable.

Using his free hand, he reached up and began rolling his mask up, doing it deftly, so that his eyes never moved from mine and his gun arm never faltered.

Doing it slowly.

The wool peeled away like a snake's molt, exposing a soft, unremarkable face with fine features.

Rosy cheeks. The hair brass colored, thinning, worn thicker at the sides, now matted by the mask.

Andrew Coburg.

The storefront lawyer's smile was wide, wet—impish.

A surprise-party smile.

He twirled the mask and tossed it over his shoulder. "Voilà."

I struggled to make sense of it—Coburg directing me to Gritz. Misdirecting me. Careful researcher . . . Mrs. Lyndon . . .

"I really *like* this place," he said. "Despite all the queer art. Nice, crisp, cruel, L.A. ambience. Much better than that little yuppie log cabin of yours. And *cliff-*

side—talk about perfect. Not to mention your little friend's *truck*—unbelievable. Couldn't have set it up better myself."

He winked. "Almost makes you believe in God, doesn't it? Fate, karma, predestination, collective unconscious—choose your dogma . . . do you have any idea what I'm talking about?"

"Delmar Parker," I said.

The dead boy's name blotted out his smile.

"I'm talking about consonance," he said. "Making it *right*."

"But Delmar has something to do with it, doesn't he? Something beyond bad love."

He uncrossed his legs. The gun made a small arc. "What do you know about bad love, you pretentious yuppie prick?"

The gun arm was board rigid. Then it began vibrating. He looked at it for just a second. Laughed, as if trying to erase his outburst.

Scratch, bump. The dog was throwing himself hard against the glass.

Coburg snickered. "Little *pit* puppy. Maybe after it's over I'll take him home with me."

Smiling but sweating. The rosy cheeks deep with color.

Trying to keep my face neutral, I strained to hear sounds from the bedrooms. Nothing.

"So you think you know about bad love," said Coburg.

"Meredith told me about it," I said.

His brow tightened and mottled.

The dog kept scraping. The old-man whining sound filtered through the glass. Coburg gave a disgusted look.

"You don't know anything," he said.

"So tell me."

"Shut your mouth." The gun arm shot forward again.

I didn't move.

He said, "You don't know a *tenth* of it. Don't flatter yourself with empathy, *fuck* your empathy."

The dog bumped some more. Coburg's eyes flattened.

"Maybe I'll just shoot it . . . skin it and gut it . . . how good can a shrink's dog be, anyway? How many shrinks does it take to change a lightbulb? None. They're all dead."

He laughed a bit more. Wiped sweat from his nose. I concentrated on the gun arm. It remained firmly in place, as if cut off from the rest of him.

"Do you know what *my* sin was?" he said. "The great transgression that bought me a ticket to hell?"

Ticket to hell. Meredith had called the school the same thing.

I shook my head. My armpits were aching, my fingers turning numb.

He said, "Enuresis. When I was a kid I used to piss my bed." He laughed.

"They treated me as if I *liked* it," he said. "Mumsy and Evil Stepdaddy. As if I liked clammy sheets and that litter-box smell. They were *convinced* I was doing it on purpose, so they beat me. So I got more nervous and pissed gallons. So then what did they do?"

Looking at me, waiting.

"They beat you some more."

"Bingo. *And* washed my dick with lye soap and all sorts of other wonderful stuff."

Still smiling, but his cheeks were scarlet. His hair was plastered to his forehead, his shoulders hunched under the designer sweatshirt.

My first thought, seeing those rosy cheeks, had been: *a beautiful baby.*

"So I started to do other things," he said. "Really naughty things. Could anyone blame me? Being tortured for something that I had no control over?"

I shook my head again. For a split second I felt my agreement meant something to him. Then a distracted look came into his eyes. The gun arm pushed forward and the black-metal barrel edged closer to my heart.

"What's the current lowdown on enuresis, anyway?" he said. "Do you pricks still tell parents it's a mental disease?"

"It's genetic," I said. "Related to sleep patterns. Generally it goes away by itself."

"You don't treat it anymore?"

"Sometimes behavior therapy is used."

"*You* ever treat kids for it?"

"When they want to be treated."

"Sure," he grinned. "You're a real humanitarian." The grin died. "So what were you doing making speeches—paying homage to *Hitler*?"

"I—"

"Shut up." The gun jabbed my chest. "That was rhetorical, don't speak unless you're spoken to . . . sleep patterns, huh? You quacks weren't saying that back when I was getting beaten with a strap. You had all sorts of other voodoo theories back then—one of your fellow quacks told Mumsy and Evil that I was screwed up sexually. Another said I was seriously depressed and needed to be hospitalized. And one genius told them I was doing it because I was angry about their marriage. Which was true. But I wasn't *pissing* because of it. *That* one they bought. Evil really got into expressing *his* anger. Big financial man, spiffy dresser—he had a whole collection of fancy belts. Lizard, alligator, calfskin, all with nice sharp buckles. One day I went to school with an especially nice collection of welts on my arm. A teacher started asking questions and the next thing I knew I was on a plane with dear old Mumsy to sunny California. Go west, little bad boy."

He let his free hand drop to his lap. His eyes looked tired and his shoulders rounded.

The dog was still throwing himself against the glass.

Coburg stared straight at me.

I said, "How old were you when they put you in the school?"

The gun jabbed again, forcing me backward against the couch. All at once his face was up against mine, breathing licorice. I could see dried mucus in his nostrils. He spat. His saliva was cold and thick as it oozed down the side of my face.

"I'm not *there*, yet," he said, between barely moving lips. "Why don't you shut up and let me *tell* it?"

Breathing hard and fast. I made myself look into his eyes, feeling the gun without seeing it. My pulse thundered in my ears. The spit continued its downward trail. Reaching my chin. Dripping onto my shirt.

He looked repulsed, struck out, slapping me and wiping me simultaneously. Wiped his hand on the seat cushion.

"They didn't *put* me there right away. They put me in another dungeon first. Right across the street— can you believe that, two hellholes on the same street —what was it, zoned H1 for hell? A real shithole run by a nincompoop alkie, but expensive as hell, so, of course, Mumsy thought it was good, the woman was always such an *arriviste*."

I tried to look like a fascinated student . . . still no sounds from the bedrooms.

Coburg said, "A nincompoop. Not even a challenge. A book of matches and some notebook paper." Smile.

Firesetters and truants . . . Bancroft hadn't said the fire was at *his* school.

"Poor Mumsy was *stymied*, out on the next plane, the poor thing. This wonderful look of *hopelessness* on her face—and she such an educated woman. Crying as we waited for our taxi—I thought I'd finally scored a point. Then *he* walked over. From across the street. This *goatish* thing in a black suit and cheap shoes. Taking Mummy's hand, telling her he'd heard what had happened, tsk-tsking and letting her cry some more about her bad little boy. Then telling her *his* school could handle those kinds of things. Guaranteed. All the while tousling my hair—twelve years old and he was tousling my fucking hair. His hand stank of cabbage and bay rum."

The gun hand wavered a bit . . . not enough.

Scratch, bump.

"Mummy was *thrilled*—she knew him from his magazine articles. A famous man willing to tame her wild child." His free hand fluttered. "The cab came and she sent it off empty."

The gun withdrew far enough for me to see its black snout, dark against his white knuckles.

Two hellholes on the same street. De Bosch exploiting Bancroft's failures. An alumnus of both schools, coming back years later, a tramp . . . the clean-cut face in front of me bore no street scars. But sometimes the wounds that healed weren't the important ones.

"Across the street I went. Mummy signed some papers and left me alone with Hitler. He smiled at me and said, 'Andrew, little Andrew. We have the same name, let's be friends.' Me saying, 'Fuck you, old goat.' He smiled again and patted my head. Took me down a long dark hall, shoved me into a cell, and locked it. I cried all night. When they let me out for lunch, I snuck into the kitchen and found matches."

A wistful look came into his eyes.

"How thorough was I tonight? Did I leave anything standing at Casa del Shrinko?"

I remained silent.

The gun poked me. *"Did* I?"

"Not much."

"Good. It's a shoddy world, thoroughness is so rare a quality. You personify shoddiness. You were as easy to get to as a sardine in a can. All of you were— tell me, why are psychotherapists such a passive, *helpless* bunch? Why are you all such absolute *wimps* —*talking* about life rather than *doing* anything?"

I didn't answer.

He said, "You really are, you know. Such an *unimpressive* group. Stripped of your jargon, you're noth—if that dog of yours doesn't shut up, I'm going to kill him—better yet, I'll make *you* kill him. Make you *eat* him—we can grill him on that barbecue you've got out back. A nice little *hot* dog—that would be justice, wouldn't it—making you confront your own cruelty? Give you a taste of *empathy*?"

"Why don't we just let him go?" I said. "He's not mine, just a stray I took in."

"How kind of you." Jab. My breastbone felt inflamed.

I said, "Why don't we let my friend go, too? She hasn't seen your faces."

He smiled and settled back a bit.

"Shoddiness," he said. "That's the big problem. Phony science, false premises, false promises. You pretend to help people but you just mind-fuck them."

He leaned forward. "How do you manage to live with yourself, knowing you're a phony?"

Jab. "Answer me."

"I've helped people."

"How? With voodoo? With bad love?"

Trying to keep the whine out of *my* voice, I said,

"I had nothing to do with de Bosch except for that symposium."

"*Except* for? *Except* for! That's like Eichmann saying he had nothing to do with Hitler *except* for getting those trains to the camps. That symposium was a public *love fest*, you asshole! You stood up there and canonized him! He tortured children and you *canonized* him!"

"I didn't know."

"Yeah, you and all the other good Germans."

He spat at me again. The knuckles of his gun hand were tiny cauliflowers. Sweat popped at his hairline.

"That's *it*?" he said. "That's your *excuse*—'I didn't *know*'? *Pathetic.* Just like all the others. For a bunch of supposedly educated people, you can't even *plead* for yourselves effectively. No class. *Delmar* had more class in his little finger than the lot of you put together, and he was *retarded*. Not that it stopped them from bad-loving him day in and day out."

He shook his head and flung sweat. I saw his index finger move up and down the trigger. The painful, hungry look on his face made my bowels churn. But then it was gone and he was smiling again.

"Retarded," he said, as if enjoying the word. "Fourteen, but he was more like a seven-year-old. I was twelve, but I ended up being his big brother. He was the only one in the place who'd talk to me— beware the dangerous pyromaniac—Hitler warned them all against having anything to do with me. I was completely shunned except by Delmar. He couldn't think clearly, but he had a heart of gold. Hitler took him in for the publicity—poor little Negro retardo helped by the great white doctor. When visitors came, he always had his hand on Delmar's woolly little head. But Delmar was no great success. Delmar couldn't remember rules or learn how to read and write. So when there were no visitors around, he kept bad-loving him, over and over. And when that didn't work, they sent in the she-beast."

"Myra Evans?"

"No, not her, you idiot. She was the *bitch*, I'm talking about the *beast*—Dr. *Daughter*. Kill-Me *Kate*—thank you, I already have."

High-pitched laughter. The gun moved back some more and I stared into its single, black eye.

The dog began scratching again, but Coburg didn't notice.

"When the *beast* finished with Delmar, he was drooling and crapping his pants and banging his head against the wall."

"What did she do to him?"

"What did she *do*? She did a number on his *head*. And other parts of his body."

"She molested him?"

His free hand touched his cheek and he arched his eyebrows.

"Such *shock*, the poor man is *shocked*! Yeah, she *molested* him, you idiot. In ways that *hurt*. He'd come back from sessions with her crying and *holding* himself. Crawl into bed, weeping. I had the room next door. I'd pick the lock and sneak him something to drink. When I asked him what the matter was, he wouldn't tell me. Not for weeks. Then he finally did. I didn't know much about sex, period, let alone ugly things. He pulled down his pants and showed me the marks. Dried blood all over his shorts. *That* was my introduction to the birds and the bees. It *altered* me, it altered me."

His lips vibrated and he swallowed hard a couple of times. The gun arm like steel.

The glass door vibrated.

"So he took the truck," I said. "To escape what she was doing to him."

"*We* took it. I knew how to drive because Evil had a farm in Connecti—a summer place, lots of trucks and tractors. One of the farmhands taught me. Planning the break was hard because Delmar had trouble remembering details. We had a bunch of false starts. Finally we made it out, late at night, everyone asleep. Delmar was scared. I had to drag him."

The gun barrel made tiny arcs.

"I had no idea which way to go, so I just drove. The roads kept getting curvier. Delmar was scared out of his mind, crying for his mama. I'm telling him everything's okay—but some idiot left sawhorses in the middle of the road—a ditch, no warning lights. We skidded . . . off the road . . . I yelled for Delmar to jump free, tried to *pull* him out, but he was too heavy—then my door flipped open and I was thrown out. Delmar . . ."

He licked his lips and breathed with forced deliberation. His finger tapped the trigger.

"Boom. Kaboom," he said. "Life is so tenuous, isn't it?"

He looked winded, dripping perspiration. The big smile on his face was forced.

"He . . . it took me two hours to walk back to hell. My clothes were torn and I'd twisted my ankle. It was a miracle—I was alive. Meant for something. I managed to crawl into bed . . . my teeth were chattering so loud I was sure everyone would wake up. It took a while till the commotion began. Talking, footsteps, lights going on. Then Hitler came stomping into my room, tore the covers off me, and stared at me —foaming at the mouth. I looked right back at him. This crazy look came into his eyes and he lifted his hands—like he was ready to claw me. I stared right back at him and pulled my pud. And he just let his arms drop. Walked out. Never spoke to me again. I was locked in my room for three days. On the fourth day, Mummy came and picked me up. Go east, young victor."

"So you won," I said.

"Oh, yeah," he said. "I was the conquering hero." Jab. "My victory bought me more dungeons. More sadists, pills, and needles. That's what your places are about, whether you call them hospitals or jails or *schools*. Killing the *spirit*."

I remembered the flash of anger he'd shown in his office, when we'd talked about Dorsey Hewitt.

He should have been taken care of . . .

Institutionalized?

Taken care of. Not jailed—oh, hell, even jail wouldn't have been bad if that would have meant treatment. But it never does.

"But you got past that," I said. "You made it through law school, you're helping other people."

He laughed and the gun retreated an inch or two.

"Don't patronize me, you fuck. Yeah, let's hear it for higher education. You know where I learned my torts and jurisprudence? The library at Rahway State Prison. Filing *appeals* for myself and the other wretches. *That's* where I learned the law was written by the oppressors to benefit the oppressors. But like fire, you could learn to use it. Make it *work* for you."

He laughed again and wiped his forehead. "The only bars I ever passed, were the ones on my *cell*. For five years, I've been going up against yuppie carcerist assholes from Harvard and Stanford and kicking their asses in court. I've had judges compliment my work."

"Five years," I said. "Right after Myra."

"Right *before*." He grinned. "The bitch was a gift to myself. I'd just gotten the gig at the center. Gave myself two gifts. The bitch and a new guitar—black Les Paul Special. You remember my guitar, don't you? All that rapport-building crap you slung at me in my office?"

The guitar-pick tiepin . . .

What do you do mostly, electric or acoustic?

Lately I've been getting into electric.

Special effects, too. Phase shifters . . .

He grinned and raised his free hand as if for a high-five. "Hey, bro, let's jam and cut a record."

"Is that the offer you gave Lyle Gritz?"

The grin shrank.

"A human decoy," I said. "To throw me off the track?"

He jabbed me hard with the gun and slapped my face with his free hand. "Shut up and stop *controlling*, or I'll do you right here and make your little friend in there clean it up. Keep those fucking hands up—up!"

I felt spit hit my cheek again and roll over my lips. Silence from the bedroom. The dog's struggles had become background noise.

"Say you're sorry," he said, "for trying to control."

"I'm sorry."

He reached over and patted my cheek. Almost tenderly.

"The bitch," he said wistfully. "She was *given* to me. Served on a plate with parsley and new potatoes."

The gun wavered, then straightened. He crossed his legs. The soles of his shoes were unmarked except for a few bits of gravel stuck in the treads.

"Karma," he said. "I was living out in the valley, nice little bachelor pad in Van Nuys. Driving home on a Sunday. These flags out at the curb. Open house for sale. When I was a kid, I liked other people's houses —anything better than my own. I got good at getting *into* other people's houses. This one looked like it might have a few souvenirs, so I stopped to check it out. I ring the bell. The real estate agent comes to the door and right away she's giving me her pitch. Da *da*, da *da*, da *da*, da *da*.

"But I'm not hearing a word she's saying. I'm looking at her face and it's the *bitch*. Some wrinkles, her boobs are sagging, but there's no doubt about it. She's shaking my hand, talking about pride of ownership, owner will carry. And it hits me: this is no accident. This is *karma*. All these years I'd been thinking about justice. All those nights I lay in bed thinking about getting Hitler, but the fuck beat me to it."

He grimaced, as if stung. "I thought I'd put *that* behind me, then I looked into the bitch's eyes and realized I hadn't. And she made it so easy—playing *her* part. Turning her back and walking right in front of me. Open invitation."

He coughed. Cleared his throat. The gun bumped against my sternum.

"Everything was perfect—no one around. I locked all the doors without her noticing, she's too busy giving me her spiel. When we reached an inner bathroom with no windows, I hit her. And did her. She fell apart as if she was made of nothing. At first it was messy. Then it got easier. Like a good riff, the rhythm."

He talked on for a long while, slipping into a drone, like a surgeon dictating operating-room notes. Giving me details I didn't want to hear. I tuned out, listening to the dog thump and bark, listening for sounds from the bedrooms that never came.

Silence. Sighing. He said, "I found my life's work."

"Rodney Shipler," I said. "He didn't work at the school, did he? Was he a relative of Delmar's?"

"Father. In name only."

"What was his crime?"

"Complicity. Delmar's mom was dead, Shipler was the only member of Delmar's family I could find.

Delmar told me his dad was named Rodney and he worked for the L.A. schools—I thought he was a teacher. Finally I located him over in South Central. A janitor. This tired old asshole, big and fat, living by himself, drinking whiskey out of a Dixie cup. I told him I was a lawyer and I knew what really happened to his son. Said we could sue, class action—even after the bitch, I was still trying to work within the system. He sat there drinking and listening, then asked me could I guarantee him a lot of money in his pocket. I told him no, money wasn't the issue. The publicity would expose Hitler for what he'd really been. Delmar would be a hero.''

Jab. "Shipler poured himself another cup and told me he didn't give a shit about that. Said Delmar's mom had been some whore he'd met in Manila who wasn't worth the time of day. Said Delmar had been a fool and a troublemaker from day one. I tried to reason with him—show him the importance of exposing Hitler. He told me to get the hell out. Tried to push me out.''

Coburg's eyes flared. The gun seemed fused to his hand.

"Another good German. He tried to push me out —real bully, but I taught him about justice. After that, I knew the only way was swift punishment—the system wasn't set up to do the job.''

I said, "One form of punishment for the underlings, another for the high command.''

"Exactly. Fair is fair." He smiled. "Finally *someone* catches on. Mrs. Lyndon was *right*, you *are* a clever piece of work. I told her I was a reporter, doing a story on you. She was so happy to help . . . her little A student.'' The gun tickled my ribs. "You deserve something for paying attention—maybe I'll knock you unconscious before I roll you over the cliff outside. Such a perfect setup . . ." Head cock toward the front door. "Would you like that?"

Before I could answer: "Just *kidding*! Your eyes will be taped *open*, you'll experience every *second* of hell, just like I did."

He laughed. Droned some more, describing how he'd beaten Rodney Shipler to death, blow by blow.

When he was through, I said, "Katarina was high command also. Why'd you wait so long for her?"

Trying to buy time with questions—but to what end? A longer ordeal for Robin—why was it so quiet in there?

My eyes shifted downward. The damn gun arm wasn't moving.

He said, "Why do you think, clever boy? Saving the best for last—and you messed me up royal. *You* were supposed to go before *her*, but then you started snooping around, sending your queer police buddy snooping, so I had to do her out of sequence. . . . I'm pissed at you for that. Maybe I'll put your girl-friend on the *barbecue*. Make you watch that with your eyelids taped open."

Smiling. Sighing. "Still, she-beast got done, and what's done is done . . . do you know how she han-dled her fate? Total *passivity*. Just like the *rest* of you." Jab. "What kind of person would want to spend his life just sitting there listening—not *doing* anything?"

He laughed.

"She got down on her knees and begged. Her she-beast throat got all clogged up like a toilet full of shit. . . . She was eating breakfast, I just strolled in, put this gun to her head, said 'bad love, she-beast.' And she just fell apart."

Shaking his head, as if still not believing. Slight shift of the gun.

"Not an ounce of fight. No fun. I had to stand her up and order her to make a run for it. Kicked her *butt* to get her to move. Even with that, all she could do was stumble into the garage and get down on her knees again. *Then* she snapped out of her trance. *Then* she started begging. Crying, pointing to her stomach, telling me she's pregnant, please have pity on my baby. Like *she* had pity . . . then she pulled a card out of her pocket, trying to prove it to me. A sperm bank. Which makes sense, who would have *done* her?'' Laughter. ''Like that was a reason. Saving her beastly fetus. *Au contraire*, that was the best reason of *all* to *do* her. Kill Hitler's seed.''

Another shake of the head. ''Unbelievable. She bloodies Delmar's shorts and thinks that's a good reason. . . . She started to tell me she was on my side, she'd helped me, killing *him*.''

''She killed her father?''

''She claimed she OD'ed him on pills. Like she'd gotten some insight. But I knew she did it as a favor to *him*. Putting him out of his misery. Making sure I'd never get to him. Giving me *another* reason to do her hard and long, she's blabbing and just digging herself deeper.'' Smile. ''I made sure to do the baby first. Pulled it out, still attached to her, showed it to her and put it back in her.''

The dog's struggles seemed to be weakening; I thought I heard him whimper.

Coburg said, ''You messed up my order, but that's okay, I'll get creative. You and your little friend will be an adequate final act.''

''What about the others?'' I said, fighting to keep my voice even. Fighting to focus my own rage. ''Why'd you choose the order you did?''

''I keep telling you, I didn't choose *anything*. The pattern constructed itself. I put your names into a hat and drew them out, eeny-meeny—all the meanies.''

''The names of the people who spoke at the symposium.''

Nod. "All you good Germans. I'd been thinking about all of you for years—even before doing the bitch."

"You were there," I said. "Listening to us."

"Sitting in a back row, taking it all in."

"You were a kid. How'd you come to be there?"

"More karma. I was nineteen, living in Hollywood and crashing at a halfway house on Serrano."

Just a few blocks from Western Peds.

". . . taking a walk on Sunset and I saw this program board out in front. Psychiatric symposium, tomorrow morning."

Tensing up, he waved the gun, arm dipping for just one second, then snapping back into place, the barrel touching my shirt.

"*His* name . . . I went in and picked up a brochure at the information desk. Shaved and showered and put on my best clothes and just walked in. And watched all you hypocritical bastards get up there and say what a *pioneer* he'd been. Child *advocate*. Gifted *teacher*. The she-beast and her home movies. Everyone smiling and applauding—I could barely sit there without screaming—I should have screamed. Should have gotten up and told all of you what you really were. But I was young, no confidence. So instead, I went out that night and hurt *myself*. Which bought me another dungeon. *Lots* of time to think and get my *focus*. I'd cut out your pictures. Pasted them on a piece of paper. Kept the paper in a box. Along with other important things. I've lived with you assholes longer than most people stay married."

"Why was Dr. Harrison spared?"

He stared at me, as if I'd said something stupid. "Because he *listened*. Right after the Hitler canonization, I called him and told him it had bothered me. And he *listened*. I could tell he was taking me seriously. He made an appointment to speak to me. I was going to show up, but something came up—another dungeon."

"Why'd you tell him your name was Merino? Why'd you tell *me* you were Mr. Silk?"

Wrinkled forehead. "You spoke to Harrison? Maybe I'll visit him after all."

A sick feeling flooded me. "He doesn't know anyth—"

"Don't fret, fool, I'm fair, always have been. I gave all of you the same chance I gave Harrison. But the rest of you flunked."

"You never called me," I said.

Smile. "November thirtieth, nineteen seventy-nine. Two p.m. I have a written record of it. Your snotty secretary insisted you only treated children and couldn't see me."

"She wasn't supposed to screen—I never knew."

"That's an *excuse*? When the troops fuck up, the general's culpable. And it was a chance you didn't even deserve—a lot more than I got, or Delmar, or any of the other *loved* ones. You muffed it, bro."

"But Rosenblatt," I said. "He *did* see you."

"He was the *biggest* hypocrite. Pretending to understand—the soft voice, the phony *empathy*. Then he revealed his true colors. Quizzing me, trying to get into *my* head." Coburg put on an unctuous look: " 'I'm hearing a lot of pain . . . one thing you might consider is talking about this more.' " Fury compressed the light brown eyes. "The phony bastard wanted to give me *psychoanalysis* to deal with my *conflicts*. Hundred-buck-an-hour *couch work* as a cure for political oppression because he couldn't accept the fact that he'd worshiped Hitler. He sat there and *pretended* to hear, but he didn't believe me. Just wanted to mess with my head—the worst one of all, bye-bye birdie."

He made a shoving motion with his free hand
and smiled.

I said, "How'd you get him to see you outside his
office?"

"I told him I was bedridden. Crippled by something Hitler had done. *That* piqued his interest, he
came right over that evening, with his kind looks and
his beard and his bad tweed suit—it was hot but he
needed his little shrink costume. The whole time he
was there, I stayed in bed. The second time, also. I
had him bring me a drink . . . serving *me*. It was a
really muggy day, the window was *wide* open for air.
Tissue box on the ledge—karma. I pretended to
sneeze and asked him to get me a tissue." Shove. "Fly
away, hypocrite bird."

Other people's houses. A financial man . . . A farm
in Connecticut. Did that mean an apartment in New
York City? *And her such an educated woman.*

She a lawyer, he a banker.

I said, "The apartment belonged to your mother
and stepfather."

He shook his head joyfully. "Clever little Alex.
Mrs. Lyndon would be so proud. . . . Mummy and
Evil were in Europe, so I decided to crash at the old
homestead. Rosenblatt's office two blocks away . . .
karma. Eight floors up, have a nice flight."

Mr. and Mrs. Malcolm J. Rulerad. Cold people,
Shirley Rosenblatt had said. Unwilling to let a private
investigator search their place. Guarding more than
privacy? How much had they known?

"You left burglar tools behind," I said. "Did you
need them to get in, or were you just setting it up as
another East Side burglary?"

He tried to mask his surprise with a slow, lan-
guid smile. "My, my, we *have* been busy. No, I had a
key. One keeps looking for home sweet home. The big
Brady Bunch in the sky . . ."

"Stoumen and Lerner," I said. "Did they meet with you?"

"No," he said, suddenly angry again. "Stoumen's excuse was that he was retired. Another flunky shutting me out, did I want to speak to the doctor on call—you people really don't know how to delegate authority properly. And Lerner made an appointment but didn't show up, the rude bastard."

The unreliability Harrison had spoken of: *it had affected his work—missed appointments.*

"So you tracked them down at conferences—how'd you get hold of the membership lists?"

"Some of us are thorough—Mrs. Lyndon would have liked me, too—what a kindly old bag, all that midwestern salt-of-the-earth friendliness. Research is *such* fun, maybe I'll visit *her* in person someday."

"Did Meredith help you get the lists?" I said. "Was she doing publicity for the conventions?"

Pursed lips. Tense brow. The hand wavered. "Meredith . . . ah, yes, dear *Meredith*. She's been a great help—now, stop asking stupid questions and get down on your knees—keep those hands up—keep them up!"

Moving as slowly as I could, I got off the couch and kneeled, trying to keep a fix on the gun.

Silence, then another impact that shook the glass.

"The dog's definitely chops and steaks," he said.

The gun touched the crown of my head. He ruffled my hair with the barrel and I knew he was remembering.

The weapon pressed down on me, harder, as if boring into my skull. All I could see were his shoes, the bottoms of his jeans. A grout seam between two marble tiles.

"Say you're sorry," he said.

"Sorry."

"Louder."

"Sorry."

"Personalize it—'I'm sorry, Andrew.' "

"I'm sorry, Andrew."

"More sincerity."

"I'm sorry, Andrew."

He made me repeat it six times, then he sighed. "I guess that's as good as it's going to get. How are you feeling right now?"

"I've been better."

Chuckle. "I'll bet you have—stand up slowly— *slowly*. Slo-o-o-wly. Keep those hands up—hands on head—Simon says."

He stepped back, the gun trained on my head. Behind me was the couch. Chairs all around. An upholstered prison, nowhere to go . . . a run for it would be suicide, leaving Robin to deal with his frustration. . . .

The dog throwing himself, harder . . .

I was upright now. He stepped closer. We came face-to-face. Licorice and rage, lowering the gun and pushing it against my navel. Then up at my throat. Then down again.

Playing.

Choreography.

"I see it," he said. "Behind your eyes—the fear— you *know* where you're going, don't you?"

I said nothing.

"Don't you?"

"Where am I going?"

"Straight to hell. One-way ticket."

The gun nudged my groin. Moved up to my throat again. Pressed against my heart. Back down to my crotch.

Taking on a rhythm—the musician in him . . . moving his hips.

I was altered . . .

Groin. Heart. Groin.

He poked my crotch and laughed. When he raised the gun again, I exploded, chopping the gun wrist with my right hand as I stabbed at his eye with the stiffened fingertips of my left.

The gun fired as he lost balance.

He landed on his side, the gun still laced between his fingers. I stomped on his wrist. His free hand was clamped over his face. When he pulled it free and grabbed at my leg, his eye was shut, bleeding.

I stomped again and again. He roared with pain. The gun hand was limp, but the weapon remained entangled. He struggled to lift it and aim. I dropped my knee full force on his arm, got hold of the hand, tugging, twisting, finally freeing the automatic.

My turn to aim. My hands were numb. I had trouble bending my fingers around the trigger. He slid across the carpet on his back, kicking out randomly, holding his eye. Blood ran over his hand. His escape was blocked by a sofa. Flailing and kicking—he looked at me.

No—*behind* me.

He screamed, "Do it!" as I ducked and wheeled, facing the hallway.

The smaller gun in my face. A woman's hand behind it. Red nails. Coburg shouting, "Do it! Do it! Do it!" Starting to get up.

I dropped to the floor just as the little gun went off.

More gunshots. Hollow pops, softer than the black pistol's thunder.

Coburg on me. We rolled. I struck out with the black gun and caught the side of his head. He fell back, soundlessly, landed on his back. Not moving.

Where was the silver gun? Arcing toward me again from across the room. Two red-nailed hands starting to squeeze.

I dove behind the couch.

Pop! The fabric puckered and gobbets of stuffing flew inches from my face.

I pressed myself flush to the marble.

Pop! Pop, pop!

Heavy breathing—gasping—but whose I couldn't tell.

Pop!

A dull noise from my back, then the windchime song of shattered glass. Scampering feet.

A small, black blur raced past me toward Meredith.

Hooking my arm around the couch, I fired the big black automatic blindly, trying to aim well above dog level. The recoil drove me backward. Something crashed.

Barks and growls and female screams.

I scuttled to the opposite side of the couch, squeezed the trigger, waited for return fire.

More screams. Footsteps. Human. Getting distant.

I hazarded a look around the couch, saw her heading for the front door, silver gun dangling like a purse.

Coburg still down.

Where was the dog?

Meredith was almost at the door now. The bolt was thrown—she was having trouble with it.

I rushed her, pointing the black gun, feeling the trigger's heavy action start to give.

Swift justice.

Screaming "Stop!" I fired into a wall.

She obeyed. Held onto the silver gun.

"Drop it, drop it!"

The gun fell to the floor and skidded away.

She said, "I'm sorry, I didn't want to—he made me."

"Turn around."

She did. I yanked off her mask.

Her face was trembling, but she tossed her hair in a gesture more suited for a teenager.

Blond hair.

My hand was still compressing the trigger. I forced myself not to move.

Jean Jeffers said, "He made me," and glanced at Coburg. He remained openmouthed and inert, and her eyes died. She tried tears.

"You rescued me," she said. "Thanks."

"What'd you do with Robin?"

"She's fine—I promise. She's in there—go see."

"Step out in front of me."

"Sure, but this is silly, Alex. He made me—he's crazy—we're on the same side, Alex."

Another look at Coburg.

His chest wasn't moving.

Keeping the black gun on Jeffers, I stooped and pocketed the silver one. Maintaining a clear view of her, I managed to pull a large, upholstered chair over the bottom half of Coburg's body. Not worth much, but it would have to do for the moment.

I walked Jeffers back to the bedroom. The door was closed. The dog stood on his hind legs, scratching at it, gouging the paint. An acetone stink came from the other side. Familiar . . .

"Open it," I said.

She did.

Robin was spreadeagled on the bed, hands and feet tied to the posts with nylon fishing line, duct tape over her mouth, a bandana over her eyes. On the nightstand were the spool of line, scissors, nail polish, a box of tissues, and Robin's manicure set.

Nail polish remover—the acetone.

A used emery board. Jeffers had passed the time by doing her nails.

She said, "Let me free her, right now."

I pocketed the scissors and let her, using her hands. She worked clumsily, the dog up on the bed, growling at her, circling Robin, licking Robin's face. Specks of blood dappled his fur. Diamond glints of broken glass . . . Robin sat up and rubbed her wrists and looked at me, stunned.

I motioned her off the bed and gave her the silver gun. Shoved Jeffers down on it, belly down, hands behind her back.

"Did she hurt you?" I said.

Jeffers said, "Of course I didn't."

Robin shook her head.

Jeffers' red nails were so fresh they still looked wet.

She said, "Can we please—"

Robin tied her up quickly. Then we returned to the living room. Coburg's head where I'd hit him was huge, soft, eggplant-purple. He was starting to move a bit but hadn't regained consciousness.

Robin trussed him expertly, those good, strong hands.

The dog was at my feet, panting. I got down and inspected him. He licked my hands. Licked the gun.

Superficial cuts, no sign he was suffering. Robin picked the glass out of his fur and lifted him, kissing him, cradling him like a baby.

I picked up the phone.

33

Three days later, I waited for Milo at a place named Angela's, across the street from the West L.A. stationhouse. The front was a coffee shop. In back was a cocktail lounge where detectives, lawyers, bailbondsmen, and felons drank and worked on their lung tumors.

I took a booth at the rear of the lounge, drinking coffee and trying to concentrate on the morning paper. Nothing yet on the "bad love" murders, orders of the brass till it got sorted out. Coburg was in the hospital, and Milo had been virtually sequestered with Jean Jeffers at the county jail.

When he showed up, fifteen minutes late, a woman was with him, thirties, black. The two of them stood in the doorway of the lounge, outlined by hazy gray light.

Adeline Potthurst, the social worker I'd seen on film, Dorsey Hewitt's knife up against her throat.

She looked older and heavier. A big white purse was clutched in front of her, like a fig leaf.

Milo said something to her. She glanced over at

me and replied. A bit more conversation, then they shook hands and she left.

He came over and slid into the booth. "Remember her? She's talking to me."

"She have anything interesting to say?"

He smiled, lit up a cigar, and added to the pollution. "Oh, yeah."

Before he could elaborate, a waitress arrived and took his Diet Coke order.

When she left, he said, "Lots happening. I've got New York records placing Coburg in Manhattan during all the East Side break-ins up till the day after Rosenblatt's death: busted for shoplifting, he was arrested in Times Square two days before the first burglary, went to court the day he shoved Rosenblatt out the window, but his attorney got a continuance. Records listed his address as some dive near Times Square."

"So he celebrated with murder."

He nodded grimly. "Jivin' Jean finally opened up —her attorney convinced her to sell out Coburg for a reduced plea to accessory. Names, dates, places, she's puttin' on a good show."

"What's her connection to de Bosch?"

"She says none," he said. "Claims the revenge thing was all Coburg's game, she didn't really know what he was up to. She says she met him at a mental health convention—advocacy for the homeless. Struck up a conversation at the bar and found they had lots in common."

"Social worker encounters public interest lawyer," I said. "A couple of idealists, huh?"

"God help us." He loosened his tie.

"Coburg probably went to lots of conventions. With his phony law degree and his public-interest persona, he would have fit right in. Meanwhile, he's looking for de Bosch disciples. *And* trying to undo his past. Symbolically. All those years he spent in institutions. Now he's in the power role, hobnobbing with therapists. He was like a little kid, thinking magically. Pretending he could make it all go away."

"We're still trying to unravel his travel schedule, place him and Jeffers together at least once: Acapulco, the week Mitchell Lerner was killed. Jeffers admits going along for the weekend—she presented a paper —but claims to know nothing about Lerner. She also admits using her position to get Coburg shrink mailing lists, but says she thought he just wanted to use them in order to advertise the law center."

"How does she explain trussing up Robin and taking potshots at me?"

He grinned. "What do you think?"

"The Devil made her do it."

"You bet. As their relationship developed, Coburg began to dominate her psychologically and physically. She'd started to have some suspicions about him, but was too afraid to back away from him."

"Does physically mean sexually?"

"She says there was some of that, but mostly she claims he used mind control, threats, and intimidation to get into her head. Kind of a mini-Manson thing: poor, vulnerable woman taken in by psychopathic Svengali. She says the night he announced he was going to get you, she didn't want any part of it. But Coburg threatened to tell her husband the two of them had been screwing for five years, and when that didn't work, he flat out said he'd kill her."

"How does she explain being so vulnerable?"

"Because she'd been abused as a kid. She says that was what drew her to Coburg—their mutual experiences. At first, their relationship was platonic. Lunch, talking about work, Coburg helping some of her clients out of legal jams, she helping *him* get social services for his. Eventually, it got more personal, but still no sex. Then one day, Coburg took her to his apartment, cooked lunch, had a heart to heart and told her all the shit he'd been through as a kid. She told him she had, too, and they ended up having this big emotional scene—cathartic, she called it. *Then* they went to bed and the whole relationship started taking another turn."

"Five years," I said. "That's when the murders began. . . . Who does she say abused her?"

"Daddy. She's free and easy with the ugly details, but it'll be impossible to verify—both parents and her only sibling, a brother, are dead."

"Natural causes?"

"We're looking into it."

"Convenient," I said. "Everyone's a victim. I guess she could be telling the truth about being abused. First time I met her she told me violating a child's trust was the lowest, she could never work with abuse cases. Then again, she could have been toying with me—she and Coburg got off on playing games."

"Even if it's true, it doesn't change the fact that she's a psychopathic witch. *Couple* of goddamn psychopaths—there's your two pathologies scenario."

"The bond between them couldn't be that deep. It didn't take long for her to sell him out."

"Honor among scumbags." His drink came and he cooled his hands on the glass.

I said, "So what about Becky? What does Jean say the link was between her and Coburg?"

"She claims to have no idea what his motive was, there." He smiled. "And guess what? He didn't have one, other than making Jean happy."

"Becky was *Jean's* thing?"

"You bet. And that's what I'm gonna get her on. All her cooperation on the other murders isn't going to help her there, because I've got independent info on a motive: Becky and Dick Jeffers were having an affair. For six months."

"How'd you find that out?"

"From the newly talkative Ms. Adeline Potthurst. Adeline saw Becky and Dick Jeffers together, sneaking off during a Christmas party at the center. Kissing passionately, his hand up her skirt."

"Not very discreet."

"Apparently Becky and Dick weren't—he used to come by to pick up Jean and end up talking to Becky, body language all over the place. The affair was semipublic knowledge at the center—I checked it out with some of the other workers and they confirm it."

"Meaning Jean knew."

"Jean knew because Dickie told her. I had a chat with him this morning—guy's a basket case—and he admitted everything. Six months of illicit passion. Said he was planning to leave Jean for Becky, and he let Jean know it."

"How'd she react?"

"Calmly. They had a nice chat and she told him she loved him, was committed to him, please give it some thought, let's get some counseling, et cetera."

"Did they?"

"No. A month later, Becky's dead. And there's no reason for anyone to make a connection—a nut hacking her up. The way I see it, it's just like you said: Jean and Coburg searched for a nut who could be *manipulated* to hack her up and came up with Hewitt—both of them had ties to him."

"What was Jeffers' tie?"

"She was his therapist before transferring him to Becky—supposedly because of a heavy workload."

"She told me Becky was the only therapist he had."

"Adeline says no, Jeffers definitely treated him.

And Mary Chin, Jeffers' secretary, confirms it. Twice-a-week sessions, sometimes more, for at least three or four months before Becky took over. We can't find any therapy notes—no doubt Jeffers destroyed them —but that only makes it look worse for her."

I said, "She made a point of telling me she didn't do therapy anymore—another mind game . . . why didn't the fact that she was working with Hewitt ever come out after Becky's murder?"

The hand went over his face. "We didn't ask, and no one volunteered. Why would they? Everyone saw it as psycho kills girl. And we killed the psycho. No one suspected a damn thing—none of the staffers at the center or Dick Jeffers. He's pretty freaked out now. Coming to grips with the monster he's been living with. Says he's willing to testify against her— whether or not he sticks with that remains to be seen."

"An affair," I said. "So goddamned mundane. Jean sleeps with Coburg for five years, but Becky gets the death penalty . . . typical psychopathic thinking, the ego out of control: you hurt me, I kill you."

"Yeah," he said, drinking and licking his lips. "So tell me, specifically, how would you get a nut like Hewitt to kill?"

"I'd pick someone with strong paranoid tendencies whose fantasies got violent when he was off his medicine. Then I'd get him off his medicine, either by convincing him to stop taking it or by substituting a placebo, and try to get as much control as I could over his psyche as he deteriorated. Maybe use some age-regression techniques—hypnosis or free association, bring him back to his childhood—get him to confront the helplessness of childhood. To feel it. The pain, the rage."

"The screams," he said.

I nodded. "That's probably why they taped him.

They got him to scream out his pain, played it back for him—you remember how hard it was to listen to. Can you imagine a schizophrenic dealing with that? Meanwhile, they're also teaching him about bad love, evil shrinks—indoctrinating him, telling him he's been a victim. And insinuating *Becky* into the delusion, as a major-league evil shrink—the purveyor of bad love. They continue to increase his paranoia by praising him for it. Convincing him he's some kind of soldier on a mission: get Becky. Then they transfer him to her. But I'll bet Jean continued to see him on the side. Prepping him, directing him. Backed up by Coburg—another authority figure for Hewitt. And the beauty of it is even if Hewitt hadn't been killed at the scene and had talked, who would have believed him? He was crazy."

"That's about the way I had it," he said. "But hearing you organize it that way helps."

"It's not hard evidence."

"I know, but the circumstantial case is building up, bit by bit. The DA's going to let Coburg's attorney know how extensively Jeffers is ratting him out, then offer a deal: no death penalty in return for Coburg ratting on Jeffers over Becky. My bet is Coburg takes it. We'll get both of them."

"Poor Becky."

"Yeah. Guess how she and Dick got started? Jean had Becky over for dinner, supervisor-student rapport and all that. Eyes across the fried chicken, a couple of knee nudges. Next day Becky and Dick are at a motel."

"Mrs. Basille said she thought Becky had a new beau. Becky wouldn't talk about it, which led Mrs. Basille to suspect it was someone she wouldn't have approved of—what she called a loser. Becky'd gone with married men before—guys who promised to get divorced but never did. Dick was *exactly* her type—married *and* disabled."

"What does disabled have to do with it?"

"Becky had a thing for guys with problems. Wounded birds. Jeffers' missing leg meshed nicely with that."

"He's missing a leg? That's what the limp is?"

"He wears a prosthesis. Becky's dad was diabetic. Lost some of *his* limbs."

"Jesus." He smoked. "So maybe there is something to this psychology stuff, huh?"

I thought about Becky Basille, trapped in a locked room with a madman. "Everything Jean and Coburg *did* was part of the ritual. Like forging Becky's therapy notes and scripting them to make it seem Becky was having an affair with *Hewitt*. In addition to diverting us, once more, to Gritz, it added insult to injury by humiliating Becky. As if that could undo the humiliation Becky'd caused Jean."

He stubbed out his cigar. "Speaking of Gritz, I think I found him. Once I realized Coburg and Jeffers were probably using him as a distraction, I figured the poor sucker's life expectancy wasn't too great and started to call around at morgues. Long Beach has someone who fits his description perfectly. Multiple stab wounds and ligature around the neck—a guitar string."

"The next Elvis. I'd check Coburg's guitar case."

"Del Hardy already did. Coburg's got a bunch of guitars. And a phase shifter and other recording stuff. In one of the cases was a set of brand-new strings. Missing the low E. The other interesting things that came up were a man's shirt too small to be Coburg's, torn up and used for a rag, still stinking of booze. And an old Corrective School attendance roster with nineteen seventy-three ripped out."

"Small shirt," I said. "Gritz was a little man."

He nodded. "And a client of the law center. Coburg had gotten *him* off a theft thing, too, couple of months ago."

"Any indication he ever knew Hewitt?"

"No."

"Poor guy," I said. "They probably lured him with notions of being a recording star—let him play with the guitars and the gizmos, make a demo. That's why he talked about getting rich. Then they killed him and used him as a red herring. No family connections, the perfect victim. Where was the body found?"

"Near the harbor. Naked, no ID, quite a bit worse for wear. He'd been in one of their coolers with a John Doe toe tag. They figure he's been dead anywhere from four days to a week."

"Right around the time you called Jeffers and asked her to speak to me. You said she thought she recognized my name. When I got there she pretended it was because of the Casa de los Niños case. But she knew it from Coburg's hit list—it must have shocked them, their next victim in their face, like that. Your making the connection between the 'bad love' tape and what happened to Becky. Someone else might have backed off, but clearing the list just meant too much to Coburg—he couldn't let go of it. So he and Jean decided to stay on track and use Gritz as extra insurance. Jeffers sends me to Coburg, Coburg just happens to remember Gritz was Hewitt's friend and directs me to Little Calcutta. Then, just in case we still weren't biting, Jeffers produces the therapy notes with all those references to 'G.' Maybe I should have wondered—Jeffers made such a big deal about Becky being a lousy note taker, then magically these appear. Mrs. Basille said Becky was a real stickler for the rules, but I figured she was just out of touch."

"There was no way to know," he said. "These people are from another planet."

"That lunch with Jeffers," I said, feeling suddenly chilled. "She sat across from me—touching my hand, letting loose the tears. Bringing Dick along was another ritual: Becky vanquished, Jean was showing off her spoils. After we were finished eating, she insisted on walking me to my car. Stood on the sidewalk, misbuttoned her sweater, and had to redo it. Probably a signal to Coburg, waiting somewhere across the street. She stayed with me all the way to the Seville—tagging the car for Coburg. He followed me up to Benedict and learned where I was hiding out."

He shook his head. "We hadn'ta caught them, they'd probably run for office."

"At lunch, I told Jeffers that I was going to Santa Barbara the next day to talk to Katarina. That got them worried I'd learn something—maybe even bring back the school roster. So they were forced to break sequence—Coburg beat me up there and killed Katarina before me. And tossed the house. Any idea why Coburg called himself Silk and Merino?"

"I asked the asshole. He didn't answer, just smiled that creepy smile. I started to walk out and then he said, 'Look it up.' So I did. In the dictionary. 'Coburg' is an old English word for imitation silk or wool. . . . Enough of this, my head's splitting. . . . How are you and Robin doing?"

"We've been able to go back to the house."

"Anything left?"

"Mostly ashes."

He shook his head. "I'm sorry, Alex."

I said, "We'll survive—we're surviving. And living in the shop's not bad—the smallness is actually kind of comforting."

"Insurance company jerking you around?"

"As predicted."

"Let me know if I can do anything."

"I will."

"And when you're ready for a contractor, I've got a possible for you—ex-cop, does nice work relatively cheap."

"Thanks," I said. "Thanks for everything—and sorry about the rental house. I'm sure your banker didn't expect bullet holes in his walls. Tell him to send me the bill."

"Don't worry about it. It's the most exciting thing's ever happened to him."

I smiled. He looked away.

"Shootout at the Beverly Hills corral," he said. "I should have been there."

"How could you have known?"

"Knowing's my job."

"You offered to drive us home, I turned you down."

"I shouldn't have listened to you."

"Come on, Milo. You did everything you could. To paraphrase a friend of mine: 'Don't flog yourself.' "

He frowned, tilted his glass, poured ice down his gullet, and crunched. "How's Rov—Spike?"

"A few surface cuts. The vet said bulldogs have high pain thresholds. A throwback to when they were used for baiting."

"Right through the glass." He shook his head. "Little maniac must have taken a running start and gone ballistic. Talk about devotion."

"You see it from time to time," I said. Then I ordered him another Coke.

34

I drove back to Venice. The shop was empty and Robin had left a note on her workbench:

> 11:45 a.m. Had to run to the lumberyard.
> Back at 2. Pls. call Mrs. Braithwaite. Says
> she's Spike's owner.

Pacific Palisades exchange. I phoned it before the disappointment could sink in.

A middle-aged female voice said, "Hello?"

"Mrs. Braithwaite? Dr. Delaware returning your call."

"Oh, doctor! Thank you for calling, and thank you for caring for our little Barry! Is he all right?"

"Perfect. He's a great dog," I said.

"Yes, he is. We were so worried, starting to give up hope."

"Well, he's in the pink."

"That's wonderful!"

"I guess you'd like to come by to get him. He should be back by two."

Hesitation. "Oh, certainly. Two it is."

I busied myself with the phone. Calling Shirley Rosenblatt and having a half-hour talk with her. Calling Bert Harrison, then the insurance company, where I dealt with some truly vile individuals.

I thought about the Wallace girls for a while, then remembered another little girl, the one who'd lost her boxer—Karen Alnord. I had no record of her number. All my papers were gone. Where had she lived—Reseda. On Cohasset.

I got the number from information. A woman answered and I asked for Karen.

"She's at school." Brilliant, Delaware. "Who's this?"

I gave her my name. "She called me about her boxer. I was just wondering if you found him."

"Yes, we have," she said edgily.

"Great. Thanks."

"For what?"

"Good news."

Mrs. Braithwaite showed up at one forty-five. She was short, thin, and sixtyish, with an upswept, tightly waved, tapioca-colored hairdo, sun wrinkles, and narrow brown eyes behind pearloid-framed glasses. Her maroon I. Magnin suit would have fetched top dollar at a vintage boutique, and her pearls were real. She carried a bag that matched the suit and wore a bejeweled American flag lapel pin.

She looked around the shop, confused.

"Robin's place of business," I said. "We're in between houses—planning some construction."

"Well, good luck on that. I've been through it, and one meets such an unsavory element."

"Can I offer you something to drink?"

"No, thank you."

I pulled up a chair for her. She remained standing and opened her handbag. Taking out a check, she tried to give it to me.

Ten dollars.

"No, no," I said.

"Oh, doctor, I insist."

"It's not necessary."

"But the expenses—I know how Barry eats."

"He's earned his way." I smiled. "Charming fellow."

"Yes, isn't he?" she said, but with a curious lack of passion. "Are you sure I can't reimburse you?"

"Give it to charity."

She thought. "All right, that's a good idea. Planned Parenthood always needs help."

She sat down. I repeated my drink offer and she said, "It's really not necessary, but iced tea would be fine if you have it."

As I fixed the drink, she inspected the shop some more.

When I gave her the glass, she thanked me again and sipped daintily.

"Does your wife fix violins?"

"A few. Mostly guitars and mandolins. She fixes and makes them."

"My father played the violin—quite well, actually. We went to the Bowl every summer to hear Jascha Heifetz play. Back when you could still enjoy a civilized drive through Hollywood. He taught at USC —Heifetz did, not Father. Though Father was an alumnus. So is my son. He's in marketing."

I smiled.

"May I ask what kind of doctor you are?"

"Psychologist."

Sip. "And where did you find Barry?"

"He showed up at my house."

"Where's that, doctor?"

"Just off Beverly Glen."

"South of Sunset, or north?"

"A mile and a half north."

"How odd . . . well, thank heavens for good samaritans. It's so nice to have one's faith in human nature restored."

"How did you find me, Mrs. Braithwaite?"

"From Mae Josephs at Frenchie Rescue—we were in Palm Desert and didn't get her message until today."

The door opened and Robin came in, carrying a bag and holding the dog by the leash.

"Barry!" said Mrs. Braithwaite. She got off the chair. The dog trotted straight to her and licked her hand.

"Barry, Barry, little Barry. You've had quite an adventure, haven't you!"

She petted him.

He licked her some more, then turned around, stared at me, and cocked his head.

"You look wonderful, Barry," said Mrs. Braithwaite. To us: "He looks *wonderful*, thank you so much."

"Our pleasure," said Robin. "He's a great little guy."

"Yes, he is—*aren't* you, Barrymore? Such a *sweet* boy, even with your snoring—did he snore?"

"Loud and clear," said Robin. Smiling, but her eyes had that pretears look I knew so well. I took her hand. She squeezed mine and began emptying the bag. Ebony bridge blanks.

The dog padded back over to us and propped his

forelegs on Robin's thigh. She rubbed him under the chin. He pressed his little head to her leg.

"Mother loved that. The snoring. Barry was actually Mother's—she kept English bulldogs and Frenchies for over fifty years. Did quite a bit of breeding and showing in her day. And obedience training."

"Did she perimeter train him?" I said. "To avoid water?"

"Oh, of course. She trained all her dogs. She had lily ponds and a big pool, and the poor things sink like stones. Then her back started to go and the English were too heavy for her to carry, so she kept only Frenchies. Then she got too weak even for the Frenchies. Barry was her last little boy. She imported him three years ago. Flew him all the way from Holland."

A linen hankie came out of the handbag. She took off her glasses and dabbed at her eyes.

"Mother passed away three weeks ago. She'd been ill for a while and Barry was her faithful companion—weren't you, sweetie?"

She reached out her hand. The dog settled on all fours but remained next to Robin.

Mrs. Braithwaite dabbed some more. "He stayed in bed with her, barked for the nurse when she started to—I do believe he was the reason she kept going as long as she did. But of course, in—when she —the last time we had to call the paramedics, *such* terror and commotion. Barry must have slipped out. I didn't realize it until later. . . ."

"Where did your mother live?" I said.

"Little Holmby. Just off Comstock, south of the boulevard."

Two miles from my house.

She said, "He managed to cross Sunset—all that traffic." Dab. "Poor little *boy*, if anything had *happened* to you!"

"Well," said Robin, "thank God he made it."

"Yes. I see that—you've made a nice little home for him, haven't you?"

"We tried."

"Yes, yes, I can see that . . . yes . . . would you like to have him?"

Robin's mouth dropped open. She looked at me.

I said, "You don't want him?"

"It's not a matter of that, doctor. I *adore* animals, but my husband doesn't. Or rather, *they* don't like *him*. Allergies. Severe ones. Dogs, cats, horses—anything with fur sets him off and he swells up like a balloon. As is, I'm going to have to take a bubble bath the moment I get home, or Monty will be wheezing the moment he sees me."

She pulled something else out of the purse and gave it to me.

An AKC pedigree sheet for "Van Der Legyh's Lionel Barrymore On Stage." A family tree that put mine to shame.

Mrs. Braithwaite said, "Isn't that noble?"

"Very."

Robin said, "We'd love to take him."

"Good. I was hoping you were nice people."

Smiling, but she took another dubious look around the shop. "He likes his liver snaps and his sausage sticks. Cheese, as well, of course. Though he doesn't seem to have any affection for Edam—isn't that odd, his being Dutch?"

Robin said, "We'll support him in the lifestyle to which he's become accustomed."

"Ye-ess . . ." She glanced furtively around the shop. "I'm sure he'll love your *new* home—will it be in the same location?"

"Absolutely," I said, scooping up the dog and rubbing his tummy. "We've been happy there."

35

It came in a plain white envelope.

Pressed into my hand as I walked out the shop's side door, Spike heeling.

I looked up to see Ruthanne Wallace's kid sister, Bonnie. Tight jeans tucked into cowboy boots, white blouse, no bra, nipples assertive.

She winked at me, tickled my palm with her finger, and ran to the curb. A dark blue Chevy Caprice with chrome wheels and black windows was idling there, blowing smoke. She jumped in, slammed the door, and the car sped off.

No postmark on the envelope, no lettering. Too thin to have anything in it but paper.

I slit it open with my fingernail.

A piece of notebook paper, torn evenly in half.

A note on the first:

Dear doctor.

I am fine. I am happy. Thank you for try to help us. Jesus loves you.

Tiffani.

A drawing on the second. Blue skies, golden sun, green grass, red flowers.

A girl sitting in what looked like an aboveground swimming pool. Fat droplets of water scattering, the girl's face a perfect circle bisected by a crescent-shaped smile.

A signature in the lower right corner: Chondra W.

A title next to the sun:

HAVING FUN.

"Sounds like a good idea," I said to Spike.
Snort, snort.

ABOUT THE AUTHOR

After a distinguished career in child psychology, JONA-THAN KELLERMAN turned to writing fiction full-time. Today there are more than fourteen million copies of his novels in print: *When the Bough Breaks, Blood Test, Over the Edge, Silent Partner, Time Bomb, Private Eyes, Devil's Waltz* (all Delaware novels), and *The Butcher's Theater*, a novel of serial killings in Jerusalem. He is also the author of two volumes of psychology and a soon to be published children's book, *Daddy, Daddy, Can You Touch the Sky?* He and his wife, the novelist Faye Kellerman, have four children.

Turn the page for an exciting preview of Jonathan Kellerman's next novel featuring psychologist-detective Dr. Alex Delaware.

SELF-DEFENSE

A Bantam Hardcover
On Sale in January 1995

1

She smiled, as usual.

From her chair she had a fine view of the ocean. This morning it was a wrinkled teal sheet gilded with sunrise. A triangle of pelicans reconnoitered overhead. I doubted she'd notice any of it.

She moved around a bit, trying to get comfortable.

"Good morning, Lucy."

"Good morning, Dr. Delaware."

Her purse was at her feet, a huge macramé bag with leather straps. She had on a light blue cotton sweater and a pleated pink skirt. Her hair was fawn-colored, sleek, shoulder length with feather bangs. Her slender face was lightly freckled, with great cheekbones and fine features ruled by huge brown eyes. She looked younger than twenty-five.

"So," she said, shrugging and still smiling.

"So."

The smile died. "Today I want to talk about *him*."

"Okay."

She covered her mouth, then removed her fingers. "The things he *did*."

I nodded.

"No," she said. "I don't mean what we've already been over. I'm talking about things I haven't told you."

"The details."

She squeezed her lips together. One hand was in her lap, and her fingers began to drum. "You have no idea."

"I read the trial transcript, Lucy."

"All of it?"

"All the crime-scene details. Detective Sturgis's testimony." Private testimony, too.

"Oh . . . then I guess you do know."

She glanced at the ocean. "I thought I'd dealt with it, but all of a sudden I can't get it out of my head."

"The dreams?"

"No, these are waking thoughts. Images float into my head. When I'm at my desk, watching TV, whatever."

"Images from the trial?"

"The worst things from the trial—those photo blowups. Or I'll flash on facial expressions. Carrie Fielding's parents. Anna Lopez's husband." Looking away. "*His* face. I feel like I'm going through it all over again."

"It hasn't been that long, Lucy."

"Two months isn't long?"

"Not for what you went through."

"I suppose," she said. "The whole time I sat there in that jury box, I felt as if I was living in a toxic waste dump. The grosser the testimony got, the more he enjoyed it. His staring games—those stupid satanic drawings on his hands. As if he was *daring* us to see how bad he was. Daring us to punish him."

She gave a sour smile. "We took the dare, all right, didn't we? I suppose it was an honor to put him away. So why don't I feel honored?"

"The end result may have been honorable, but getting there—"

She shook her head, as if I'd missed the point. "He *defecated* on them! *In* them! After he—the *holes* he made in them!" Tears filled her eyes.

"Why?" she said.

"I couldn't even begin to explain someone like him, Lucy."

She was silent for a long time. "Everything was a big *game* for him. In some ways he was just like an overgrown kid, wasn't he? Turning people into dolls so he could play with them. . . . Some kids play like that, don't they?"

"Not normal kids."

"Do you think he was abused the way he claimed?"

"There's no evidence he was."

"Yes," she said, "but still. How could someone . . . could he really have been in some kind of altered state, a multiple personality like that psychiatrist claimed?"

"There's no evidence of that either, Lucy."

"I know, but what do you *think*?"

"My guess is that his crazy behavior at the trial was faked for the insanity plea."

"So you think he was totally rational?"

"I don't know if rational's the right word, but he certainly wasn't psychotic or the prisoner of uncontrollable urges. He *chose* to do what he did. He *liked* hurting people."

She touched a wet cheek. "So you don't think he was sick."

"Not in the sense of benefiting from a pill or surgery or even psychotherapy." I handed her a tissue.

"So death's what's called for."

"What's called for is keeping him away from the rest of us."

"Well, we did that, all right. The DA said if anyone's going to get gassed, it's him." She gave an angry laugh.

"Does that trouble you?" I said.

"No . . . maybe. I don't know. I mean, if he ever makes it to the gas chamber I'm not going to be standing around watching him asphyxiate. He deserves it, but . . . I guess it's the calculated aspect that gets to me. Knowing that on such and such a day, at such and such a time . . . but would I do anything different? What would be the alternative? Giving him a chance of getting out and doing those things again?"

"Even correct choices can be agonizing."

"Do you believe in the death penalty?"

I thought for a while, composing my answer. Normally, I avoided injecting my opinions into therapy, but this time evasion would be a mistake. "I'm where you are, Lucy. The idea of someone being calculatedly put to death bothers me, and I'd have trouble pulling the switch. But I can see cases where it might be the best choice."

"So what does that make us, Dr. Delaware? Hypocrites?"

"No," I said. "It makes us human."

"I didn't jump at it, you know. I was the holdout. The others were really on me to finish up."

"Was it rough for you?"

"No, they weren't nasty or anything. Just persistent. Repeating their reasons and staring at me, like I was a stupid kid who'd eventually come around. So I guess I have to wonder if part of it was good old peer pressure."

"As you said, what would have been the alternative?"

"Guess so."

"You're in conflict because you're a moral person," I said. "Maybe that's why the images have started returning."

She looked confused. "What do you mean?"

"Maybe at this point in time you *need* to remember exactly what Shwandt did."

"To convince myself what *I* did was right?"

"Yes."

That seemed to calm her, but she cried some more. The tissue in her hand was wadded tight, and I handed her another one.

"It all boiled down to sex, didn't it?" she said, with sudden anger. "He got off on other people's pain. All that defense testimony about uncontrollable impulses was bull—those poor, poor women, what he made them —God, why am I starting my day *talking* about this?"

She looked at her watch. "Better be going."

The clock on the mantel said fifteen minutes to go.

"We've got time left."

"I know, but would you mind if I left a little early? Stuff's been piling up; my desk is a—" She grimaced and looked away.

"It's what, Lucy?"

"I was going to say a bloody mess." Laughter. "The whole experience has warped me, Dr. Delaware."

I reached over and touched her shoulder. "Give it time."

"I'm sure you're right. . . . Time. I wish there were *thirty*-four hours in the day."

"Are you backlogged because of your jury duty?"

"No, I cleared the backlog the first week. But my workload seems heavier. They keep shoving stuff at me, as if they're punishing me."

"Why would they be punishing you?"

"For taking three months off. The firm was legally obligated to grant me leave, but they weren't happy about it. When I showed my boss the notice, he told me to get out of it. I didn't. I thought it was important. I didn't know what trial I'd be assigned to."

"Had you known, would you have tried to get out of it?"

She thought. "I don't know. . . . Anyway, I've got eight new major corporate accounts to clear paper on. Used to be only tax season was like this."

She shrugged and stood. Behind her, the pelicans began a dive in formation.

When we reached the door, she said, "Have you seen Detective Sturgis lately?"

"I saw him a couple of days ago."

"How's he doing?"

"Fine."

"What a nice guy. How does he deal with this kind of stuff constantly?"

"Not every case is like Shwandt."

"Thank God for that." Her skirt was in place but she tugged at it, smoothing the thin fabric over hard, narrow hips.

"Are you sure you want to leave early, Lucy? We've gotten into some pretty disturbing stuff."

"I know, but I'll be fine. Talking about it's made me feel better."

We left the house and walked across the footbridge

to the front gate. I turned the bolt and we stepped out to Pacific Coast Highway. This far north of the Malibu Colony, coastal traffic was thin—a few commuters from Ventura and produce trucks rattling down from Oxnard. But the vehicles that did pass were speeding and deafening, and I could barely hear her when she thanked me, again.

I watched her get into her little blue Colt. The car fired up and she gave the wheel a quick turn, peeling out, burning rubber.

I went back inside and charted the session.

Fourth session. Once again, talking about Shwandt's crimes, the trial, the victims, but not the dreams that had brought her to me in the first place.

I'd mentioned them the first time, but she changed the subject abruptly and I backed off. So maybe the dreams had ceased as she got some of the horror out of her system.

I started some coffee, went out to the deck, and watched the pelicans while thinking about her sitting in the jury box for three months.

Ninety days in a toxic dump. All because she didn't eat meat.

"*Pure* vegetarian," Milo had told me, over his glass cf scotch. "SAVE THE WHALES sticker on her car, donates to Greenpeace. Naturally the defense had the hots for her."

"Compassion for all living things," I said.

He grunted. "Defense thought she'd be too knee-jerk to send that piece of shit to the apple-green room."

He gave an ugly laugh, drank his Chivas, and ran his hand over his face as if washing without water.

"Bad guess. Not that he's likely to eat cyanide soon, what with all the paper his lawyers are churning out."

He was pretty much drunk, but maintaining. It was 1 A.M. and we were in a half-empty cocktail lounge in a half-vacant high-rise office building downtown, a few blocks from the Hall of Justice where Jobe Rowland Shwandt had held court for one-quarter of a year,

eering, giggling, picking his nose, squeezing black-
heads, rattling his chains.

The press turned every twitch into news and
Shwandt luxuriated in the attention, loving it almost as
much as the pain he'd caused. The trial was a rich dessert for him after a ten-month banquet of blood.

The Bogeyman.

The more repulsive the testimony got, the more he
smirked. When the death penalty verdict was read, he
yanked his crotch and tried to expose himself to the victims' families.

"No fish," said Milo, putting his glass down on the
bar. "No eggs or dairy products either. Just fruits and
vegetables. What's that called, a vegan?"

I nodded.

The bartender was Japanese, as were most of the
patrons. The bar food was soy-flavored trail mix, cucum-
ber and rice wrapped in seaweed, and tiny, pinkish,
dried shrimp. Conversation was low and polite, and
even though Milo was talking softly, he sounded loud.

"Lots of do-gooders are full of shit, but with her you
get the feeling it's real. Real soft-spoken, gentle voice;
pretty but she doesn't make a thing out of it. I knew a
girl like that in high school. Became a nun."

"Does Lucy seem nunnish?"

"Who'm I to say?"

"You're a pretty good judge of character."

"Think so, huh? Well, I don't know anything about
her love life. Don't know much about her, period, other
than that she's having bad dreams."

"Is she single?"

"That's what she said at the voir dire."

"What about a boyfriend?"

"She didn't mention any. Why?"

"I'm wondering about her support system."

"She said her mother's dead and she doesn't see her
father. In terms of social life, she comes across a little like
Miss Lonelyhearts. Defense guys probably loved that,
too."

"How come the prosecutors didn't eliminate her?"

"I asked George Birdwell about that. He said they were running out of disqualifications and figured her fo* a fooler. Inner toughness that would make her do th* right thing."

"Do you sense that too?"

"Yeah, I do. There's a . . . solid core there. You know the old joke about a conservative being a liberal who's been mugged? She impresses me as someone who's been through rough times."

"What does she do for a living?"

"Crunches numbers for one of those big accounting firms in Century City."

"CPA?"

"Bookkeeper."

"Did she mention any problems other than the dreams?"

"Nope. And the only reason the dreams came up is I told her she looked tired and she said she wasn't sleeping well. So I took her out for a piece of pie and she told me about having them. Then she changed the subject fast, so I figured it was something personal and didn't push. Next time she called, she still sounded wiped out so I suggested she see you. She said she'd think about it; then she said okay, she would."

"How'd she hook up with you in the first place?"

"I was studying the jury the way I always do, and we happened to make eye contact. I'd noticed her before because she always seemed to be working real *hard*. Then, when I went up to testify, I saw her staring at me. Intense. After that, we kept making eye contact. The day the trial ended, the jury was being escorted out back and I was parked there, too. She waved at me. *Really* intense look. I felt she was asking me for something, so I gave her my card. Three weeks later she calls the station."

He pressed one hand down on the bar and inspected his knuckles. "Now I've done my good deed for the year. I don't know how much she can afford—"

"I don't imagine bookkeepers are investing in bullion," I said. "We'll work something out."

One hand pulled at his heavy jowls, knockwurst finers tugging heavy flesh down toward his bull neck. In the ice-blue light of the lounge, his face was a pock-marked plaster cast and his black hair hung over his forehead, creating a hat-brim shadow.

"So," he said. "Is a day at the beach really a day at the beach?"

"Bitchin', dude. Wanna come by and catch some waves?"

He grunted. "You ever saw me in a bathing suit, you wouldn't offer. How's the house coming along?"

"Slowly. *Very* slowly."

"More problems?"

"Each trade seems to have a sacred obligation to ruin the work of the previous one. This week, the drywallers covered over some electrical conduit and the plumbers damaged the flooring."

"Sorry Binkle didn't work out."

"He was competent enough, just not available. We needed more than a moonlighter."

"He's not that good of a cop, either," he said. "But other guys he did construction work for said it came out fine."

"As far as he got, it was fine. With Robin taking over, it's even better."

"How's she handling that?"

"Now that the workers are taking her seriously, she's actually enjoying it. They've finally learned they can't snow her—she gets up on the scaffold, takes their tools, and shows them how."

He smiled. "So when do you think you'll be finished?"

"Six months, minimum. Meanwhile, we'll just have to suffer along in Malibu."

"Tsk, tsk. How's Mr. Dog?"

"He doesn't like the water but he's developed a taste for sand—literally. He eats it."

"Charming. Maybe you can teach him to shit adobe bricks, cut your masonry costs."

"Always the practical one, Milo."

2

It had been a nomad year.

Thirteen months ago, just before Jobe Shwandt ha
started climbing through bedroom windows and rippin
people to shreds, a psychopath high on vengeance ha
burned my house down, reducing ten years of memorie
to charcoal. When Robin and I finally mustered th
strength to think positively, we began plans to rebuild
and looked for a place to rent.

The one we found was on a beach on Malibu's fa
west end. Old rural-route Malibu, nudging up against
the Ventura County line, light-years from the glitz. The
recession made it affordable.

I'd never lived at the beach, thinking it too remote
too cut off from the urban pulse. Now I welcomed the
isolation—just Robin, Spike, and me, and patients willing to make the drive.

I hadn't done long-term therapy for years, limiting
my practice to forensic consultations. Most of it boiled
down to evaluating and treating children scarred emotionally and physically by accidents and crimes and trying to untangle the horror of child-custody disputes.
Once in a while something else came along, like Lucy
Lowell.

The house was small: a thousand-square-foot gray
wood saltbox on the sand, fronted on the highway by a

high wooden fence and a double garage where Robin, after deciding to sublet her storefront in Venice, had set up her luthier's shop. Between the house and the gate was a sunken garden planted with succulents and an old wooden hot tub that hadn't been serviceable for years. A planked footbridge was suspended over the greenery.

Almost all the houses were bungalows owned by weekenders too busy to recreate, and even on holiday weekends, when central Malibu jammed up like a freeway, we had the beach to ourselves: tide pools, driftwood, and enough sand to keep Spike licking his chops.

He'd been trained as a pup to avoid water and hated the ocean, keeping his distance from the breakers and growing enraged at high tide. Sometimes a stray retriever or setter showed up and he romped with them, ending up winded and drooling. But his new appetite for silica more than made up for those indignities, as did a lust for barking at shorebirds in a strangulated gargling tone that evoked an old man choking.

Mostly he stayed by Robin's side, riding shotgun in her truck, accompanying her to the jobsite. This morning, they'd left at six and the house was dead quiet. I slid open a glass door and let in some heat and ocean noise. The coffee was ready. I took it out to the deck and thought some more about Lucy.

After getting my number from Milo, she'd taken ten days to call. Not unusual. Seeing a psychologist is a big step for most people, even in California. Somewhat timidly, she asked for a 7:30 A.M. appointment that would get her to Century City by 9:00. She was surprised when I agreed.

She arrived five minutes late and apologizing. Smiling.

A pretty but pained smile, rich with self-defense, that stayed on her face almost the entire session.

She was bright and articulate and full of facts—the small points of the attorney's legal wranglings, the judge's mannerisms, the compositions of the victims' families, Shwandt's vulgarities, the yammerings of the press. When the time came for her to leave, she seemed disappointed.

When I opened the gate to let her in for the second session, a young man was with her. Late twenties, tall, slender, with a high brow, thinning blond hair, Lucy's pale skin and brown eyes, and an even more painful version of her smile.

She introduced him as her brother, Peter, and he said, "Nice to meet you," in a low, sleepy voice. We shook. His hand was bony and cold, yet soft.

"You're welcome to come in, take a walk on the beach."

"No, thanks, I'll just stay in the car." He opened the passenger door and looked at Lucy. She watched him get in. It was a warm day but he wore a heavy brown sweater over a white shirt, old jeans, and sneakers.

At the gate Lucy turned to look back, again. He was slumped in the front seat, examining something in his lap.

For the next forty-five minutes, her smile wasn't as durable. This time, she concentrated on Shwandt, intellectualizing about what could have led him to sink to such depths.

Her questions were rhetorical; she wanted no answers. When she began to look beaten down, she switched the topic to Milo and that cheered her up.

The third session, she came alone and spent most of the time on Milo. She saw him as the Master Sleuth, and the facts of the Bogeyman case didn't argue with that.

Shwandt had been an equal-opportunity butcher, choosing his victims from all over L.A. County. When it became apparent that the crimes were connected, a task force involving detectives from Devonshire Division to the Sheriffs substation in Lynwood had been assembled. But it was Milo's work on the Carrie Fielding murder that closed all the cases.

The Fielding case had brought the city's panic to a boil. A beautiful ten-year-old child from Brentwood, snatched from her bedroom in her sleep, taken somewhere, raped, strangled, mutilated, and degraded, her remains tossed on the median strip that bisected San Vicente Boulevard, discovered by joggers at dawn.

As usual, the killer had left the crime scene impeccable. Except for one possible error: a partial fingerprint on Carrie's bedpost.

The print didn't match the little girl's parents' or those of her nanny, and neither was it a mate for any swirls and ridges catalogued by the FBI. The police team couldn't conceive of the Bogeyman as a virgin and went looking through local files, concentrating on newly arrested felons whose data hadn't yet been entered. No leads emerged.

Then Milo returned to the Fielding house and noticed planters' mix in the dirt beneath Carrie's window. Just a few grains, virtually invisible, but the ground beneath the window was bricked.

Though he doubted the importance of the find, he asked Carrie's parents about it. They said no new planting had been done in their yard since summer, and their gardener confirmed it.

The street, however, had been planted extensively—magnolia saplings put in by a city crew to replace some blighted old carrotwoods—in a rare show of municipal pride stemming from the fact that one of the Fieldings' neighbors was a politician. Identical planters' mix had been used around the new trees.

Milo set up fingerprinting sessions for the landscaping crew. One laborer, a new hire named Rowland Joseph Sand, didn't show up, and Milo went to his apartment in Venice to see why. No sign of the man or his registered vehicle, a five-year-old black Mazda van.

The landlord said Sand was paid up for another two months but had packed some bags and driven off yesterday. Milo got permission to search and found the apartment scrubbed neat as a surgical tray, reeking of pine cleaner. A little more searching revealed a disconnected hot water heater and the seams of a trapdoor barely visible underneath.

An old cellar, said the landlord. No one had used it in years.

Milo removed the heater and climbed down.

Straight down to hell, Alex.

Spatter and shreds and gobbets in formalin. Needles and blades and beakers and flasks.

In one corner of the cellar stood sacks of peat moss, sphagnum moss, planters' mix, human excrement. A shelf of pots planted with things that would never grow.

A background check showed Sand had given the city a false name and ID. Further investigation showed him to be Jobe Rowland Shwandt, alumnus of several prisons and mental hospitals, with convictions for auto theft, exhibitionism, child molestation, and manslaughter. He'd been in prison most of his life but had never served more than three years at a time. The city had given him a chain saw.

He was picked up a week later, just outside of Tempe, Arizona, by a highway patrolman who spotted him trying to change a tire on the black van. In his glove compartment was a mummified human hand—a child's, not Carrie's, and never identified.

The fingerprint on the bedpost turned out to be a false lead, belonging to the Fieldings' maid, who'd been in Mexico during the week of Carrie's murder and hadn't been available for comparison printing.

I sat silently through Lucy's recitation, recalling all those meetings with Milo for late-night drinks, listening to him go over it.

Sometimes *my* head still filled with bad pictures.

Carrie Fielding's fifth-grade photo.

Shwandt's Methedrine eyes and drooping mustache and salesman's smile, the oily black braid twisting between his long white fingers.

How much restoration of innocence could Lucy hope for?

Knowing more about her background might educate my guess.

So far, she'd kept that door closed.